Fatal Ground

Love, Betrayal & Death in Montana Territory

D.A. Galloway

Continuous MILE

Fatal Ground

Frontier Traveler Series - Book 2

First published by Continuous MILE 2022

To my wife, Leesa.
She is my past, present, and future.

I myself would rather die an Indian than live a white man
- Sitting Bull

Contents

Prologue

May 1872

B eads of sweat accumulated on the forehead of the young Crow woman, soaking the roots of her braided black hair and trickling down her cheeks as she emitted a series of wails.

She had been in labor for ten hours. The contractions were now occurring at regular intervals, and she was fully dilated. With each set of contractions, she rose to a squatting position and used gravity to assist her pushing. She briefly sat on a woven grass mat and took deep breaths between cycles. The effort was taking a toll.

"You need to drink," the midwife implored as she handed Makawee a cup of tea made from red raspberry leaves.

The mother-to-be gratefully accepted the strong herbal concoction from Among the Grass, feeling the liquid moisten her lips and throat, which were dry from constant open-mouth breathing. The two women were alone in the small tepee, although other family members and neighbors had gathered and were talking beside a fire outside the pole lodge.

When the contractions started again, Among the Grass helped Makawee into a squatting position and urged her to push. The pregnant woman obliged, shouting in pain as the baby became more visible.

"Touch the child," Among the Grass said, as Makawee sat back down for another brief rest. She guided the first-time mother's hand between her legs, where Makawee felt the top of the infant's head. It was soft and wet. "Remember, this is not bad pain. It is *good pain*. You will soon be a mother!"

When the next urge came, Makawee squatted and pushed with renewed energy. Gradually, then suddenly, the baby's head cleared the cervix. The infant dropped onto the mat and let out a loud cry. Makawee sat down and collapsed onto her back, exhausted.

Among the Grass retrieved the wailing newborn from the mat and laid it on Makawee's belly, using a cloth to wipe the child's nose and mouth.

"It's a girl!" the midwife announced in a loud voice.

A loud roar erupted outside the tepee, followed by shouts. Men fired rifles and women shrieked with happiness.

Tears of joy streamed down the mother's face as she gazed at the swollen pink face and wet hair of the infant, who was crying and flailing her tiny arms. Instinctively, she soothed her daughter by humming in soft tones. *Indeed,* Makawee thought, *birthing is a good pain.*

Among the Grass returned to her work. She used thin strands of elk-hide cord to tie two knots on the umbilical cord before cutting it with a knife. After wrapping the baby in a blanket, she handed her to Makawee.

A short time later, Makawee felt the contractions start again. The midwife urged her to push one more time. Soon the placenta was delivered onto the woven mat. Makawee watched as the midwife carefully cleaned the afterbirth in a pail of water before bringing it for the new mother to admire. She turned it over to reveal the fetal underside of the organ, where the remains of the translucent amniotic sac clung to the placenta. A dense network of blue-black veins and scarlet arteries radiated from the twisted white umbilical cord.

"This baby was born with a healthy tree of life," Among the Grass noted as she pointed to the beautiful and intricate network of vessels on the wet placenta resembling branches of a tree.

Makawee nodded as she sat up and encouraged her newborn to suckle at her breast.

"But this is strange," the midwife said, as a frown creased her forehead. She used her index finger to trace several arteries from the outside edge of the organ to the umbilical cord.

"What do you see?" Makawee asked, with a hint of anxiety.

"This vessel pattern says your baby is not from here. She is from a distant place. Is this true?"

Makawee's eyes widened. She was alarmed the identity of the child's father might be discovered.

"The baby's father is not from our village. Perhaps that is what you see in the vessels," she replied evasively.

"And where is the father's home?"

Everyone in the village had wanted to know the answer to this question for the past nine months. She would not divulge this information to anyone, especially not a midwife who had a reputation for gossiping and spreading rumors.

Makawee quickly changed the subject. "I know the mothers in our tribe bury their placentas. Where should I take mine?"

"This is a decision for every mother. Choose a sacred site or a place that has special meaning for you and the child."

Makawee immediately knew where she would return the placenta to the earth.

The child's father, Graham Davidson, had connected with the spirits last summer at a sacred spring her Kiowa ancestors called *Tó-sál-dàu*. The Dragon's Mouth, as it would be referred to in the future, was on the banks of the Yellowstone River upstream from the canyon. Graham had traveled to her ancestral land from one hundred years in the future. The couple had fallen in love while members of the Hayden Expedition of 1871, which was charged with exploring and mapping the wilderness area.

The baby daughter she now cradled was conceived on the shores of Yellowstone Lake. At the conclusion of his Hayden duties, Graham had reluctantly returned to his own time. Makawee missed him terribly. Perhaps if the placenta of his child was returned to Tó-sál-dàu, her former lover would sense his connection to the earth at this sacred place and return to her time.

"I know where I must go," Makawee said with tears welling in her eyes. "Please leave the afterbirth here. And thank you for helping me."

"Would you like Long Horse to visit?"

"Yes, of course."

Long Horse was Makawee's adoptive father. He was the chief of this clan of Mountain Crow she called family.

Makawee had a difficult childhood. Her parents and siblings had died of smallpox when she was an infant. She had been raised by a white man who had married a Crow woman and kidnapped by Blackfeet when she was ten. After four years in captivity, the enemy tribe traded her to another white man, who taught her to read and write. When she turned sixteen, she was granted her freedom and taken in by Long Horse.

Although she lived among the Crow people, most considered her an outsider because she was not from their clan. She was an unwed twenty-two-year-old mother who refused to identify the father of her child. And for good reasons. Not only was Graham a *baashchiile*—a white man, but he was not from the present time. He was from the future! No one would believe her even if she spoke the truth.

The midwife gently laid the wet placenta on the mat, picked up the pail of bloody water she had used to wash the organ, and ducked outside the tepee. Makawee carefully covered the afterbirth with a blanket, as Crow traditions forbade men to be near a woman while she was menstruating or giving birth. She did not want to offend her adoptive father.

A minute later, Long Horse lifted the flap and entered. He sat cross-legged beside the new mother.

"Among the Grass says you have a strong baby girl," he said, stroking the newborn's black hair while the infant nursed. He paused before saying, "She looks healthy, but seems a little pale. What will you name her?"

"This honor is given to the child's grandfather."

"I am not that person."

"But you adopted me. Now you have a granddaughter. I would like you to give her a name."

The request touched the chief. He noticed the necklace with an obsidian pendant shaped like a tortoise hanging from Makawee's neck. Long Horse regarded the baby suckling at her mother's breast.

"She will be known as Nahkash," he pronounced, taking inspiration from the necklace. The chief rose and lifted his hands skyward, chanting a quick prayer to the spirits and thanking them for the gift of a new life. He flashed a thin smile to his adopted daughter and her newborn before departing.

Makawee was pleased. Nahkash translated as "Turtle" in English. The name linked the child to her mother. It had a connection to her own name, which meant "Earth Maiden." Both mother and infant were given names strongly associated with Mother Earth. She was glad Long Horse did not know the seed planted in Makawee nine months ago had come from a young man who was from *another time* on this earth.

"Nahkash," the mother whispered to the suckling infant. "We will travel to the *Land of Burning Ground* and leave a piece of us where your life began."

Patches of snow remained on the north-facing slopes of the hills surrounding the Yellowstone River Valley in late May. After a four-day ride from the Crow

Reservation in Montana, the group arrived at Tó-sál-dàu just before sunset. Makawee handed baby Nahkash to Rides Alone before dismounting.

Rides Alone was the eldest son of Long Horse. He had become a brother to Makawee when his father adopted the young Crow woman. The two were very close and became even more so when they rode together with the Hayden Expedition for nearly forty days last year. While Makawee served as a guide, her brother hunted to keep the large survey team supplied with wild game during the journey.

Rides Alone was initially resentful of Graham's affections toward Makawee, but the baashchiile saved him from a grizzly bear attack. He respected the man from Pennsylvania and allowed him to spend time with his sister. When Graham never returned from a walk to the sacred spring on a moonlit evening last August, Makawee sobbed for hours. It was obvious she loved him.

Now he was holding an infant he strongly believed had been fathered by Graham Davidson. Out of respect for his sister's privacy, he never directly asked her to confirm this. But he had no doubts. He hoped Makawee's sorrow would be lessened if she could return the placenta of Graham's child to the earth and move on from her past.

Makawee removed a parfleche from her horse and carefully opened the supple elk skin folds to reveal a flattened, dried placenta. The salted organ had lost most of its coloring over the last two weeks. The collection of collapsed gray vessels emanating from the shrunken umbilical cord created an ethereal pattern resembling a leafless tree in winter.

The siblings walked up the hillside to the Mud Volcano, a thermal feature situated a short distance from the Dragon's Mouth. Last year the hyperactive mud spring had periodically blasted clay a hundred feet or more from a tall cone, plastering trees with the sticky brown substance. Since their previous visit, an enormous eruption had destroyed the conical structure. Now it was reduced to a crater of bubbling mud.

Makawee carried the placenta, while Rides Alone cradled Nahkash in his arms as they approached Tó-sál-dàu. Hidden forces were heating the water inside a darkened grotto. Steam spewed from the entrance, and boiling water was violently splashing against the internal walls of the cave. The hot water collected and sloshed in a small pool at the entrance. A roaring noise accompanied each burst of steam and surge of water against the rock walls. The distinctive odor of sulfur permeated the hillside. This hot spring was only one of many in the area that had earned Yellowstone the moniker *Land of Burning* Ground by the Crow people.

Holding the placenta in both hands and lifting it above her head, Makawee intoned the spirits to bless this symbol of life and the child who had been nurtured by it in her womb. She lowered her arms and tossed it into the dark recesses of the cacophonous cave.

When Nahkash started crying, Makawee unlaced the top of her elk-hide dress. She took the infant from Rides Alone and turned her back to him before dropping the dress over one shoulder and exposing her breast. The baby girl latched on and immediately became quiet. As the young Crow woman walked alone down the hillside toward the river, she sang to her child. It was an ancient song about the tree of life and how all people and animals are joined.

She sat on the riverbank in the gray dusk, basking in the wondrous miracle of becoming a mother to a beautiful child. Low on the horizon, a full moon appeared in the early evening sky. Earth Maiden closed her eyes and silently asked the spirits to grant the request of a certain young man from the future who may petition them to reunite with his family from the past.

When Makawee opened her eyes, she gazed at the rising moon. "We are waiting for you, Graham," she whispered as Nahkash drifted to sleep in her arms. "Please come."

Chapter One

Ashes to Ashes

November 1971

A steady line of mourners queued at the entrance to the chapel of the funeral home, waiting to pay their respects to Leroy Davidson. Graham and his mother stood beside his father's open casket and greeted each person. Helen frequently replenished the tissue in her hand as she dabbed her cheeks to soak up tears blackened by mascara. Graham smiled as each visitor remarked on what a great man his father had been, and it was a shame his life had ended at a young age.

Well-intentioned visitors leaned over the casket and responded with sincerity, "He really looks like himself!" Graham thought this observation was absurd.

He recalled his aversion to a famous photo of three men killed at the O.K. Corral in Tombstone, Arizona. The undertaker had displayed the open caskets of the men dressed in formal clothes in a funeral parlor window. Now his father's body was on full display for spectators. Graham cringed at the thought of others passing judgment on the suitability of the clothing selection for a burial or admiring the funeral director's skills in making a corpse look like the deceased was only sleeping. He gritted his teeth and made a mental note to specify cremation in his will.

The receiving line dwindled. People whispered to one another while sitting in neat rows of folding chairs facing the casket. Graham escorted his mother to a chair in the front row and sat beside her, while his aunt Ruth sat on Helen's opposite side and held her younger sister's hand.

Funerals assault our senses. This thought flashed through Graham's mind as the minister began the eulogy. He tried to be attentive to the pastor's words of assurance. But in this time of grieving, the sensations of his environment overwhelmed him.

As he glanced behind him at friends and family listening to the pastor reading scriptures, the absence of color struck Graham. Everyone was adorned in monotonous shades of black and gray that underscored the somber mood in the room. Most men wore wide black kipper ties that blended with a matching dark sport coat or suit. Even though they were in Pennsylvania, some opted for a bolo tie — a men's fashion accessory that was popular throughout the country in 1971, not just in the western states. Women wore tea-length black dresses, sometimes accented by either faux pearls or a necklace with a cross pendant.

It was a stark contrast to the explosion of color surrounding the casket. Baskets of flowers competed for space. The arrangements sat on staggered shelves and pedestals on both sides of the casket. There were arrangements of white lilies and orchids, purple gladioli, pink roses, yellow chrysanthemums, and blue hydrangea. An enormous spray of roses, carnations, gerbera, hydrangea, spider mums, dianthus, and delphinium adorned the bottom half of the casket.

How odd, thought Graham. *We dress gloomily, yet we try to overcome our melancholy with vibrant flower arrangements.*

Besides the pleasing visual sensation, the bouquets emitted a sweet blend of fragrances. But these transient floral scents concealed the odor of death. Graham had attended the funerals of three siblings over the last decade. His younger brother Billy, sister Susan, and older brother Frank each had their turn lying in a casket while family and friends gazed at their empty bodies and expressed their condolences to his mother and father. As the lone surviving Davidson child, he knew what death smelled like. And it wasn't a bouquet. The odor of death was the sterile disinfectant in a hospital emergency room. It was the earthy odor of a freshly dug grave plot. It was the peculiar stench of musty gravestones.

His father's death had once again pushed these malodorous memories to the fore. In Graham's mind, the flowers guarding the casket masked the hidden fetor of the dead like the air freshener his mother used after their puppy had urinated on the carpet.

Graham was familiar with funeral and burial routines. A line of cars with their headlights on and miniature purple flags stuck to their front fenders would proceed to the cemetery. After a brief graveside service, close friends and family would gather back at the Davidsons' home.

A group of women had prepared a variety of foods for the mourners. Everyone would socialize while munching on macaroni salad, baked beans, potato chips, fruit salad, and sheet cake. They would wash down the food with coffee or a Coca-Cola. It was another peculiar tradition, in Graham's opinion. In an awkward moment like this, people could temporarily avoid thinking about their mortality by doing something only the living can do — eat. Yet Graham knew the food would taste bland to him. It was one o'clock, and he hadn't eaten breakfast. But he had no appetite.

Helen broke his train of thought by nudging his ribs. She turned toward him, furrowed her brow, and mouthed, "Are you okay?"

Graham nodded and turned his focus to the pastor, who was asking everyone to sing the hymn in the funeral program. He turned on a tape recorder of organ music. Almost everyone knew the tune and attempted to sing. The collective sour melody that filled the room left no doubt most in this group lacked vocal talent. They sang the ancient song with sincerity and sorrow in their voices.

Rock of Ages, cleft for me,
Let me hide myself in thee;
Let the water and the blood,
From thy wounded side which flowed,
Be of sin the double cure;
Save from wrath and make me pure.

Not the labors of my hands
Can fulfill thy law's demands;
Could my zeal no respite know,
Could my tears forever flow,
All for sin could not atone;
Thou must save, and thou alone.

...

Helen stood with her son at the graveside under the tent. Everyone had departed after the service for the Davidson home, but she wanted a moment alone with Graham.

"Let's sit for a while," she said.

Mother and son stared at the double headstone. Unlike some of the ostentatious granite stones with winged cherubs or trumpeting angels scattered throughout the cemetery, the marker for the open grave in front of them was simple. *DAVIDSON* was engraved in capital letters at the top. A matching set of roses had been carved into the granite near both edges. Leroy's name and birth date were etched in one half. "November 21, 1971" would be engraved later as the date of Leroy's death. The other side had Helen's name and birth date with a blank area for her date of death.

"Your father and I purchased this headstone and the burial plots last year. We wanted to be buried close to our children. This is as close as we could get."

Graham looked out the side of the tent and saw his siblings' gravestones in the same row.

"I'm sure distance won't make a bit of difference when we all meet in Heaven."

"Of course, you're right. It's just that we didn't…I mean, we never expected to use one of these plots so soon." She paused. "I wish I would have taken better care of your father."

Graham reached over and squeezed his mother's hand.

"Don't blame yourself, Mom. The doctor told Dad he had high blood pressure, and he was at higher risk of a stroke. But we both know he was never fond of taking medication. It's easy in hindsight to second-guess what might have been done."

After Helen dabbed her eyes with a tissue, she turned to Graham.

"Before we leave the cemetery, I want to tell you something. Do you see anything missing?"

He studied the headstone but was puzzled by his mother's cryptic question.

"No, Mom. What do you mean?"

"There is no burial plot reserved for you next to ours," she remarked. "Your father and I talked about buying an additional plot for you, but I advised against it."

She searched her son's eyes for a reaction.

"Oh…"

This revelation took him aback.

"And why did you decide not to purchase one?"

"That's what I wanted to explain."

His mother turned toward him in the chair and looked into his eyes while she spoke.

"Graham, I love you dearly. It would comfort me knowing our entire family would share the same small parcel of earth as our last resting places. But since you came back from Yellowstone, you are a different young man. You have changed. I can sense you love that place — or perhaps even someone from that region. I didn't want you to feel tied to Pennsylvania if your future lies elsewhere."

Graham leaned over and hugged his mother.

"Oh, Mom! You don't realize how much this means to me. You have always been so supportive of my dreams. Dad couldn't understand why I wanted to go to Wyoming and Montana the first time."

He felt a twinge of guilt after his last statement. It sounded like he was disparaging his father, although that hadn't been his intention. He glanced toward the casket lowered into the ground.

"Sorry, Dad. No offense," he mumbled.

"I don't think he heard you."

There was a release of tension in their shared joke. They laughed. Graham reached over and hugged his mother again.

As quickly as laughter had erupted, it ceased. Mother and son broke into tears as they shared their grief.

"I miss him so much!" she said, weeping into her son's shoulder. "What will I do without him?"

"I'm here for you, Mom," Graham said, reassuring her between sobs. "I'll take care of you."

Most of the guests had left the Davidson home by late afternoon. The church volunteers had cleaned up everything and packaged the leftover food. Graham's mother and his aunt Ruth were washing a few dishes when there was a knock at the door. When Graham opened the front door, a tall man in his late forties with dark skin, braided hair, and high cheekbones greeted him.

"Afternoon, Gra'am."

"Redfield! I'm so glad to see you! I wasn't sure if you would make it. Come in!"

The Crow Indian used his heels to slide off his boots and stepped into the room. He was wearing blue jeans, a western-style shirt with snap closures, and a sheepskin vest.

Graham took his friend's vest and ushered him into the dining room.

"Mom, Aunt Ruth, please come meet my friend Redfield."

"Redfield, it's so nice to meet you!" Helen said as she shook his hand. "Graham always speaks highly of you. Thank you for watching over him while he was at Big Hill Farm."

"Well, ma'am, the regard goes both ways. He's a fine young man."

Ruth introduced herself as Helen's sister. She retrieved a pot of coffee, cups, and a cream pitcher. Everyone had a seat.

Graham explained to Ruth how he had met Redfield while working at Big Hill Farm. The middle-aged man had taken him under his wing to make him feel at home.

Redfield briefly told the women about his Crow heritage. He explained he was born on the reservation in Montana and migrated east after the war to find work.

"Now I understand why Graham wanted to spend time with you," Helen said. "Your people have a strong connection to Yellowstone, where he worked this past summer."

"Yes, ma'am."

"Please, call me Helen."

Redfield cleared his throat before speaking. "I'm sorry for your loss. Please accept my condolences, but I preferred not to attend your husband's funeral. I didn't want to witness a spirit being trapped."

This comment surprised Graham. He peered across the table at his mother and Ruth, who shared a puzzled look.

"Could you explain what you mean?" Graham asked his friend sitting next to him.

"Every tribe has different beliefs about death. Many, including the Crow, believe our spirit lives on after we die."

"Christians believe this, too," Helen interjected.

"True. But I understand in your burials the body is preserved by removing blood and other body fluids and replacing these with a chemical. We believe this violates the sacred vessel that is the human body. Is that what was done with your husband's body?"

"Well... well, yes," Helen responded.

"And they placed his body in a sealed coffin in the ground."

"That's right."

"The spirit must be free to leave the body to travel to the next life. Our ancestors believed you must wait four days before burying a body. Until they exposed the Crow to Christianity, we placed the bodies of our dead in trees or scaffolds to decompose naturally. We collected the bones later and buried them. The spirit was released. The body returned to the earth — from which we all came."

"Ashes to ashes, dust to dust," Helen murmured as she stared into her coffee cup.

Graham could see his mother was getting upset going through the burial scene again. It was very fresh in her mind. He tapped Redfield with his foot to get his attention and tilted his head toward his mother. The Crow Indian glanced at Helen and realized a woman in the depths of grieving was not receptive to his plainspoken explanation.

"Mrs. Davidson, I did not choose my words well. I'm sorry. Perhaps I should leave," he said while standing.

"Don't be silly!" Helen replied immediately, reaching across the table and touching Redfield's arm. "Please sit down and have a cup of coffee. We're glad you are here. Your beliefs are not wrong. And your words were not hurtful. There are many things to think about right now, and I am very emotional."

"That's what sisters are for," Ruth said, as she patted Helen's forearm. "I'll be here as long as you need me. I've given this some thought. My house has plenty of room. Why don't you come stay with me until we get things sorted out? Or at least until Graham finishes school in the spring. There's no sense in both of us living alone right now."

Ruth had become a widow over a decade ago when Graham's uncle was killed in a railroading accident. He had been crushed between the couplers of two cars being joined. Three months after Graham's younger brother Billy drowned in the family pond, the family had mourned the loss of Ruth's husband. Aunt Ruth never remarried. The couple didn't have children, so she doted on her niece and nephews.

Although he had been only eleven years old when his uncle died, he remembered his mother sitting him down for a talk. She forbade him from walking on the railroad tracks that ran through a hollow several hundred feet behind their home. He and Frank had spent hours walking the rails on Sunday afternoons. This edict seemed like an unjustified punishment. When he protested, his mother gave him a look that signaled her directive was not negotiable.

When he was older, Graham realized his uncle's accidental death had triggered his mother's reaction. Unfortunately, his mother's decisive action to protect her children from the dangers of a railroad couldn't prevent his sister from dying in an auto accident or his older brother from being killed in Vietnam.

"Perhaps you're right," Helen said to Ruth. "I'll plan to stay with you when Graham returns to school after the Thanksgiving holiday. But only for a short while — until I figure some things out."

"Wonderful!" Ruth exclaimed, as she hugged her younger sister.

"Ma'am, I'd best be leavin'. It'll be dark in a few hours, and I've got a bit of a walk," Redfield said. He went to the front door and pulled on his boots.

"Did you walk all the way from Big Hill Farm?" Helen asked.

"No. Miguel, one of the farm hands, dropped me off. But it's only six or seven miles."

"Redfield, I'll drive you home," Graham said. He handed Redfield his vest and grabbed a coat.

"Much appreciated, Gra'am."

"I hope you will visit again," Helen said, walking around the table and shaking Redfield's hand.

"I look forward to it. Thank you, ma'am."

"It's Helen."

Redfield opened the front door. He stopped and turned to Helen.

"During your time of grief, perhaps you will find comfort in an old saying of our people — 'There is no death. Only a change of worlds.'"

Redfield nodded his head and hurried out the door.

Graham smiled at his mother. He turned and followed his friend outside, gently closing the door behind him.

Chapter Two

Secrets of the Past

December 1971

C hristmas at the Davidson home started as a somber occasion. When Graham came downstairs in the morning, he found his mother standing in the kitchen wearing a robe and slippers. She was sipping a cup of coffee and peering out the window at the frozen pond situated several hundred feet below the house.

"Merry Christmas!" Graham said.

"Oh... yes. Same to you," she replied, without turning around.

"What are you thinking about?"

"Billy would have been fifteen this Christmas. Your father would have taught him to operate the tractor — like he did with you and Frank at that age. You boys would have cut a spruce tree for our living room. And Susan would have helped me bake cookies. But it seems the Lord had other plans for our family. That's what I was pondering."

Helen had a deep sadness in her voice. Her reminiscing brought an air of melancholy into the house.

Her words were like a sack of rocks placed on his shoulders. His legs felt unsteady, and he sat down heavily in a ladder-back chair. Was she going to spend her time grieving the loss of three children and a husband on a holiday that celebrated the birth of the Christ child?

Graham experienced a range of emotions while he looked at the back of his mother as she clasped the coffee cup and continued to stare out the window. Images of each family tragedy flipped in front of his eyes like a presentation on a Kodak slide projector.

His despondency grew into anger. He missed his siblings and father. But couldn't they enjoy today instead of dwelling on the past? His mother spoke before he said something he might regret.

"What would you like for breakfast?" she asked, turning away from the window and forcing a smile.

"You don't need to fix anything. I can just have a bowl of Cheerios."

"Nonsense! It's Christmas. Our company won't arrive until the afternoon. Let's have a leisurely breakfast and talk."

"Okay. How about slapjacks?"

"Slapjacks?"

"Uh, I meant pancakes," Graham corrected himself.

"You must have picked up that expression when you were in Yellowstone. Is that what they call pancakes out West?"

"Yeah. They sure do."

His mental slipup was another reminder of the discussion he planned to have with his mother. "Slapjack" was a common term in 1871 Wyoming, but not in 1971 Pennsylvania. He had informed Redfield he would reveal his time travel experience to Helen. Graham invited his friend to Christmas dinner to be part of the conversation.

"Nothing we eat today will come from a box," she pronounced. "I know how much you love pancakes made from scratch. Let's have the real thing!"

The prospect of doing something she enjoyed brightened her mood. His mother had always loved cooking and baking. As she gathered the ingredients, she began humming Irving Berlin's "White Christmas." It was one of her favorite songs from a Johnny Mathis album played every December in the Davidson home for as long as Graham could remember.

He considered the pending discussion with his mother. He hoped her disposition would not sour like the carton of buttermilk she pulled from the Frigidaire.

Helen, Graham, and Redfield sat down to a feast. Bowls of mashed potatoes, corn, green beans, and cranberry sauce surrounded the stuffed turkey.

Helen bowed her head and said grace, thanking God for the food and their many blessings. She singled out Redfield in her prayer by expressing gratitude for new friends and closed by asking the Lord to "watch over everyone in our family wherever we are."

Graham lifted his head and glanced across the table at Redfield, wondering if his friend heard the irony in his mother's closing petition.

"Amen," Helen said. "Okay, Graham. Would you serve the turkey?"

As Graham stood wielding the serrated knife to carve the roasted bird, Redfield spoke.

"Ma'am, I ain't seen such a spread in a long time. I'm much obliged by the dinner invitation."

"Helen. Please call me Helen. No need to refer to me as ma'am."

"Yes, ma.... Helen."

"Why did you make so much food? You knew there would only be three people for dinner," Graham asked as he placed a large slice of turkey on her plate.

"I know. Your aunt Ruth was going to join us, but she is spending the holidays in Florida with a friend. It doesn't matter. I like leftovers from a turkey dinner. And I'll bet Redfield would appreciate taking some food home with him tonight," she said with a wink.

"That would be wonderful. Thank you, Helen."

The trio enjoyed the meal, with Helen carrying most of the conversation. It was clear she appreciated the company and relished the opportunity to display her culinary skills. Although she prompted Redfield many times by asking questions, he responded with courteous but brief answers. Graham hoped his mother would overlook Redfield's reticence to talk. Having worked closely with the man on Big Hill Farm for months, Graham had learned he was soft-spoken and thoughtful.

After the men cleared the table and Helen stored the leftovers, she came into the dining room holding a half empty bottle of Johnnie Walker Red Label Scotch Whiskey.

"I almost forgot where Leroy kept this. He only drank liquor on holidays or special occasions. Today is both! Not only is it Christmas, but we also have a guest to break bread with. That makes our meal special. Redfield, would you like me to pour you a glass?"

Graham drew in a breath and looked at his friend. He had learned from Floyd, the farm manager at Big Hill, if Redfield consumed any hard liquor, he would often drink until he passed out. Graham later confirmed this. When he had visited Redfield at the migrant worker's camp on weekends, Redfield was often hungover. Yet Floyd valued Redfield's work ethic and his gift as a peacemaker between the Hispanics and the Black workers. The farm manager overlooked the Indian's "liquor problem", as he called it, because Redfield was a good man who would do anything asked of him.

"I think I'll just have a cup of coffee, if it's not too much trouble."

Graham was grateful his friend had declined the offer of a Christmas drink.

A few minutes later, Helen came into the dining room with a pot of coffee and a plate of cookies. Graham waited until his mother had filled the cups with the steaming liquid before clearing his throat.

"I wanted to share some details about my trip to Yellowstone this past summer. It's something I've told no one except Redfield."

Graham regretted starting the conversation with these words, but it was too late to retract them.

"What could you share with Redfield before telling your mother?" she asked. "Does this have something to do with your disappearance for six weeks?"

"Yes. It does."

Helen furrowed her brow and leaned across the table.

"Let me guess. You were not kidnapped by a young couple and held against your will, as you said earlier."

"No, I made up that story."

"You lied about being kidnapped? We were worried sick thinking about all the terrible things that could have happened to you!" She drew a quick breath before squinting her eyes and asking, "Does this involve a woman?"

"Well, yes. Sort of. But…"

"Oh, Graham! How could you? Your father was right! When you disappeared, he mentioned this as a likely explanation. The authorities asked if you might have run away with someone when they interviewed us. I defended you. I said, no! Not my Graham. He would do nothing like that. And now you're telling me…"

"Mother! Please! I did not run off with a woman!"

"Okay. Okay. Good," she said. Searching her mind for another explanation, she asked, "Did you get into some trouble? Because we have a friend who's an attorney and…"

"No. I did nothing illegal."

This wasn't true. Lying about being kidnapped put him in legal jeopardy. But he hoped his false claim about being abducted would never surface to the authorities.

She composed herself before continuing. "Then where on God's green earth were you for six weeks last summer?" she asked, sitting back in her chair while crossing her arms.

Graham blew out a long breath before answering.

"It's not where I was. It's more like *when* I was there."

Helen clutched her cup of coffee and shook her head.

"I don't have the foggiest notion of what you're talking about, young man. You're not making any sense." She paused before addressing their dinner guest. "Redfield, you've been quiet. Do you know what my son is about to tell me?"

"Yes."

"And do you believe his story?"

"It is true," Redfield said. He turned to Graham and said, "Tell your mother everything you told me."

Graham nodded. "Mother, all I ask is that you listen to my story. And please keep an open mind, because what I'm about to say will not seem possible."

"I'm listening."

Graham started by explaining Redfield's vision quest, where he sent an eagle west. He described the sacred spring known as Tó-sál-dàu or Dragon's Mouth. Redfield corroborated Graham's story by occasionally nodding or providing a more detailed explanation of the Crow ritual of a vision quest, but he let Graham do most of the talking. It was his story.

After Graham described his supernatural experience of waking in 1871, he gauged his mother's reaction.

She pursed her lips and shook her head.

"You should have stayed with your kidnapping story. At least that was a believable lie," she said. "I don't know whether to be angry at you for lying or afraid that you've lost touch with reality. Probably both."

"Helen, your son entered the spirit world. He was transported to another time. If you let Graham finish his story, we will convince you it happened," Redfield interjected.

Helen put her elbows on the table and rested her chin on her hands. "Go ahead. Finish your fantasy tale."

Graham sighed. His mother was incredulous, but he didn't blame her. Forging ahead with the story, he explained he was no longer deaf in one ear. He recalled the various people he had encountered on the Hayden Expedition and its military escort, the fateful day a soldier fell into Firehole Spring, his near drowning experience in Yellowstone Lake, the grizzly bear attack on the Crow guide named Rides Alone, his altercation with Lt. Gustavus Doane, his capture by hostile Piegan Blackfeet, and his return to the present day at the Dragon's Mouth almost forty days later.

Graham leaned back in his chair, mentally exhausted from retelling and reliving his adventure in such detail.

"You've omitted something," Redfield said, turning toward the younger man sitting beside him.

"What?" Graham recoiled at this accusation. He had thought Redfield was an ally!

"You didn't share everything with your mother. She won't believe you if you withhold information."

"Thank you, Redfield. I already figured out what you didn't say," Helen said, looking at her son. "You hinted earlier there was a woman involved in this... this escapade. Tell me about her."

Graham threw a quick glance at Redfield before answering his mother.

"Her name is Makawee. She served as one of the Crow guides for the Hayden Expedition. She is the sister of Rides Alone, who I told you was attacked by a grizzly but survived. We're very close friends."

"You *are* very close friends?" Helen had noted Graham's use of the present tense to describe his relationship.

"Yes. Makawee is a real person whom I met in 1871. She is not alive in our time. But she is very much alive one hundred years in the past. We are the same age. Would you like to see a photo?"

"Of course!"

Graham got up from the table and ran upstairs to his bedroom, retrieving his backpack. Returning to the dining room, he unzipped the pack and pulled out a bright yellow Kodak envelope of the photographs he had taken in Yellowstone.

He extracted a picture of Makawee sitting on the edge of a rock outcropping. [The slender Crow woman had straight black hair worn in two thick braids. Dark brown eyes, high cheekbones, and an aquiline nose accented her diamond-shaped face. She wore leggings, moccasins, a fringed elk-hide dress adorned with elks' teeth, and a necklace of black-and-yellow chevron seed beads. She gazed into the camera, with Yellowstone Lake shimmering in the background. Graham smiled as he handed the photo to his mother.]

Helen studied the picture. "She is lovely, but..."

"I know. It doesn't prove when the photo was taken," Graham said, finishing his mother's thought. "I just wanted you to see how beautiful Makawee is. She's also intelligent! She can ride a horse, shoot a rifle, catch rabbits with a snare, build a wickiup, and treat wounds with herbal medicine. This young woman knows her way around the wilderness of Wyoming better than most men!"

"Yes, I can understand how a young man would be charmed by a woman endowed with such talents," Helen responded. "Was she a summer employee who studied acting or theater?"

"She's not an actor! Makawee is a special woman who..." Graham composed himself. Anger would not help convince his mother. He held up his finger, showing he had more to share.

Flipping through the stack of photos, he selected another picture taken with his Kodak Instamatic. It was a side view of his docile molly mule. She was standing in an area that had burned several years earlier. The open canopy had allowed extensive patches of magenta fireweed to grow where dense lodgepole pines once stood.

"This is Lindy," he said, sliding the photo across the table to his mother. "I rode her around Yellowstone Lake while I was with the Hayden Expedition."

"It's a picture of a mule standing among wildflowers. They're beautiful, by the way. What's unusual about this picture?"

"Look at Lindy's bridle. Do you see the brass rosette?"

"I don't know what the parts of horse tack are called. Where is it?"

"It's the decoration where the crownpiece and the brow band are connected," he said, pointing to the round button below the mule's ear.

Helen put on her reading glasses and held the photograph closer.

"You mean this circular piece with 'US' stamped in the middle?"

"Yes. Do you know when they used this rosette design?"

"Of course not."

"The US Cavalry used it during and after the Civil War. A company from the Second Cavalry escorted the Hayden group. They loaned me a carbine, a mule, and tack. The rosette on Lindy proves the approximate year of the photo."

"I'm not a military historian, Graham. I'll just take your word for it." She handed the picture of the cavalry-issued mule to Redfield, who glanced at it for a few seconds, nodded, and gave it back to Graham.

Okay, he thought, *at least she isn't discounting this photograph. I need to provide more evidence I spent time in 1871.*

"I have more pictures," he said, handing two photos to his mother.

He had taken the first image on the day he had assisted photographing Castle Geyser with William Henry Jackson. It showed the photographer removing his bulky camera from a tripod with the geyser cone steaming in the background. The bearded man wore a black kepi, a short single-breasted frock coat, and gray woolen pants.

The second photo was even more remarkable. A group of men and horses were standing within a hundred feet of the Old Faithful geyser.

"Look at these. Do you see the cavalry soldiers and horses? Do you notice the clothing styles of the civilians? See how close they are to the geyser? I took this picture near the Firehole River while facing southwest. I know you haven't been to the park. Today there are many buildings and walkways on the land in the background of this photo — most notably the Old Faithful Inn. But they did not build it until 1904! You are looking at a color photograph taken before 1900. I can assure you I took it in <u>1871</u>. I was there!"

Graham could see she was struggling to comprehend what he was telling her. He pressed on, eager to seize on the momentum of his mounting evidence. Unbuttoning his shirt, he pulled a necklace over his head and laid it on the table.

Helen leaned in to get a closer look.

"Redfield gave me this necklace before I left for Yellowstone. It has a very special meaning for him," Graham explained, as he looked at his friend.

"Helen, I talked about the Crow vision quest earlier," Redfield started. "This is the necklace I created after my vision quest. The bear spirit gave me special powers, and that's why the original necklace had a single grizzly bear claw when I loaned it to your son. It enables the wearer to be seen by the spirits under certain conditions. Gra'am needed this necklace to enter the spirit world at the Dragon's Mouth. And because the bear spirit endows powers of healing, I knew it would also protect young Gra'am if he was ever in danger."

"Mother, I'm convinced this sacred necklace provided protection and healing," Graham interjected. "I avoided being hurt by a grizzly twice. Remember the soldier who was burned when he fell into the hot spring? That could have been me, because I walked the same ground as he, but I didn't fall through the thin crust. I also survived falling into a frigid lake. And it saved me from being shot in the chest by a Blackfeet warrior."

"Shot?" Helen exclaimed. "You said earlier this hostile Indian group had taken you prisoner, but you said nothing about almost being killed!"

Oh my, he thought. *I should never have mentioned the Piegan incident. It caused her to worry needlessly.*

"Yeah, well... it worked out. After all, I made it home," he said. "Anyway, let me tell you the significance of each item strung on this elk-hide cord."

"Look at these," he said, pointing to six dark gray bear claws. "As Redfield explained, his original necklace had only a single claw. I added the pendant from my Eagle Scout award because Redfield had seen an eagle in his vision. Remember the grizzly that attacked Makawee's brother? After I saved his life by shooting the bear, Rides Alone named me Eagle Bear. He gave me five claws from the slain bear, and I added these."

"A white man being named Eagle Bear by a warrior is a true sign of respect," Redfield said as he looked at his protégé.

Graham smiled before continuing his explanation. "Notice the five beads. Redfield placed two beads on this sacred necklace before I traveled west."

"That's right," Redfield chimed in. "The red bead represents me and the white one is Gra'am."

"The other three beads were a gift from Makawee," Graham said. "She wore a necklace with black-and-yellow chevron beads and a green obsidian turtle pendant. She gave me three beads from her necklace the night I traveled back to my own time at the Dragon's Mouth."

Redfield reached under his shirt and pulled a beaded turtle necklace over his head. He laid it beside the eagle-bear-claw necklace. The beads on both were identical.

"Helen, my grandmother Nahkash, which translates as "Turtle," passed this necklace down to me. Her mother gave her the necklace as a young girl, but I never knew my great grandmother's name," Redfield said, letting Graham pick up the story.

"When I returned from Yellowstone, I wanted to learn more about that time and the people I met. So, I went to the university library and did some research. I discovered the name of Redfield's great grandmother. Her name is Makawee."

Graham pushed the color photo of the beautiful young Crow woman he showed earlier across the table in front of his mother.

"Look what Makawee is wearing," he said, pointing first to the necklace in the photo, then to the necklace lying on the table.

Helen's eyes grew wide with excitement. "Are you telling me... Do you mean that...?"

"Yes. The woman in this photograph is Redfield's great-grandmother. She is the same person. Her name is Makawee. And I love her!"

He hadn't intended to share his passion for Makawee at this moment, but the reminder his lover was waiting for him in the past triggered the emotion that fueled a spontaneous response.

Helen rested her elbows on the table and placed her fingertips on her forehead. She paused before fondling the matching glass beads and contemplating what she had heard.

Without looking up, she said, "You keep using the present tense when referring to Makawee. But... it seems you are in love with someone who isn't among the living."

"Makawee is not alive today. But she is very much alive a century earlier," Graham said. "Mother, there's more. Please look at me."

As Helen looked up, Graham opened his mouth and folded his tongue into multiple bends until it formed a cloverleaf. It was a unique lingual contortion. While playing one day in front of a mirror as a boy, he had discovered he could twist his tongue into this shape. Only his mother and father knew of this bizarre talent. Because he was deaf in one ear, he was concerned his friends might ridicule him if they learned about a second physical anomaly.

"Yes, Graham. I'm aware of your ability to form a cloverleaf with your tongue. Our family doctor told us it's a rare inherited trait."

Graham nudged Redfield, who opened his mouth and duplicated the feat. As Helen stared at her son and their dinner guest, her jaw dropped in amazement.

"You can do it too?"

Redfield nodded. "It's something we share."

"What are the chances of two strangers inheriting the same rare trait?" she marveled.

"Well, that brings me to the last thing I want to share," Graham said. "I did some genealogy research in the library using census records of Indians on the Crow Reservation. I found Makawee's name. She was never married, but she gave birth to Nahkash in 1872."

Graham paused. He couldn't think of a gentle way to break the astounding implication to his mother.

"I made love to Makawee several times in August 1871 while I was in Yellowstone. The records show Nahkash was born nine months later, in May 1872. When I shared this information with Redfield, he confirmed that was his grandmother's birth month."

He took a deep breath before saying, "Redfield's grandmother is my child."

Helen put her hand to her mouth and scooted back in her chair. She gawked at Graham, then at Redfield, then back to Graham.

"It's true. I know it seems impossible. But there's no other explanation," Redfield said, placing an arm on top of the younger man's shoulders and looking into his eyes. "Gra'am and I are not strangers. We share the same blood."

Chapter Three

Go West, Young Man

March 1972

Winter stubbornly refused to end in central Pennsylvania. Although it was late March, snow swirled and formed eddies in the gray sky as Graham trudged across the Penn State campus. Large wet flakes stuck to his knit cap, quickly melting when they landed on his cheeks and nose. The twenty-minute walk from his dorm to the student parking lot gave him a chance to ponder what he would do after graduation in May.

His plans had changed dramatically in the last six months. When he had returned to the present day after his time travel journey to the uncharted 1871 Yellowstone wilderness last summer, his path and his destiny seemed clear. After discovering he was the father of Makawee's child, he resolved to be there for the birth of Nahkash, who would be born in May of 1872. But his life was irrevocably different after his father passed away. As much as his heart yearned to be with Makawee and his daughter, he simply couldn't leave his mother alone.

After Helen's shock from the Christmas Day conversation subsided, she had become pensive. The night before Graham drove to school after the holiday break, he tried to encourage his mother to share her thoughts. Although she insisted she wasn't upset, her introspective mood betrayed this claim. And who could blame her? He had disclosed his love for a woman from the previous century, with whom he had fathered a child.

Helen knew her son wanted to be with Makawee. This meant the possibility of losing the last member of her family — not to death, but to another time.

No, Graham thought. *I cannot go back in time and leave my mother. That would be selfish. I need to find my way in the present and cherish the moments I had with Makawee in the past.*

When Graham reached the lot, he located his Studebaker parked near a fence. Most of the students had already left for the weeklong spring break. After placing his suitcase in the trunk, he fetched an ice scraper and removed a layer of wet snow from the windows before sliding behind the wheel and starting the engine. As he

25

waited for the heater to warm the vehicle, he reached under his coat and removed the eagle-bear-claw necklace. He had worn the necklace every day as a reminder of the past — and his future.

Graham fondled the black-and-yellow chevron beads. Tears welled in his eyes as he remembered the night Makawee had given these to him. Feeling the bear claws against his chest had always been oddly reassuring. But now that he was in the present, continuing to wear the sacred necklace would only be a painful reminder of a world he would never see again.

It was time to put the past behind him. He kissed the beads before laying the necklace in the glove box and latching the door.

The wet snow had turned to rain as he left the mountains and drove southeast along the Susquehanna River toward Harrisburg. It was late afternoon when he eased the Studebaker into the parking area next to the carport.

"Mother, I'm home!" Graham shouted as he closed the front door behind him and slipped off his wet shoes. He set his suitcase down and removed his coat.

"We're in the kitchen!" came the reply.

When Graham walked to the back of the house, he was startled to see Redfield sitting at the table drinking a cup of tea.

"Afternoon, Gra'am."

"Redfield! I didn't expect to see you here!" he exclaimed, reaching out to shake his friend's hand.

"I invited him to dinner," Helen said. "I know you haven't seen each other since the holidays, and I thought it would be nice to share a meal."

"That was a wonderful idea!"

He leaned over and kissed her on the cheek.

The trio chatted and drank tea. Helen periodically rose to check on the beef roast in the oven and the pot of boiling potatoes on the stove.

Graham marveled at his mother's cheerful disposition. It was a stark contrast to her temperament when he'd last seen her. Perhaps she had concluded her only son would not abandon her. Seeing his mother smile again eased some of the heartache he had felt a few hours ago sitting in the Studebaker.

Helen surprised Graham after dinner by walking into the dining room with a layer cake. A half dozen lit candles flickered on top of the cake as she carried it to the table.

"Happy twenty-second birthday!" she said.

Graham was pleased.

"You remembered coconut is my favorite."

"Of course. Redfield, I won't make you sing 'Happy Birthday.' Graham, just make a wish and blow out the candles. And try not to blow coconut flakes all over the table," she said, teasing her son.

Graham closed his eyes while he conjured up a request. It was a silly ritual. Yet somehow he found it comforting to petition an unknown entity to grant a birthday wish. There was no harm in asking.

I wish I could see Makawee again. As he silently mouthed these words, a tinge of guilt swept over him. He chastised himself for reneging on a decision he had made hours earlier to stay with his mother.

He quickly opened his eyes and blew out the candles. His mother clapped, and Redfield smiled at the birthday boy.

After serving the cake, Helen looked at Graham and said, "I have some news to share."

"Oh?"

"Well... you know I've been staying with your aunt Ruth since January. And it's really been quite pleasant. She and I have become close. It feels like we are making up for all those years when we didn't visit each other nearly enough. Two weeks ago, she asked me to move in with her."

Graham stopped eating and put down his fork.

"Really? And what did you say?"

"I said I couldn't decide until I talked with you."

"It's your life, Mother. Do what makes you happy."

"But where does that leave you? I'm sure you would also be welcome in Ruth's home, but I know you'll want a place of your own after graduation."

"True."

"And we have the question of what to do with our home."

"Sell it, of course," he said, before forking a piece of cake into his mouth.

"Yes, well, that's an option. But I started thinking about your father's chair-making business. I hate to auction the shop and all his woodworking equipment. He had built a reputation for building quality chairs."

"Mother, if you're hinting I should take over the business, I'm sorry to say I'm not interested. I'm not sure what I will end up doing, but crafting rocking chairs isn't on my list of career choices."

Graham hoped his words weren't too harsh.

"Okay. I just needed to confirm you weren't interested. Last Sunday at our church, a man approached me when he heard Ruth and me talking about living together. He made a very attractive offer to buy the chair business."

"There you go! It sounds like the stars are aligned. Sell the house and the business. The proceeds will provide a nice nest egg. And Aunt Ruth would be pleased to have your company!"

"Thanks, Graham. I'm so glad to have your approval," she said with a smile. "But there's one thing that gives me pause."

"What's that?"

"Well... I went down to your father's workshop the other night. I hadn't been in that building since last summer when Leroy was... was still living. I discovered something. We'll walk down to the shop when we've finished our cake."

After she had served coffee, Helen reached into a closet and pulled a package from a shelf.

"Happy birthday," she said, handing it to him. "Before you open it, you should know it is a used item. But you will love it."

Graham's curiosity was piqued. What could he love as a gift that was used?

He tore off the paper. The label on the shoebox indicated it was a pair of size eleven Oxford wingtips. He recognized the style his father wore on Sundays. Was she gifting his father's old dress shoes? He hoped not.

"Open it," Helen said, encouraging him.

Graham flipped off the lid and folded back several layers of white tissue paper to reveal a pistol. He pulled it out and immediately recognized the .38 Special Colt Cobra revolver. He grabbed the rounded-butt grip with his right hand and rubbed his fingers across the stubby two-inch nickel-plated barrel. His older brother Frank had purchased the double-action revolver in 1966, a few months before he was sent to Vietnam.

As Graham admired the weapon, memories of his late brother came flooding back. While Frank allowed his younger brother to fire his .30-06 Springfield, he refused Graham's repeated requests to try the Colt Cobra. Frank had promised to teach him how to use the handgun safely when he came home on leave. But Frank came home in a casket, and the lessons were never given.

"Graham!" he heard his mother's voice, breaking him from his despondent state. "Do you like it?"

"Yes. Yes, of course. Thank you."

"I was going through some of Frank's things in the attic, and I discovered his handgun. I thought you would like it. There's a box of ammunition under the paper. It was in the same cardboard box as the revolver, so I assume it's the right caliber."

"This is a perfect birthday present. Thanks," he said, standing and walking over to his mother to give her a hug.

"Let's go to the workshop, shall we?" Helen said, heading toward the front door.

The trio donned coats and strolled the short distance to the shop, where Helen unlocked the door and flipped a light switch. A pair of overhead fluorescent lights flickered before gradually brightening the room.

"Looks like I may need to replace the starters on these lights if you plan on coming to the shop very often," Graham commented.

A pleasant fragrance of sawdust lingered in the stagnant air. It had been four months since his father had used any of the woodworking equipment. The workshop evoked a contrast of memories for Graham. He had spent many hours contentedly helping his father build the chairs from oak and hickory. The shop was once a refuge for his father. It was a place to withdraw from family life as he became increasingly embittered over the premature deaths of three children.

"Over here," Helen said, as she weaved through a collection of equipment including a band saw, a lathe, a splitting machine, and a belt sander. Leroy had assembled three oak rocking chairs with hickory split seats and backs. Two were sitting upright. One had been turned upside down.

"Do you notice anything unique about these chairs?" she asked.

Graham inspected the chairs, peering from several angles. He searched for something different about these chairs compared to the hundreds of others he had helped his father assemble. The pattern on the two vertical spindles was the most distinguishable feature. This design was a unique identifier for each chair maker. Leroy had not changed this crucial design element.

"Nothing looks different to me."

"Look," she instructed, pointing to the exposed bottom of the rocker rail on the overturned chair.

Graham and Redfield leaned over for a closer look.

Graham expected to see an imprint of his father's custom mark. His initials "LCD" were centered on an apple.

Leroy Charles Davidson had developed this simple design when he started his chair-making business twenty years earlier. He would heat a metal template and burn the custom logo onto the bottom of a rocker rail on every chair. Besides the finial pattern, this pyrographic design was another way to identify Leroy Davidson as the artisan. He had chosen it because Adams County was known for its myriad fruit farms, where apples were the dominant crop.

Leroy had replaced his custom apple logo with a unique design.

Graham gasped.

"Why would he change his mark from an apple to a bison and only use the initial of our family's last name?" Graham wondered aloud.

"That's what makes me uncertain about selling his chair-making business. Perhaps he envisioned passing the Davidson business along to you. I couldn't think of any other reason he would use the letter *D* in place of his initials."

How could his father have assumed he would take up chair-making? Graham had made his view clear to Leroy. And Graham had confirmed his career intentions only ten minutes ago when his mother asked if he was interested in taking over his father's business. As he stood there contemplating the meaning of the bison logo, he could feel anger welling up inside him.

"How dare he dictate my future!" he blurted out. "It's not fair that..."

"Gra'am!" Redfield said forcefully, interrupting his friend. "There's another explanation."

"Yeah? What?" Graham asked, with a tone of bitterness.

"Maybe it was his way of blessing your return to Wyoming. Perhaps your father recognized the future of the Davidson legacy would be built in the Land of Burning Ground. I know that's true for me. Remember, I wouldn't be here unless you had traveled to Yellowstone and met my great grandmother, Makawee."

Graham sighed. Maybe his friend was right. He felt his anger slowly morph into confusion. He didn't know what to believe.

Helen thought about Redfield's comments for a moment. She walked around the chair and put one hand on her son's broad chest and gently stroked his beard with the back of her other hand.

"Graham, we'll never know your father's intentions. But I can tell you this. He loved you deeply, and he wanted you to be happy. I think Redfield is right. Each time he burned this design into wood, it reminded him of how proud he was of you. I can imagine his pride growing with every chair. The bison isn't his mark. It's *your* mark! It's your father's approval for you to head west."

Helen reached around his waist and gave him a hug. Graham was stunned. He hugged his mother in return, trying to comprehend her assertion. He chastened himself for jumping to conclusions about his father's intentions. Only Leroy Davidson knew why he had changed from a Pennsylvania to a Wyoming logo. And he took that decision to his grave.

Graham gently pulled away from his mother. He rubbed his watery eyes and walked to a nearby workbench to collect his thoughts. When he had returned from Yellowstone after having been reported missing for six weeks, his father seemed overjoyed to see him. But Graham always wondered if Leroy's reaction was genuine. He was touched by the possibility his father had tacitly acknowledged his only living son should pursue his dreams wherever they may take him.

Looking at the scattered hand tools on the bench, he spied a small square of leather. The bison design had been etched into the leather by a woodburning instrument. Graham held the tanned cowhide to his nose and breathed in the raw scent of leather tinged with sawdust. He tucked the memento of his father into his coat pocket before turning around.

"Gra'am, you're fortunate to have such a loving family," Redfield said.

"I know," Graham said, choking back tears.

Standing amid scattered piles of sawdust, the three members of the Davidson family embraced one another while a cold rain fell on the tin roof of the workshop.

It was difficult for Graham to focus on his studies when he returned to school. Now, with his mother's blessing, he could prepare for a future with Makawee. There were so many things to consider as he planned his return to Yellowstone.

He made a list of items to take and quickly realized he would have to limit his packing.

Graham had to learn about the history of Wyoming and Montana in the 1870s, especially as it related to the white man's interactions with the Crow people in that era. He spent evenings and weekends in the library reading about these topics. It would be challenging to marry a Crow woman and raise a mixed-race child if he didn't understand their culture.

He contacted his former supervisor of the Bridge Bay Marina and asked if he could hire on as a scenicruise operator. Jeff was glad to have Graham back and teased him about working the entire season this year. He needed a place to stay until the first clear night with a full moon. Then he could make his journey through time. Graham felt guilty for deceiving his old boss about his true intentions, but he knew they could train a dockhand as a replacement when he failed to show up for work.

Helen suggested she, Graham, and Redfield meet on a Saturday in mid-April. She wanted to discuss the events around Graham's graduation and his travel plans. Redfield immediately agreed, since he needed to advise Graham on his second spiritual journey. At Redfield's request, Helen bought maps of Wyoming and Montana, while Graham committed to visiting the university's library and gathering information about the Bighorn Medicine Wheel.

As the trio sat at the kitchen table on a sunny afternoon, Helen was more loquacious than usual. Graham listened in amusement as his mother chatted about how excited she was for the graduation ceremony, the assorted food she planned to have for the guests, and the thrill of having her son be the first Davidson to graduate from college.

When she stopped talking and rose to refill their glasses with iced tea, Graham prompted his friend.

"Redfield, you said earlier I won't be able to use the Dragon's Mouth for my vision quest. Is that why you asked me to research the Bighorn Medicine Wheel?"

"Yes. But before we talk about the Medicine Wheel, I want to show you our people's land before they confined us to a reservation. Helen, do you have the maps?"

"Yes. I got these from the AAA office in Gettysburg," she said, pulling two road maps from a plastic bag. Graham and Redfield opened the accordion-folded maps and laid them on the table.

The Crow Indian rubbed his chin as he studied the highway maps. "These don't show all the streams and mountains. I need to know where these are."

"This may help," Graham chimed in. He retrieved a folder from his backpack and handed a document to Redfield.

It was a photocopy of a map produced by the US Army Office of the Chief of Engineers titled Map of the Yellowstone and Missouri Rivers and their tributaries. The map had originally been produced in 1860 and updated in 1876. It covered all of present day Montana and Wyoming, as well as parts of the Dakotas, Nebraska, Idaho, and Utah.

"I found it while doing my research," Graham said. "I thought it would be helpful because it shows what the area looked like in the 1870s."

"Just what I need," Redfield said. "After I mark it up, it will be a very useful reference for your journey. Helen, do you have a pencil?"

Graham smiled while his mother walked to a small writing desk in the next room. He was pleased with his friend's reaction.

Redfield spoke as he fetched a pair of reading glasses from his shirt pocket and accepted the pencil. "I'll start by labeling the familiar landmarks."

Graham and Helen leaned over the table to observe.

"So, here is Yellowstone National Park," he said, drawing a dotted-line square in the northwest corner of the Wyoming Territory. "Now I'll label the major waterways."

After writing the names of the Missouri and Yellowstone Rivers on the map, he penciled in the names of the Musselshell, Powder, North Platte, and Snake Rivers.

"Okay, now I can draw an approximate boundary of the Crow Territory as it looked after the Fort Laramie Treaty of 1851."

He narrated as he moved his pencil over the map.

"Starting on the Yellowstone River just north of today's park, the boundary went due north to the Musselshell River. It followed the river until it meets the Missouri River. Then it turned southeast to where the Yellowstone River meets the Powder River. It followed the Powder River south until it meets the North Platte River. From there, it turned westward to the Snake River, north of Jackson Hole. It turned back northeast to the Upper Yellowstone River and followed the river through the park to the northern entrance, where we started."

"That's an immense area!" Helen exclaimed. "Can you outline today's Crow Reservation?"

Redfield nodded and drew an irregular shape in the center of the original Crow Territory, with its southern boundary on the Montana-Wyoming border. The Bighorn River bisected the reservation diagonally.

"Wow!" Graham exclaimed. "It looks about the same size as Yellowstone Park. Your reservation is less than one-tenth of the original territory. How did you lose so much land?"

"Directly and indirectly, we lost our territory because of the white man. Two of our enemies, Sioux and Cheyenne, slowly encroached on our land. They did this because white hunters slaughtered the buffalo herds. All regional tribes relied on bison for their livelihoods. Everyone had to compete for fewer animals. Let me show you where the neighboring tribes lived."

He started by penciling in Piegan and Blood Blackfeet northwest of the original Crow Territory. He moved clockwise around the map, writing the names of the Crow's other tribal neighbors — Hidatsa to the northeast; Lakota Sioux to the east; Arapaho and Cheyenne to the southeast; Shoshone, Bannock, and Utes to the southwest; Nez Perce to the west.

"The white man invaded our territory when they discovered gold in southern Montana during the Civil War. After the Bozeman Trail was opened and the Union Pacific Railroad was finished, pioneers and miners soon flooded into our land." He drew two parallel lines with a series of hatches as a symbol for the railroad that traversed from Nebraska through southern Wyoming to Ogden, Utah.

"The largest portion of our land was eventually sold to the government in the late 1860s. It shrank to its present size after more land was ceded over the next twenty years."

Redfield scribbled a few additional notes on the map before turning it on the table so Helen and Graham could inspect his handiwork.

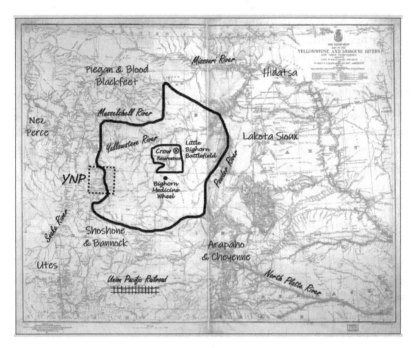

As they studied the annotated map, Redfield spoke again. Thinking about the plight of his people had filled him with melancholy. It was reflected in his voice.

"Is it okay if I step outside for a smoke?"

"Sure. Go ahead," Helen said. She waited until he stepped onto the front porch before turning to her son.

"Oh, Graham! Look at this world you want to go back to!" she said, looking at the names of the tribes. "There are so many dangers, so much uncertainty, so much greed, so much..."

"Beauty," Graham finished. "Beauty of the land. Beauty of the people. And the beauty of Makawee."

Helen nodded. "I know I won't change your mind. And I will support your decision, it's just that..."

"I know. You're concerned, Mother. But my journey will be less dangerous than Frank's time in Vietnam. My destiny is in this land a century ago," he said, emphatically tapping his forefinger on the map without looking.

Helen's focus shifted to her son's finger on the map. Graham followed her gaze. When he lifted his hand, they both gasped when they saw where he was pointing. Redfield had placed a circled 'X' in the northeast corner of the current Crow Reservation.

He had labeled this place "Little Bighorn Battlefield."

Graham stared at the marking. Helen's eyes grew wide, and she clamped her hand over her mouth. They stood in silence for a moment.

"I... I didn't know the battle took place inside the Crow Reservation," Graham said weakly.

"We learned about this battle in history class, but I don't remember when it happened. Do you?" his mother asked.

Graham responded by hurrying into the living room. He scanned a set of World Book Encyclopedias on a bookshelf. Pulling out the *Ci* through *Cz* volume, he thumbed through the pages until he found the listing he was searching for.

The entry featured a black-and-white photograph of a handsome uniformed young man with curly shoulder-length hair wearing a slouch hat. He had a neatly trimmed horseshoe mustache and was staring into the camera in a defiant pose with crossed arms. The biographical data of the famous military officer answered his mother's question about the date of the battle. "George Armstrong Custer. Lieutenant Colonel, Seventh US Cavalry Regiment. Born December 5, 1839. Died June 25, 1876," Graham said in a loud voice. He snapped the book closed before shelving it and walking back to the kitchen.

"If you go back, will it be 1872?" Helen asked.

"You mean *when* I go back? I certainly hope so."

"Graham, promise me you will be nowhere near Custer in the summer of 1876," she pleaded.

"Mother, I have no intention of being with the cavalry. I have no reason to be on any battlefield, let alone the Little Bighorn."

"Promise me."

"Okay. I promise I will not be with Custer on June 25, 1876."

Redfield opened the front door and entered the kitchen. A faint aroma of tobacco smoke followed him into the room.

"I sure could use a drink," he commented.

"I'll get a pitcher of iced tea from the refrigerator," Helen replied. "While you were outside, Graham and I discussed the other markings on your map. Can you tell us why you noted the location of the Little Bighorn Battlefield?"

"It's an important event not only in US history but also for the Crow people. We had several warriors serving as scouts on that famous expedition against our enemies, the Sioux. And as you can see, the battle took place within our reservation's borders. A large party of Sioux, Cheyenne, and Arapaho were on Crow land without permission that day in June. The battle took place in our homeland."

Helen filled three glasses with iced tea and invited everyone to sit. She glanced worriedly at Graham.

"My mother is concerned about my whereabouts on the day of the battle," he explained to Redfield. "I assured her I had no intention of joining the Seventh Cavalry."

"Well, I'm glad we're discussing this. I need to remind you of a limitation of your vision quest. This battle is a perfect example. Let me say this clearly. The spirits will not allow you to change history."

"Why would I want to do that?"

"Because you will know the future. History tells us about two hundred and sixty cavalry and one hundred Sioux and Cheyenne will be killed in the Battle of the Greasy Grass."

"Battle of what?" Helen asked.

"Greasy Grass. It's the Lakota name for the battle because it describes the look of the grass in the waters near the battlefield," Redfield explained. He turned to fix his gaze on Graham. "This is a warning. At some point, it may tempt you to influence the outcome of a key event. You will fail. The spirits will not allow it. What will be, will be. What's done is done."

Graham nodded.

Helen breathed a sigh of relief. Redfield's words assuaged her fears. It meant her son was less likely to put himself in harm's way.

"Now, I think we're ready to talk about the Medicine Wheel," Redfield said, pointing to a dot he had penciled on the map about ten miles south of the Crow Reservation in north central Wyoming. "Gra'am, what do the reference books say about the Medicine Wheel? I'll tell you whether it's true."

Graham opened his folder and removed several papers.

"Well, it's a pattern of stones arranged in the shape of a wheel. The one you marked on the map sits at the summit of Medicine Mountain in the Bighorn Range. Researchers have identified over one hundred and fifty medicine wheels in Wyoming, Montana, the Dakotas, and some Canadian provinces. But this is one of the largest and best preserved."

Graham laid a picture on the table.

"The wheel is about eighty feet in diameter," he continued. "As you can see, there are twenty-eight spokes radiating from a central cairn, which is a ring-shaped pile of rocks. Six other cairns are spaced along the circumference."

"What is the significance of the twenty-eight spokes?" Helen asked, picking up the photo to study it more carefully.

Redfield started to speak, but Graham held up his hand.

"I can answer that. Makawee told me twenty-eight represents one lunar cycle. It's also why she kept ten black and yellow beads on her turtle necklace. It is ten lunar months, or two hundred eighty days, from conception to birth of a child." Graham's voice grew louder as he finished the explanation. "If Nahkash goes full term, Makawee will deliver our daughter one month from now — in the middle of May 1872. And I will be there!"

"Calm down," Redfield said in a low voice, while gently squeezing the younger man's shoulder. "One step at a time. You need to understand this sacred place before you visit. Is there anything else you learned?"

Graham inhaled deeply, exhaled, and looked down at his papers. "Archaeologists believe the Bighorn Medicine Wheel is likely of Crow and Shoshone origin. A recent article by an astronomer claims they used this stone wheel as a sort of astronomical observatory and a predictor for the summer solstice."

"Very good," Redfield said. "Everything you said is accurate. However, there are things about this sacred place you did not mention. Young men seeking a vision quest have visited this site for thousands of years. I was one of those youths. I made a horseshoe-shaped fasting bed on the western slope of Medicine Mountain and completed my vision quest at *Annáshisee.*"

"Is that what your people call the Medicine Wheel?" Helen asked.

"That's right. You can only visit Annáshisee during the summer months and early fall."

"Why?" Graham asked.

"Because the mountain is nearly ten thousand feet high, snow covers the mountaintop from late September through June. The road leading to the Medicine Wheel is closed until mid-to-late June. Besides, the spirits are not active when Annáshisee is covered with snow."

"Oh," Graham replied. He had not considered the seasonal impact on visiting this sacred site. He had noticed many mountains over ten thousand feet high in Yellowstone's Absaroka Range were covered with snow in June. Suddenly, he realized the implications for his vision quest. "But... but I have to go back in May. That's when Nahkash will be born! How can I do that if Annáshisee is covered in snow?"

"You cannot go in May. You'll have to wait a month or two."

Graham was dejected, but he didn't give up easily.

"Wait! Why can't I travel back in time at the Dragon's Mouth? There may still be snow, but I'm sure I could reach the thermal spring in May."

"We discussed this. Since you already used the time portal at T̲ó̲-s̲á̲l̲-d̲à̲u̲, it is closed. You must petition the spirits at another sacred place."

"Is there any other sacred site I can visit in May?" he asked in desperation.

"There are other places at lower elevations like the Bear Lodge. Those would be more accessible in the spring."

"I've never heard of Bear Lodge. Where is it?"

"It's a solitary butte that rises about six hundred feet above the plains in northwest Wyoming. It has nearly vertical sides which are heavily striated. These fissures look like giant bear claws could have created them. The site is sacred to the Crow. It is also a spiritual place for Arapaho, Lakota, Cheyenne, Kiowa, and Shoshone."

Redfield pointed to a location on the Wyoming highway map labeled "Devils Tower National Monument."

"The Lakota word for 'evil spirit' or 'bad god' is *wakansica*, and their word for bear is *wahanksica*. Unfortunately, white explorers confused these two words. They mistranslated the name of this sacred rock as 'Bad God's Tower' instead of Bear Lodge. Devils Tower was adopted as the official name on maps and documents."

Graham made a mental note to visit this site near the Black Hills, either before or after he traveled back in time.

"But let's get back to the Bighorn Medicine Wheel. As a practical matter, this sacred site is much closer to Yellowstone than Bear Lodge. Go in July or August. You will have several fair-weather months when you can appeal to the spirits on a clear night under a full moon at Annáshisee. Have patience."

"Patience? I have to be there when Makawee gives birth!"

"Gra'am, you do not have to be there. You want to be there. Baby Nahkash will be born with or without you. What will be, will be. What's done, is done."

Graham slumped in his chair. He leaned forward, placed his elbows on his knees, and despondently bowed his head.

Helen sat down and put her hand on Graham's shoulder while she spoke.

"Son, please listen to Redfield. I know how much you want to be with Makawee and your child. You have been impatient ever since you were a little boy. This attribute often served you well because you always pushed yourself to get things done quickly. But it can also be a weakness."

The room was silent. The only sound was the quiet hum of the refrigerator and the rhythmic ticking of the grandfather clock in the dining room.

"Gra'am, you have spoken highly of Rides Alone. Would you consider him a noble warrior?" Redfield asked in a soft tone.

Graham nodded but didn't look up.

"Is he a patient man?"

Another nod.

"There is an old saying: 'The two most powerful warriors are patience and time.' You must arm yourself with *daasátchuche* — patience."

Graham inhaled deeply and blew air out of his lungs. "I think I've figured out a way to communicate with you from the past," he said, still looking at the floor.

"Oh? Communicate across time? How can we do that?" Helen asked. She was skeptical.

Graham slowly raised his head and scooted his chair closer to the table. He gulped some iced tea before providing an explanation.

"Actually, it would only be one-way communication. It would be from the past to the present — from me to you."

"We're listening," Redfield said.

"While I was with the Hayden Expedition in Yellowstone, the men wrote letters to their families. These were sent to Fort Ellis, then forwarded via stagecoach and train to their loved ones. I didn't have a family in 1871, so I wrote a brief description of the region and addressed it to the newspaper editor in Adams County, Pennsylvania. When I came back to the present time and returned to school, I did some research in the library. That's how I discovered the name of Redfield's great-grandmother Makawee and that Redfield is my descendant."

"Yes. You explained this earlier," Helen replied.

"Well, I also examined microfilm copies of the local newspaper published in the previous century. It wasn't always called the *Gettysburg Times*. They published it under the name *Adams Star and Sentinel*. I discovered the article I had written in August 1871 published in the Miscellaneous section!"

"Hmm," Redfield replied. "I see where you're going with this reasoning. After you travel back in time, if you write to the local newspaper, we could see what you submitted by looking up historical copies of the *Adams Star and Sentinel*."

"That's right. I plan to use the pseudonym David Graham."

"This assumes the newspaper prints your letters," Helen said.

"Yes. There's no guarantee they will publish everything I submit. You would only see published letters after one hundred years had passed since they had been written. I don't know how often I will write. But if you scan the microfilm every month, you might see what was happening at the time I wrote the letter."

Helen nodded thoughtfully. "It would give me some comfort hearing from you, but..."

"You would be reading about events that occurred a long time ago. I know. It's not the same as receiving a letter from me today."

"Okay. Why not? It's better than never knowing what happened to you," Helen replied. She shook her head. "I can't believe we're discussing time travel. Even though you convinced me earlier that's what happened to you, common sense tells me it's a preposterous concept!"

"You're only questioning it now because you know I will soon leave you, Mother."

"Perhaps you're right," she said with a sigh. "Although I will lose my son to the past, I have gained a previously unknown Davidson child. Redfield, why don't you come live with me in Ruth's home? You're part of our family."

"That's mighty generous, Helen. But I need to stay with my people on Big Hill Farm. They need me from time to time. In a way, I need them too."

"Mother, I feel the same way. You, Redfield, and Aunt Ruth are my family in 1972. But I also have a family in 1872. Their names are Makawee and Nahkash. They need me, and I need them."

"I just want you to lead a happy life — wherever and whenever that may be."

Graham stood and walked to the kitchen window. The rays of the setting sun cast a soft yellow hue on the western side of the small building where his father had once assembled rocking chairs. It triggered a memory, which he shared while gazing out the window.

"One day last fall, when we were working in the shop, Dad gave me some brilliant advice. He told me, 'Never leave something unless you are also going to something.' It's true, I'm leaving my present-day family. It's also true I'm going to my family in the past."

Graham pulled the patch of leather with the bison burned into its surface from the front pocket of his Levi's. He had carried it with him ever since the rainy night he discovered it in the workshop. He turned from the window and laid it on the table.

"If this is my father's stamp of approval, as both of you suggested several weeks ago, I plan to follow his advice of going *to* something. I will go to a place and a time when bison are plentiful. Wyoming in 1872."

Chapter Four

Like No Place on Earth

May 12, 1972

A two-thousand-mile solo drive across America afforded Graham plenty of time to think. Sometimes his thoughts were focused on the here and now, like finding a place to stop for fuel and relieve himself. Other times, his mind drifted to the recent past. Only two days ago, he had said a bittersweet goodbye to his mother and Redfield; it was painful to realize he would never see them again.

But mostly he pondered his future, which awaited him in the previous century. His powerful yearning to reconnect with Makawee and their soon-to-be-born child salved the emotional wound caused by leaving his twentieth-century family behind.

As the Studebaker hummed along Interstate 90 in western South Dakota on a cloudless day in mid-May, Graham's attention suddenly shifted from his pending time-travel journey to the present when a large sign appeared indicating he was crossing the state line. A Wyoming highway sign featured a bucking horse and rider in the foreground with the Teton Range as a backdrop. The slogan *"Like No Place on Earth"* was printed in white letters on a dark blue background at the bottom of the sign.

Graham smiled at the ambiguous phrase. It implied this state wasn't like anywhere else on the planet; it seemed to be from another world. He agreed with the enigmatic expression. Indeed, in Wyoming, he hoped to enter a different world when the spirits would again transport him back in time at the Bighorn Medicine Wheel.

Twenty minutes later, he approached the small town of Sundance, just south of the Black Hills National Forest. A dark green grain silo squatted alongside the highway. It doubled as a billboard to entice potential visitors. "Welcome to Sundance — where the kid got his name" was painted in bright yellow letters on the rotund metal storage tank. Graham grinned. He instantly made the connection with the popular movie *Butch Cassidy and the Sundance Kid*, which had premiered three years earlier.

Less than a mile later, a green highway sign identified the exit for Devils Tower. Graham pulled to the side of the road and consulted his map. It was only thirty miles from the interstate to the national monument. He considered taking the quick side trip to visit the sacred site Redfield had mentioned as an alternative location for consummating a vision quest. It was three o'clock, and he still had another seven hours of driving time to reach Yellowstone Lake. Although tempting, he couldn't explore the area around the famous butte and still reach his destination before midnight. Reluctantly, he folded the map and pulled the Studebaker back onto the highway.

The truck stop on the outskirts of Cody was busy. After he filled the tank of the Studebaker, Graham walked inside. He poured a cup of black coffee, snapped on a lid, and walked to the front counter to pay for his fuel. Racks of chewing gum, potato chips, packs of cigarettes, and cans of snuff tobacco framed the clerk at the register. As he handed a ten-dollar bill to the woman in her fifties with a cigarette dangling from her lower lip, he asked about conditions on the East Entrance Road.

"A fella was in here 'bout an hour ago. Came over the mountains in a tandem," she said, in the raspy voice of a heavy smoker. "Said the snow was deep in places from that big storm we had three days ago, but the road was open. It rained down here, but it dumped a bunch o' the white stuff in the mountains."

"Good to know," Graham said, glancing at his watch. It was nine o'clock, and he had two more hours of driving to reach Yellowstone Lake.

"You headed over the mountains tonight?" she asked, handing him the change.

"I sure am."

"Best be careful. Been sunny and near sixty last couple of days. Might've caused that heavy snow to loosen up," she cautioned.

"Thanks. Appreciate it."

He walked back to the fuel pumps and slid into the driver's seat. Before starting the car, Graham opened the glove box. He retrieved his eagle-bear-claw necklace, slipped it over his head, and tucked the pendants under his sweater. He would soon enter Yellowstone, the *Land of Burning Ground*. It was time to wear the necklace.

Graham paused for a moment to weigh his options. He could find a motel and stay the night, but that would lighten his thin wallet. He decided to push on.

The first segment of the highway heading west out of Cody was clear. After passing the Buffalo Bill Reservoir, the road followed the North Fork of the Shoshone River, gaining elevation as it snaked through the deep and narrow Wapiti Valley. The weather and landscape changed when the river and the road diverged.

As the road climbed out of the valley between Top Notch Peak and Hoyt Peak, Graham regretted his earlier decision. The temperature had dropped precipitously, falling from the upper forties to the twenties as the Studebaker labored up the steep incline. The East Entrance Road had been opened only one week earlier. Giant snowblowers had carved a channel with twelve-foot vertical walls on both sides of the road. The higher the car climbed, the more the road narrowed, and the higher the walls grew. Soon, the road was barely wide enough for two vehicles to pass, although he had seen no vehicles traveling in either direction for the last twenty minutes.

Snow swirled in front of the headlights as a brisk wind picked up and deposited powdery drifts at the base of the frozen walls. Graham alternated the headlight settings between high and low beams, experimenting to find the best visibility. He strained to see the double yellow dividing line. He even tried winding down his window and sticking out his head to get a better view. Opaque clouds of snow and immense frozen facades gave the illusion the white walls on either side of the road were not parallel to one another but formed a funnel. The visual effect was unsettling.

The Studebaker's headlights suddenly illuminated a small brown rectangular sign jutting from the snow at the apex of the ascent.

SYLVAN PASS
ELEV 8530

At least now I will descend, and there will be less snow, he thought with relief as he guided the car through the narrow passage. Five minutes later, the walls were only six feet high. Graham's anxiety level dropped with the height of the snow. He leaned forward and peered through the windshield at the gradient of the mountain. He could see gigantic snow fields on the treeless slopes next to the road. Rounding a curve, he spotted a large yellow sign reminding motorists stopping was not permitted because this section of road was an avalanche zone. He had no intention of stopping. He just wanted to...

Boom!

An explosive noise near the top of the mountain to his left sounded like artillery fire. He slammed on the brake pedal. The Studebaker skidded to a halt. He cranked his window down and squinted into the darkness. A thunderous commotion convulsed the frigid night. Graham's eyes grew wide with fear when he recognized the source of rumbling above him.

Avalanche!

He removed his foot from the brake and jammed it on the accelerator. The Studebaker fishtailed as the rear wheels spun, ejecting ribbons of snow from under the tires. He stole a quick glance up the mountain. A shadowy white cloud of snow and rock was tumbling down the slope. Graham eased off the gas pedal just long enough to give the tires a chance to bite into the packed snow. This time he gradually stepped on the gas pedal and urged the Studebaker forward, knowing he had only seconds before the roiling mass of snow would cover the road. Large chunks of snow mixed with bits of scree rained on the car. Rocks thumped on the roof and hood, creating dents and cracking the windshield. The tires gained traction, and the squatty car sped away from the imminent path of destruction.

[The cacophonous noise reached a crescendo as hundreds of tons of snow slid across the road and continued down the mountainside.]As quickly as it had begun, the snowslide ceased. The night was again silent. He stopped the Studebaker and peered into the rearview mirror. Less than one hundred feet behind him, the road was buried in twenty feet of snow. The brake lights cast an eerie reddish tinge on the mammoth snow pile blanketing the road.

Graham shifted the car into park. After taking a moment to calm his racing heart, he put on his emergency flashers. He donned the cowboy hat lying on the passenger seat, buttoned his coat, and climbed from the vehicle. Walking to the rear of the car, he realized how close he had come to dying. If he had driven through this area thirty seconds later, the Studebaker would have either been entombed or swept down the mountain.

A set of headlights appeared in the distance, coming toward the Studebaker from the west. [Graham walked back to his car and watched as a white four-wheel-drive truck pulled up.]A man with a short salt-and-pepper beard wearing a green fur-lined coat emerged from the truck, which had a park service emblem on the door.

"Are you okay?" asked the park official as he approached Graham.

"Yeah. I made it through just in time."

"Anybody right behind you?"

"Don't think so. Yours is the first vehicle I've seen for a while."

"Good. Your path is clear the rest of the way to the lake. I'll get on the radio, and we'll close the road until we can get a crew up here. Let me move my truck to the side so you can pass."

As Graham steered the Studebaker around the pickup and eased down the road toward the lake, he considered his close brush with death. Or was it luck? He reached under his sweater and felt the eagle-bear-claw necklace suspended around his neck. Five grizzly bear claws from Rides Alone, three chevron beads gifted from Makawee, two solid beads from Redfield, and the pendant from his Eagle Scout award were all strung on an elk-hide cord.

When he had traveled back to 1871 Yellowstone last summer, he had escaped serious injury or death several times. There was no doubt in Graham's mind this necklace had provided healing *and* protection. It may have done that tonight. He shuddered when thinking about what might have happened if he had left the sacred necklace in the glove box instead of wearing it. Would he have taken his final breaths in a car buried under tons of snow? From now on, he resolved the necklace would be part of his daily attire.

Sunlight filtered through the dirty glass of the window, stirring Graham from a brief night of sleep. Rubbing his eyes, he sat up, unzipped his sleeping bag, and swung his legs over the side of the creaky bed. The room was cool. He pulled on the Levi's he had left on the floor the previous evening and padded to the rusty electric heater near the door. He fiddled with the knobs, turning the temperature setting as high as it would go. When there was no response, he donned a wool sweater to ward off the chilly air.

When Graham arrived at the H-block building late last evening, he had retrieved his room key under a rock at the base of the steps. Jeff Martindale, his supervisor and the manager at Bridge Bay Marina, had placed it there when Graham wrote to accept the job offer and explained he would arrive very late in the day. He had carried only his backpack and a sleeping bag into the rustic employee dormitory room. Exhausted from the long day's drive and the harrowing near-miss with the snowslide on Sylvan Pass, he had left his suitcase in the trunk of the Studebaker. He had slipped off his jeans, rolled out the sleeping bag on the sagging mattress, climbed into bed, and had fallen asleep almost immediately.

Now, he walked over to the heater and blew into his cupped hands. Glaring at the wall unit, he gave it a swift kick with his heel. To his surprise, the dormant heater rattled and hummed as the internal fan started spinning. The vent spewed a cloud of dust and debris, causing him to step back from the tiny particles. After the dust cloud settled, he held his hand over the vent and felt warmth on the tips of his cold fingers. He grinned at his crude but effective heater repair skills.

Graham put on his cowboy hat, fished the car keys from his jeans pocket, and walked outside to fetch his suitcase. As he placed the key in the trunk lid, he could see in daylight what had not been noticeable last night. Dents and scratches covered the trunk. He stuffed his hands in the front pockets of his bulky sweater and strolled around the car to assess the damage.

The roof and hood had suffered the same damage as the trunk lid. Debris carried down the slope by the avalanche had landed on the vehicle as it sped away from the chaotic tumble of snow, rocks, and sticks. A rock had hit the windshield, fracturing it into a spiderweb pattern. A large crack emanated from the center and snaked across the width of the glass. To the casual onlooker, it appeared as if he had driven through a hailstorm.

Oh well, Graham thought, *I only need the Studebaker to get me to the Medicine Wheel.*

Graham removed the suitcase from the truck and carried it inside. Tossing his hat on the bed, he retrieved his LL Bean backpack and laid it on a small table under the window. He emptied the pack and took an inventory of the items he planned to carry with him.

He had purchased topographical maps of northern Wyoming and southern Montana. A similar map of Yellowstone had proven beneficial in navigating the wilderness when he was with the 1871 Hayden Expedition. He also brought the map Redfield had drawn on his mother's kitchen table. It would be a useful reference for tribal lands in the 1870s, as well as the boundaries of the Crow Reservation.

He smiled when he laid a color photo of Redfield on the table. He was eager to show Makawee a picture of her great grandson!

Graham pulled two United States Notes out of the pack. Alexander Hamilton's portrait was printed on the twenty-dollar bill, and Daniel Webster was featured on the ten-dollar bill. James Stevenson had given these to him as payment for his services with the Hayden Survey team in 1871. No one would recognize the US dollars in his wallet in 1972 as legal tender in the previous century.

Next, he removed a chrome Eveready flashlight and a Zippo lighter. He had taken both on his first time travel journey. He gave a flashlight to the Piegan leader who had spared his life at the Norris Geyser Basin. The lighter was his gift to Makawee. She had been fascinated with the magical ability of the tiny box to create an instant fire with a flick of a thumb.

He extracted a leather pouch of *kinnikinnick*, a willow bark and tobacco mixture used in ceremonies by the Crow, as well as a briar pipe. He needed to duplicate a rite he had learned from Redfield last summer to prepare his path for a successful vision quest.

Two non-essentials were removed from the pack — a toothbrush and three Hershey's chocolate bars. While a willow chewing stick had done an acceptable job while he was with the Hayden Survey, he had missed the ability to clean his teeth with a modern tool designed for that purpose. And Makawee loved the flavor of the milk chocolate. He knew she would be delighted to taste the sweet confection again.

Graham remembered his conversation with Makawee near Old Faithful. She had learned to read and speak English well since she had spent time with several white families. When she asked about his favorite book, he had said *Alice in Wonderland*. This was not true. Graham loved the story spun by Mark Twain in *The Adventures of Huckleberry Finn*. He wanted Makawee to read the story even though it would not be published for a dozen years after they met again in 1872.

He extracted the square of leather with the bison logo burned into the surface. This item had no practical purpose, but it had great sentimental value. It was a tangible sign his late father had blessed his venture westward to follow his dreams.

The heaviest items were at the bottom of the pack. He laid a box of .38 special jacketed hollow-point cartridges on the table before removing the Colt Cobra revolver from a black felt fabric. Park regulations allowed visitors to possess firearms if they were unloaded and in a case. Frank had never bought a case for the pistol. A hard-shelled case would be too bulky to fit into Graham's pack, so he had wrapped the handgun in the soft cloth.

Graham held the snub-nosed double-action revolver in his hand. Many in law enforcement preferred the aluminum alloy weapon because it weighed less than a pound. This made it easier to carry than the heavier all-steel revolvers. He opened the cylinder, loaded it with six cartridges, and snapped it closed. Then he reversed the process and emptied the gun using the ejector rod.

Everything seemed in good working order. He hoped to find a place outside the park to fire a few rounds before the night of his second vision quest. One thing was certain. A firearm was essential for anyone in Wyoming or Montana in the early

1870s. When he'd arrived at the Yellowstone River in 1871, he had felt vulnerable without a firearm to protect himself. He had been fortunate the cavalry had been willing to loan him a Spencer carbine.

Satisfied he had what he needed for his time-travel journey, he repacked everything and put the backpack in the trunk of the Studebaker for safekeeping.

He strolled to the Lake Hotel for breakfast. The employee dining hall would not be open for two more weeks. That's when most of the seasonal summer park employees would arrive. Jeff had told him to take his meals in the venerable hotel's dining room.

Graham stopped at the gift shop and picked up a newspaper on his way to the restaurant, which he paged through while eating a hearty breakfast of scrambled eggs, toast, and bacon. As he finished his coffee, he noticed the weather summary for northern Wyoming on the back page. It listed local sunrise and sunset times, as well as the phases of the moon. His eyes widened when he saw the next full moon would occur in three nights under a cloudless sky. He laid the newspaper on the table, excited to see his trip back to the past was only days away! His pulse quickened as he thought about his imminent journey to the Medicine Wheel.

And then he remembered the events of last night. The Absaroka Range had a lot of snow. Medicine Mountain was almost fifteen hundred feet higher than Sylvan Pass. Even if the road to the Bighorn Medicine Wheel was open, the sacred site would be covered with snow.

"Shit!" he said aloud in frustration.

An older couple sitting at a table nearby turned and glared at him. The woman gave a look he had seen his mother use when she was extremely displeased with something he'd said. He silently mouthed, "Sorry," and picked up the newspaper to hide from the woman's disapproving stare.

Okay, he thought. *If I can't get to the Medicine Wheel, what are my other options?*

It didn't take long to envision the obvious answer.

I'll go back to the Dragon's Mouth! It's less than an hour from here. Maybe Redfield was mistaken about not using the same sacred site twice. Why should I wait until next month for my vision quest if a full moon is only days away?

Graham's mood quickly brightened. He checked his watch. Jeff was expecting him at the marina soon. He pushed away from the table, placed the napkin on his chair, and started whistling "*Raindrops Keep Fallin' on My Head*" as he sauntered toward the exit.

The couple looked up from their oatmeal and shook their heads in bewilderment at the bearded young man passing by their table. What could cause someone to be angry enough to swear, then quickly become exuberant?

Chapter Five

Portals to the Past

May 15, 1972

S everal inches of wet snow had fallen overnight. Snow wasn't unusual for mid-May. It routinely fell at higher elevations within the park. Morning had revealed a brilliant, deep blue sky and calm winds. It was going to be a frosty night at the Dragon's Mouth Spring. Other than Graham's Studebaker, there were only two cars in the parking lot when he arrived at the Mud Volcano thermal area in the late afternoon. He wanted to make sure any visitors had left before heading to the hot spring. He pondered his situation while he sat in the car with the engine running.

He had worked at the marina for only three days. Jeff had no clue he would not be showing up for work on the fourth day. He would not forgo the perfect combination of ideal weather and a clear night to travel through the time portal. The authorities would launch a missing person investigation after they found the abandoned car in the Mud Volcano parking area the following morning. A tinge of guilt swept through him, but he dismissed the uncomfortable feeling. He was ready to take the leap into the past.

By the time the last car left the parking area, it was nearly dusk. The sky was rapidly transitioning from deep purple to gray to black when he turned off the engine. He opened the car door, retrieved his hat and backpack, and placed the car keys under the floor mat. It was unlikely anyone would want an eleven-year-old car pocked with dents. It was dispiriting to think his faithful car would end up in the salvage yard.

The familiar sulfurous smell of rotten eggs filled his nostrils as he followed the trail to the Dragon's Mouth. A group of bison lumbered above the hot spring. The visible portion of the hot spring was a small, shallow pool sitting against a hillside. It was spewing steam and violently splashing water against the hidden internal walls of a darkened grotto, generating a roaring noise with each *whoosh* of boiling water.

Graham could understand why Redfield's ancestors might revere Tó-sál-dàu, the Kiowa name for this hot spring. The sights, sounds, and malodorous gases made this site a prime candidate for the mystical birthplace of a people.

He leaned forward, placing his elbows on a wooden rail while listening to the raucous roars emanating from the spring. He watched as the massive bison slowly made their way north along the hillside. Soon he could discern only the silhouettes of trees on the surrounding landscape.

A first-time visitor who stood in the darkness next to this angry-sounding hot spring would likely experience a modicum of anxiety. But the din of the thermal feature comforted Graham. It was here he had been transported to the previous century. And it was at this sacred site he had returned to the present day. Something about this place revitalized him.

His contentment was rooted in more than just familiarity with this hot spring. He felt something tugging at his soul. It was like someone was calling him. He imagined he heard a muffled voice in the water-filled cave. After straining for several minutes, all he could detect were intermittent sounds of hot water splashing against the rock walls. He eventually gave up and turned around to lean against the railing.

Suddenly, an explanation for this odd sensation came to him. *This is where I lost my hat when I returned to the present,* he thought. *Makawee found it and passed it along to her offspring, and it ended up with Redfield. That must be why I feel such a strong connection tonight.*

Graham removed his chocolate-brown, diamond-crown faux-leather hat freckled with brown spots. These were tiny mementos of his encounter with the neighboring Mud Volcano, which had spewed sticky clay particles during a violent eruption in the last century. Not wishing to lose his hat again, he held it and his backpack.

He checked his watch. A full moon was required so the spirits could see him. While he waited for the moon to clear the horizon, he double-checked his backpack to be sure he had forgotten nothing. He silently rehearsed his petition to the spirits. And he allowed himself to think about seeing Makawee when he arrived in the past.

By ten o'clock, the celestial orb was visible over the Yellowstone River Valley. May's flowering moon hung low in the sky, illuminating the vaporous clouds of steam from Dragon's Mouth Spring, casting ghostly shadows on the surrounding landscape.

He completed a mental check of the requirements for a spirit to heed his request. He was standing under a full moon at a sacred place. His one-sided deafness satisfied the requirement for everyone on a vision quest to be vulnerable. He was wearing the eagle-bear-claw necklace, which he pulled from beneath his shirt and placed on the front of his jacket.

It was time to smoke the pipe. Setting the pack and his hat on the boardwalk, he retrieved the leather pouch and packed the briar pipe with kinnikinnick. He returned the pouch, lit the pipe, and prepared to replicate the ceremony Redfield had taught him last summer.

Graham turned to face the rising moon. He pointed the pipe skyward and entreated, "Holy Spirit, I am here at Tó-sál-dàu. Hear my prayer."

Extending the pipe toward his feet, he said, "Thank you for the blessings of the earth."

He turned to the north and said, "Open my eyes."

He turned to the east and said, "Open my ears."

He turned to the south and said, "Open my heart."

Finally, he faced west and said, "Guide my path!"

Graham closed his lips around the stem, pulled air through the bowl of the pipe, and blew a thick cloud of pungent smoke toward the moon. He watched as the white vapors slowly dissipated in the still night air.

He sat down immediately. Clutching his pack and hat close to his chest, he waited for the heavens to accelerate. This would be the first sign he was being propelled backward in time.

Seconds passed, then a minute. Graham checked the position of the moon. It had remained stationary.

There were no alternating lunar and solar cycles. No rotating sky. No urge to lie down because of vertigo-induced celestial movements. No stiff breeze showing a spiritual presence.

Nothing.

The spirits had ignored his petition.

The disillusioned time traveler rose, donned his hat, and shouldered his pack. He banged the pipe against the wood railing several times to empty the smoldering tobacco mixture onto the sinter next to the spring. He waited for another few minutes, holding out a faint hope for a delayed response.

Frustrated, he trudged down the hill to the Studebaker, where he tossed his hat and pack onto the passenger seat. He placed his arms on the top of the opened car door and looked back toward the noisy hot spring, mulling over his failed attempt to connect with the spirits.

He knew why he had been unsuccessful. Redfield had explicitly told him the Dragon's Mouth was not an option for his second vision quest. But he had ignored his mentor's counsel. When he had pulled the Studebaker into the parking area before sunset, he was sanguine about the possibilities that lay before him. Now he was doleful and crestfallen.

Graham roused from his self-pity when a shadow silently passed in front of the moon. He followed the path of a great horned owl as it perched on a high branch of a lodgepole pine overlooking the Yellowstone River. He gazed at the enormous bird with long, earlike tufts. Had the spirits sent this creature to deliver a message?

The raptor underscored his despondency when it emitted a deep call with a distinctive cadence. It sounded to Graham like the giant owl with intimidating yellow eyes was saying, *who's awake, me too.* Unfortunately, he was still awake. He had not lost consciousness. He was still in the twentieth century. And he would miss the birth of his daughter in May 1872.

Sighing, he climbed into the Studebaker and closed the door. He peered at the belching hot spring. His hopes for reuniting with Makawee had been fractured like the windshield of his car.

As he drove back toward Yellowstone Lake, he considered his next opportunity. It would be twenty-eight days before the next full moon. His disappointment gradually turned to determination, as he deepened his resolve to be successful in connecting with the spirits at the Bighorn Medicine Wheel in June.

The days lasted longer as the daylight hours increased. That was what it seemed like to Graham. Surely there were twenty-five hours in each day as May transitioned to June. He circled the date of the next full moon. While everyone savored the additional sunlight, he crossed off each day on a calendar. It was his *raison d'être* each day.

Graham remained guarded with his fellow employees about his personal life. He avoided most social gatherings and kept to himself. While those with whom he worked viewed him as somewhat aloof, this didn't bother him. He reasoned it would be better if he didn't get close to anyone. It would be less painful if he remained an enigma. That way, when he made a sudden departure, few people would truly miss him.

He was fortunate in not having a roommate. Yellowstone Park Company had hired the usual number of seasonal employees, but fewer had reported for work, so he had the small room to himself. This suited Graham. It was easier to remain private if he wasn't sharing living quarters. Although he kept everyone at arm's length, one person had almost breeched his emotional defenses.

Mirabelle was an athletically built strawberry blonde from Minnesota. The business major was an accounting clerk in the marina office. Graham saw her almost every day when he turned in the tour tickets after a cruise. She always found some reason to strike up a conversation. He listened politely as she talked about the beauty of the land near her hometown of Duluth, ice fishing with her father, or hiking trips along Lake Superior. They shared a love of the outdoors, and he enjoyed their conversations.

One Saturday evening, Graham had broken his antisocial norm and joined a small group at the employee bar. After drinking a few beers, he called it a night. When he rose to excuse himself, Mirabelle asked if he would escort her back to the Lake Hotel since it was well after dark.

As they passed by the H-block building, she inquired about seeing his room. He led her up the rickety steps and opened the door. After he flipped on the lights and closed the door, she surprised him by turning off the lights.

"I hoped we might get to know each other a little better," she said, slipping off her jacket and letting it fall to the floor.

Graham's eyes were still adjusting to the abruptly darkened room as he removed his jacket and tossed it onto the bed. He could see the silhouette of her slender body framed by the window.

"Well... what would you like to know, Mirabelle?"

"That name is too formal. My close friends call me Mira."

"Oh, all right. Why did your parents give you that name?" He was struggling to say something.

"My father is from Sweden and my mother is from France. They met when he was a foreign exchange student attending university. Mirabelle is a plum in the North of France. I guess my mother wanted to name me something that reminded her of that region."

"Mira. That's nice."

She took a step closer in the dark.

"Why haven't you asked me out on a date?" she asked, hands on hips.

"We had a good time talking with the others at the bar."

"That's not a date. That's just friends talking," she replied. "I had something else in mind. Something more personal." She placed her hands on his chest.

"Oh, well, you see I..." His mind went blank when he breathed her intoxicating perfume.

She leaned forward, tilted her head back, and parted her lips.

Graham instinctively placed his hands on the small of her back, pulled her toward him, and leaned down to meet her lips. When her breasts pushed against him, he felt a pinch from the bear claws on his necklace. It was an instant reminder of Makawee and jolted him out of his sexual stupor.

He grabbed Mira's wrists and stepped back.

"I... I can't do this."

"Can't do what? Kiss on our first date?"

"I'm not looking for a relationship. I'm sorry if I led you on," he said, letting go of her wrists.

"There's another woman in your life?"

"Yes."

"She must be very special."

"More than you can imagine."

Mira sighed as she picked her jacket up off the floor.

"It figures. Every guy I've met has tried to put moves on me. After a few drinks, all they want is to get me into bed. Yet the one guy I pursue isn't interested."

"Mira, in another time or place, I would get to know you better. But I'm committed to someone else."

"Graham, your fidelity makes you even more desirable. I hope this woman realizes she has someone exceptional," she said, while opening the door.

"Can we still be friends?"

"Sure. It's refreshing to meet a guy who doesn't change his mind the first time he's in the dark with a woman. Good night," she said, closing the door behind her.

Graham flipped on the lights and checked the calendar on the wall. It was only three days before he would venture to the Bighorn Medicine Wheel. They could not pass quickly enough.

The Bighorn Mountains loomed in the distance as the Studebaker left Lovell, Wyoming and headed east. Graham estimated he would arrive at the base of Medicine Mountain within thirty minutes. It was only six o'clock. He had planned to arrive while there was still plenty of daylight. Nighttime temperatures had been much lower than normal for early June, and he had brought an extra layer of clothes, anticipating cold weather and windy conditions on the mountaintop.

He was in good spirits, knowing the night he would complete his vision quest was finally here. He had traded his day off with another scenic cruise operator so he could leave early and make the four-hour drive. It felt strange not saying goodbye to anyone before he left Yellowstone Lake. So as not to raise any suspicions, he told his coworkers he was going to use his free time to explore the Bighorn Mountains.

His upbeat mood turned sour when he reached the mountains. A pair of barriers with "road closed" signs had been placed in the middle of the highway. He stopped the car and peered over the wooden barricades. Why would the road be closed? It looked clear ahead. He drummed his fingers on the steering wheel, debating his options. He would not be deterred. Not after waiting almost thirty days and driving all this distance!

A quick glance in his rearview mirror showed no other vehicles were behind him. He slammed the transmission into park, threw open the door, and ran to the front of the car. Grabbing an end of the wooden trestle in the eastbound lane, he quickly pivoted it out of the way. He ran back to the car, jumped in, and sped through the opening. He braked, exited the vehicle, and repositioned the barricade across the road behind him.

A minute later, he was ascending the mountain on a narrow, winding road. As he rounded a sharp curve, the headlights revealed a coating of snow on the road. Soon the Studebaker was slogging through several inches of snow. The tires repeatedly lost traction on the untreated asphalt. Reluctantly, he acknowledged the car could go no farther.

He sat for a minute and considered his situation.

I'm not giving up. There's no way I'm going back! he thought. *I'll just leave the car here and walk the rest of the way.*

He turned off the engine. As he reached for his pack and his hat on the passenger seat, he recalled Redfield's counsel:

"The spirits are not active when Annáshisee is covered with snow. You must arm yourself with daasátchuche — patience."

"Dammit!" he shouted through the windshield. He gripped the top of the steering wheel and rested his forehead on the backs of his hands. How could this happen? He was less than a mile from the site that could re-unite him with his nineteenth-century family. Yet it seemed he would fail again.

I may not have an abundance of patience, but I don't give up easily, he thought.

Suddenly, an idea seized him. He clicked on the dome light, opened his pack, and yanked out a flashlight and the Wyoming road map, which he rapidly unfolded. He clicked on the flashlight and used a finger to trace a route over the southern edge of the Bighorn Mountains, then east through Buffalo and Gillette. His finger stopped on Devils Tower National Monument. A quick calculation of the distance yielded an estimated driving time of nearly six hours.

A smile slowly creased his face. He could be at the Bear Lodge shortly after midnight. He tossed the unfolded map onto the passenger seat, started the engine, and carefully backed the Studebaker down the slippery mountain road, looking for a good place to turn around.

The solitary butte rose almost nine hundred feet above the grasslands. It stood like a sentinel watching over the Ponderosa pine forest and grasslands at its base.

Vertical hexagon-shaped columns of igneous rock created deep striations. It was easy to imagine why Indigenous people had named this geological anomaly Bear Lodge. It looked as if a giant grizzly had scraped its claws on the sides.

Graham leaned against the front fender of the Studebaker and marveled at the astounding natural monument. The reflected light from the full moon illuminated the sides. It created a stark contrast with the shadows between the vertical rock channels. From his vantage point, the lunar satellite appeared as though it were perched just above the flat top of the massive tower.

It was an easy walk from the parking lot to the base of the butte. After gathering his belongings, he placed the keys to the Studebaker under the floor mat and mouthed a silent goodbye to his faithful car. Graham flipped on his flashlight, but he could see the paved footpath remarkably well in the moonlight.

When he came to Tower Trail, he had to decide which direction to go, since this path encircled the butte. Unlike the Dragon's Mouth, there didn't seem to be an obvious place to stand where the spirits may be most active. An information display showed a small trail branched from the main path on the south side of the butte. This choice would also allow him to keep the moon in full view. Ten minutes later, he was snaking his way through a huge boulder field as he approached the base of the butte. He stopped when the path ended several hundred feet from the base.

Taking off his hat, he tilted his head back and scanned the massive aggregate of rock pillars as they jutted into the night sky. A hundred feet up, he could faintly make out a bird's nest on the narrow ledge of a broken column. He knew this was a nesting area for peregrine falcons and regretted not being able to see one of these dark-plumed raptors.

It was time to replicate his vision quest ritual from last month.

As he removed the sacred necklace from under his shirt and placed it on the outside of his jacket, he considered the potential connection between wearing an eagle-bear-claw necklace and standing at the Bear Lodge. Hopefully, this was a good omen.

Graham packed the briar pipe and lit the tobacco-willow bark mixture. He turned to face the moon, which was near its apex. Because there were no streetlights, a vast array of stars was visible in the inky black sky.

Pointing the pipe skyward, he petitioned, "Holy Spirit, I am here at Bear Lodge — Wakansica. Hear my prayer. Thank you for the blessings of the earth."

He turned to each of the four cardinal directions as he repeated the phrases he had learned from Redfield. "Open my eyes. Open my ears. Open my heart. Guide my path!"

Graham pulled air through the pipe, held it momentarily, and blew white smoke toward the moon. He leaned against a large boulder and stared at the moon, looking for the slightest movement that would indicate it had reversed its arc across the night sky. He awaited the telltale swirling breeze that showed a spiritual presence. One minute passed. Three minutes. Five minutes.

The earth and the chilly black sky were motionless. He stood and faced the gigantic rock tower, desperately searching for indications of a spiritual presence among its jointed columns. There were no signs of movement or shadows on the inert walls.

For the second time in less than a month, the spirits had refused his petition. They had denied Graham Davidson passage through the time portal.

"No! No! No!" He slammed his hat to the ground and shook a fist at the sacred mountain.

No, no, no. His words echoed as the sound waves from his voice reflected off the massive mountain and returned a second later, as if to mock him.

Graham sat down heavily and leaned against the smooth boulder, pulling his knees toward his chest, and cradling his head in his hands. What had he done wrong? Why weren't the spirits listening to his plea?

His anger morphed into melancholy as he contemplated the significance of another missed opportunity. His daughter, Nahkash, was at least a month old. With each passing month, Makawee would believe she would remain a single mother. She didn't realize her lover was trying everything within his power to get back to her. Yet he had been unsuccessful. His only option was to try again in the next lunar cycle.

Graham slowly rose to his feet. He swiped his hat from the ground and dusted it off by beating it against his leg before placing it on his head. Shouldering his pack, he checked his watch. It was almost one o'clock. He was scheduled to take the first cruise onto Yellowstone Lake at eight o'clock. He would need to drive all night to make it back in time.

He trudged back to the Studebaker and fetched the keys from under the floor mat. Before he slid into the driver's seat, he looked back at the Bear Lodge. Nothing about the appearance of the massive butte was different. However, the sky had darkened considerably. A passing cloud in an otherwise perfectly clear sky had drifted in front of the moon, temporarily occluding it from view.

The concealed moon seemed like another sign the spirits had denied his appeal. It was a fitting conclusion to the night's failed quest.

The phone booth was empty on the first Saturday evening in July. He had sent a letter to his mother with the number of the pay phone and asked her to invite Redfield on the call. Since his mother had moved in with her sister Ruth, they added an extension line. This made it convenient for two people in the same household to share a telephone conversation.

Graham stepped into the narrow booth, closed the folding glass door, and sat on the narrow wooden seat. He looked at his watch. The local time was eight o'clock, which meant it was ten o'clock in Pennsylvania. He had chosen this day and time because long-distance calls were less expensive on weekends and after ten o'clock. When the phone came alive with two quick rings, he picked up the receiver.

"Hello?"

"Graham! Oh, honey, it's so nice to hear your voice!"

"It's great to hear you as well, Mother!"

"Redfield is on the extension."

"Hi, Gra'am," a deep voice responded.

"Hey, Redfield! Thanks for joining the call. I know these calls are expensive. We won't talk long, but I wanted to see how you're doing."

Graham listened as his mother talked about her living arrangements with Aunt Ruth and how much she enjoyed being with her sister. He was gratified his mother seemed content, especially because he would soon leave the twentieth century. At least, that was what he had planned.

Redfield said very little about his life on Big Hill Farm. He was a man of few words.

Graham briefly spoke about his two failed attempts to travel back in time — at the Dragon's Mouth in May and the Bear Lodge in June. He shared that his next attempt would be next month at the Bighorn Medicine Wheel.

"Redfield, I'm disappointed and frustrated. I haven't been able to connect with the spirits," he said glumly. "I followed your instructions and did everything like I had last summer. But there was no response."

There was a moment of silence on the other end of the line. Graham imagined Helen and Ruth were looking at each other while holding the receivers to their ears in adjacent rooms. It was Redfield who responded.

"Did you not understand when I said Tó-sál-dàu was closed to you?"

"Yes. But it was close by. I'm eager to return to Makawee. I had to try."

"Uh-huh."

"Well, I understand why my first attempt failed. But the conditions were perfect at Devils Tower last month. I carefully followed all the steps in the ritual. I even used the Crow word for Bear Lodge — Wakansica."

"That's one reason you were unsuccessful."

"Why?"

"Wakansica means Bad God's Tower. You were at Wahanksica, which means bear. Benevolent spirits would never appear at a place designated for evil spirits."

"Shit!" Graham mouthed silently inside the phone booth. He had made the same mistake as the early explorers by mispronouncing the name of the sacred butte.

"That's not the only reason you failed," Redfield said.

"How so?"

"What was the last thing you said in your petition?"

Graham thought for a few seconds, silently repeating the words.

"Guide my path!"

"And what were you thinking while you said those words?"

"I don't know. I guess I just needed the time portal to be opened. And the spirits were the key for making that happen."

"That's the problem."

"What do you mean?" Graham asked as he furrowed his brow.

"Gra'am. Listen carefully. It's not only *what* you say but *how* and *why* you are saying it. The spirits interpreted the last three words you spoke at the Bear Lodge as a demand. You cannot demand anything. You must humbly make a request. Do you understand the difference?"

"Yeah. I do," a gloomy voice replied from Wyoming.

"Your failures are rooted in a personal fault we discussed before you left. You are impulsive. You have not displayed daasátchuche. The spirits sense you are impatient."

Redfield's words stung. He knew his mentor was right.

There was an uncomfortable silence. The only sound was the faint breathing of three people sharing the line.

Graham asked the obvious question.

"What can I do to guarantee a successful quest at the Medicine Wheel — Annáshisee? Did I say that correctly?"

"You pronounced the name correctly. But there is no guarantee your next attempt will succeed. The most important thing you can do is *request* guidance rather than demand it."

Helen jumped into the conversation. "Graham, I believe Redfield is right. Remember the words of our Lord's Prayer?"

"Of course."

"When Christians pray the words: 'thy will be done,' we are saying it is up to Him to guide and direct us. It isn't our will. It's His will."

Graham nodded, even though his mother couldn't see he understood what she had explained.

"We should hang up. This will be an expensive phone call. I'll send you money to pay for it, Mother."

"When is the next full moon?" Helen asked.

"Ten days."

"Graham, please continue to write letters while you are in today's world. And send updates to the newspaper when you travel back in time. I...I miss you even more now that we've talked. I love you so much and want you to lead a happy life with Makawee, but..."

Helen placed the receiver on her bosom and held her hand to her mouth as she softly wept. Graham heard the muffled sound of crying and knew his mother was grieving the loss of her son.

Redfield spoke to fill the void.

"Gra'am," he said in a fatherly voice, "I will watch over your mother when you are gone. We will be thinking about you from the future. Remember, to become a powerful warrior, you must arm yourself with patience."

"Thanks for everything. I love you both," he said, using his index finger to depress the hook switch.

He hung the handset in the cradle and leaned against the glass side of the booth. His heart ached knowing the emotional stress he had caused with his decision. But it also ached to see Makawee and Nahkash.

"Hey! Are you finished?" a man shouted outside the phone booth.

Graham nodded, pushed open the folding doors, and stepped into the hallway to allow the man to use the pay phone. If he connected with the spirits in ten days, this was the last time he would hear the voices of Redfield and his mother.

The road to Bighorn Medicine Wheel was familiar. Graham was certain he would reach his destination this time. It was a warm day in mid-July under partly cloudy skies. His only concern was whether there would be a break in the clouds long enough for him to be seen in the light of the full moon that was forecast for this evening.

He turned the Studebaker off Highway 14A onto a gravel road and drove about a mile and a half to a parking area, where a half dozen cars awaited their owners. A forest ranger advised the visitors to hike the remaining mile or so to the top of Medicine Mountain.

Graham parked his battered car in a remote part of the lot. He donned his jacket and hat, then opened his LL Bean pack to check the contents one last time. He had tossed some food into the pack with his personal gear, including three apples, a can of nuts, and a pack of beef jerky. It would be impossible to predict where his next meal would come from if he were successful with his quest.

Not if he was successful! When he was successful! He chastised himself for this temporary lapse into negative thinking.

He tossed the car keys under the floor mat and closed the door, running his fingers along the roofline as he headed to the trail. It was (he hoped) his last goodbye to the trusty car that carried him all the way from Pennsylvania — and several times across northern Wyoming.

Graham followed a gravel road up a gentle rise and was quickly above the timberline. Ten minutes later, he passed a signpost showing the elevation was 9,642 feet. He had reached the Medicine Wheel.

Visitors had tied a variety of offerings onto a post-and-rope fence encircling the sacred site. These included tobacco bundles, feathers, dream catchers, and even locks of hair. The most prominent sacred gifts were colorful prayer flags, which fluttered in the constant breeze that swept across the exposed mountaintop.

Although it was an hour before sunset, there were still a dozen people walking around the circumference and studying the rock structure from all angles. Graham walked around the fence to the highest point on the slightly sloping limestone surface to get the best view of Annáshisee. He counted twenty-eight spokes radiating from a ring-shaped central cairn. Someone had placed a bison skull on top of the hollow rock structure.

Graham thought about the picture of this ancient, hallowed site he had shared with Redfield and his mother. The photograph did not come close to conveying its true beauty or the spiritual presence he felt standing here.

He slowly pivoted while scanning the horizon. He was rewarded with a magnificent view of distant mountain peaks and the immense Bighorn Basin. He sat down a short distance from the wheel and waited for the visitors to leave.

After dusk settled over the mountaintop, Graham stood and followed the fence around the circumference. Satisfied everyone had made their way down the gravel road to their cars, he stepped over the fence. He walked to the central cairn and admired the bison skull.

He spotted the first outline of the full moon rising above the Bighorn Basin low on the southeastern horizon. A few clouds lingered in the early evening sky, but the chances of the moon being fully visible after sunset were promising.

This would be his third attempt to connect with the spirits. He needed to repeat the protocol of the previous vision quest attempts, but this time, he had to set his mind right. Redfield had made it clear Graham's petition was to be raised as a request, not an impatient demand. He closed his eyes and meditated, focusing on being vulnerable rather than trying to maintain control.

"Alaxxíche!" a voice called out in the darkness.

It startled Graham. He opened his eyes and spun around, looking for the source of the voice.

"Stop right now!" a stranger repeated in English.

Graham could see the silhouette of a man standing near the western edge of the Medicine Wheel. The shadowy figure gracefully stepped over the rope and walked toward him. As he drew near, Graham could discern the features of an elderly Native American. His loose gray shoulder-length hair framed a wrinkled brown face. He was wearing a simple elk-skin tunic and leggings.

"Only tribal members are allowed inside the sacred circle."

"Oh, I understand. But can I tell you why I'm here?"

The old man crossed his arms over his chest and nodded.

Graham attempted to explain his presence without raising suspicion. "I'm not a member of a tribe. But my close friend is Crow. He advised me to come to Annáshisee for a vision quest. I mean no disrespect. Just the opposite. I know this is a sacred place for many Native people."

The stranger's eyes narrowed as he spoke. "Prove you have a personal connection to a Crow."

Graham realized he was wearing the proof. He unbuttoned his coat, pulled the eagle-bear-claw necklace over his head, and handed it to the man.

"My friend Redfield gave me this necklace. He made it after he received *Baaxpée* from the bear spirit during his vision quest," he said, while the old man inspected the necklace. "I have a photo of him."

His hand brushed against the snub-nosed Colt revolver when he reached into the pack. He hoped the stranger would not search his belongings.

Graham retrieved the picture and offered it to the stranger.

The gray-haired man took the photo. He tilted it toward the moon and squinted at the picture before returning it.

"This necklace has bear claws. But it also has an eagle. Why?"

"I added the eagle pendant because that is my animal spirit."

The man rubbed the glass beads between his thumb and index finger like a rosary. He gave the necklace back to Graham, who placed it over his head.

"What are you called?"

"Graham Da-," he started to say. He changed his answer. "I am Graham Eagle Bear."

The stranger's eyebrows raised. He reached out his hand. "Wind at Night."

Graham accepted his hand and shook it.

"I safeguard this place from vandals. To Natives, Bighorn Medicine Wheel is not a monument. It is a living part of our spiritual traditions. Tourists disrupt the harmony of this sacred place. Sometimes they try to take home rocks as souvenirs."

The ignorant behavior of his white brethren embarrassed Graham.

"I'm sorry to hear that. Are you here every night?"

"Tonight, I am here. Tomorrow, I may be in another place."

"I promise to leave everything as I found it. The moon needs to be fully visible before I meditate and try to connect with the spirits."

"What is your offering?"

"I, uh, I didn't know one was required."

"If you want the spirits to heed your prayer, leave something as a sign of respect. Something simple."

An idea quickly came to him as he looked at the rope fence. He reached into his back pocket and pulled out a blue kerchief with a white paisley design.

"How about this?"

The old man accepted the square cloth and nodded. "You may proceed."

"Thank you."

Graham was relieved. He had not expected someone guarding the Medicine Wheel might thwart his third vision quest.

Wind at Night ambled to the fence and stepped effortlessly over it. He held the blue cloth above his head with both hands, said something Graham didn't understand, and tied the bandanna onto the rope. He faded into the darkness.

Graham peered to the southeast, where the moon was now bright and fully visible. He packed the pipe with kinnikinnick, removed his hat, and set his pack on the ground beside the cairn.

He prepared himself mentally, picking up on his meditative thoughts before the old man interrupted him. A candid self-examination was crucial if the spirits were to heed his supplication. He closed his eyes and considered the meaning of his words.

Opening his eyes, he started the ritual as he had twice before. Lighting the pipe, he repeated the series of phrases and blew the smoke toward the moon. This time, he let the words speak for themselves. If this was the time for him to enter the spirit world, it would happen. If not, he would wait until next month and try again.

After saying the last phrase, "Guide my path!" he grabbed his pack and hat before sitting with his back against the cairn.

A moment later, a soft breeze tickled his cheeks and tussled his hair. Suddenly, a gust swept over the mountaintop and pushed the bison skull off the top of the cairn. As quickly as it had arrived, the zephyr moved on, swirling dust from the gravel road as it ventured to an unknown destination.

Graham fixed his gaze on the brightly lit full moon. It began moving slowly but perceptibly lower in the sky. He blinked several times to make sure his eyes were not deceiving him. The moon moved from right to left in an arc toward the southeastern horizon, where it had appeared earlier.

When the full moon disappeared, the night sky dimmed. It brightened to a dark gray as a waxing gibbous moon reappeared over the southwestern horizon. This celestial sequence was continuously repeated, and the time for the moon to traverse the sky became shorter with each circuit. The moon rose, arced across the sky, and waxed or waned into a new phase with increasing speed. The heavens moved in concert with the moon, causing the constellations to shift positions and the stars to blur as the sky sped up its whirling rotation.

Graham had witnessed an identical supernatural occurrence at the Dragon's Mouth last summer and realized what was happening. The spirits had granted his petition! He was overjoyed, despite being disoriented and nauseous. He lay down beside the cairn, clutched his pack and hat, and closed his eyes to reduce the swirling sensation in his brain. A moment later, he lost consciousness.

The hundreds of colorful prayer flags affixed to the rope encircling the Bighorn Medicine Wheel hung motionless in the calm evening air. All except one. The blue paisley-patterned kerchief fluttered and flapped for twenty-eight seconds before going limp.

On a moonlit night in 1972, in the middle of the Bighorn Medicine Wheel, Graham Davidson vanished.

Chapter Six

Humbled by a Hatchet

July 16, 1872

S irius glittered in the eastern sky. The multi-colored star pulsed and flickered in the deep purple predawn. The heliacal rising of the morning star near the horizon was an impressive sight.

Little Wolf observed the brief celestial show while sitting in a fasting bed. The original coffin-shaped rock structure had been built hundreds of years ago and used by countless vision questers. It was situated a short distance from the Medicine Wheel on the east slope of the mountain. Little Wolf had an excellent view of the bright early morning star because the bed was oriented with its long axis running west to east. He had spent three days meditating on Medicine Mountain and three nights in the fasting bed. His stomach was empty, and he felt light-headed. This morning was his last opportunity to connect with the spirits.

It discouraged the young quester when the bright, distant star faded into the blue sky as the sun cleared the horizon. The dog days of summer were here now that Sirius and the sun shared the same eastern sky. Another August morning had arrived. Another day and another night had passed. But the spirits were nowhere to be seen or heard.

It was disheartening. A few months earlier his father, Long Horse, had granted Little Wolf permission to pursue a third vision quest. He was excited about the opportunity and had listened to the elders who instructed him on how to prepare. He especially valued the counsel of his older brother Rides Alone. But he would return to the Crow Reservation without so much as a hint of a spiritual encounter.

The young Crow rolled up his buffalo hide from the fasting bed and secured it with an elk-hide cord. He strode to the top of the mountain for a last visit to the Medicine Wheel before starting the journey back home.

As Little Wolf approached the center of the wheel, he spotted a man lying next to the central cairn. He stopped, walked backward for a few steps, then turned and sprinted down the slope to his horse to fetch his weapon. He returned to the

Medicine Wheel, creeping toward the cairn with his bow raised and an arrow in place. The bearded stranger remained motionless. When he reached the sleeping man's feet, Little Wolf pointed the tensioned arrow at the intruder.

"Iluú!"

Graham awakened with a start and sat up. He shielded his eyes from the low bright rays of the morning sun and was alarmed to see a nocked arrow six feet from his chest. He extended his hand in front of his face to protect himself.

"Wait! Don't shoot!"

Little Wolf took a few steps back but kept his weapon drawn.

"Iluú!"

"I don't speak your language. Speak English?"

"Stand up!" the young Crow said with perfect English.

Graham held both hands in the air as he struggled to his feet. He was relieved they could communicate.

"Why are you here?"

"I...I fell asleep after a long journey last night. I am Graham Eagle Bear. What's your name?" He kept his hands raised to reassure the young man he meant no harm.

"Little Wolf, son of Long Horse."

Graham's eyes widened. "Son of Long Horse? You...You are brother of Rides Alone!"

This statement surprised Little Wolf. He lowered the bow and cocked his head to one side.

"You are baashchiile. How does a white man know Rides Alone?"

"I became friends with him and Makawee when we rode together through the Land of Burning Ground last summer."

"You know Makawee? She is my sister."

"She is your *adopted* sister," Graham said. "Your father brought her into his family when you were a young boy."

Little Wolf took the tension off the bow and removed the arrow from the string, keeping a watchful eye on the white man.

Graham took a deep breath, exhaled, and lowered his hands. He was fortunate this young man was from a Mountain Crow tribe. If a Lakota Sioux or Blackfeet warrior had come upon him, they would have pierced his heart with an arrow while he slept. And who could blame them? A strange white man had violated their sacred place.

"I'm on my way to see Makawee and your brother. If you're headed back to Crow Mission, I would like to join you," Graham said hopefully.

"My family is not at Mission Creek. The Crow Agency is located inside Fort Parker. We are camped on Buffalo-Jumps-Over-the-Bank River. It is about three days' ride from here."

"I don't know that river."

"White men call it Stillwater River. Where is your horse?"

"It...it was stolen."

Graham had developed a skill for fabricating stories the last time he had traveled back in time. He wasn't comfortable doing it, but often felt he had no choice.

"This way."

Little Wolf walked down the slope to his horse, which was tied to a tree.

"You can come with me, but I only have one horse. I do not have food for two men."

Graham noted the abandoned fasting bed. Looking in that direction, he asked, "Did you come to Medicine Mountain on a vision quest?"

Little Wolf nodded.

"How long has it been since you've eaten?"

"Three days."

Graham knew the discomfort of hunger pangs after fasting for twenty-four hours. What would it feel like if he had not eaten for three days? He saw this as an opportunity to gain the young man's favor. He reached into his pack and proffered an apple.

The aspiring warrior hesitated before snatching it from the white man's hand. Graham watched as the famished young man devoured the firm fruit, including the core. As Little Wolf was savoring his last bites, Graham queried his young friend.

"Makawee was pregnant when I last saw her. Did she give birth to a girl or a boy?"

Graham wanted Little Wolf to confirm what he already knew from the Crow Indian census report.

"She had a girl. Named her Nahkash," he said, after swallowing the last piece of apple.

Graham was indeed the father of a baby girl! He thought of the obsidian turtle necklace Makawee wore around her slender neck.

"That name means 'turtle,' doesn't it?"

"Yes. It does."

"I'm eager to see Makawee, Nahkash, and your brother Rides Alone."

Little Wolf nodded. "We should go. My horse cannot carry both of us. We will take turns riding and walking."

"I will walk first. You are weak from fasting," Graham said.

He fished another apple from his pack and handed it to Little Wolf, reserving the third apple for himself. After thirty minutes of walking, Graham removed his pack and extracted the package of jerky. He handed several strips to Little Wolf, who accepted the savory dried beef.

The traveling partners switched every hour between walking and riding as they made their way northwest toward Montana Territory. Little Wolf was not talkative. Graham wasn't sure if this was his nature or if he was not feeling well from lack of food. When he complimented Little Wolf on his English, the young Crow explained Makawee had taught him the white man's language.

They stopped to rest along the banks of the Shoshone River around midday. Graham filled his canteen, and Little Wolf filled a water bag made from a bison stomach. After splitting the remaining jerky, Graham shared his small can of nuts. It was the last food he had in his pack. They needed to secure more provisions. The teen warrior claimed to have a few dried fish, but these would provide only a small meal.

"We will hunt before sundown," Little Wolf said.

"Are you an expert hunter?"

Graham regretted his question and hoped he had not offended the young man.

Little Wolf expanded his chest and looked into Graham's eyes. "I am the best hunter among the boys in my village."

Graham nodded. He hoped Little Wolf was truthful and not just boasting. Their stomachs might depend on his friend's skills. Graham thought about the Colt revolver in his pack, but decided he would use it only as a last resort. Because of its short barrel, the unusual-looking pistol might raise suspicions. He didn't have confidence he could hit a rabbit or other small game unless he was very close to his target.

They broke camp and packed their belongings. As Little Wolf mounted the horse, Graham held up his hand.

"Did you hear that?" he asked.

Little Wolf leaned forward on his horse and listened. The only sounds were the gurgling of water flowing around large rocks in the river and trees rustling in the sultry breeze.

A voice suddenly called out from a cluster of cottonwoods on the opposite riverbank.

"Stop!"

Both men scanned the shady wooded area where the voice had originated. Graham reached into his pack for the revolver, while Little Wolf started to remove the bow slung over his shoulder.

"Hands up!" the voice bellowed.

Graham left his pack on the ground at his feet and raised his hands. Little Wolf held one hand in the air but kept the other on his bow.

A dark-skinned man with shoulder-length hair emerged from the trees on horseback. He wore a short-brimmed hat with a round dome, a white shirt, a sack coat with a single chevron on the upper sleeve, wool pants, and an ammunition belt around his waist. He pointed a Winchester repeating rifle at the pair as he approached, riding across the shallow river.

"Where you headed?" asked the man with the rifle.

"Absarokee," Little Wolf said.

Graham could see his companion still had one hand on the bow slung across his shoulder. The young warrior wouldn't have enough time to whip an arrow onto the bowstring before the stranger shot him.

Don't do anything rash, kid, Graham thought.

"You are Crow?" the stranger asked.

"Yes. I am Little Wolf. Son of Long Horse."

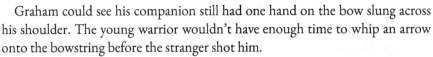

"I am NeesiRAhpát of Arikara tribe. Some call me Bloody Knife," he said, sliding the Winchester into a scabbard. He urged his horse forward. "Long Horse is respected chief. Our people are friends."

"This is Eagle Bear," Little Wolf said, nodding at Graham and removing his hand from the bow. "We met on Medicine Mountain this morning."

"Only one horse?"

"My horse was stolen," Graham chimed in.

"Sioux?"

"I...I don't know. It happened while I was sleeping."

"Sioux always take things. Horses, women, land..."

Unsure how to respond, Graham nodded.

"Wait here," Bloody Knife said, before wheeling his horse and crossing the river. He rode up the opposite bank and disappeared behind a dense stand of trees. Little Wolf and Graham looked at each other, puzzled by what Bloody Knife was doing.

He emerged a few minutes later leading a large bay roan and handed the lead rope to Graham.

"Scouting. Saw this pony. Sioux took your horse. We take theirs," he said, unfastening a blanket from behind his cantle and throwing it to Graham.

The horse had been stolen. But he would not refuse the Arikara scout's offer. It was literally a gift horse!

"I can pay," Graham offered. He laid the blanket on the ground, removed his pack, and reached inside to retrieve the United States notes.

"No money," he said, shaking his head. "We stand together against Sioux. Have food?"

Graham opened his mouth to speak, but Little Wolf interjected.

"We have plenty. Thanks for the horse. I will tell my father of your help."

Bloody Knife touched the brim of his hat, turned his horse, and rode across the river. He was soon out of sight.

"Why did you tell him we have plenty of food? We only have some dried fish and..."

"If we cannot find food, we deserve to starve."

There was an edginess to his words. Little Wolf's failure to connect with the spirits on Medicine Mountain had undoubtedly hurt his pride. Graham knew how the young man felt, having twice failed on a vision quest before last evening's success. The young Crow needed to prove he could kill or trap game to regain his self-esteem.

Graham handed the blanket to Little Wolf, who tucked it behind his saddle. He shouldered his pack and donned his hat. It occurred to him he wasn't sure how to mount an unsaddled horse. He had learned to ride a saddled mule last summer, but he had never ridden a mule or horse bareback. As he pondered the best way to get on the horse without the aid of stirrups, Little Wolf spoke.

"Jump onto her back!"

Graham grabbed the reins, hopped once, and swung his right leg high onto the horse's back. The horse turned abruptly and stumbled. Graham quickly lost his balance and tumbled backward. The mare bobbed her head and gave a puzzled look at the man sitting in the dirt.

Little Wolf cackled at this feeble attempt to mount a bareback horse. "Watch," he said after dismounting his horse.

The young Crow stood at the mare's front legs with his back to her head. He grabbed a tuft of mane just in front of her withers. In one smooth movement, he hopped on his left leg, threw his right leg over the horse's back, and grabbed the withers with his right hand to pull his upper body over. He made it look effortless. Little Wolf swung his right leg over the horse's neck and slid off.

"This horse is taller than most in our herd. She looks to be a little over fifteen hands. You are a big man. She can carry you. All you need to do is get on."

Graham sighed, positioned himself beside the horse, grabbed the mane, and hopped. A second later, he was seated on the ground, his cowboy hat lying several feet from where he landed.

Little Wolf shook his head. He took the bay roan's reins and led her toward the river, where he stopped beside a large boulder on the riverbank. He cocked his head, motioning for Graham to come to the horse. The embarrassed baashchiile used the rock as a step and mounted the mare without trouble.

After riding all day, Graham was glad when they stopped by a small creek and made camp. Riding bareback required him to use his inner thigh muscles to maintain his balance. When he slid off the sweaty mare at the end of the ride, his sore muscles compelled him to walk with a stiff gait.

While Graham gathered firewood, his traveling partner used a hatchet to cut willow sticks. Graham watched as the young man searched for small animal paths along the creek. After discovering one, he pushed an arched willow branch into the soft soil and fastened a sinew snare at the end of the supple limb. He set up several other snares within several hundred yards of their camp.

Little Wolf had not overstated his hunting prowess. An hour before sunset, he came back to the fire holding a fat sharp-tailed grouse by its neck. He used the hatchet to behead the bird. He offered the raw heart and liver to Graham, who politely declined, telling Little Wolf he should eat the nutrient-rich organs to regain his strength after fasting.

The young man's ability to be self-sufficient in the wilderness impressed Graham. He was reminded of his own ineptitude in basic survival skills. As they sat by the fire at dusk enjoying the roasted fowl, he attempted to strike up a conversation.

"Is this the first time you went on a vision quest?"

Little Wolf stopped chewing and wiped his mouth with the sleeve of his tunic. "Third time. I was ten years old when I traveled to Pryor Mountains on my first quest. I went to the same mountains again when I was twelve. The village shaman instructed me to go to Annáshisee this time. He said Medicine Wheel has a very strong spiritual presence."

Indeed, the spirits are very active there, Graham thought. "And how old are you?"

"Fourteen."

Graham almost choked on a piece of grouse and took a swig of water from his canteen. He couldn't imagine a ten-year-old boy spending three days and nights by himself in the wild. Or a fourteen-year-old riding solo three days to a sacred site. It was no wonder he had developed strong survival skills.

"It is clear the spirits do not deem me worthy of receiving a vision," Little Wolf continued as he tossed the breastbone of the prairie chicken into the fire and wiped his hands on his leggings. "Without a vision, I will not have any standing in my tribe. And I will dishonor my father."

"I'm sure when the time is right, the spirits will hear your prayer." He recalled the counsel given by Redfield and repeated it. "You must arm yourself with daasátchuche."

Graham was glad he remembered the Apsáalooke word for patience. But he cringed at the hypocrisy of his advice. It was easy to tell others to be patient. It was much harder to exercise this self-discipline. His previous vision quest failures were testaments to his own impatience.

"This may be true. But I have not yet humbled myself. I will not let pride prevent me from connecting with the spirits."

Little Wolf grabbed the hatchet lying beside him. He placed his left hand on a flat rock by the fire and folded his first three fingers into his palm. He swung the hatchet above his head. The sharpened edge of the small ax glinted in the flickering firelight.

When Graham realized what was about to happen, he jumped up and shouted, "No!"

"Thwack!"

It was too late.

The steel blade hurtled down, instantly severing Little Wolf's finger, which flipped into the fire beside the breastbone of the bird. Blood spurted from the severed digit and trickled down his forearm when he raised his hand. He gazed detachedly at his shortened finger.

"Shit!" Graham exclaimed as he rushed to Little Wolf and grabbed his hand to inspect the wound. His little finger had been amputated between the first and second joint. Graham clamped the stub of the teenager's finger to stop the bleeding. He desperately searched his brain for a way to wrap the wound.

"Lie down and hold your hand in the air."

The injured Crow obliged.

"You need to clamp your finger. Give me your other hand. I will show you where to apply pressure."

After Little Wolf pinched the stub of his amputated finger, Graham swiftly removed one boot and a sock. He used his pocketknife to cut off the elastic portion of the sock above the ankle. Then he cut the bottom portion into several strips. He dashed to the stream and soaked the cotton strips. Coming back to his patient, Graham waited for a few minutes until the blood stopped oozing from the wound. He fashioned a multilayered gauze from the damp strips. The stretchy top of the sock was used to bind the injured finger to the three healthy fingers.

"This will do for now," Graham said. "I need to get something. I'll be right back."

Graham discreetly fetched the flashlight from his pack. He slipped his sockless foot into his boot and stumbled upstream to the snare where the grouse had been captured. After a few minutes of searching in the dark, he located a second snare. Bringing the animal traps to the fire, he used his pocketknife to remove the sinew loops and used these to hold the bandage in place.

As he finished wrapping the wound, he noticed Little Wolf's extended arm had gone slack. Looking down, he could see the young man had lost consciousness from shock. Graham laid Little Wolf's arm on his chest. He fetched a blanket, lay it on top of his companion, and placed more wood on the fire.

Graham checked on the horses and returned with another blanket, which he laid on the opposite side of the fire. He stared at the flames and contemplated the self-mutilation ritual. His thoughts drifted to Redfield, who had also amputated a finger in pursuit of a successful vison quest. Redfield had done it for the same reason as Little Wolf — to show vulnerability and to prove he was imperfect to the spirits.

Somewhere in the prairie grass a chattering male cicada started its resonant calls. No sooner had the shrill sound of one insect faded when another began vibrating its abdominal membrane. It seemed as if Graham was in a giant amphitheater surrounded by dozens of eager insect performers. As Sirius was a visual sign in the early morning sky, these winged insects were audible signs of the dog days of summer.

While some found cicada sounds annoying, he was delighted by the summer symphony. It was further confirmation he had traveled back in time because he could hear insects from *every* direction. Earlier in the day, he had also heard the faint sound of the Arikara scout moving in the cottonwood trees by the river before Bloody Knife appeared.

His profound one-sided deafness was one reason he had been successful in connecting with the spirits. He didn't need to mutilate himself for a successful vision quest. He was *already* vulnerable and imperfect. Like the last time he had time-traveled to the previous century, his hearing had been restored!

Little Wolf regained consciousness, moaned, and tried to sit up. Graham scooted to his side and told him to lie down. The wounded warrior was soon asleep. Graham wondered if the aspiring warrior would regret his impulsive decision to amputate a finger when he awoke. He was also worried Long Horse might find Graham at fault for allowing his youngest son to mutilate himself.

He lay back on the horse blanket with his hands behind his head. As he gazed at the starry sky, he thought about his pending visit to the Crow camp. Would he be able to assimilate into the tribe? Would Long Horse give him permission to marry Makawee?

Graham was eager to see the love of his life. But he wasn't sure how or whether Makawee would welcome his return. He hoped he had not mutilated his chances of reuniting with Makawee by abandoning her and returning to his own time last summer.

Chapter Seven

Reunited

July 19, 1872

G raham counted a dozen Crow lodges along the banks of the Stillwater River as they approached the camp at dusk. They had erected the tall tepees in a staggered line several hundred feet from the river. The tops of twenty-one lodgepoles diverged at odd angles from the apex of each conical structure. Internal cooking fires illuminated most of the lodges.

Little Wolf reined his horse and turned to Graham.

"We will visit the ashé, or tepee, of my father, Long Horse. Have you ever been a guest in a Crow home?"

"No."

"There are a few simple rules. The rear of the lodge is the place of honor. That is where Long Horse will sit. Do not sit at the door. This is reserved for the bravest man."

Graham nodded. *Don't sit at the rear. Don't sit at the front. Got it,* he thought.

"Say nothing that will make the owner of the lodge unhappy."

Another nod. *Looks like I must choose the right time and place to ask for Makawee's hand in marriage.* "Anything else?"

"The tepee is the property of my mother, Fox Woman. Even though my father is our clan's chief, it is she who will determine if you are welcome as a guest in her home."

"Will Makawee be there?"

"Perhaps. Our family often shares an evening meal."

Little Wolf urged his horse forward, and Graham followed the young warrior toward camp. His heart started pounding, and his palms were sweating. He had waited an entire summer (and one hundred years!) to see his lover. He longed to hold her in his arms and kiss her until they couldn't breathe. However, a small part of him almost hoped she was not in Fox Woman's tepee. It would be difficult to keep his emotions in check, and he needed to make a favorable first impression on his future in-laws.

A boy saw the two riders and ran into the largest tepee in camp. He emerged a few seconds later with a warrior and pointed in the direction where Little Wolf and Graham were approaching. The warrior held a Sharps rifle in one hand and placed his other hand over his eyes to scan the horizon.

"Kahée!" Little Wolf shouted, waving his bow above his head.

"Kahée!" the man with the rifle replied.

When they got closer, Graham was delighted to see the warrior was Rides Alone. If it shocked him to see the young man from Pennsylvania again, he didn't show it.

The two riders dismounted. Rides Alone embraced his younger brother. "You have much to tell. I am eager to hear about your vision quest at Annáshisee."

"Not much to say," Little Wolf said. He changed the conversation by nodding at Graham. "I met this baashchiile on Medicine Mountain. His name is Graham..."

"Eagle Bear," Rides Alone finished, looking at Graham. "I rode with Eagle Bear in Land of Burning Ground last summer."

"Rides Alone, it's good to see you," Graham said sincerely.

"Did not expect you to return from long journey."

Graham caught the hidden meaning in his friend's words. Although he had never told Rides Alone about his time travel, the warrior sensed Graham had a spiritual presence and had not been born in this time. He was the only person other than Makawee who knew about this secret.

"I missed Makawee," Graham said. "That's why I came back."

"She has child."

"Yes. Little Wolf said her name is Nahkash."

"Nahkash has *blue eyes.*"

Graham was stunned. Rides Alone knew Graham was the father of Makawee's child! He threw a furtive glance at Little Wolf, who seemed oblivious to the significance of his brother's bold statement about the baby's eye color.

"Have you eaten, Eagle Bear?" Rides Alone asked.

Graham was speechless. This revelation elevated the anxiety he was already experiencing in anticipation of meeting with Makawee's family. Had Rides Alone shared this knowledge with others? If Makawee's family knew he was the baashchiile who had abandoned her after she was pregnant, they would not welcome him. He had planned to tell her father, but not so soon. And not without talking to Makawee first!

"We would like to share the meal," Little Wolf responded to his brother's query.

Rides Alone spoke in Apsáalooke to the boy, who took the reins of both horses and led them away. Little Wolf entered the tepee.

Graham turned to Rides Alone and asked, "Does anyone else know...?"

"Talk later. Enter," Rides Alone said, holding open the flap.

Graham took a deep breath and exhaled. He grabbed his backpack, removed his hat, and ducked into the lodge.

He paused and let his eyes adjust after he stepped inside. The only light came from a cooking fire, its smoke wafting to the opening at the top. He scanned the lodge. Six or eight indistinct figures were seated along the periphery, cloaked in the shifting shadows cast by the light of the fire. He could only see the faces of those sitting closest to the fire. An older man and woman were sitting at the rear of the tepee, away from the opening. Based on their age and the place of honor, Graham concluded they were Chief Long Horse and his wife Fox Woman.

"Father, I have returned," Little Wolf said, bowing his head. "I met this man at Annáshisee. He is Eagle Bear."

Long Horse extended a hand to his side, inviting both travelers to sit in an area to his right. After Graham and Little Wolf were seated, Fox Woman rose and ladled stew into wooden bowls. When she offered Graham a bowl, he nodded in appreciation, wishing he knew the Crow word for "thanks."

Little Wolf raised a bowl to his lips and made a loud slurping noise as he sipped the warm meat broth. Graham also drank the flavorful soup, grateful for a hearty meal after three days on the trail eating prairie chicken and dried fish. Little Wolf made exaggerated slurping noises as he sucked liquid from the bowl. As he tilted the bowl toward his lips, the young man elbowed Graham in the ribs and caught his eye.

For a second, Graham was confused. Was he doing something wrong? The young man had given him a cue to follow his lead. The host *expected* noises from her guests while they ate. If they didn't make any noise, she would think they did not like her cooking. Graham tilted the bowl and allowed a small amount of air to be sucked in while he guzzled the broth. He imitated Little Wolf's sonorous slurping sounds.

When he lowered the bowl from his lips a minute later, he could see Fox Woman smiling. He held out the empty bowl and nodded to the steaming kettle on the fire. Little Wolf's mother rose and ladled another helping into his bowl before returning to Long Horse's side.

"I speak some English," Long Horse said. "Welcome to our home. This is my wife, Fox Woman."

Graham nodded again to show his appreciation of the flavorful stew. This was her home. Thanks to Little Wolf, he knew it was important for Fox Woman to see him as a polite guest.

The chief looked to his right. He moved his arm counterclockwise around the tepee, pointing to each person as he spoke.

"Little Wolf, youngest son. Rides Alone, oldest son. Among the Grass, widow of my brother Falling Rock. Black Hawk, son of Falling Rock."

The cry of a baby interrupted Long Horse's introductions.

A woman rose, emerged from the shadows, and stepped toward the center of the lodge. She bowed her head and sang softly to an infant. When she looked up, the firelight illuminated her features. Graham gasped and almost dropped his bowl.

"I am Makawee, daughter of Long Horse and Fox Woman. This is Nahkash," she said in a familiar, pleasing voice that was music to Graham's ears.

He struggled to suppress his desire to jump up and embrace the beautiful Crow woman. He searched her face for clues about how she felt seeing him for the first time in over a year. She beamed while holding their daughter, and her dark brown eyes glinted in the faint light. She retreated to the dark recesses of the lodge and sat down.

"Young woman with child is my daughter, Makawee," Long Horse said with a hint of pride in his voice. "You know her?"

Graham was so distracted with thoughts of Makawee, he hadn't heard the chief's question.

"Huh? Did you ask me something?"

"You know Makawee?" Long Horse repeated his question.

"Oh...yes. I rode with her and Rides Alone through the Land of Burning Ground last summer. We are... friends."

His heart was bursting with joy. He could see by Makawee's body language and the look on her face she was glad he had returned. Oh, what a reunion it would be! He had so much to tell her. And he had many questions. In his mind, he fast-forwarded to the day when they would be married and have their own home.

"Little Wolf!" The chief's deep voice snapped him from his reverie. "What is this?" he asked, clasping his fingers.

Graham looked over at his riding companion sitting beside him. Earlier this morning, he had used his other sock to wrap the amputated finger with a clean bandage. Although the wound had stopped bleeding, he hoped the young warrior wouldn't contract a bacterial infection from the rusty hatchet. There would be no tetanus vaccine for another fifty years.

Little Wolf looked down at his bandaged hand. "To prepare for my *next* vision quest."

Long Horse used one hand to make a circular motion around his other hand. He wanted Little Wolf to remove the bandage.

Little Wolf obliged. He untied the sinew holding the crude bandage and unwrapped the cloth strips. He held the wounded hand in his lap.

"Alóowee!" ["You show!"], Long Horse commanded.

Little Wolf stood. He extended his left arm toward the fire and spread his fingers. Even in the dim light of the lodge, everyone could see the shortened fifth digit.

A gasp came from the dark.

"Áxpiichiwee." ["Tell about what happened."]

Little Wolf spoke in his native tongue, gesturing with his hands as he spoke. The first part of his story was about his experience on Medicine Mountain. He used expressions and body language to portray a fasting bed, the rising sun, meditation, and prayers to the spirits. When the storyteller looked at him, Graham assumed Little Wolf was explaining their encounter at the Medicine Wheel three days ago.

Graham flinched when Little Wolf concluded his story by swiftly bringing his hand down into his left palm with a slap. It was a shocking depiction of the moment he had used a hatchet to amputate a finger.

Long Horse was stoic during the young man's story. He turned and said something to Among the Grass, who approached Little Wolf and motioned for the teen to come with her.

Rides Alone leaned over to Graham. He whispered that Among the Grass was a midwife who had learned about herbal medicines from a shaman in another village. The chief had instructed her to treat Little Wolf's wound.

"Why you here?" Long Horse asked Graham after they had departed.

Graham took a deep breath. He squinted across the lodge toward Makawee, but could only see the shadowy outline of a woman cradling a baby. He wished he could have spoken with her before he said anything to her father.

"I traveled through the Land of Burning Ground with Rides Alone and Makawee last summer. I decided to come back," he said vaguely but truthfully. He prayed Rides Alone would not choose this moment to disclose the secret behind the birth of the chief's granddaughter. Graham stole a quick glance at the warrior, whose gaze remained fixed on his father.

"How long you stay?"

"I'm not sure."

The chief sat back, crossed his arms, and studied Graham's face.

"You help Little Wolf. Rides Alone calls you friend. Stay," he announced.

"Eagle Bear stay in my tepee," Rides Alone said. He stood and indicated Graham should follow.

Graham picked up his pack and hat, but paused before leaving. He turned toward the back of the lodge and respectfully nodded to Long Horse and Fox Woman before stooping at the entrance and stepping into the darkness.

The lodge where Rides Alone slept was smaller than the spacious one used by Chief Long Horse. After leading Graham into the tepee, he rekindled the fire under a suspended kettle. He explained the lodge was also home for Little Wolf, Makawee, and Nahkash.

"Thanks for allowing me to stay with you," Graham said, removing his hat and setting his pack down. "And for giving me a chance to explain to your father what happened last summer. I promise to tell him the truth about Nahkash, but wanted to speak with Makawee first."

Rides Alone acknowledged him with a nod. "I will get Makawee."

The young white man looked around the dwelling and noted its simple furnishings. Clusters of buffalo hides and blankets around the walls defined sleeping areas. Several willow-rod backrests had been set up. One of these had been placed alongside a wooden cradleboard in an area designated for Makawee and Nahkash. Twigs and logs were piled near the fire. Elk-hide bags and pouches served as containers for knives, pots, pans, herbal medicines, and other necessities. They had hung several sacred objects. A bow, a quiver of arrows, and a rifle leaned against the front wall, where they could be accessed quickly.

Graham smiled when he spied a smudging stick suspended from a pole near the back wall. He pulled it to his nose and breathed in the fragrance of sweetgrass and sage. Memories of the sensual evening he spent with Makawee came flooding back. Last summer they had smudged each other's clothes inside a temporary wickiup on the shores of Yellowstone Lake. They had made love on a buffalo hide. They conceived their daughter on that night of passion in the Land of Burning Ground.

"You came back," a voice said softly from the opening.

Graham let go of the smudging stick and spun around to see Makawee holding Nahkash.

"Yes. I couldn't live in my world without you," he said, walking toward her.

"A part of you was always with me," she replied with a smile, looking down at her infant daughter.

Graham stepped closer. He pulled a blanket fold away from the baby's face and gazed at her. "Rides Alone was right. She has blue eyes," he commented aloud.

"She has *your* eyes."

Graham leaned over the swaddled child and kissed her mother. As he pulled away, Makawee leaned forward and pressed her lips against his. He clasped his hands around her nape and met her lips. They separated and kissed again and again. They sought each other's lips hungrily, as if they could never get enough. Graham felt sensuous impulses course through his body for the first time in a year. Tears of joy streamed down their faces and dripped onto the baby's blanket.

"Wah! Wah!"

Nahkash started crying, oblivious to the passionate reunion between the two people hovering over her.

"Chitchíssee," ["Quiet"] Makawee said soothingly. "She needs to eat. She can nurse while we talk."

Makawee sat on a backrest made with a seat of thin willow branches fastened into a trapezoidal shape and edged with wool. The narrow end of the backrest was hung on a short tripod by an elk-hide cord.

Graham set up another backrest beside the cradleboard. The young mother slipped her loose-fitting dress over a shoulder and removed her arm from the sleeve. Nahkash latched on to her exposed breast and became quiet.

"Did you return through the Medicine Wheel?" she asked.

"Yes. That's where I met Little Wolf. I tried to come back through the Dragon's Mouth several months ago. Redfield told me it would not work a second time. But I had to try. I felt your presence there and was sure the spirits would guide me to you."

"I was at Tó-sál-dàu right after Nahkash was born. I had taken the afterbirth and tossed it into the noisy cave. Many Crow women bury the afterbirth of their babies at a sacred place to connect them to the earth."

"I can't think of a more appropriate place. Was she born healthy?"

"Yes. Among the Grass is a midwife. She helped me to deliver. However, she suspects Nahkash is not from our tribe."

"She probably noticed our baby's blue eyes."

"Perhaps." Makawee looked down at the suckling baby. "Among the Grass makes me uneasy. I'm not sure why. She has treated me well. It's just a strange feeling I have."

"Did you tell anyone I'm the baby's father?"

"No one. Everyone wanted to know. There was plenty of gossip in our camp. But I kept this secret close to my heart."

Graham nodded. "Rides Alone knows," he said, observing Makawee for a reaction.

"I did not tell him. He was with us the entire time we were in Yellowstone last summer. He knew we were in love. It was easy to determine what happened. Don't you remember he gave us time together near the end of our journey?"

"Yes, I do. I respect him for keeping this secret."

"As do I. Graham, Rides Alone respects you as well. He would never say this, but I believe he is almost as glad you returned as I am. Almost," she said with a smile.

"Would you like to hold her?" she asked abruptly.

"Of course!"

Nahkash had drifted into a light sleep induced by filling her stomach with warm milk. When Makawee pulled the baby away, Nahkash instinctively sucked as if she were still attached to her mother's breast. Makawee handed the three-month-old child to Graham. She pulled her dress up over her shoulder to cover her breast.

Graham cradled his daughter and immediately knew he was unprepared to hold an infant. His arms, shoulders, and jaw stiffened. He had faced a grizzly bear, a belligerent cavalry officer, and hostile Blackfeet. But this was an unknown fear. She seemed so fragile. Was she comfortable? What if he dropped her?

Makawee chuckled. "She won't break."

Graham nodded and tried to relax. He studied the baby's features. Her light brown skin and her dark hair. Her tiny hand that poked from beneath the warm blanket. She was beautiful and amazing. She was a miracle!

"I'm a father," he said, beaming.

When Nahkash had fallen sound asleep, Makawee took the baby from Graham, swaddled her, and strapped her onto the cradleboard. They moved their willow backrests to the opposite side of the tepee so they could talk without disturbing Nahkash.

"Can you tell me about the other family members I met in the lodge?" Graham inquired.

"Among the Grass is a widow to Falling Rock, the younger brother of Long Horse. She had lost two girls at birth before her son Black Hawk was born. They joined our band last year. They lived with the River Crow for many years. I understand Long Horse and Falling Rock had a disagreement as young men and they separated."

"How did Falling Rock die?"

"He fell from his horse during a buffalo hunt and was trampled to death."

Graham cringed at this horrible death.

"Among the Grass came to Long Horse's camp after this happened?"

"Yes. She and her son also came because the government started passing out annuities at the Crow Mission in Fort Parker. They wanted to be sure to get their share."

"Tell me about Black Hawk."

Makawee sighed. "He is an angry young man."

"Do he and Rides Alone get along?"

"They tolerate one another. They are about the same age. Black Hawk thinks his cousin is too soft in reacting to the white man's actions. I overheard them arguing. Rides Alone believes the best approach for our people is to follow the advice of Plenty Coups, a young chief whose vision calls for us to be allies with the white man to preserve more of our territory. Black Hawk thinks we should fight the white man like our enemies — the Sioux, Cheyenne, and Blackfeet. He would like to become a chief so he can lead our tribe to war."

"I see. Is Rides Alone the successor to Long Horse?"

"It will most likely be him, followed by Little Wolf. So long as both brothers are alive, Black Hawk is not likely to become a chief — unless he proves himself more capable than Rides Alone. Long Horse said he will decide later who will inherit the reins of leadership."

"So Black Hawk sees Rides Alone and Little Wolf as rivals?"

"Yes. Any male offspring from the house of Long Horse would be given first consideration as the next leader."

"I am not a threat to Black Hawk. Neither are you or Nahkash," he said, glancing toward the cradleboard where the infant girl was sleeping.

"That's right. Only male offspring from the lodge of Long Horse."

Graham breathed a sigh of relief. "Thanks for sharing this. If I am to be a part of your family, I want to know a little about who these people are."

"I would ask you to return the favor and tell me about your family, but..."

"Yeah, they haven't even been born!" he finished her thought.

Graham stood and tossed some wood on the fire. He cherished these moments alone with Makawee.

He turned to face her and said, "I plan to tell Long Horse I'm the father of his granddaughter. Will you go with me tomorrow?"

"Yes. I am not ashamed. We will do this together," she said, as she stood and grabbed his hand.

"Thank you!"

Graham pulled her to him and placed his hands on her hips. She wrapped her arms around his neck and stood on her toes as they shared a deep kiss.

He dropped to one knee while still holding her hands. He looked up at her face in the flickering light of the fire.

"Makawee, I love you. I want to care for you and spend my life with you. Will you marry me?"

"Éeh!"

"Is that yes or no?"

"Yes! Yes! Yes!"

He jumped up and pulled her so close he could feel the eagle-bear-claw necklace pressing against his chest. They shared another passionate kiss, their lips pressing together as if to seal these words. His hands moved from her hips to her breasts, which he cupped in his hands. She responded by closing her eyes and tilting her head back. Graham kissed her neck while unlacing the top of her dress. He slipped it over one shoulder to expose her breast. He felt a surge of pleasure in his loins and unbuttoned his shirt.

She stepped back abruptly.

"Graham, we can't do this right now. Rides Alone or Little Wolf could return," she said, pulling her dress back in place and retying the laces.

He inhaled and blew out a long breath while buttoning his shirt.

"When can we make love?" he asked in an exasperated tone.

"I don't know. We have to wait for the right moment."

Wait. There's that cursed word again, he thought. *She's right. This isn't the time or the place. Damn, it's hard being close without becoming intimate!*

Graham refocused on the excitement of a few minutes earlier. Makawee had accepted his marriage proposal! They were going to be man and wife. He grinned at the prospect of spending time with her and Nahkash.

"Can I at least have a hug before I leave?" he asked, reaching out and pulling her back to him.

She stepped into his embrace. They kissed, held each other, and swayed back and forth for a minute. This time it was Graham who stepped away.

"I'm sorry my proposal wasn't in a more romantic setting. But I thought this might be the perfect place for us," he said, looking over his head.

She followed his gaze. They had kissed while standing beneath the smudging stick. A bundle of sage and sweetgrass had ignited their inner flames of passion a year ago. Tonight, they committed to each other under the Crow equivalent of mistletoe.

Chapter Eight

Seven Horses

July 20, 1872

I t was well after midnight when Graham drifted off to sleep. He had stared for hours at the clear sky through the narrow opening at the apex of the tepee, his thoughts consumed by the pending conversation with Long Horse. One minute he was convinced the chief would grant his request to marry Makawee; the next minute he became despondent after concluding Long Horse would ban him from the tribe for making his adopted daughter pregnant before marrying her.

He was grateful to be welcomed into the lodge of Rides Alone. But it felt awkward to share sleeping quarters with the warrior, Little Wolf, Makawee, and baby Nahkash. Everyone quickly fell asleep. Loud snoring and soft breathing resonated throughout the buffalo-hide enclosure. When the baby awakened during the night, Makawee comforted and nursed her, while the men slept. Graham longed for the day when he would sleep with Makawee in their own home.

Rides Alone rose at dawn. He rekindled the fire and boiled water in a kettle. The lodge occupants shared a meal of dried deer strips, huckleberries, and tea. Makawee strapped Nahkash onto a cradleboard and joined Graham for the walk to the lodge of Long Horse.

Fox Woman offered tea to the visitors. Among the Grass and Black Hawk were sitting on one side of the large tepee. When the guests were seated, Makawee addressed her father.

"Eagle Bear would like to speak."

Long Horse nodded.

Graham took in a deep breath and exhaled. "Thank you again for welcoming me. I respect you and your people. I promise to help however I can."

Another nod.

"Last evening, I said Makawee and I are friends. We are more than friends. We are in love." He didn't wait for the chief to respond. He pressed on before his courage dissipated. "We met and fell in love last summer in the Land of Burning

Ground. I traveled back East after the Hayden trip finished, but I always knew I would return. Makawee gave me several beads from her turtle necklace, which I put on my eagle-bear-claw necklace to represent our commitment to each other."

He stood, removed the sacred necklace, and handed it to the chief before returning to sit beside Makawee.

Long Horse inspected the necklace with the Eagle Scout pendant and five grizzly bear claws. He paid special attention to the black-and-yellow chevron seed beads strung onto the elk-hide cord.

"When I left, I did not know Makawee was with child." Graham gave a fleeting glance at Nahkash sleeping in Makawee's arms. Returning his gaze to Long Horse, he said, "I am the father of Nahkash."

Fox Woman raised a hand to her mouth in surprise.

Among the Grass whispered something to Black Hawk. The white man had just confirmed her suspicions about the baby not having been fathered by a local tribe member.

"I wish to marry Makawee, and I am asking for your permission," he concluded.

Makawee flashed an approving smile at Graham. She was pleased with his words.

Fox Woman leaned over and muttered something in her husband's ear. Long Horse clasped his hands together in front of him and appeared to be deep in thought. After a moment, he spoke.

"Makawee my only daughter. You give seven horses. Prove worthy. Then you can marry."

Graham was crestfallen. Seven horses? He had only one horse — the one Bloody Knife had stolen and given to him! And what must he do to show the chief he was worthy? *This is crazy*, he thought. *I love this woman. She has a child with me. By marrying her, I am doing the right thing.*

His disappointment morphed into anger. "Is this because I am baashchiile?"

The chief's countenance changed. He leaned forward, his eyes narrowing as he spoke. "*Anyone* who wants to marry Makawee gives seven ponies and proves worthy."

"But I'm this child's father!" he exclaimed, pointing to the sleeping baby.

Makawee squeezed Graham's elbow. It was her signal for him to be silent.

"All noble warriors have daasátchuche," was the chief's reply.

Dammit, Graham thought. *Once again, I'm told to have patience.* Redfield had given him the same advice.

"Father...," Makawee said.

Long Horse held up his hand.

"I have spoken."

The chief held out the eagle-bear-claw necklace draped across the palm of his hand.

"Go."

Graham stepped forward and retrieved the necklace. He started to speak, but reconsidered after noting the steely gaze of Long Horse. Continuing to argue with the chief would only make things worse.

Lifting the cradleboard, Makawee rose to her feet and hurried to the front of the tepee. Graham followed, but paused at the opening. He calmed his emotions and suppressed his bitter disappointment long enough to turn and bow to the chief. He pushed the flap aside and entered the bright morning sun.

"This is a good day!" Among the Grass exclaimed. The midwife and her son had walked to the river in silence after the meeting in the tepee of Long Horse. The humid air and cloudless skies were harbingers of another hot day in southern Montana. They had sought refuge from the August sun under a mountain alder adorned with small woody cones.

"Why do you say this?" Black Hawk asked.

"Now we can join the house of Long Horse."

"We are already family."

"No. We are guests. After your father died, Long Horse welcomed us into his tepee. But we are people from another land."

"We are all Apsáalooke," Black Hawk objected.

"We are River Crow. Long Horse's people are Mountain Crow. Not the same."

Black Hawk knew this was true. He had been the leading candidate to be chief among the River Crow. But because they had moved from the Missouri River to southern Montana to live with their cousins, he had to prove himself as a potential leader.

"What can we do?"

"You must marry Makawee," Among the Grass said without hesitation. "It is clear Long Horse favors her. After you marry into his family, you will be an equal to Rides Alone."

"But Cousin Rides Alone is the oldest son. He is the obvious choice to take his father's place as chief."

"Listen to me, son. I believe Long Horse would like to fight the white man to keep our lands. He secretly complains about how the Crow are treated, but he does nothing. Several times I overheard Rides Alone advise his father to listen to Plenty Coups."

The veins in Black Hawk's neck became prominent as his muscles tightened. His voice became louder as he spoke.

"Is Plenty Coups the young Crow who had a vision? I've heard his prophetic dream. He saw weird buffalo with odd tails coming out of a hole and spreading over the land. This is supposed to represent cattle overtaking the buffalo. He says the only way to save our people is to cooperate with the white man. Warriors fight. They do not surrender!"

"I agree. Rides Alone is not a true warrior. He does not think we can fight our traditional enemies and the white man," Among the Grass said. "You must marry Makawee. Get close to Long Horse and influence his thinking. Convince him you can unite our people against *all* enemies, including the white man."

Black Hawk nodded. "Even if Long Horse does not support Rides Alone as the next chief, what about Little Wolf? He is also a son of Long Horse."

"Many things can happen to a young man as he tries to prove himself as a warrior when counting coup," she said with a shadowy smile. "Prove yourself as a warrior, and become Makawee's husband. Do these things and your path to being a chief will be assured."

"How do I convince Makawee to marry me? The baashchiile Eagle Bear has already proposed."

"You don't have to persuade Makawee. Long Horse decides who will marry his daughter. Did you hear what Long Horse wants for her hand in marriage? He wants seven horses and a warrior as his son-in-law. You can steal seven horses from our enemies and prove you are worthy. Eagle Bear will fail. He is a poor white man who lacks the heart of a warrior."

Black Hawk pondered his mother's advice.

"Makawee is a beautiful woman. But she is already a mother. I could never accept her half-white child as my own."

"You are wise to see the world this way," Among the Grass said, as she gripped his elbow and looked into his eyes. "Some Crow women have married white men and given birth to mixed-race children. When you become chief, forbid marriages with our enemies. Proclaim that you will welcome only those with pure

Apsaàlooke blood into your lodge. Treat baby Nahkash as a half-breed orphan. When Makawee bears your son, he will be the legacy of *Chief Black Hawk.*"

Among the Grass had presented a compelling future scenario in which her son would be a respected warrior. He would lead his people to fight against the never-ending hordes of white people invading their land. He would be revered among the Crow as a powerful leader, equal in stature with Chief Sitting Bull and Chief Crazy Horse of their Sioux enemies. Her words were encouraging and inspiring.

"I will do as you say," Black Hawk said with steely resolve.

Graham was miserable. It had been six weeks since Long Horse had listed his requirements to marry Makawee. The message had spread through camp. Eagle Bear was welcome, but he had not earned the right to marry Makawee. Although the lovers had a few brief moments alone, there never seemed to be an opportunity for Graham and Makawee to share their affections. He had to settle for holding baby Nahkash and stealing an occasional kiss with his bride-to-be when no one was watching. Even Rides Alone was unwilling to give his sister and Graham privacy in the tepee they shared, respecting his father's ultimatum.

The disconsolate young white man spent most of his time trying to be helpful. He gathered firewood, assisted with the horses, and took his turn standing guard at night. Little Wolf taught him how to make and set snares to catch rabbits, grouse, and other small animals. Every few days, he accompanied the men on hunting trips. They preferred killing bison, but the immense bovids were becoming scarce. The hunting party had to travel farther from camp each time to locate the dwindling herds.

One early October afternoon, Graham ventured up the river on his own. He needed time alone to consider his options for starting a new life with Makawee and their daughter. His initial month with Makawee had not unfolded as he had hoped or envisioned. The only thing he knew for certain was his current lifestyle was not sustainable.

Graham shouldered his backpack, placed a saddle on his horse, and tied a blanket to the rear pommel. Rides Alone had given him an old wooden frame saddle covered with buffalo hide. It had two elk-horn pommels, one in front and one in back. Although the crude saddle was more comfortable than riding bareback, he yearned for a traditional leather western saddle.

He followed the Stillwater River upstream toward the Beartooth Mountains for thirty minutes. When he came to a thick grove of black cottonwood trees, he dismounted. The heart-shaped leaves of the fast-growing trees were a bright yellow-gold, signaling that summer had transitioned to fall. Scattered among the cottonwoods, willow bushes competed for space along the riverbank.

After tying his horse, he spread the blanket at the base of the largest tree. He sat down beside his pack and leaned against the cottonwood. The late afternoon sun made him drowsy, and he nodded off to sleep.

He was awakened by a squawking great blue heron. The long-legged bird flew low over the river and landed in a shallow area a few hundred feet away. He watched as the majestic gray-blue bird with a curved neck waded into the stream. A few minutes later, it speared a frog and swallowed the prey head first before taking flight and continuing upstream, seeking its next meal.

Graham peered under the cottonwood branches at the sun hanging low on the horizon. He could see a small herd of elk grazing in the distance. Two bulls were sparring, pushing one another with their antlers and raising clouds of dust from the dry grass. The clacking sound of the dueling antlers carried to the river. This bucolic scene seemed to clear his head. It enabled him to think about his immediate future.

Horses cost money. Saddles cost money. But he had only thirty dollars in his pocket. He needed to secure a paying position. Those opportunities didn't exist in eastern Montana. He faced a conundrum. As much as he wanted to be with Makawee and Nahkash, he would have to leave them to earn enough money to buy the horses and secure his family's freedom to live together.

"Kahée!" someone shouted from the other side of the tree.

Graham reached into the pack and retrieved his Colt Cobra revolver. He jumped up and cautiously peered around the tree, aiming the gun in the voice's direction. He was relieved and surprised to see Makawee sitting on a horse.

"Kahée!" he replied, lowering his weapon and placing it in his pack. In the short time Graham had lived among the Crow, he had learned some basic Apsáalooke words and phrases. He was determined to speak both Crow and English to his daughter as she learned to talk.

Makawee dismounted and led her horse to the cottonwood grove, where she tied the brown-and-white mare to a tree.

"This is a beautiful place," she said, approaching him with a smile.

"Yes, it is. How did you know I would be here?"

"I saw you leave camp and travel in this direction. I asked Fox Woman to watch Nahkash, and I followed your trail."

"How is baby Nahkash?"

"She is healthy. We are so blessed to have her."

"I am blessed to have both of you."

Makawee tilted her head slightly as she touched his forearm. "Are you glad I came?"

Graham responded by swiping the cowboy hat off his head with one hand and pulling her close with the other. Their lips met in a long, sensual kiss.

"Does that answer your question?" he asked, stepping away but holding her hand.

Makawee smiled. This time, she pulled him in. She leaned her head back and stood on her toes to kiss him again.

"I'll take that as a yes," he said, grinning. "Sit with me on the blanket. I'm so happy we have some time alone!"

"Let me get a buffalo hide from my horse."

Makawee retrieved the buffalo hide and joined him on the blanket. She removed her moccasins. Graham followed her cue and removed his boots and socks. She draped the buffalo hide over their laps to guard against the chilly early evening air and snuggled close to him. They sat in silence for several minutes, watching the sky turn muted shades of pink and purple as the sun lowered further on the horizon.

If life could only be this simple, he thought. *I could be content spending my days sitting under a cottonwood tree with the woman I love.*

"I brought some things from the future," he said, unzipping his backpack. "Would you like to see your great-grandson?"

"Of course!"

Graham handed her a color photograph of himself with Redfield. They were standing outside his mother's house in Pennsylvania. His friend was just a few inches shorter than Graham, who was six feet two. He had high cheekbones and dark eyes. His straight black hair was shoulder length and gathered into two braids.

"How old is he in this picture?"

"I don't know. But I'd guess he is almost fifty."

Makawee studied the picture, holding it close to her face. Graham couldn't imagine the feeling someone would have if they gazed into the eyes of a family member who was yet to be born.

"What is he like? Is he a good man?"

"He is one of the finest men I've met. He has the gift of keeping the peace between men who argue with one another. I respect and admire him."

"Does he have a happy life?"

How could he truthfully answer this question? Should he tell her Redfield was an alcoholic who lived in a migrant worker's camp? What would she think if he described his small room in a dilapidated cinder block building? Should he disclose that her great-grandson drank most of his take-home pay each week? Or should he lie?

"Graham, is he happy?" Makawee repeated, looking into his eyes.

What is a happy life? he thought. *Is it measured by material possessions? A good-paying job? Being married and having children?* By any of those measures, Redfield was poor and unhappy. But by a different standard, he was wealthy and contented.

"Redfield is doing a job he loves. Those around him respect him. The bear spirit is in him. He is a modern warrior. Yes, he is happy."

Makawee nodded and held the photo against her heart.

"Oh, here's something I know you'll like!" he said, reaching into his pack. "Close your eyes and hold out your hand."

She laid down the photo and obliged.

He placed two Hershey bars in dark brown wrappers in her open hand.

"I remember tasting this!"

Graham had first shared the milk chocolate when they sat beside Yellowstone Lake last year. The sweet flavor was a wonderful treat when compared to the bitter baking chocolate available in the 1870s. She tore open the wrapper, broke off a small piece, and placed it into her mouth. A smile came to her face as she experienced the luscious combination of cocoa, milk, and sugar.

"May I have a bite?" he asked.

She broke off another piece and placed it into his open mouth. After they finished the last bite, she leaned over and kissed him, the chocolate lingering on their lips and breath.

"Thank you. I will keep the other bar for a special occasion."

"Good idea. I was thinking this could be a special place for us. It is a beautiful spot. Do you think we could secretly meet here?" he asked.

"I don't see why not."

"Let's stake our claim to this small slice of heaven on earth!"

He jumped up and fished a pocketknife from his jeans, which he used to remove the outer layers of fissured bark to form the letter *G*.

"Your turn," he said, passing the knife to Makawee. She sculpted the letter *M* into the dark outer bark next to his initials, then handed the knife back.

"We need one more thing to complete our family," he said. Graham carefully carved a small letter *N* below the *G* and the *M*.

"Oh! For baby Nahkash," Makawee said approvingly.

He stepped back from the tree and admired their handiwork.

"That's right! We have our very own family meeting tree."

They sat on the blanket and pulled the bison hide over their legs. Graham leaned over and kissed her. He pulled her close until the top of her head rested under his chin. There was something very satisfying about the simple act of carving out a place to call their own. It was uncertain how long it might be before they would have a home. This would have to do for now. It was a secret spot where they could discuss their future. Perhaps it was even a place to love.

She sat up abruptly, interrupting his reverie. "Oh, Graham! What are we going to do?"

"I think the question is, 'What am *I* going to do?' I'm the one who has to prove himself and deliver seven horses to marry you. That's why I rode here. I can think of only one option. I need to go somewhere to earn enough money to buy those horses. But if I leave camp, I won't see you and Nahkash."

"There is a way to accomplish both."

"Oh?"

"Steal seven horses from our enemy. You get the horses *and* prove your bravery."

He furrowed his brow and returned her gaze. "I won't do that."

"Won't or *can't?*"

Graham became indignant. "It's illegal and wrong to take someone's property. If they convict a white man of stealing a horse, they hang him!"

"You are living among the Crow. We see things differently. You steal from the Sioux. They try to steal our horses all the time. By taking their horses, you are striking our enemy. It will prove you are a warrior in the eyes of my father. We call this counting coup. Long Horse will consider how many coups you have collected as a measure of your worth."

Graham flipped the buffalo hide from his legs and stood. He paced back and forth for a moment before walking down to the river in his bare feet, pondering her advice while rubbing his chin. He kneeled on a rock, cupped his hands, and drank the cold water. Would the bearded young man reflected in the clear water become a horse thief? Even if he could rationalize these thefts as acceptable, he had no experience in horse stealing. He would need someone to teach and assist him in such a dangerous endeavor. Perhaps Rides Alone or Little Wolf would help him? He was uncertain about the best course of action.

Eagle Bear rose from his knees and strolled back to the cottonwood tree. She'd made it sound so simple. It wasn't. Not to him.

"I need to think about it," he said, looking down at Makawee, who had pulled the buffalo hide up around her neck.

Makawee saw his frustration and softened her voice. "Think about it tomorrow. Let's enjoy each other tonight."

She stood and let the buffalo hide slip to her feet. Graham's mouth dropped open. Makawee had removed her elk-hide dress. She was naked except for the obsidian turtle pendant suspended between her breasts. The last golden rays of the sun setting behind her created an aura around her lithe silhouette.

Graham removed his shirt and jeans. He stepped forward to embrace her. She tugged at his underwear, which he slid to his ankles and kicked off. She lay on the blanket, and Graham lowered himself on top of her. His eagle-bear-claw necklace clacked against her turtle pendant. He pulled the buffalo hide over their bodies. Their lips met and separated. While she gripped his muscular triceps, his hands traveled to her breasts and caressed them. Breast milk started seeping from her nipples.

"Careful. I need to nurse Nahkash when I return," she whispered, reaching between his legs to stroke him.

As he became aroused, he moved his hands to the inside of her thighs. She became wet as he gently massaged her. He was hungry for her love and yearned to enter her warm body.

Distant words of advice emerged from his subconscious and echoed in his brain. *"You must arm yourself with daasátchuche — patience."*

The voice in his head startled him, and he pushed himself up from her body.

"What's wrong?" Makawee asked, seeing the uncertain look in Graham's eyes.

"I...I thought I heard a voice telling me to be patient."

She wrapped her hands around his neck. "There's no one here."

"But what if your family finds out that we...?"

"You are the father of my child. We should not be ashamed. Even though we are not married, we are committed to each other," she said. "Graham, I have waited a year for this moment."

"As have I."

"Remember when I resisted making love that first night? It wasn't the right place or the right time." She pulled him onto her and slid her hands onto his buttocks. "Tonight is the night. This is the place. Love me."

Their initial sex was physical and urgent, with both lovers seeking to satisfy an intense carnal need. Following an erotic explosion, they lay on their sides and caressed one another until they were mutually aroused. Their second encounter was lovemaking. The couple fell into a deliberate rhythm as each sought to prolong their partner's sensual pleasure as long as possible before the climax.

In thirty minutes, Graham unleashed a year's worth of pent-up desire with the Crow woman who would one day become his wife. Makawee welcomed the opportunity to share her passion with the man she loved.

Sweating and exhausted, they enjoyed the aftermath of their sensual connection. Graham lay on his back while Makawee draped her arm across his chest and placed her leg over his thigh. *This woman is worth more than seven horses,* he thought. *Hell, I'll steal a herd of horses if that's what it takes to make her my wife!*

A full moon had appeared in the eastern sky. In the distance, a bull elk bugled. The distinctive mating call began with a guttural noise and transitioned into a muted scream before ending in a series of grunts. The bull in rut was sending a message to the cows in the herd that he was ready to mate.

Under a cottonwood tree by the Stillwater River, another mating ritual concluded. After a century apart, Graham and Makawee had rediscovered one another.

Chapter Nine

Fireworks

October 30, 1872

A group from Long Horse's band traveled to Fort Parker during the Hunter's Moon. The government had promised the Crow people annuities at the end of the month. Tribal representatives planned to gather at the fort to receive goods in proportion to the number of people in their respective families. Long Horse, Rides Alone, Black Hawk, Graham, and Makawee (carrying baby Nahkash) were among three dozen camp residents making the trip.

The two-day ride afforded Graham a chance to reflect on the last thirty days. A series of clandestine meetings under their private cottonwood tree had assuaged his concerns about securing Makawee's hand in marriage . Sometimes Makawee brought Nahkash along; other times, she came alone. They almost always made love. They spent hours sitting by the Stillwater River sharing their dreams of a future when they could express their love for one another. These emotional moments strengthened Graham's resolve to make Makawee his bride.

The party arrived at Fort Parker on the afternoon of the second day. The fortified settlement was on Mission Creek between the Crazy and Absaroka Mountain Ranges on the banks of the Yellowstone River.

Crow families had erected clusters of tepees several hundred feet from the fort. Thin trails of smoke wafted into the air from the cooking fires. Women were sewing elk-hide clothing and mending buffalo hides. Dogs barked and chased small children as they scampered among the lodges. It was a carnival-like atmosphere. As they rode through the camps, the scene reminded Graham of the county fairs he had attended as a boy. He envisioned a carousel tucked among the tepees.

After checking the identities of the travelers, a soldier opened the gates of the log palisade and allowed them to enter. They informed Long Horse annuities would be distributed early the next day. His band would camp outside the fort with the others who had made the journey from remote parts of the reservation. Graham said goodbye to Makawee as she left with the rest of the group to set up camp. He wanted to inquire about potential employment within the agency.

When he asked who was in charge, a soldier directed him to a single-story building that served as headquarters for the civilian Indian agent. Graham removed his hat and knocked on the door of the small cabin.

"Yes?" came a voice from inside.

"Hello. I'm a civilian traveling in the area. May I have a minute of your time?"

"Wait," the man behind the desk responded.

Graham heard papers being shuffled, followed a short time later by the sound of a chair sliding across the plank floor. The door opened to reveal a balding man in his late thirties with a bushy horseshoe mustache.

"Fellows Pease," the man said, extending his hand.

"Graham Davidson," he stated, shaking the Indian agent's hand.

"Come in," Pease said, gesturing to a chair as he sat behind the desk. "So, young man, what can I do for you?"

"Thanks for seeing me. I came west from Pennsylvania last year. I need to pay for my education and wanted to try my hand at mining. I thought if I got lucky..."

"You would become a wealthy man?" Pease finished the sentence. "Sounds like you've got the gold bug like thousands of others pouring into Montana Territory."

"No, sir. I just wanted to pay for school."

"Uh-huh."

Graham could see the agent wasn't impressed with his opening statement, so he moved on. "When I was in Wyoming Territory last year, I linked up with the Hayden Expedition," he said, hoping to establish some credibility.

"The group led by Ferdinand Hayden into the Yellowstone area?"

"That's the one."

"Well, now that trip had to be worth its weight in gold! I understand the photographer William Jackson was part of Hayden's team. He was here just a few months ago and took a photo of this fort."

"Yes, sir. He is quite talented. Anyway, let me get to the point of why I'm here."

"Please do."

"While in Yellowstone, I fell in love with a Crow woman. We want to be married. Her father, Long Horse, is asking seven horses for her hand."

"And you're looking for a job to earn the money needed to buy these horses," Pease said, stating the obvious conclusion.

"That's right."

Pease stood and paced behind his desk, stroking his mustache using his thumb and forefinger.

"Well," he said after a moment, "you seem like a sincere young man. We have two things in common. We're both from Pennsylvania, and we both love a Crow woman. In fact, I married a Crow. The problem is this agency is small. We have a modest group of employees: a butcher, an engineer, a blacksmith, a miller, and a schoolteacher. None of these tradesmen are hiring. We had a physician, but Dr. Frost was killed during a Sioux raid last month. I'm hoping to find another doctor soon."

Graham felt his heart sink. His hopes of earning money at Fort Parker were dimmed. He was also reminded of the dangers, where intertribal conflicts and invasion of native lands by whites inevitably led to lethal confrontations. It was not a coincidence they established the Crow Agency inside a fort with a permanent detail of soldiers.

"But..." Pease said, raising a finger in the air. "The sutler could use a pair of hands."

Graham furrowed his brow. "What's a sutler?"

"He's a civilian storekeeper who sells goods and items not considered necessary or supplied by the army. We've had a sutler at Fort Parker ever since it was built three years ago. It's very helpful to have Uriah Brown and his store here. Otherwise, we would have to travel forty miles to Bozeman or Fort Ellis for any of these items. Would you like to meet with him?"

"That would be great!"

Graham's spirits lifted.

Pease grabbed his coat from a wooden peg on the door. The two men walked to a small building at the north end of the fort. The Indian agent rapped his knuckles on the door and entered without waiting for a response.

"Uriah, got a minute?"

A skinny man in his fifties with thinning gray hair and wearing wire-rim glasses looked up from a desk, where he was writing in a large ledger book.

"Sure."

"This is Graham... What's your last name, son?"

"Davidson."

"Right. Graham Davidson is looking for work. I told him you may need a strong back. I'll let the two of you talk. Good luck, young man," Pease said before exiting and closing the door behind him.

Uriah extended an arm with his palm up, gesturing for Graham to have a seat in a ladder-back chair opposite the desk.

"What's your story?" he asked, after removing his eyeglasses and placing one of the temple tips in his mouth.

Graham repeated the same narrative he had shared with Fellows Pease earlier. He ended by requesting work.

"You showed up at a good time," Uriah said. "It's a lot of work to distribute these annuities. Hundreds of Crow families will show up to receive their allocations over the next week. It's a full-time job just keeping the books straight. I need help to unload wagons as they arrive and retrieving goods from the warehouse. It's hard work, but you look like a strong young man. Mr. Story pays a handsome wage for annuity distribution work — two dollars a day. He pays thirty dollars per month for general labor."

"Who is Mr. Story?"

"Nelson Story. He's a businessman from Bozeman and my boss. He has the government contracts for Fort Parker and Fort Ellis. Are you interested? You could start today."

"Absolutely!" Graham said. He had no reference for wages in the 1870s. And he was in no position to negotiate. This was an opportunity to earn the cash needed to buy horses.

Uriah Brown stuck his hand across the desk. Graham accepted, and they shook to seal the deal.

"Let me show you around," he said.

The sutler pointed out the other buildings inside the perimeter of the fort. There were two bastions at opposite corners of the fort. The two-story structures jutted out from the fort and afforded good visibility from all directions. The soldiers' quarters were in a building next to the south bastion. Several one-room wooden buildings had been constructed for Crow families who had committed to transition from a nomadic lifestyle to farming, but none of these were occupied. There were separate structures for the butcher, the miller, and the blacksmith.

Stables and corrals were outside the walls. The largest building was tucked into a corner next to the north bastion.

The sutler stopped at the warehouse, where two wagons of goods were waiting to be unloaded.

"There are a dozen soldiers and a sergeant from Fort Ellis stationed here. Each bastion houses a twelve-pound howitzer and two ammunition boxes. All boxes contain twenty-round shot, eight spherical cases, and four canister rounds. I know this because I'm charged with keeping a precise inventory of everything on site. When the soldiers conduct any practice firing, I insist they count the remaining ammunition and report it to me. I've heard of sutlers at other government installations who give away items from their store for favors. That's illegal, wrong, and bad business. I insist on accurate accounting and integrity from those who work with me."

Uriah Brown was making a point. If you want to stay employed, don't cheat or steal. Graham got the message.

"Yes, sir."

"This is where I keep our inventory," he said with a measure of pride. He reached into his trousers pocket, extracted a key, and opened a padlock on a hasp. He swung the large double doors open to reveal a large room with extensive wood shelving along three walls. There was nothing haphazard about this storage facility. Everything was organized. This was not surprising, given his diatribe about accurate accounting.

Graham stepped inside with the sutler and surveyed the supplies.

Dozens of brown packages of smoking tobacco from Thomas Hoyt & Company and William H. Goodwin were stacked on a shelf. The same shelf held squares of wrapped chewing tobacco packaged by A.H. Mickle & Sons. Uriah pulled a box of cigars from the shelf to show his new employee. A colorful portrait of a bearded man wearing a musketeer-style hat adorned the box lid of Masseto Cuban cigars.

"We receive cigars in boxes of one hundred, but we sell them in singles. These are very popular among the soldiers and officers. Right now, we have three boxes. I open only one box at a time. We need to keep the others fresh."

Uriah Brown walked along the shelves and pointed out other items as Graham followed. There were boxes of hard candy, bags of flavored teas, balls of yarn, kitchen utensils, knives, a keg of nails, rope, hand tools, sewing needles in a variety of lengths, pins, stationery, ink, matches, candles, buttons, trousers, shirts, hats, and socks. Another wall was reserved for food items, including Borden's condensed milk, canned fruit, dried apples, beans, sardines, molasses, smoked hams, salt pork, and dried fish. An entire shelf was dedicated to Arbuckle's ground coffee in one-pound brown paper packages. Twenty-pound sacks of flour and cones of sugar wrapped in blue wax paper were stacked near the rear of the building.

"Notice anything missing?"

Graham scratched his chin. "No. It looks like a nice variety of goods." He didn't know what dry goods or hardware were common in the late nineteenth century.

"Alcohol," Uriah said, answering his own question. "I am permitted to sell just about anything, but it is forbidden to sell ardent spirits to enlisted men or Indians. Nor do I want to sell alcohol. Mr. Story is a businessman. But unlike others in this territory, he will not profit by catering to men who wish to become drunk — be they white or red."

"I understand."

As they exited the building, Uriah pointed to the wagons. "There's your first job. Lock the warehouse doors and come see me when you're done."

It was after dark when Graham shouldered the last bag of flour and carried it to the rear of the warehouse. He was careful to place the items in neat stacks with their labels visible. There was no doubt Uriah Brown was a stickler for organization and detail. He wanted to make a good impression. The sutler was still working at his desk by lamplight when Graham knocked on the door to announce he had finished unloading the wagons.

The two men walked to the warehouse, where the sutler unlocked the doors and held the lantern up to inspect the job. He gave a satisfied nod.

"Where are you sleeping tonight?"

"With my Crow family in one of their lodges."

"Would you like to earn an extra two dollars?"

"Sure. How?"

"Sleep in the warehouse tonight. I have a folding wooden frame field cot and bedding."

"Why do you want me to sleep in the warehouse?" Graham asked, although he had a hunch.

"I've been missing some inventory. At night, I think someone picks the lock and takes things. The thief is still getting inside even after I changed the lock twice. Leave the door unlocked. If he shows up in the middle of the night, you can catch him red-handed."

"What about the soldiers? Don't they patrol the area?"

"Sure. But they may be part of the problem. If the thief is someone living inside the compound, he may pay them off to look the other way."

Graham nodded.

"Do you have a gun?"

"Yes."

"If the rascal shows up, hold him at gunpoint and yell for me."

By ten o'clock, Graham was lying on the cot in the dark warehouse. While sharing an evening meal with Makawee and Rides Alone, he had explained he would stay inside the fort for the evening. Now he wondered whether this was a good idea. One minute he was a simple warehouse laborer; the next, he was an armed security guard. He fished the flashlight from his pack and checked the Colt revolver for the third time. After making sure the cylinder was loaded, he placed it back under his pillow. His mind raced, imagining a scenario where an intruder opened the warehouse doors, only to see a .38 Special aimed at his chest. What if the alleged thief ran? Would Graham pull the trigger and wound or kill the man? Should he?

He had to admit the cot was an improvement over sleeping on the ground. The combination of a thin feather mattress laid on top of an iron wire mesh made a comfortable bed. He was tired from unloading the wagons and relaxed, despite his anxiety over his security duty. The mingled smells of coffee, dried fish, salt pork, and stale tobacco pervaded his nostrils as he drifted off to sleep.

A few hours later, the door burst open. A shadowy figure wearing a kepi poked his head inside and yelled, "Anybody in here?"

Graham bolted upright, swiped the revolver from under his pillow, and aimed it at the intruder.

"Don't move or I'll shoot!"

"Whoa! Who the hell are you?" the man asked, holding a hand up and backing out of the doorway.

Graham tossed the blanket aside and jumped off the cot, keeping the Colt aimed at the stranger while he walked toward the door.

"Hands up!"

"Hey, mister! I'm jes' followin' orders and tellin' people ta get outta here. The fort's on fire!"

Graham lowered the pistol. "On fire?"

"Yeah, get out!" the soldier said as he turned and ran across the courtyard.

Graham stuck the revolver in his coat pocket and ran out the door. The pungent odor of smoke filled the night air. He sprinted to Uriah's cabin and pounded on the sutler's door.

"Mr. Brown! Fire! Get up!"

The door swung open. Uriah was in a nightshirt. He fumbled with his glasses, trying to fit them over his ears.

"The fort's on fire! I'm going back to the warehouse!"

The courtyard was a chaotic scene of men running and yelling. Flames were shooting from the north bastion directly behind the storage building. The sergeant had ordered soldiers to grab buckets, pots, and pans. They were running back and forth from wood barrels holding drinking water, desperately trying to douse the flames a few gallons at a time.

Graham ran to the warehouse and flung both doors wide open. He tossed his backpack onto an empty wagon. Starting at the front of the building, he threw things out as fast as he could grab them. Some things landed in the wagon. Others bounced away and tumbled into the courtyard. He focused on removing the most valuable items first, uncertain if he had time to save everything.

Within minutes, smoke entered the warehouse. Graham started coughing. He held his breath each time he ran into the building to fetch another armload of goods. The pile grew higher in the courtyard as shelves were emptied.

Uriah Brown appeared with a horse and hitched it to a wagon. He tossed a bunch of dry goods onto the deck that had fallen around the wheels, then climbed on the seat.

"Ha!" he yelled, snapping the reins. The frightened horse responded. The wagon lurched away from the smoking building and headed to the gates.

As Graham entered the warehouse for another load, he saw heavy winds were fanning the flames on the two-story tower. Clusters of hot embers floated in the swirling winds and landed on adjacent buildings. The back corner of the warehouse roof caught fire. This would be his last trip.

Thirty seconds later, he stumbled out of the building with an armful of coffee and fell to his knees. His eyes stung from the irritating smoke. He coughed violently, trying to expel the thick smoke from his lungs.

Boom!

An explosion from the top of the bastion echoed in the night, blowing a hole in the burning roof and shooting sparks skyward. Fragments of burning debris showered down, igniting small fires on the buildings below.

"The cannon! She's gonna blow! Everybody out! Now!" screamed the sergeant.

Graham heard feet running past him as he lay on the ground. He stood, but his eyes were watering, and his vision was blurry. He blinked but couldn't see the entrance, even though the raging fire had illuminated the courtyard. Someone grabbed his arm and guided him as they half walked and half ran toward the open gates of the fort. As they cleared the front gate, Graham heard a familiar voice from the rescuer who had escorted him from danger.

"Eagle Bear is safe," Rides Alone said.

Graham looked at his friend but erupted into a coughing fit when he tried to speak.

A crowd had gathered several hundred yards from the fort to watch the spectacle. Rides Alone eased Graham to the ground and ran to fetch some water. Graham rubbed his watery eyes with his coat sleeve and watched the fort burn through a filmy haze.

A series of resonant sounds erupted from the bastion. The ammunition for the smoothbore muzzle-loading artillery piece had heated up. It was igniting at regular intervals. Iron balls released by the bursting charge of the spherical case shot produced a dazzling exhibit of light and noise. The micro-blasts created fireworks that rivaled many Fourth of July celebrations.

The unplanned fireworks display was spectacular. But everyone watching realized this was an unmitigated disaster. The army would lose a fort. The sutler would suffer huge losses of inventory. And the Crow would not receive their promised annuities.

Rides Alone returned with a small pail of water and a tin cup. He offered the cup to Graham, who drank the cool water to soothe his parched throat. A few minutes later, Makawee arrived. She sat beside Graham and hugged him, then rubbed his back as he continued to cough.

The stunned spectators were silent.

All they could do was watch and wait until the fire burned itself out.

The stench of burned wood permeated the chilly October morning. Dawn revealed the extent of the damage. The cottonwood structures had been perfect fuel for the blaze. It had reduced two walls of the log palisade and many buildings to charred rubble. Thin trails of smoke climbed skyward from smoldering ashes.

Uriah Brown and Graham stood in the courtyard and surveyed a pile of blackened wood and ashes that had been the warehouse. Despite the devastating loss, Graham's efforts had been successful. The second wagon had been far enough from the flames to be spared. A jumble of assorted dry goods was littered around the wagon where they had been tossed.

"How much was left behind?" Uriah asked.

"I'm not sure. I didn't have time to save the flour, sugar, or any bulk items."

"Well, my office is a pile of cinders. At least I saved this," he said, tapping the green ledger book with his finger. "We can't cry over spilled milk. All we can do is move ahead. The first order of business is to take an inventory. I'll count the items on the first wagon. You sort these things so I can tally them when I return."

Graham nodded. He marveled at the single-mindedness of the sutler. His housing and personal possessions had been destroyed. But he was concerned with getting an accurate count of goods saved from the blaze.

"Do you still have your gun?"

"Yeah."

"Good. There may be looters. Most civilians and soldiers lost everything. This pile of goods is all we have until the next shipment arrives from Bozeman. We'll take care of everyone and extend them credit. But we'll do it in an organized way. Got it?"

"Yes, sir."

The destroyed fort gradually came alive, with men sorting and sifting through rubble for items to be salvaged. A cheer rose from the discouraged men around midmorning. Graham looked up to see a soldier on horseback leading a dozen men and two wagons into the courtyard. An army officer dismounted and spoke with Fellows Pease and the sergeant. The officer's back was to Graham, but he could hear them discussing the calamitous event of the previous night. He explained the men in his command had been scheduled to relieve those on duty at Fort Parker, and the wagons contained annuities for the Crow.

There was something familiar about the officer's voice, but Graham couldn't quite place it. When Fellows Pease and the officer turned and walked toward his pile of stacked goods, Graham's heart sank. He immediately recognized the tall officer with his distinctive handlebar mustache and confident gait.

"Graham Davidson, I'd like you to meet Lieutenant Gustavus Doane of the Second Cavalry, based at Fort Ellis," Pease said.

Doane nodded before stating, "We've already met."

"Oh? When was that?" a surprised Pease asked.

"Last year on the expedition I led through Yellowstone," Doane said, with a steely gaze directed at Graham.

"The Hayden Expedition? I've read about that group's exploits. The photographs, paintings, and descriptions of that trip are marvelous!" Pease exclaimed.

"A more accurate name would be the Yellowstone Expedition of 1871. It was organized by Ferdinand Hayden. But I was the one who guided him and his team through the Yellowstone wilderness," he said. "Hayden was following my footsteps from the previous year when I explored the area with minimal resources. Unlike my exploration, Hayden had the benefit of generous government sponsorship."

Graham bit the inside of his lip. Seeing Doane and hearing him brag about his role in the expedition made him wince. He had locked horns with Doane frequently during their time exploring the future park. And with good reason. Doane resented Graham's land navigation and guiding skills. The lieutenant had demanded all loaned supplies be returned at the expedition's conclusion. But the final blow was the incident where Makawee fended off the lieutenant's advances. If Graham had not arrived, his future wife might have been assaulted. He had hoped to never see Doane again.

"I have to meet with the Crow leaders and let them know the annuity distribution will be delayed. And we have to erect temporary housing right away. Lieutenant Doane, I'll check in with you later. We're so glad you showed up with men and supplies," Pease said as he pivoted and walked toward his partially burned office.

"What are you doing here?" Doane asked with a sneer when the Indian agent was out of earshot.

"I came to Fort Parker with my Crow family. They are here to receive their annuities."

"Your Crow family? Ah, yes. You must still be sweet on Makawee. Perhaps I'll stop by and say hello to that lovely young woman," he said with a twinkle in his eye.

Graham felt his face flush with anger. He knew Doane was goading him and struggled to suppress his ire toward the man. "I'm working for Uriah Brown, the sutler," he said, ignoring the lieutenant's statement.

"Being a warehouse helper isn't as glamorous as exploring a wilderness, is it?" Doane asked, casually placing a hand on the butt of his revolver. "We got off on the wrong foot in Yellowstone. Perhaps you can make amends for your insolence last year."

Graham gritted his teeth but remained silent. Doane surveyed the stacked items by the wagon. He picked up an unopened box of cigars and held it to his nose, sniffing the rolled tobacco.

"I don't smoke. But many of the officers at Fort Ellis do. And my commanding officer, Major Baker, always seems to have a cigar in his mouth. These could be very useful to curry favor."

"I'm not allowed to give anything away."

"Oh, come on. No one would ever know about a missing box of cigars. These could have been lost in the fire!"

"Put the cigars back."

Now it was Doane's face that turned red.

"I'm giving you a chance to clear the slate! Do you think your boss wants a reckless employee who doesn't follow orders? You were with one of our soldiers when he fell into a hot spring last summer. You nearly caused a man to drown. And you ignored my orders to stop giving Hayden advice. Either you allow me to take this box of cigars, or I'll tell your boss who you are. The military determines who may operate inside this fort, not civilians. So what's it gonna be — your job or a box of cigars?"

Graham grimaced at Doane's false assertions. None of those things were true. But it would be his word against those of the egotistical lieutenant. Although he needed this job, he wasn't about to be bullied.

"Put the cigars back."

Doane tossed the box of cigars on the ground. "Sergeant!" he yelled over his shoulder.

"Yes, sir!" came a reply from across the courtyard.

"Find Uriah Brown. Tell him to meet me outside the front gates. I need to speak to him."

The sergeant saluted and hurried off.

"Pack your things. You will be gone by day's end!" Doane said as he pivoted and walked toward the entrance.

"Ever smoked a good cigar? One that is top rail?" Uriah Brown asked.

"A good cigar? No," Graham said. His father had forced him to smoke a King Edward cigar as a young teen, hoping to dissuade him from smoking. Graham had become nauseous and puked halfway through the cigar. He never had the urge to smoke again.

"Try one of these," Uriah said, offering a hand-rolled Cuban.

"I appreciate the offer, Mr. Brown, but I'd rather not."

"I understand. It's an acquired taste. Mr. Story wanted me to pass along his appreciation."

It was quite a turn of events. Three days ago, Lieutenant Doane had spread lies to Uriah Brown about Graham. He painted a picture of an untrustworthy and careless young man. Under pressure from the cavalry officer, Brown committed to letting Graham go after the Crow annuities had been distributed.

Graham defended himself against the spurious attacks. He cited James Stevenson as a reference. Stevenson was Hayden's survey manager, who had organized the material and supplies for the expedition. Graham had reported to Stevenson during the 1871 Yellowstone Expedition and proved the opposite of the slanderous accusations put forth by Doane. This information carried much weight with Brown, as he had worked with Stevenson on assembling the supplies for the Hayden Expedition. The two men had mutual respect. However, because the military determined the success of any sutler, Brown initially honored the demand to dismiss Graham.

Two days later, a courier delivered a message to Uriah Brown from Bozeman. It was from Nelson Story. The businessman had heard about Graham Davidson's heroics in saving the warehouse goods. His bold move had saved thousands of dollars of inventory. Story had given Uriah explicit instructions to thank the young man with a generous gift.

Now they were standing in a temporary building cobbled together from the cottonwood lumber salvaged from the fire.

"Well, Mr. Story has given me permission to grant you any reasonable request. What would you like?"

Graham didn't hesitate.

"I'd like to keep my job."

"That's already taken care of. You will continue to work for me after we complete the annuity work." Brown leaned forward and whispered. "I don't like that mealymouthed Doane. But I didn't have a choice. I couldn't keep you employed without Mr. Story's blessing."

"Thanks!"

"Is there something from our inventory you would like but can't afford?"

Graham thought for a moment before speaking. "A nice saddle. I have an old Indian saddle. It's not very comfortable."

"Hmm," Brown said, rubbing his chin. "That's not something we carry. The army supplies everyone in the cavalry with a saddle. But I can have one freighted here from Bozeman."

"That would be great!"

A knock on the door interrupted their conversation.

"Enter!" Brown said.

Fellows Pease appeared and closed the flimsy wood door behind him.

"Brrr. It's gettin' cold," he said, rubbing his hands together. "I came by to share good news. We can't bivouac through the winter. There aren't many trees left in the area. So I've contracted with my good friend Charlie Hoffman from Bozeman to construct twenty adobe buildings to replace the wooden ones that burned. He's going to have a crew here within the next few days."

"That is good news!" Brown said. "Does he have enough men?"

"Nope. That's a problem. Seems like everybody 'round here would rather get rich quick by mining than pick up a hammer or a trowel. Good labor is as scarce as hen's teeth."

"What if I loaned Graham? The Crow will leave soon to return to their camps for the winter. I won't have much work until we get the warehouse rebuilt. Whaddaya say, young man?"

"Sure. I'd be glad to help."

"That's wonderful!" Pease said. "I'll hook you up with the supervisor when he gets here. I'm sure he will appreciate all the help he can get."

After Pease left, Graham asked for permission to leave. He planned to stay with Makawee and Rides Alone in their lodge tonight. Long Horse's clan were headed back to their camp on the Stillwater River in the morning.

Graham found Makawee tending the fire inside the tepee when he arrived. He smiled when he saw Nahkash sleeping on a cradleboard propped up along one side of the lodge. He was eager to share the good news of his employment. It meant he could start earning money toward the purchase of horses.

His wife-to-be stood when he entered the lodge, and Graham gave her a hug. As he leaned down for a kiss, she raised a hand to her mouth and brushed him aside as she ran outside. A few seconds later, Graham could hear her vomiting onto the frozen ground. He stepped outside to see her stooped over with her hands on her knees, gagging on chunks of undigested food caught in her throat.

He fetched a water bag and brought it to her. She rinsed out her mouth and spat, then tottered into the tepee and sat down by the fire.

"Are you okay? When did you get sick?" he asked, sitting beside her.

"I've been throwing up for two weeks."

"That's a long time," he said in a worried tone as he rubbed her back. "Do you want to see a doctor?"

"No need. It's worse in the morning. But I'm sure I'll feel better in a month," she said, smiling.

Worse in the morning? Better in a month? Graham thought. "Are you...pregnant?"

"I am."

Graham's jaw dropped. He didn't know what to say. He stared at Makawee in the flickering firelight.

"Are you happy?" she asked.

"This is wonderful!" he exclaimed, pulling her close to him and squeezing her shoulder.

An instant later, the dark side of this otherwise joyous news rocketed into his brain. Their clandestine rendezvous beside the Stillwater River would soon produce a second child. How would Long Horse and Fox Woman react? Would he be ostracized? Would the price of Makawee's hand in marriage escalate?

"Graham," she said, grabbing his chin and turning his face toward her. She could see his worried look. "Do not concern yourself about Long Horse. I am happy. That's what matters."

"Yes. Of course, it is."

Another negative thought emerged.

"I can't leave you in a camp two days' ride away to care for Nahkash while you are pregnant. I should be with you! But I need to stay at the agency to earn money."

"I will be fine. Among the Grass is an experienced midwife. She has good medicine."

"I'll come every few months to visit. If I work hard, I'm sure Uriah Brown will give me some time off."

"It will work out," she assured him. "Our baby will be born next summer. It will be a happy time."

"When will you tell your family?"

"I will wait until the baby is showing."

Graham nodded and pulled Makawee to his chest. His head swirled with the events of the past few days. He'd found a job working for a sutler, but a fire had destroyed the fort. An old nemesis showed up to have him fired. He was going to be a father...again! But this could prevent him from marrying the mother of his children. There was so much joy mingled with the anxiety of an uncertain future.

For Graham and Makawee, tomorrow would bring a bittersweet parting.

Chapter Ten

Baby Angst

February 1873

T he winds made it feel much colder than the actual temperature, which was in the twenties. Flames from the fire flickered and danced in the sporadic stiff breezes. Snow flurries swirled in the evening air. Graham tossed a small log onto the fire and clasped the buffalo robe under his chin to ward off the cold. He had ridden thirty miles from Fort Parker and would arrive at the camp of Long Horse by midmorning tomorrow. At least his new western saddle made long rides more comfortable. It came with a pommel bag holster, which gave him a place to keep his Colt Cobra after stuffing the bottom of the holder with a rag to accommodate the short barrel of the snub-nosed revolver.

When his horse snorted, Graham rose and checked on the large mare. He fed her a few slices of dried apple as a treat, then scratched her neck just behind the ear. He had named the horse Blade, in honor of Bloody Knife, who had stolen the bay roan from the Sioux. A second horse nickered and pushed its nose against Graham. He had bought the brown-and-white mare a few days earlier.

"Okay, girl. I have some apples for you too," he said, reaching into his coat pocket and holding them in his open palm.

Graham was eager to present the mare to Long Horse. He hoped this gesture would underscore his commitment to earning Makawee's hand in marriage. One horse down, six to go. He returned to sit by the fire and consider tomorrow.

He had visited Makawee for a few days over Christmas. It was a joyous time for their family. Nahkash had learned to roll over and was crawling. They enjoyed watching her scoot across the buffalo hide in the tepee. Rides Alone had assumed the role of uncle, occasionally watching the baby girl to give his sister a break from her motherly duties. Even Fox Woman seemed to relish being a grandmother, despite Nahkash being a mixed-race child from an illegitimate relationship. She cuddled the child and sang to her in the evening to put her to sleep.

For Christmas, Graham had given Makawee a copy of *The Adventures of Huckleberry Finn* he had brought in his backpack. It would not be published for another thirteen years. For this reason, he told her not to show the classic book to anyone. He knew she would enjoy reading the tale of a runaway boy and an escaped slave's travels on the Mississippi. He expected she would find Twain's story especially poignant, as the book explored racism and the lack of freedom. Native Americans shared these experiences with their Black American counterparts.

During his December visit, they had agreed Makawee would reveal she was expecting a second child when he visited again in February. At fourteen weeks, her body would almost certainly show a child was growing inside, especially since this was her second pregnancy. Some camp residents had viewed Makawee with suspicion because she was an unmarried mother. They may be even less tolerant of an unmarried woman who was expecting a second child. He especially fretted about how Long Horse would react. Perhaps the extra horse would assuage the chief's anger or disappointment when he learned of Makawee's pregnancy.

Graham rode into camp leading the recently acquired mare the next morning. He dismounted in front of the chief's tepee and was greeted by Rides Alone. When Graham explained the mare was the first payment toward his marriage to Makawee, the warrior smiled. Rides Alone walked around the horse and stopped when he saw a fresh brand on the horse's left shoulder.

"What is this?"

Graham had used a branding iron to burn a symbol with four straight lines into the hairs of the horse. The letters *L* and *H* were offset and overlapped; the base of the *L* was also the crossbar for the letter *H*.

"This is the mark of Long Horse," Graham said.

"White men who raise cattle use these marks."

"That's right. They brand cattle to identify strays or those that are stolen. Every rancher has a unique brand."

Rides Alone glanced at the letters burned into the horse's hide. "Don't need to mark horse. If enemy steals it, we steal one of theirs. Maybe two."

Graham could tell his friend was unimpressed.

"Look, I paid a hundred and twenty hard-earned dollars for this mare. It seems like horses come up missing a lot around here. So I asked the blacksmith at Fort Parker to make a branding iron. I wanted him to make a brand that placed the *LH* inside a shape of a buffalo, like this design my father used for his wooden chairs back in Pennsylvania."

Graham removed his backpack and pulled out the piece of leather displaying an outline of a buffalo with the initial *D* for *Davidson*. He handed it to Rides Alone, who examined it.

"The smithy said I should keep the brand simple. That's how I came up with an overlapping *LH*. If any horses go missing, we can identify the stolen mustang or mare. I will handpick each of the remaining six horses. I want your father to know the ponies that came from Eagle Bear. They will bear his mark."

Rides Alone nodded and returned the leather. Even though he didn't believe branding was necessary, he could understand why his friend was doing it. He lifted the mare's front legs to look at her hooves and opened her mouth to examine her teeth.

"You chose well."

Long Horse emerged from his lodge.

"This is for you. I am delivering the first of seven horses," Graham said, offering the lead rope to the chief.

Long Horse ignored the extended rope. Instead, he walked around the horse. He stopped to point at the brand on the left shoulder and furrowed his brow.

Graham stepped forward. "The mark of Long Horse," Graham said proudly, outlining the *L* and the *H* with his finger.

The chief understood. He flashed a thin smile and nodded.

"Strong first pony," he said. The chief motioned for a young boy to lead the horse away before ducking into the tepee.

"My father speaks few words but is pleased," Rides Alone said.

Graham breathed a sigh of relief. *The chief may be contented with the horse. But his approval may dissipate when he learns about Makawee's pregnancy,* he thought.

The couple stared at the swaddled sleeping child who lay between them. Graham stroked Nahkash's hair. He smiled when she wrinkled her nose before settling back to sleep. He couldn't imagine he could love the next child as much as his firstborn. Makawee had shown Graham how their baby girl was pulling herself up. It wouldn't be long before she would be a toddler.

"She is beautiful," he said.

"Yes. She is." Makawee scooped up Nahkash and placed her on an adjacent buffalo hide before returning to lie next to Graham by the fire.

It was a pleasant surprise to have a few hours in private. Rides Alone had taken Little Wolf on a hunting trip. He had told Graham they would not return until several hours after sundown. Graham and Makawee would have the hide-covered lodge to themselves.

"How are you feeling these days?" Graham asked, propping himself up on an elbow.

"The morning sickness is gone. I get leg cramps, and my lower back hurts, but these aren't too bad."

Graham reached over and touched Makawee's swollen belly.

"You're showing. How did you hide it from the others?"

"I made a loose-fitting elk-hide dress to wear. Because of the cold weather, I always had a blanket or robe draped over my shoulders. Would you like to see my belly?" she asked, her eyes sparkling with excitement.

Graham nodded.

Makawee got to her knees, unlaced the dress, and pulled it down to her waist. Her expanding uterus and excess fluid had caused her midsection to push outward, producing a smooth bump centered at her navel. Her breasts were larger compared to the last time they had seen each other at Christmas, and her skin glistened in the firelight. Graham had heard people speaking of women having a "glow" while pregnant. *She looks radiant as an expectant mother,* he thought.

Makawee reached for Graham's hand and placed it on her navel. He rose to his knees in front of her.

"Sometimes I can feel the baby," she said. "It's a faint and brief fluttering."

The parents faced each other on their knees. Graham surrounded her round belly with both hands like he was holding a basketball, hoping to detect some movement. The only sounds were the crackling of the fire and the soft snoring of Nahkash. After a minute, he leaned forward and kissed her belly several times.

Makawee took him by the wrists and pulled his hands to her bosom. He cradled her swollen breasts, feeling the weight caused by nurturing milk that had developed. He leaned in and found her mouth. She lay back and slipped the dress over her hips, kicking it off at her feet. He rapidly undressed. Soon they were lying on their sides, facing one another, entwined in a naked embrace.

"Let's do it like this," she whispered while lifting her top leg. "It will be more comfortable for me."

Making love in this position was sensual. Perhaps it was because their thrusting movements were subtle. Maybe it was because their bodies were touching in so many places. The bump in her belly was a visible reminder of their intimacy several months ago on the banks of the Stillwater River. It was also a reminder of their devotion to each other and fueled their passion.

"Graham?" Makawee asked as they lay together afterward, her head nestled under his chin.

"Yes?"

"I'm anxious about tomorrow — when we tell Long Horse and Fox Woman our news."

"Me too. Whatever happens, I'll do whatever it takes for our family to live together."

"I believe you," she said, tilting her head back to look in his eyes. "And I believe in you."

Fox Woman had prepared a stew for the family from an elk Rides Alone had shot. She added wild rice and a few spices to make a dish everyone enjoyed as they sat in the tepee of Long Horse. While Fox Woman held her granddaughter, Among the Grass boiled water for coffee and passed out steaming cups of the strong beverage to everyone after the meal.

"How long you stay?" Long Horse asked as he sipped the coffee.

"I leave in two days. But I will be back during the flowering moon." Graham had learned some basic Crow terms and remembered this was the name given the month of May. Graham looked at Makawee. He raised his eyebrows, signaling her to go ahead with the announcement.

Makawee spoke in her native tongue of Apsáalooke. "Father, I have some news to share. I am expecting a second child."

"Kalatchíishee!" ["Repeat what you said!"]

Makawee swallowed hard. She spoke again, announcing she was pregnant.

Long Horse rose to his feet. He spoke in Apsáalooke. Although he appeared calm, an observer could only interpret his facial expressions and hand gestures to mean one thing. He was not pleased. The chief alternated between looking at Makawee and looking at Graham. After speaking for two minutes, he sat down and waved his hand toward the opening of the tepee.

Makawee had tears in her eyes. She took Nahkash from Fox Woman and followed Graham into the night. They walked the short distance to the tepee of Rides Alone in silence.

Graham sat beside her in the tepee and held Nahkash on his lap. He was desperate to know what Long Horse had said, but waited until Makawee was ready to speak. After a moment, she turned to him and spoke.

"My father is angry," she finally said.

"That was clear. What did he say?"

"Long Horse said my unborn child would not pay for the faults of his parents. He said you continue to lack patience and are not disciplined. These are critical traits of a warrior."

Graham nodded. He couldn't argue this point.

"You now have to deliver three spirit guns besides the seven horses so we can marry."

Graham recalled the hostile Blackfeet who had captured him last year referred to modern rifles as spirit guns — so named because it appeared the spirits were reloading the weapon between shots. Warriors from all tribes recognized the superior firepower of a breechloader over a muzzleloader. Repeating rifles were the most desirable spirit guns. The Crow leaders had petitioned Fellows Pease, the civilian Indian agent, to provide weapons so they could defend themselves against the ever-encroaching Lakota Sioux. The Crow considered repeating rifles and horses more useful than oxen or plows. Although Pease had passed along these requests to the army, their pleas had fallen on deaf ears.

"Anything else?"

"You are not welcome in the lodge of Long Horse until you prove yourself worthy," she said. Her eyes teared up as she finished her father's proclamation. "We can still see each other, but you may stay in his camp only two days at a time."

This final edict stung the most. Graham was already living forty miles apart from his family. He could only get away from the Crow Agency at Fort Parker every few months. Having only two days to spend with Makawee during a visit was a harsh punishment.

"It will be okay. I'll just work harder," he said, comforting Makawee as Nahkash drifted off to sleep in his lap.

Graham knew what needed to be done to deliver horses and weapons. The larger obstacle was proving his worthiness to Long Horse. After today's revelation, that task had just become substantially more difficult.

"The white man has proven his weakness again," Among the Grass said to Black Hawk as he tended to his horse. "Long Horse favors Makawee, but he will never allow her to marry a baashchiile even if he delivers the horses and spirit guns."

"I agree."

"But there is a potential threat growing inside of her."

Black Hawk stepped back and looked at his mother standing in front of the horse he was grooming.

"What do you mean?"

"The only men Long Horse may consider taking his place are his sons. Rides Alone does not have a fighting spirit. Little Wolf is young, but we need to watch him. He has a strong will. But Makawee has a baby on the way."

"How can a baby be a threat?"

"If she has a son, the baby boy would be another male heir to Long Horse."

"Let's wait to see if she has a boy," he said, shrugging.

"We cannot take that chance."

Black Hawk blinked a few times.

"What are you saying?"

"As a midwife, I have learned to predict whether an unborn child will be a boy or a girl. I look at the shape of the mother's belly. I see how high she is carrying the child in her womb. The color and odor of the mother's pee are also signs. I will know soon if the unborn child is a boy."

"And if you determine Makawee is carrying a boy?"

"Babies are born early for many reasons. Certain herbs and medicines encourage this to happen."

Black Hawk stared at his mother and wondered, *Would she abort a child?*

"We cannot do this. *You* cannot do this."

"Do you want to be a chief?" It was a question with only one answer. And they both knew it.

"Yes."

"Then our path is clear," the midwife said. "You attack our enemies. I remove threats from within."

Chapter Eleven

Unborn Spirit

March 1873

The horse stood quietly while Graham adjusted the cinch straps. He mounted the rifle scabbard by wrapping the upper strap around the pommel and attached the lower strap to the rear cinch ring. He admired the Springfield Model 1866 in the gray light of dawn before inserting it into the scabbard. Graham placed a box of .50-caliber centerfire cartridges for the breechloading rifle in his backpack, then grabbed the lead rope for a second horse before mounting Blade.

He smiled, recalling the good fortune that allowed him to buy a gun and a horse at a discount. Two days ago, he had been working with Uriah Brown, when a man with rumpled white hair and a scraggly beard sauntered into the warehouse.

"I be lookin' for the storekeeper," the stranger had said as a greeting.

A small storefront with a few shelves and a counter had been added when the burned warehouse was rebuilt.

"That would be me," Uriah said, looking up from his ledger book. "How can I help you?"

The man placed a Springfield rifle on the tall table. "How much ya give me fer it?"

The sutler pulled his eyeglasses from a front pocket, unfolded them, and slipped them over his ears. He picked up the weapon and held it to his shoulder, then opened the hinged trapdoor at the breech.

"Got any ammo?"

The old man fetched a box of cartridges from his coat pocket and plunked it on the table.

Uriah loaded a cartridge into the chamber and closed the trapdoor. When he reopened it, the cartridge remained in the chamber.

"The ejector spring is broken."

"Yep. I jest fish out the spent cartridges by hand. But she shoots true."

"Why are you sellin'?"

"Need the money. I still got a good pistol."

Uriah paused, inspecting the heavy rifle at several angles before making an offer. "Twenty-five dollars."

"It's worth more!"

"Maybe. But this converted musket isn't reliable, and repeaters are in higher demand than single-shot rifles."

The man scratched the small chin hidden under his beard.

"Been siftin' the dirt for gold over at Clark's Fork. Ain't had much luck. Amos Benson at the tradin' post downriver won't buy or trade. I ran up a whiskey bill, and he says no more credit if'n I don't pay up." The stranger paused before asking, "That the best you can do?"

"Got anything else for sale or trade?" the sutler inquired.

"My horse. Don't wanna give 'er up. I have a good ol' mule. Trouble is, I can't afford ta feed both of 'em."

"Let's take a look." Uriah held out his arm, indicating they should step outside and inspect the animal.

As Graham walked around the horse with Uriah, he whispered, "I'll pay for both the rifle and the horse if you can get them at a good price."

Uriah nodded.

"Tell you what," the sutler said, looking at the prospector. "Ninety dollars for the rifle and the horse."

"Add ten dollars, and it's a deal."

The men shook hands. Ten minutes later, the unlucky miner was riding his mule out of Fort Parker with cash in his pocket but without a rifle and a horse.

"I feel bad for him," Graham said as they watched the old prospector pass through the front gates.

"Don't be. That's why we don't sell whiskey or liquor. Strong spirits eat at a man's judgment. Make him do stupid things."

Graham reached in his pocket and handed seventy dollars to Uriah. "You can take the balance out of next month's pay."

"Fair enough. Now let's get back to work."

Now, Graham urged Blade forward and headed east with the second horse in tow. His mood was upbeat. He planned to make the forty-mile ride in one day, bringing a rifle and another horse with the *LH* brand to the chief. It had only been two weeks since he had seen Makawee. Uriah had granted permission for a quick visit to his wife for working extra hours. He was eager to see how she was feeling four months into her pregnancy.

The midwife measured a teaspoon of mugwort and an equal quantity of pennyroyal into a tin cup, then poured boiling water over the herbal mixture and set it aside. She turned and attended to her patient, who was sitting on a willow-rod backrest and wincing in pain.

"How are you feeling, Makawee?" Among the Grass asked.

The pregnant woman drew in a deep breath and exhaled. "Not well. I don't understand. I've been sick for many days. Why hasn't your medicine made me better?"

"Give it time. This tea will help your lower body relax. It will relieve your cramps."

"But I've been drinking several cups of tea for over a week. I feel more contractions each day, and now I'm bleeding."

"Let me see."

Makawee pulled her dress up to the top of her thighs and parted her legs. A thick, pink excretion had puddled onto the chair seat.

"The tea is working. It is helping your body rid itself of bad medicine."

Among the Grass wiped the seat with a cloth and retrieved the fresh cup of herbal tea.

"Drink. I'll get a medicine smudging stick."

Among the Grass draped a buffalo hide over her shoulders and stepped outside into the cold.

Makawee gripped the cup and breathed in the minty aroma released by the golden-brown herbal concoction. Surely something with such a pleasant fragrance would be good for her unborn baby. She sipped the tea and hoped the contractions would soon abate.

Outside, the midwife hurried to the river, where Black Hawk was waiting.

"How is she?" he asked, as his mother approached.

"Makawee is quite ill. Pennyroyal is a powerful herb. It is poison to a pregnant woman."

"Is it working?"

"It will soon be done. I expect the child to be expelled at any moment," she said with a sardonic grin.

"You are a clever shaman," he acknowledged.

"Aah!"

A distant scream pierced the early morning air.

Among the Grass hurried back to the lodge. When she arrived, Rides Alone was on his knees beside Makawee. He was holding his sister, who was sobbing.

"What is the trouble?" Among the Grass asked.

His face was flushed with anger. "Where were you?"

"I went to get a smudging stick. I was only gone for a moment."

"She has lost the child," Rides Alone said, pointing to the bloody wet mass on a buffalo hide. "I should not be here. Only a woman should see these things."

"I will take care of it," the midwife said, reaching down to place the aborted fetus onto a cloth.

"No! Don't touch! He's mine!" Makawee shouted between sobs.

Among the Grass nodded. She squatted to look at the apple-sized fetus. The unborn child had distinctive human features, including eyes, ears, nose, and mouth. The hands and feet were fully developed. Blood vessels could be seen through translucent skin. The external genitalia were visible. Had Makawee gone full term, she would have delivered a son.

"I will take care of Makawee," the midwife said calmly.

"Your medicine did not prevent this!"

"It's true my medicine was not strong enough to save her baby. But no medicine can overcome the will of the spirits. This child was not meant to come into the world."

Rides Alone swallowed hard. The midwife was correct. The spirits were more powerful than any medicine.

"To protect the mother, I need to reach into her and pull out anything remaining," she said, pushing the sleeves of her tunic up over her forearms. "You should leave."

The warrior glanced at his sister. Makawee was moaning, sitting with her knees pulled to her chest. She had clutched her legs and was rocking back and forth with her face pressed into her thighs. A mixture of vaginal fluids and blood had pooled between her legs.

Rides Alone stood and quickly exited the tepee. Having heard wailing, the camp residents gathered outside. When he paused outside the lodge and shook his head, no words were needed. The villagers' worst fears were confirmed.

Long Horse was stoic when he heard the news. Fox Woman handed Nahkash to another woman and hurried to Makawee's tepee.

"Someone should tell Eagle Bear," Rides Alone said to his father.

The chief nodded. "Send Little Wolf."

Within ten minutes, the young warrior had packed a few things and prepared for the full day's journey to the Crow Agency. As Little Wolf mounted his horse, Rides Alone gave instructions to his younger brother.

"Do not tell him Makawee lost her child. Tell Eagle Bear she is sick. He will discover the truth when he arrives."

Little Wolf nodded. He turned his horse and galloped west, hoping to make Fort Parker by sunset.

Graham had stopped to rest the horses and give them a drink when he saw a rider approaching from the east. He pulled the Colt revolver from the pommel holster and held it by his side, squinting to identify the horseman. He relaxed when he recognized his young friend and greeted him.

"Kahée!"

"Kahée, Eagle Bear."

"Are you headed to the Crow Agency at Fort Parker?"

Little Wolf dismounted and led his horse over to Graham.

"I was coming to see you. I have a message from Rides Alone."

"Oh? What is it?"

"Makawee is *baakuhpée*."

"I don't understand this word."

"She is not feeling well."

"Makawee is sick? What kind of illness does she have? How long has she felt this way? Is the baby okay?"

"Too many questions. I don't know these answers. I will water my horse. We will ride together to camp."

They were soon headed toward the Stillwater River at a fast trot.

They arrived in the camp of Long Horse as the sun was slipping below the western horizon. Graham slid off the saddle and ducked into the tepee, leaving his horses with Little Wolf. Rides Alone was sitting cross-legged inside the entrance and stuck out his arm to stop the visitor. He put his index finger to his lips and pointed to Makawee, who was sleeping under a wool blanket.

Graham nodded and padded to his future wife. He kneeled beside her and removed his hat. She surprised him by her appearance. Her wan face was framed by hair matted from sweating. Her eyelids were puffy, and her nose was red around the nostrils. As he studied her face and gripped the brim of his cowboy hat, Rides Alone touched him on the shoulder and tilted his head toward the entrance. Graham followed his friend outside into the cold early evening.

"There is bad news," Rides Alone said.

"Is Makawee going to die?" Graham's mind raced to the worst outcome.

"No. She lost blood. But she will live."

"Lost blood? How? What illness would cause her to...?" He clasped his hand over his mouth. Tears welled in his eyes. "Did she lose the baby?"

Rides Alone nodded.

Graham felt his legs weaken. He sat on the cold ground, stunned.

"But she was healthy last time I saw her. I don't understand."

"Among the Grass helped. Makawee drank medicine tea seven nights. Baby not to be."

Graham wiped his eyes as he scrambled to his feet.

"I should be with her," he said, gripping his hat. "Is someone taking care of Nahkash?"

"Fox Woman."

Graham walked back to the tepee. He gathered his thoughts, telling himself he needed to be strong for Makawee before ducking inside.

To his surprise, Makawee had pulled herself onto the willow-rod backrest. A wool blanket was resting on her lap. She looked pale and had a blank expression on her face. Graham walked over and kneeled beside the backrest. Her eyes brightened when she saw him. He leaned over and kissed her forehead.

"Did they tell you?"

"Yes. I'm so sorry, Makawee."

"I asked Fox Woman to keep him for me. She collected our baby and wrapped him in a parfleche. It's over there if you want to see him," she said in a monotone voice, pointing to a small elk-hide wrap near the fire.

"Perhaps later," Graham said. The truth was he didn't think he could handle seeing a fetus, especially one that was his child.

Makawee had a blank stare as she spoke. "He would have been a beautiful baby boy. He had fingers and toes. He had eyes and was sucking his thumb."

"The main thing we need to do is get you better," he said, pulling the blanket up to her chin. "Now you get some sleep. I will check in later to see if you can eat something."

As he started to get up, Makawee gripped his forearm and pulled him back down.

"We need to have a proper burial for our baby."

"Yes, of course," he said, laying his hand on top of hers. He lifted her arm and placed it under the blanket, then smoothed the hair above her forehead. He tossed some logs on the fire and turned to look at his future wife. She gave him a faint smile before closing her eyes.

Graham exited the lodge, where Rides Alone and Little Wolf were waiting.

"We pray to the spirits for Makawee to heal," Rides Alone said.

Graham nodded absently. He trudged to the riverbank, where he dropped to his knees. He buried his face in his hands and wept, his tears dripping from his fingers into the swift-flowing river.

The day dawned bright and cold. Three days after she had lost the baby, Makawee felt well enough to make tea and warm a kettle of soup. A heavy silence hung in the air as they shared a morning meal. Makawee seemed detached as she ladled a serving into a bowl. Graham grimaced when he saw the scars on her arms as she was serving the soup.

The day after her miscarriage, Graham had come back to the lodge after a hunting trip with Rides Alone to find her sitting by the fire. She had repeatedly slashed her forearms and calves. She had also cut her long black hair at the neckline. Her severed braids were lying beside a bloody knife. Graham's instinctive reaction was to rush to her aid and ask why she had carved her smooth skin and cut her beautiful hair. But Rides Alone pulled him aside and explained this was the way some Crow women grieved the loss of a loved one. He advised Graham to give her time and space for suffering.

The small funeral procession started up the Stillwater River in the late morning. Graham was in the lead, holding Nahkash in front of him. Makawee followed. The parfleche with the fetus was slung over her shoulder by a strap. Little Wolf was next, and Rides Alone was in the rear. Graham had expected more people to attend. But Rides Alone explained the Crow did not believe an unborn child possessed a spirit. For this reason, the camp residents did not follow their traditional burial customs.

He was resentful toward Long Horse and Fox Woman for their refusal to acknowledge the death of a grandchild, even if the fetus was only sixteen weeks when it was miscarried. He wondered if their absence was influenced by Makawee conceiving for a second time before she was married. Graham was grateful the chief had granted additional time in camp to grieve with Makawee. Long Horse had also sent a messenger to Fort Parker, informing Uriah Brown of the reason Graham would be delayed in returning to work.

Thirty minutes later, the funeral party arrived at the familiar grove of black cottonwood trees along the river. Graham led the group to the large tree where he and Makawee had made love and carved their initials. They had spoken about where to hold the ceremony and agreed they should send the unborn child on his journey where he had been conceived.

Graham positioned Blade under a large branch. He stayed on the horse while the others dismounted. Rides Alone took Nahkash from Graham. Makawee slipped the parfleche over her neck and laid it on the ground. She kneeled and pulled the two braids of her hair from a bag, then opened the flap of the hide enclosure and tucked them inside. After closing the flap, she placed her hands on the precious remains of her unborn child. When she started chanting, Rides Alone and Little Wolf joined in.

Graham removed his hat. Although he only recognized a few words of the Apsaàlooke prayer, their sorrowful tones communicated the feelings of the mourners. He silently recited the Lord's Prayer multiple times while the Crow family chanted.

After a moment of silence, Makawee stood and handed the parfleche to Graham.

"Our baby should have a name," she said, looking up at Graham on his horse. "I would like to name him Nahsa Eish. It means 'Small Heart.'"

"That's beautiful," Graham said, staring at the parfleche in his lap. A lump formed in his throat and tears welled in his eyes. Now that the fetus had a name, his family's tragic loss was magnified. He was not holding the remains of a failed pregnancy. He was cradling a little one who never had seen the light of day. A son who never knew his father or mother. A boy whose name was appropriate for a tiny unborn child — Small Heart.

While Makawee steadied his horse, Graham stood on the saddle. He used a length of rope to tie the parfleche onto a forked limb overhead, then lowered himself back onto the saddle before dismounting.

"This is our tree. It is also the resting place for Nahsa Eish," Makawee said, touching the initials they had carved into the trunk of the cottonwood.

"We need to add something," Graham said.

He fished a Barlow knife from his pocket, unfolded the blade, and scraped away the outer bark into a distinctive shape. When he was finished, the initials *G*, *M*, and *N* were in the center of a heart.

"Small Heart will always be in our hearts," he said, putting his arm around Makawee's shoulders while admiring his handiwork.

"Can we stay here for a while?"

"Yes. As long as you want."

Makawee took Nahkash from Rides Alone and said he and Little Wolf could return to camp. They sat under the tree, and she opened her tunic to allow Nahkash to nurse. Graham draped a blanket over her shoulders. He reached out and touched her exposed neck. He thought she was beautiful, even with short hair.

"Do they hurt?" he asked, pointing to the cut marks on her forearms which had scabbed over and started to heal.

"Yes. I want them to hurt. If these cuts hurt, it lessens the hurt I feel inside. I will reopen these wounds tomorrow."

"Makawee, please don't," Graham said, pleading. "I'm hurting as well. And when I see these cuts on you, I feel worse. I understand it is how you grieve. Can you please allow your cuts to heal?"

"I will see how I feel tomorrow. But I will consider your request."

Graham pulled her close to his side and looked down at the nursing Nahkash. He understood what it meant to grieve. In the twentieth century, he had attended the funerals of three siblings. He still carried survivor's guilt. They had died young. He was not only still alive, but living in another time!

The Crow practice of self-mutilation when under duress or grieving was a foreign concept to Graham. Little Wolf had amputated his finger. Makawee had dozens of self-inflicted wounds. These actions made no sense to him.

When Nahkash finished, Makawee closed her tunic and cradled the toddler in her arms. Makawee leaned against Graham, who was reclined against the cottonwood tree. He tilted his head back and gazed at the parfleche overhead. Soon thousands of buds would emerge from hundreds of bare branches, a sign the venerable tree had awakened from a long Montana winter. Unlike the tree, the tiny fetus in the elk-hide pouch would never come alive. His unborn child never had a chance to breathe the crisp March air he was breathing.

Graham felt anger welling in his chest. He wanted to jump up and shake his fist at God for abandoning him. What had he or Makawee done to deserve to lose a child? Was this punishment? For what?

He took deep breaths to calm his emotions. When he looked down, Makawee and Nahkash had drifted into sleep. But he couldn't rest. He wanted answers, dammit!

While he sulked over this personal tragedy, the words of Redfield crept into his consciousness: *"The spirits will not allow you to change history. What will be, will be. What's done is done."*

Graham brought his hand to his forehead and closed his eyes. *I am not allowed to change the future,* he thought.

He had researched the 1890 Crow Indian census rolls when he returned from his trip to Yellowstone last year and discovered Makawee had only one child, Nahkash. By making Makawee pregnant, he had potentially changed the future. If the baby had been born, Nahkash would have had a brother. How would this boy affect future generations? Would he have made a tiny ripple in the pond of time, or would he have created a much bigger wave? The spirits did not allow him to change the future. Makawee could not go full term and deliver a baby boy who was never meant to be born.

Who had caused all this heartache and suffering? He had.

It was a tough pill to swallow. But he had no other explanation. Why else would a vibrant young woman with a healthy first pregnancy have a miscarriage?

This question prompted another thought — one that had immense ramifications for their future relationship. He would need to be careful when they had sex. Knowing Nahkash would be her only child, he could not allow Makawee to become pregnant only to have her experience another miscarriage. That would be cruel, especially when he could predict the outcome of a future pregnancy.

As he pondered these recent revelations, Makawee stirred. She rubbed her eyes and gave him a serious look.

"Graham, do you think we will see Small Heart in the next life?"

"Why do you ask?"

"I was just dreaming I saw him."

"What did he look like?"

"He was not a person. He was a wolf. I knew it was him when he looked directly at me."

"I'm sure we will see him, whatever shape he takes in the next life."

She snuggled back against his chest and dropped asleep again.

If she believed their unborn child had been reincarnated as a wolf, he would not argue. This possibility might ease her suffering and prevent her from cutting herself again.

As for Graham, he didn't know what to believe about the future, let alone the afterlife. He was determined to focus on the present. And right now, he needed to earn the right to marry the woman sleeping in his arms.

Chapter Twelve

Shrinking Land

July 1873

The massive bull bison wheezed as it lay dying on the prairie grass, hot breath whistling from its nostrils. A .50-caliber bullet had punctured a lung and fractured the distal end of a humerus bone, causing it to stumble and collapse after being shot. The hunter dismounted, pulled a revolver from his holster, and silenced the suffering bison with a single shot to the brain. He used his bowie knife to make a long cut from the anus to the chest cavity. Steaming guts spilled out of the animal.

The stocky man with a gray-streaked beard and thick shoulder-length hair wiped his bloody knife on the hide. He removed his hat and wiped sweat from his forehead with the back of his hand.

He stood and removed a small leather pouch with a drawstring from his front pocket, then kneeled by the extruding entrails. After a few quick slices, he was holding a fist-sized chunk of fat carved from the belly of the bovine. He punched a small hole in the fatty blob and slipped on leather gloves before pouring a white crystalline powder into the center and squeezing it closed. He scooted on his knees next to the steaming pile of intestinal organs and performed the same procedure a dozen times along the length of the carcass, concentrating most of them between the ribs and the hindquarters.

The wolfer stood to inspect his work. Strychnine was an efficient and cheap method to harvest wolf pelts. All a man had to do was lace the carcass of a bison, elk, or other ungulate with poison and wait for wolves to arrive. The key was to make sure there was no residual strychnine on the fat chunks, as the bitter taste would cause a wolf to spit it out.

Satisfied the carcass was prepared, the wolfer used a hatchet to cleave the front leg of the bison. He tied a rope around the limb and wrapped the other end around the pommel of his saddle. As he mounted his horse, he thought about the potential payoff from an hour's work. With any luck, he could return to the slain bison tomorrow and find six or eight dead wolves. There could be as many as a dozen. Each pelt brought between two and three dollars, depending on size and quality.

This was more lucrative than mining. He would never get rich selling wolf pelts. But the work was easier than scratching in the dirt or sluicing for gold. And he was providing a valuable service to the ranchers, who wanted every wolf killed in areas where they grazed cattle.

He clucked and urged his horse forward. The severed bison leg dragged behind, wetting the grass with blood. Every so often he dropped a strychnine-laden ball of fat along the trail. This scented dragline would attract any wolves within several miles. As he approached a line of cottonwoods along a stream, he spotted a small herd of elk. He reined up, raised the Springfield to his shoulder, and fired. One animal dropped immediately.

As the surviving *wapiti* bounded away, he smiled. The cow he had just killed would become his next poisoned wolf trap.

Rides Alone dismounted and handed the reins of his horse to Graham. The Crow Indian stooped and inspected the bird lying on its back, its sharp talons pointing skyward.

"Red-tailed hawk," he said, looking up at his riding partner.

"How did it die?"

"Not sure. No marks from horned owl. No bullet hole."

The friends were on a hunting trip. They had ridden northeast to the Yellowstone River, hoping to find elk feeding on willows along the river. The dead raptor was an unusual sighting. But nothing could prepare them for what they saw as they approached the south bank of the river a short time later.

A bison carcass lay in the late afternoon sun. A tiding of magpies had gathered around the dead animal for a feast. Clouds of blowflies were feeding on the blood and intestinal fluids of the slain animal. Lying near the bison were a half dozen dead wolves. Rigor mortis had set in. Extreme extensor rigidity had caused the animals to assume a "sawhorse" stance before falling on their sides and dying.

Both riders dismounted and surveyed the gruesome scene. Graham walked around the dead canines scattered in a thirty-foot radius of the bison carcass. He used his boot to turn over the stiffened bodies of the wolves. There were no visible marks.

"Wolfer," Rides Alone announced, inspecting a canine.

"What's that?"

"White man who poisons buffalo or deer. Wolves eat meat and die. Wolfer sells fur."

Graham could see the disgusted look on his friend's face as he spoke.

"Hawk also poisoned."

"Why would someone do this?"

Rides Alone did not reply. He turned and walked to a nearby tree, seeking a moment alone.

Graham felt ashamed of being a baashchiile. Thousands of white men disrespected and interrupted the circle of life. Not only were the herds of bison disappearing from indiscriminate killing, but poisoning wolves had become a lucrative occupation. Of course, wolves were not the only scavengers to eat the poison-laced carcasses. Any animal that fed on the carcass would die a slow and painful death.

A faint whimper shook Graham from his thoughts. He removed his Colt Cobra from the pommel bag holster and guardedly walked toward the sound. He soon discovered a poisoned wolf that had stumbled and fallen in the grass. It was suffering from seizures, its swollen tongue hanging out. This animal had ingested less poison, and the toxin had taken longer to work its way through the canine. The exhausted wolf was asphyxiating.

The dying wolf's muscles had stiffened. The animal could not move its legs and struggled to turn its head as Graham approached. He raised the revolver and aimed it at the wolf's head. Since it was his first time firing the Cobra, he cocked the weapon to minimize the trigger pull.

His hand shook as the wolf looked at him with pale yellow eyes. As he stared at the helpless creature, Makawee's dream about a reincarnated Small Heart echoed in his head.

"Small Heart was not a boy in my dream. He was a wolf. When he looked at me, I knew it was him."

Graham didn't believe in reincarnation. But what if it were true? What if their unborn child was a wolf in the next life? What if Small Heart was behind those eyes? What if...

He shook his head to rid his mind of these foreboding thoughts.

Crack!

A gunshot echoed through the river valley.

Rides Alone ran toward the sound. He found Graham staring at the poisoned canine, holding a pistol to his side. The wolf lay on the grass, blood seeping into the ground from the fatal shot.

"It was suffering," Graham said, with a blank stare.

The event rekindled a memory from his time with the 1871 Hayden Expedition. A soldier had fallen into a hot spring and was badly burned. The soldier's horse had panicked and reared, punching through the thin crust near the spring and scalding its front legs. Graham was ordered to shoot the horse with his Spencer carbine to put the horse out of its misery. It had been an unpleasant but necessary task.

"Come," Rides Alone said, putting his hand on Graham's shoulder and leading him back to the carcass.

When they reached the slain bison, Rides Alone nodded at a large male wolf lying near the entrails.

"Help."

Graham grabbed the stiff rear legs of the carcass while Rides Alone took the front legs. They carried the one-hundred-and-twenty-pound animal to the horse and used a swinging motion to heave it onto the rump of the horse, which shuddered under the weight and stepped sideways until Rides Alone calmed it. While the Crow warrior used a rope to secure the animal to the rear of the saddle, Graham ran his hand over the mottled gray-and-cream coat of the animal, admiring the sleek and powerful predator.

"Scent trail," Rides Alone said, pointing to the bent, blood-stained grass along the river. "We follow."

Graham mounted Blade, and they rode upstream. To Graham's eyes, the blood trail vanished. But Rides Alone stopped every few minutes, dismounted, and ran his hands across the tops of the fescue and wheatgrass. Sometimes he would put a few blades in his mouth, grunt, spit them out, then climb back on his horse and continue riding upriver. Other times, he pointed to a small white blob of animal fat on the ground. The wolfer had created a baited trail, luring wolves and other animals toward his next poison trap.

Rides Alone abruptly held up his hand and stopped. Then he swung his rifle onto his lap, and Graham followed his lead, pulling his snub-nosed revolver from the pommel holster while urging his own horse alongside Rides Alone.

The Indian pointed to the sky. A kettle of turkey vultures was circling on thermals of hot air a short distance ahead. A second carcass had attracted their attention.

Rides Alone used hand gestures to instruct Graham to approach from the south. Rides Alone would take a wide path and approach from the west. They would meet at the carcass. Rides Alone held a finger to his lips before he left.

Graham waited until his partner positioned himself under a juniper perched on a small knoll a hundred yards to his left. Rides Alone raised his rifle over his head, signaling they should advance.

Graham tugged the brim of his hat and squeezed his legs together, urging Blade forward. He held the Colt in his right hand and the reins in his left. His heart was pounding. He strained to see what was lying in the tall grass ahead. He glanced at Rides Alone to be sure they were advancing on their quarry at the same pace. A slight breeze caused the prairie grass to sway. Graham could feel beads of sweat form on his chest and soak his shirt.

An elk carcass came into view. A dozen crows had perched on the ground near the animal's midsection. They were pulling at the exposed intestines with heavy, straight bills. There was no sign of anyone.

When the riders dismounted, the crows flew away, emitting a raucous series of caws before perching in a silver-leafed rabbitbrush a short distance away. They continued cawing and cackling, hoping to return to the tasty meal when the human intruders left. The noisy birds would soon have to compete with the turkey vultures circling overhead.

Rides Alone examined the carcass. He knelt and pulled several carved pieces of fat from the gut cavity. Retrieving a parfleche, he fished among the warm, slick intestines until he found a dozen additional chunks of poisoned fat and placed them into the leather pouch.

"We go to Fort Parker," he said with a surly tone as he tucked the parfleche of strychnine-laced elk fat under the ropes holding the body of the poisoned wolf carcass.

Graham had never seen his friend this angry. As they reined their horses and headed southwest, he wondered what Rides Alone planned to do when they arrived at the fort. He started to ask when Rides Alone pressed his horse into a fast trot. The Crow warrior was on a mission.

The Crow chiefs sat on a long wooden bench inside the fort and watched the man in the courtyard with the picture-making equipment.

A photographer poured collodion solution from a bottle onto a glass plate, then tilted it to allow the sticky substance to coat the entire surface. The thin, bearded man dipped a wet plate into a silver nitrate bath while shielding the process under a black cloth draped over a tripod. After three or four minutes, he removed the plate, wiped off the excess chemicals, and inserted it into a shallow lightproof box. He emerged from the portable darkroom and snapped the wooden holder onto the back of the camera mounted on another tripod, where a black cloth completely covered the camera so that only the lens was visible.

"Okay, gentlemen. Please look right here," the photographer said, pointing to the protruding lens.

The men gazed at the small circle ten feet away.

"Now is the time to smile," he said, placing his index fingers at the corners of his mouth to make his point.

They responded with straight-lined mouths and slack cheeks. The biggest man in the quintet cradled a spike tomahawk in his left hand. The sharpened blade of the fifteen-inch weapon rested near his elbow. His steely gaze and somber expression made it clear he was a chief among chiefs.

The photographer sighed and shrugged. "Don't move until I tell you."

He removed a slide from the wooden holder that covered the sensitized glass plate, then removed the lens cap. He counted five seconds before replacing the lens cap, followed by the slide.

"That's good," he said, raising his hand. "You can move."

After the photographer disappeared under the black covering, the Crow leaders gathered around the man with the tomahawk.

"I know you are not pleased to have your picture taken," Sits-in-the-Middle-of-the-Land said. "We have to do these things to get the best outcome for our people."

"Baashchiile want to take our lands. We get little in return," Poor Elk said.

The big man rubbed the handle of his weapon before responding. Even if they didn't say it, everyone felt the same way.

"I agree. More and more settlers and miners are coming each year. They push us from our lands. The bison herds are shrinking. Yet we need to remain friends with the government. The Crow Nation does not have enough warriors or weapons to fight the Lakota Sioux. I am told they will soon put down the iron rails where we stand today. I dislike losing our way of life. But we must move east. I see no other choice."

A well-dressed, clean-shaven man in his mid-fifties walked toward the circle of chiefs.

"Now that we have a photo to mark the occasion, let's finish our talks for today," Felix Brunot said. He held one arm to the side and invited the chiefs to the wooden boardwalk in front of the Indian Agent's office building.

After the Crow chiefs were seated in front of the building, Brunot stepped up on the raised wooden structure. Two other men, Eliphalet Whittlesey and Dr. James Wright, sat behind him, along with Fellows Pease. A sergeant leaned on a support post and smoked a pipe while watching the proceedings.

"Our negotiating team is pleased with the progress we have made on these talks. I have sent a telegraph to Washington telling them how cooperative you have been. I will ask my secretary and interpreter, Thomas Cree, to summarize the key statements and what we have agreed to so far."

Cree stepped up and faced the group. He opened a book and read from his notes, alternating between English and Apsáalooke.

"These are the circumstances which have brought us to these talks," he began.

"First, the farming efforts have been unsuccessful. The winds never stop blowing in this part of the country. Frosts and freezes come early, shortening the growing season. Because of this, corn, beans, and squash have not produced good yields. Second, we need to rebuild this agency after last year's fire. These adobe buildings are temporary. Third, the Northern Pacific Railroad has charted a course that will cut straight through this part of the reservation. Fourth, the buffalo herds are diminished. Most of the remaining herds are east of this location. Last, the Crow people need the support of the US government to defend themselves from the Lakota Sioux."

Cree paused and looked up from his notes. "Any comments?"

Poor Elk stood. He spoke for a short time, then sat.

Cree turned to the men behind him and interpreted.

"He says with enough spirit guns, they can defeat their enemies. These were never provided, even though they were requested many times."

"What's a spirit gun?" Wright asked.

"A repeating rifle. When the Indians saw these rifles years ago, they believed only spirits could load and fire a gun so rapidly," Whittlesey said.

"Poor Elk speaks the truth," Pease said. "I've made it clear in my reports it is in the best interest of everyone if the Crow are armed. They can keep the non-treaty Sioux from invading this territory and protect the settlers. But their request has fallen on deaf ears in Washington."

"Tell the chiefs we will consider this request," Brunot said.

Cree repeated the Commissioner's words in Apsáalooke. It was obvious from the expression on Poor Elk's face he was skeptical.

"Would anyone else like to speak?" Cree asked.

Sits-in-the-Middle-of-the-Land stood. He raised his chin and spoke passionately. When he was finished speaking, he paused and remained standing while Cree interpreted.

"The Sioux must have good white men friends on the Platte and Missouri. They get guns and ammunition. They are better armed. The Great Father in Washington must not know the Sioux get these arms and kill white men with them. Crow do not kill white men; the arms and ammunition we receive are used to hunt. We use these to defend ourselves and our white friends. Without these arms, the Lakota will annihilate our people."

Brunot looked at his colleagues for their reaction.

"How can we ask the Crow to be our allies if we don't trust them to have rifles to defend themselves?" Pease asked the others sitting beside him.

Brunot spoke to Sits-in-the-Middle-of-the-Land, then asked Cree to interpret. "We will provide one hundred repeating rifles when they sign the agreement."

The big chief sat down.

Cree cleared his throat. "I have shared this information at our last gathering. However, I would like to state it again. I will read the official agreement all of us will sign today.

"In consideration of ceding half your reservation land, moving east to the Judith Basin, and establishing a new Crow Agency, the US government will provide the following. One million dollars will be put in trust for the Crow people to be held in perpetuity with the interest expanded or reinvested at the discretion of the president for the benefit of said tribe. This agreement will dissolve the 1868 Treaty of Fort Laramie and relinquish right, title, and claim to the previous reservation."

"Add the rifles," Brunot whispered to Cree.

"And we will deliver one hundred repeating rifles with ammunition," Cree said while making note of this change on the agreement.

Sits-in-the-Middle-of-the-Land turned to his fellow chiefs and spoke in a low tone.

"Brothers, I do not see a choice. As bitter as this decision is, our fate is sealed. Either we align with the white man and survive, or we try to fight the white man and the Lakota. Our children will not survive if we do nothing. It appears the young warrior Plenty Coups, who saw a better future by remaining friends with the Great Father in Washington, is correct. What do you say?"

One by one, the chiefs nodded. The reality of their plight weighed heavy on their hearts.

The five men formed a line at the raised platform, with Sits-in-the-Middle-of-the-Land last. Cree and Pease pushed a long wooden table to the edge of the walkway. Brunot, Whittlesey, Wright, and Pease stood behind the table, while Cree dipped a quill into an ink bottle and pointed to the bottom of the page where each Crow chief was to make his mark.

After four marks were on the parchment, Sits-in-the-Middle-of-the-Land stepped forward. As he took the quill in his hand, a voice called from the other side of the courtyard.

"Oochia!" ["Stop!"]

Everyone at the signing ceremony looked up to see two horses trotting toward them. The sergeant dropped his pipe, pulled a pistol from his belt, and ran in front of the table. He aimed the gun at the unknown riders as they approached.

"Easy, sergeant. I recognize these men," Pease said. He placed a hand on the shoulder of the soldier, who lowered his weapon.

"Kahée!" Pease greeted the riders.

Rides Alone and Graham dismounted. The Crow warrior walked to the back of his horse, removed a knife from a sheath on his belt, and cut the ropes. A wolf carcass and parfleche fell to the ground. Rides Alone scooped up the stiff wolf. He carried it past the five Crow chiefs and tossed it onto the table on top of the parchment. The ink bottle tumbled from the table, dark liquid splashing onto the wooden planks. The officials stepped back, unsettled by this brash behavior.

The carcass had bloated in the August sun. It reeked of rotting flesh. The open yellow eyes of the canine were glazed. Its tongue had swollen and spilled out of a mouth ringed with white foam.

"This is Rides Alone, son of Long Horse," Pease said to the others. "Chief Long Horse attended our meetings last week but was too ill to make the trip today."

"Why did he bring a wolf?" asked Brunot, looking at Fellows Pease.

"I understand your language," Rides Alone said before Pease could reply. "This wolf killed."

"One less varmint. You collect your bounty in Bozeman, not here," Brunot said.

"Eagle Bear, show how wolf died," Rides Alone said to Graham.

Graham nodded. He carried the parfleche to the table, opened the flap, and turned it upside down. A dozen greasy chunks of fat spilled onto the wolf carcass. Some slid onto the wooden planks and skittered across the walkway.

"We discovered a bison carcass. A wolfer had placed these poison-filled pieces of fat in the body cavity. We also found poison in an elk carcass. Six wolves died," Graham said.

"Well now, look here, young man. Poisoning is legal," Brunot said. "Ranchers appreciate any coyotes or wolves that are trapped or shot. These predators kill less cattle with a wolf bounty in place. With any luck, we will rid ourselves of all wolves within a few years."

Rides Alone's eyes narrowed. He clenched his fists and stepped forward.

Sits-in-the-Middle-of-the-Land stuck out his muscular arm and held back the angry warrior. He turned to face Rides Alone.

"Thank you for bringing the wolf. Let me talk. Stand with the others."

Rides Alone and Graham retreated from the table. They stood with the four chiefs as their leader spoke.

"It is true the Crow hunt and kill wolves. But we do not trap them. And we never poison them — or any other creature. It is wrong. The spirits are angry with anyone who interrupts the natural circle of life."

Fellows Pease jumped in.

"Thank you, chief. Well said. Let me say something to my white brothers."

Pease huddled with the others and spoke in a low voice.

"Gentlemen, this is an important issue to the Crow. We cannot discount it. It could be a deal-breaker for the agreement we worked so hard to negotiate. Poisoning an animal is a practice anathema to all Indians, not just the Crow."

"What are we supposed to do? We don't set policy in Washington. There are hundreds of wolfers making a living in this territory. And the ranchers want their lands rid of these predators," Brunot said.

"We don't set the laws on public lands, but we have discretion on what is in the agreement concerning setting up the reservation," Pease suggested.

Brunot smoothed the hair on the back of his head and clasped his hands. What the Indian agent said made sense.

"Yes. You are correct. Gentlemen, would you support a provision that discourages the poisoning of wolves on the reservation?" he asked Wright and Whittlesey.

Both men nodded.

Brunot turned toward the chiefs and spoke.

"We would like to thank Rides Alone for bringing this to our attention. We propose an amendment to the agreement that stipulates the government will punish any poisoning of wolves within the boundary of your territory."

After a long discussion among the chiefs, Sits-in-the-Middle-of-the-Land nodded in consent.

"Wonderful! Let's take a break while Mr. Cree drafts a new agreement that includes these changes. Let's meet in two hours."

The chiefs turned and walked toward the gates.

Rides Alone crossed his arms and stayed behind. He seethed with anger at the proposal.

"Would you remove this wolf from our table?" Brunot asked the Crow warrior.

Rides Alone ignored the request. He glared at the negotiator from Washington. Someone else could dispose of the rotting wolf carcass. He pivoted and retrieved the reins of his horse.

Graham walked beside his friend. The absurdity of a clause in this agreement that punished those who poisoned wolves on the reservation was not lost on Rides Alone or Graham. It would be another broken commitment among many between the government and Indigenous tribes.

No one in Fort Parker could imagine the wolf policy that would unfold over the next century.

By 1880, Yellowstone Park superintendent Philetus Norris would state in his annual report that "the value of wolf and coyote hides and their easy slaughter with strychnine-poisoned carcasses has almost led to their extermination." In 1885, the federal government would establish the US Bureau of Biological Survey, which focused on wolf extermination. Predatory animals would be destroyed by trapping, shooting, den hunting during the breeding season, and poisoning. In 1906, the US Forest Service would enlist the help of the bureau to clear cattle ranges of gray wolves. In 1940, they would combine the Bureau of Fisheries and the Bureau of Biological Survey to form the Fish and Wildlife Service. Gray wolves would not be given protection until the Endangered Species Act was passed in 1973.

As they reached the gates of the fort, Graham could hear Brunot shouting.

"Sergeant! Get this stinking dead wolf off my table!"

Chapter Thirteen

An Only Child

September 1873

B eaver Tail waved a hand above his head, signaling the crowd to be quiet. The middle-aged Crow man addressed the spectators gathered in a grassy area outside the palisades of Fort Parker.

"We have two contestants remaining to determine the winner of *Abatsink'isha*. Every spear that enters the outer portion of the hoop is worth one point. Any spear that passes through the center of the hoop scores three points. I will roll the hoop until one person accumulates ten points and wins the game."

A series of traditional Indian skill games had been organized to help pass time while the Crow awaited the distribution of their annuities. Graham looked down at Makawee, who was kneeling beside Nahkash and pointing to the young men holding four-foot-long willow spears with a trident on the trailing end. All young men under eighteen had taken part in the hoop game. After elimination rounds, there were only two contestants left.

Beaver Tail placed the twelve-inch willow sapling hoop on the inside of his curled arm. The hoop was laced with elk-hide strips in a spiderweb pattern. There was a small hole in the center. Little Wolf stood on one side behind a log ten feet away. Bull Half White, who everyone called Curly, stood behind another log facing his opponent.

"Ready? Go!"

When Beaver Tail released the springy willow hoop, it bounced several times and quickly sped between the crowd gathered on both sides. Both contestants launched their spears. The hoop was knocked over and pinned to the ground. A cheer went up from behind a log. Beaver Tail fetched the hoop and announced that Little Wolf had scored the first point. The competitors retrieved their spears and took their places for the next throw. After twenty hoops had been rolled, the score was knotted at seven points each.

The spindly hoop was released yet again. Seconds later, it was knocked over. Beaver Tail held up the hoop to show a spear had pierced the center of the lacing for the first time.

"Three points to Curly. He is the winner!" he announced.

A loud ovation and shrieks erupted from Curly's supporters. The wiry fourteen-year-old raised the hoop over his head to more cheers. Little Wolf bowed to his friend and opponent.

"Our last game of skill is the arrow shoot," Beaver Tail announced. "We have narrowed the contestants to the three young men with the highest scores in earlier rounds. They are Curly, Spotted Owl, and Little Wolf. Young warriors, bring your bows and arrows."

The spectators strained their necks to get a good view of the three young men.

"This game is simple," Beaver Tail said loudly so everyone could hear. "Each young man will shoot arrows as rapidly as possible. The goal is to see how many arrows can be shot into the air before the first one hits the ground. Curly, you will go first."

Curly adjusted the quiver of arrows slung over his shoulder, nocked an arrow, and pulled back the bowstring. He aimed the arrow skyward, hesitated for a second, then released the string.

Thwish!

An arrow vaulted into the late summer sky. The young archer quickly reached over his shoulder, extracted another arrow from the quiver, nocked it, and let it fly. He did this in rapid succession.

Beaver Tail yelled, "Oochia!" ["Stop!"]

"Five arrows," he said. "Nice shooting."

Spotted Owl was next. He could launch six arrows before the first one landed.

Rides Alone walked over to Little Wolf holding a special bow. He got the weapon from the Mountain Shoshone while on the Hayden Expedition the previous year. The Sheep Eaters make bows from the horns of bighorn sheep. It is a time-consuming process that involves reversing the curl, straightening and drying the horns, and joining the horns together using sinew backing and hide glue. Rides Alone taught his younger brother how to shoot the elegant weapon, which was perfectly balanced and had exceptional evenness of bending. It was a superior weapon in terms of power and accuracy compared to bows made from wood.

"Remember how we practiced. You will do well," he counseled.

Little Wolf nodded and slung a quiver over his shoulder. He nocked an arrow, pulled back the bowstring, and adjusted his firing angle.

Thwish! Thwish! Thwish!

In the blink of an eye, Little Wolf started launching arrows in rapid succession.

Thwish! Thwish! Thwish!

After firing each arrow, he reached over his shoulder to retrieve the next one from his quiver, placed it on the bowstring, and sent it skyward. He accomplished this in one fluid motion. Each arrow arced into the bright afternoon sky, nearly disappearing before reaching its apex and hurtling toward the earth.

Thwish! Thwish!

"Oochia!"

Everyone knew the winner before it was announced. The eighth arrow had just been released from Little Wolf's bow when the first one landed. It was an awesome demonstration of archery skills and agility. The crowd erupted in appreciation. Spotted Owl and Curly lay their bows at his feet in recognition of his victory.

"That was a wonderful display of shooting," Graham said as he and Makawee approached Little Wolf. "It doesn't seem like the missing finger of your left hand has impaired your skills."

"Having one less finger keeps me humble. The spirits give me strength," he replied. "A horn bow requires much force to pull."

Graham turned to Curly. "You were very accurate in winning the hoop game."

"Much practice with Little Wolf," he replied. "We sharpen hunting and shooting skills together since we were *shikáakkaate.*"

Makawee saw Graham furrow his brow and realized he didn't understand the last word.

"He said they have practiced these things since they were little boys," she whispered.

Little Wolf returned the compliment. "Curly is good at hoop games because he has good eyes. He can spot an eagle in a tree when no one else can see it. He would make a great scout," he said.

It was clear they were great friends who shared a passion for becoming warriors. The young men joined Rides Alone and walked toward the temporary camp, talking in Apsaàlooke about their achievements in the youth games.

"You have become strong," Makawee said, clutching Graham by his upper arm while holding the hand of Nahkash.

Graham had indeed grown stronger over the past six months. Constructing adobe buildings at Fort Parker and lifting heavy loads from the wagons to the warehouse had broadened his chest and shoulders. His leg strength had also increased. His thighs felt tight under his jeans. It helped to have a good diet. He had three good meals each day, courtesy of the food provided by Uriah Brown.

"Thanks. I'm glad you noticed."

She reached up and stroked his cheek with the back of her hand.

"My people have little hair on their skin. But I dislike your smooth face," she said with a smile. "You should grow back your beard."

Her comment took Graham aback. He had shaved when he returned to Fort Parker after the funeral of Small Heart. He had resolved to stay clean-shaven until the time was right to grow a beard. It was his way of recognizing the death of their unborn child, just as Makawee had cut her beautiful long hair. Her hair had grown to shoulder-length in the past six months. Soon she would braid it.

"Hold out your arms," he ordered.

Makawee dropped the hand of Nahkash and complied.

Graham pushed the long sleeves of the tunic over her forearms. He turned her wrists to look at the underside of her arms. Pink scars were faintly visible reminders of her self-inflicted wounds. He was glad to see there were no fresh cuts.

"Are you done grieving?" he asked.

"A mother never stops grieving the loss of a child. But I have learned how to carry my sorrow. I have accepted what happened to Small Heart."

"I will grow a beard under one condition," he said. "You will see a doctor at Crow Agency. I want him to make sure you are okay."

"Why? I feel good."

"You were weak for quite a while after your...after the baby came early. You lost a lot of blood. I want a physician to look at you."

"Among the Grass says that..."

"I don't care what she says!" he snapped.

When Makawee flinched and took a step back, Graham realized his words were harsh.

"I'm sorry," he said, grabbing her hand. "But a midwife only has knowledge of herbal medicine. I want you to see someone trained in Western medicine. I will feel better if the doctor says you are healthy. Will you do this for me?"

"Yes. Now stop shaving!"

"Gladly," he said. "Oh, and I have a surprise for Long Horse."

"What's that?"

"I bought another pony and branded it. I'm eager to give it to him. It's a powerful stallion."

"How many horses does this make?"

"Three. I also got another rifle at a good price. I need only four more horses and one more rifle. It's taking a long time, but I'm saving every dollar. We can be married in eighteen months if my luck holds."

"Eighteen moons? That is a long time," she said gloomily.

"Yes. I agree. But with each horse or rifle, we are one step closer to being a family!"

He removed his hat and handed it to Makawee before picking up Nahkash. He swooped the child over his head and sat her on his shoulders. Her tiny legs dangled on either side of his head. He reached up and grabbed the little girl's hands. The toddler giggled as she anticipated the ride.

"Let's get something to eat. I wonder what Fox Woman has in the stew pot."

The physician slipped on his glasses before assembling the monaural stethoscope by screwing the two wooden pieces together. He placed the trumpet-shaped end of the instrument on the young woman's chest before placing the other end to his ear.

"Deep breaths, please," he said.

Makawee pulled air into her lungs, then released it through her mouth. She repeated this several times.

"Now breathe normally."

The middle-aged balding man placed the bell of his stethoscope in several positions on her chest, briefly stopping to listen. He moved behind the woman and placed the listening tube on her back.

"Let me see your tongue."

His patient complied.

He grabbed her wrists and raised her arms. When he turned them over, a frown creased his forehead. Scars from self-inflicted wounds crisscrossed the underside of her arms from wrist to elbow.

"What's this?" he asked.

"I lost a child. I cut myself so I could heal," Makawee responded indifferently.

Taken literally, this statement was absurd. The physician peered over his glasses and turned toward Graham, who was standing along the wall of the small examination room.

"Is this true?"

"Yes. It is common for Crow women to express their grief this way upon losing a child."

"My dear young woman," he said, looking at his patient. "Bloodletting should only be performed by someone trained in the practice."

"Do you practice bloodletting?" Graham asked. He was incredulous people in the medical community were still using this barbaric method in the late nineteenth century. It was a stark example of medical knowledge in the 1870s. He was regretting the decision to set up an appointment with this doctor, who visited Fort Parker every two weeks.

"I find bloodletting of limited use," he replied, shrugging. "I only use it where I need to clear out infected or weakened blood. Done properly, it can stop a hemorrhage."

Graham shook his head. He found it ironic a physician would chastise a patient for cutting herself yet endorse draining large quantities of blood as long as it was performed under medical supervision.

"Well, your heart and lungs sound fine," he reported.

"Doctor, can you determine if everything is healthy with...uh...with her reproductive system?" Graham asked, struggling to find the right words.

"Why do you ask?"

"She had a miscarriage earlier in the year and was weak for some time."

Makawee flashed a worried look. Graham had not mentioned this as a reason for the examination.

"I will not let you inside of me!" she blurted out, jumping up from her chair.

"Calm down," the doctor said, holding out his arms. "I can do a simple noninvasive exam."

Graham took the hands of his future wife and looked into her eyes.

"He will not hurt you. I will be right here."

Makawee nodded and slowly sat down.

"For this exam, I need you to lie down," he said, pointing to a cot on the other side of the room.

Makawee walked over to the narrow bed and lay on her back. Graham pulled up a chair and held her hand.

"Now, please raise your legs. Bend your knees and hold them in that position."

The doctor picked up his stethoscope and placed it over her lower abdomen. He squinted his eyes as he listened.

"I need you to pull up your dress so I can touch your pelvic area."

Makawee turned her head to the side and looked at Graham, who reassured her by squeezing her hand. She placed her feet on the table, raised her hips, and pulled the elk-hide dress over her buttocks.

"Spread your legs apart slightly."

Another glance at Graham, who silently mouthed, "It's okay. I love you."

She parted her legs and closed her eyes.

The doctor placed his hands on her lower abdomen and palpated, moving across the pelvic region. He returned to the vulva and pushed firmly several times. He furrowed his brow, said something under his breath, then stood.

"You may sit up."

The doctor clasped his hands behind his back and walked behind his desk.

"How long after your miscarriage did you bleed?"

"Several weeks. It was heavy at first. But it slowly stopped."

"Did you have any other symptoms?"

"My stomach felt sore for a long time."

"Hmm," he said, stroking his mutton chops. "I've delivered quite a few babies in my time. I think the uterine wall was torn or damaged. I can feel an abnormality like scar tissue, but of course I can't be certain unless I use my fingers to..."

"No!" Makawee said emphatically.

Graham sat on the edge of the bed and put his arm around Makawee.

"How could something like this happen?" he asked.

"Don't know for sure. It's not common. Did the midwife use any sharp objects during or after the baby's birth?"

Makawee thought for a moment before answering.

"Among the Grass reached inside me and removed the afterbirth, but I was in so much pain I don't remember everything."

The doctor pursed his lips and shook his head.

"Will she be all right?" Graham asked.

"Well, if the bleeding and pain have stopped, it means the wound has healed. But there's a big scar in her womb."

"And what does that mean?"

"She cannot carry a child full term. If she became pregnant, it would be a threat to the child — and the mother."

"What kind of threat?" Graham asked, even though he knew the answer.

The physician removed his glasses and looked at the couple sitting on the edge of the cot.

"The baby would not live, and the mother could bleed to death."

"So that means..."

"No more children. At least by natural childbirth. I'm sorry."

Graham's ears pricked up. "Does that mean a baby could be delivered by C-section?"

The doctor retracted at this suggestion. His face grew red, and his voice rose as he spoke.

"You obviously know nothing about this other than what you've read in a newspaper or overheard in a saloon. Do you realize over half the women who underwent C-sections died? Anyone who advocates a cesarean birth other than in the most extreme circumstance is practicing sacrificial midwifery!"

The physician walked behind his desk and sat heavily in a chair.

Graham helped Makawee from the bed and steered her toward the exit. She stared blankly ahead, in shock from the news she would not be a mother again. As he opened the door, the doctor called out from behind his desk.

"I'm sorry for the outburst. I've seen too damn much dying in my profession. First in the war, now on the frontier. We should preserve life, not continually end it."

"Amen," Graham said, as he donned his hat and latched the door behind him.

Graham sat by the Stillwater River and gazed at the water as it flowed around a cottonwood that had fallen into the stream. A western spiny softshell turtle basked on the tree trunk in the late morning sun. Its distinctive brown pancake-shaped shell glistened in the sunlight. A row of spiked bony protrusions encircled the upper edge of its domed carapace.

At this moment Makawee was telling her family about her visit with the doctor at Fort Parker. He wanted to accompany her when she shared the news about her infertility after the miscarriage, but he was still banned from the tepee of Long Horse. Seeing the sluggish reptile on the tree trunk reminded him of his daughter. *Nahkash* translated into English as "turtle." Perhaps it was destiny that Nahkash would be an only child. Graham was perfectly happy with having a girl, but Makawee had spoken of raising a family after he could secure the horses and rifles for the privilege of marrying her. She had planned to be a mother again.

Graham leaned against the cottonwood where they had carved their initials. He looked up at the parfleche tied to the tree branch overhead containing the remains of Small Heart. There was no way he wanted to go through another failed pregnancy. If the tree of life for Makawee and him had only one branch, then perhaps that was their destiny.

Several miles downstream, Makawee was speaking to her extended family about the examination.

"...and so the doctor told me I will not have any more children," she concluded.

"You cannot get pregnant?" asked Fox Woman.

"It is possible but not likely. If I become with child, the baby would not live, and I would suffer much loss of blood."

Among the Grass was sitting to the side with her son. She gave a furtive glance at Black Hawk. This was welcome news to both of them.

Long Horse nodded slightly. "The spirits have blessed you with one child. Be thankful for this gift."

Makawee looked at Nahkash, who was sitting beside her, playing with a string of glass beads.

"Yes. I love her. It's just that..."

Her eyes welled with tears.

"I was hoping she would have a brother. I wanted you to have a grandson."

Long Horse was nonplussed. He had not expected his adopted daughter to express these feelings openly. He struggled to regain his composure before responding.

"I would like to have a grandson," he said poignantly. "It is not to be."

Makawee nodded. She stood and swung Nahkash onto her hip. Mother and child exited the tepee, the beads clacking in the toddler's hand.

Black Hawk and Among the Grass followed them out of the chief's lodge but turned in the opposite direction. The pair walked to the area where the horses were picketed before speaking.

"This turned out better than I had hoped," Among the Grass said in a whisper. "This means there are no threats of a male heir from Makawee. The only persons who stand in your way of being the next chief of our clan are Rides Alone and Little Wolf."

"Makawee is very sad," Black Hawk said. "Did your bad medicine damage her woman parts?"

"The medicine did not cause any harm. But I made sure she could not carry any more babies. I used an obsidian scraper to remove the afterbirth."

Black Hawk winced at this news.

"Why would you do this?"

"I did it for us," she replied, putting her hand on his forearm. "I did it to ensure you will be chief."

Black Hawk shook his head slowly. His mother's grisly act upon an innocent woman appalled him.

"Let's talk about what we should do next," she said with anticipation. "Remember our plan?"

"Yes. I am to marry Makawee. But now she cannot give me a child."

"That's right. After you are named chief, you can have your pick of a second wife. I have my eye on the daughter of Old Onion. She is a big-boned and strong woman who can bear many children. She can deliver a grandson for Long Horse."

"Do you mean Otter Woman?"

"Yes. She is only fourteen. She has many years left to have children."

"But she is...she is ugly!"

"Otter Woman is not attractive, but she is fertile. Makawee is beautiful, but she is barren. How wonderful to have two wives! You will learn to love each woman for what she can offer."

Black Hawk stroked the neck of the horse they were standing beside as he considered his mother's advice. Like the number of horses, the number of wives was another measure of a man's wealth and power. Two wives would be nice. Perhaps even three...

"Yes. This is a good plan."

"We will wait until Makawee recovers from her sadness about losing her ability to be a mother. When the bearded white man is at Fort Parker, you will ask Long Horse for permission to marry her. He will welcome someone from his own bloodline to take his adopted daughter as a wife. You are a better man than the baashchiile Eagle Bear."

"And if Makawee refuses to marry me?"

"Long Horse will decide. It is not her choice."

Chapter Fourteen

A Second Suitor

October 1873

"Did you see the newspaper this morning?" Uriah Brown asked his assistant, peering over his glasses from behind the counter.

Graham paused from stacking coffee bags on the wooden shelves in the warehouse.

"No. I haven't."

"Look," Brown said, spinning the paper around for Graham to see. "Seems like your Crow friends got a good send-off."

Graham read the lead article of the October 3, 1873, issue of the *Bozeman Avant Courier* with great interest.

> *A delegation of chiefs of Mountain Crow Indians left Bozeman yesterday morning for Washington in charge of Major F.D. Pease, on a visit to the president. We doubt if a finer body of Indians ever visited the Great Father before. They are fine-looking, remarkably intelligent, and have always been true friends of the whites. Sits-in-the-Middle-of-the-Land and Iron Bull are the most prominent chiefs in this party. We bespeak for these noble red men a kind reception and hope that the president and Indian Department will be liberal and generous to them, for these Crows have conducted themselves toward the whites in this section much better than Indians generally do on the border.*

"I hope they have a good reception in Washington," Graham said, scanning the paper for other stories. A newspaper seemed like a luxury on the frontier. He had forgotten how much he had taken for granted access to current events.

"I'm sure they will," Uriah said confidently. "We need them as allies to fight the savages who refuse to stay on lands reserved for them. The Crow are more reasonable than many other tribes."

Graham bit his lip. He knew the history of Washington visits by Native Americans. Many tribes would send representatives to the capital city in the latter half of the nineteenth century. It must have been quite an experience for Plains Indians to see a modern city — and a little overwhelming for people who had never traveled east of the Mississippi River.

There would be photos and handshakes. There would be banquets and speeches. Words would be spoken. Promises would be made, and commitments by government officials would be ignored or broken.

He recalled Redfield drawing the initial boundaries of the Crow territory on a map laid on his mother's dining room table, then redrawing these lines after their lands had been reduced by a series of treaties and agreements. These proud people would eventually end up on a parcel of land less than 10 percent the size of their original territory.

"Ah, here's more good news," the sutler said, turning the page and placing his finger on a grainy photo. "This is how the government will get non-treaty Indians in line. It says they took this photograph near Detroit. Looks like a tremendous success, wouldn't you say?"

Graham picked up the newspaper to get a closer look. He gasped at the immense pile of bison skulls. A brief explanation accompanied the photo.

Secretary of the Interior Columbus Delano reports he is pleased with progress on ridding the plains of bison. A reminder to our readers that the secretary previously proclaimed if the bison become extinct, the Indians of the Great Plains would have to surrender to the reservation system. In his annual report of 1872, Delano wrote, "The rapid disappearance of game from the former hunting-grounds must operate largely in favor of our efforts to confine the Indians to smaller areas and compel them to abandon their nomadic customs."

"Doesn't this bother you?" Graham blurted out, looking up from the macabre mountain of skulls.

"Does *what* bother me?"

"This! Slaughtering hundreds of thousands of bison!" Graham said, stabbing his finger at the photo.

Uriah furrowed his brow and tilted his head to one side. "I don't know why you're all riled up. You see the remains of wild beasts in this photograph. I see something else. I see evidence of a policy effectively implemented. It's a beautiful thing, really. We eliminate the bison. The savages are tamed. As a bonus, we process the buffalo bones into fertilizer so these people can grow crops instead."

"So you support mass annihilation of a species and a way of life?" he asked. He was seething at his employer's ignorance.

Rides Alone had recently stood in this courtyard and appealed to the authorities to stop poisoning the wolves. Bison were also under threat — not by poison but by rifle. They were becoming more difficult to find with each passing month. Graham shook his head and stared at the ghastly proof bison were being systematically decimated.

"I support whatever gets these savages onto their designated land and stops them from attacking settlers," Uriah said calmly. "If that's what it takes, so be it. That's why the Crow are different. They realize their future is in farming, not following buffalo herds."

Graham gritted his teeth. *They don't want to be farmers,* he thought. *The government forced them onto a reservation just like all the other tribes.*

Eliminating the primary resource of native people was a strategy employed by the military as part of the Indian Wars. It was analogous to the scorched earth policy of General William Sherman in the Civil War. It would be decades before this horrendous decision would be corrected. By the turn of the century, fewer than three hundred of the massive bovids would remain. If Congress had not set aside Yellowstone as a national park, the American bison would have been hunted to extinction.

Uriah casually folded the newspaper and removed his glasses.

"I understand Long Horse is among those in the delegation to Washington," he said, changing the subject.

"Yes," Graham said, quelling his anger. "Sits-in-the-Middle-of-the-Land invited him and other chiefs to go with him. They want to hear directly from those in power in Washington about their intentions for the Crow people."

"I suppose that means you'd like a few extra days off this month?"

"Why...yes, how did you know?"

"C'mon, Graham. You're not welcome in Chief Long Horse's tepee. I figured if he's away, you could steal some private time with Makawee," he said with a twinkle in his eye.

Graham blushed. Indeed, he had planned to ride to the camp along the Stillwater River and see Makawee.

"Yes, sir. That's right. I would appreciate if I could..."

"Take two extra days at the end of the week. I can manage while you're away," Uriah said, waving his hand to show the matter was settled. "Now let's get back to work."

"Thank you."

Graham turned and exited the double doors of the warehouse. A wagon of supplies was waiting to be unloaded. He leaned on the tailboard with his elbows and placed his chin in his hands. By the end of the month, he would have enough money to buy another horse. He was eager to present the animal to Long Horse when he returned from Washington.

It was hard living apart from Makawee and Nahkash. But he had no choice. The only alternative was to steal horses from the Sioux. But he wasn't a horse thief. Besides, he wouldn't have a clue how to steal a horse without getting caught or killed. No, he would just have to be patient and earn the money to buy one horse at a time.

His thoughts shifted back to the Bozeman newspaper. The paper reminded him it had been a while since he had written a letter to his mother by mailing an article to the *Adams Star and Sentinel*. He found it challenging to write something that would allow his mother and Redfield to know what had happened to him one hundred years earlier. Tonight, he would pen a quick note to the editor of the Pennsylvania newspaper. He would let them know he was well. He would also report on the delegation of Crow chiefs going to Washington.

But how could he let his mother and Redfield know Makawee had a miscarriage and could not have more children? Should he? Perhaps this was an insignificant event destined to be forgotten — a personal loss that only the people who stood under a cottonwood tree and witnessed the remains of his unborn son being strapped to a branch would remember.

Graham sighed. It was painful to dwell on the past. He needed to focus on the present and take one day at a time. Unload the wagon. Write a letter tonight. Visit with Makawee in a few days. Buy another horse and present it to Long Horse when he returned next month.

The fire crackled and smoked inside the tepee of Long Horse. A dozen people had squeezed into the large pole lodge to welcome the chief and hear about his trip to see the Great Father.

Long Horse spoke at length about the long journey. He talked about meeting President Grant and Interior Secretary Delano in the White House, which he described as very large, with big round poles at the entrance. He complained about the noise since horses and carriages were everywhere on the streets. The delegation had ridden in a large carriage that sat on rails like a train and was pulled by a horse. He spoke of tasting some local food, including the strange texture and salty flavor of fried oysters. Everyone in attendance realized the wealth and power of the government had impressed the chief.

And yet, beneath the excitement of his experience, there was a sadness in his demeanor. Perhaps it emanated from the realization that even if they wanted to maintain the lifestyle of their ancestors, the Crow people were powerless to resist. The white man would ultimately have his way.

The chief reached under his tunic and pulled out a tintype photograph. He smiled as he handed the thin sheet of metal to Fox Woman, who stared at the image before handing it back. Rides Alone, Makawee, Little Wolf, and the others quickly crowded around to glimpse the souvenir from Long Horse's trip.

"This is me," Long Horse said, pointing to a man in the back row with a single upright feather adorning his head. "Agent Pease," he said, moving his finger to the bearded man wearing a top hat.

He named others in the photograph, including the two white interpreters who had accompanied the delegation. Unlike some chiefs who had taken their wives along, Long Horse had not taken Fox Woman to accompany him. Makawee glanced at her adoptive mother and wondered if she was disappointed when she saw the other wives in the photo.

"I am tired from my journey and would like to rest," Long Horse said after everyone saw the group portrait.

As everyone slowly made their way to the opening, Among the Grass leaned over and whispered to Black Hawk.

"This is your opportunity. I will wait outside."

When the others had gone, Black Hawk turned to the chief.

"I will not stay long. I have something to say," Black Hawk stated.

Long Horse and Fox Woman sat cross-legged in their customary places. The chief nodded to his nephew.

"My mother and I are grateful you accepted us into your lodge after my father died. We have been treated well," he began.

"My brother and I did not agree on many things. But it is my duty. Families should help one another."

Black Hawk nodded. The chief's proclamation was a perfect setup for what he was about to say.

"I agree. In the spirit of keeping families together, I have a request."

Long Horse stretched out his arm with his palm up. "Speak."

"I would like your permission to take Makawee as my wife."

Fox Woman put her hand over her mouth. She turned to her husband to see his reaction.

Long Horse was stoic. He placed his hands on his thighs and studied the Crow warrior standing in front of him. This was his deceased brother's only son. Granting his request would be the right thing to do. But two considerations prevented him from making an immediate decision.

Something about his nephew's behavior did not sit well with him. Rather than acting as a future leader, it seemed everything he had done since joining the band was for personal gain. While others worked together for their collective well-being, Black Hawk was centered on himself. The people in their camp came second.

The other reason for postponing his decision was less important, but it was still a factor. The white man, Eagle Bear, had already asked for his daughter's hand in marriage. He would prefer Makawee to marry another Crow. But he would not renege on the conditions he had set for Eagle Bear to marry Makawee. If he did, he would be guilty of the same deplorable behavior of the baashchiile who violated the terms of countless treaties.

"Eagle Bear has already asked permission."

"I know this. But he is baashchiile. I am Crow. He is a stranger. I am family," Black Hawk said proudly, raising his chin.

"Nahkash is the child of Eagle Bear. Would you accept her as your own?"

"Makawee and Nahkash will be my family."

This wasn't a lie. It was misleading. He didn't mention his plans for a second wife.

Long Horse nodded and folded his arms on his chest.

"You need to meet the same requirements to marry Makawee as Eagle Bear. Give seven horses and three *spirit guns*. Prove you are a true warrior."

"And then I can marry her?"

"If you and Eagle Bear provide the same number of horses and rifles, I will decide who is most worthy of my daughter's hand in marriage."

"I already have four horses and two rifles stolen from our enemy, the Sioux. I will deliver these today," he replied.

Long Horse raised his eyebrows, surprised at his nephew's initiative. Perhaps Black Hawk had more potential as a leader than the chief thought.

"Thank you, Chief Long Horse," Black Hawk said. He smiled as he pushed the flap aside at the entrance to the pole lodge and ducked outside. He was eager to find his mother and share the good news. This was going to be easier than he imagined. With any luck, one or two raids of a Sioux camp or a settler's ranch would provide the additional horses and rifle. His superior warrior skills would make him the obvious choice.

Eagle Bear was a weak rival. Makawee would be his bride by spring.

"How could Long Horse do this? I was promised your hand if I delivered the horses and rifles. Now Black Hawk wants to marry you?"

Graham was angry. Makawee had learned of Black Hawk's proposal only a few hours earlier when Long Horse called her into his lodge. She had begged her father not to allow another man the opportunity to claim her as his bride. The chief countered by reminding his adoptive daughter of his obligation to do what was best for his family. He assured her the best candidate would be selected.

Makawee took Graham's hands in hers as she spoke.

"I do not understand. I wish I could do something," she said in a quivering voice.

"Do you love Black Hawk?"

"No! Of course not. I only love you. You are the father of my child!" she sobbed.

Graham pulled her in and held her tightly. His head was spinning at this turn of events. He felt a mix of rage and frustration. Surely he could reason with her father.

"I will talk with Long Horse," he said while holding Makawee's head against his chest.

"No," she said, pulling away and looking up into his eyes. She wiped tears from her cheeks. "If you argue with him, he might demand even more horses or rifles."

"So, what am I supposed to do?"

"If both of you deliver the horses and guns, Long Horse will choose the man who is most worthy. I am confident it will be you."

"But I have to work at Fort Parker for months to earn enough money to buy one horse. Black Hawk has already stolen four horses and two rifles!" he lamented. "Can't you tell Long Horse that you will only marry me?"

"I already tried. He said it is not my decision," she said tearfully.

"Then let's run away! I can make a good life for us. We will take Nahkash and move to a place where we..."

Makawee placed her index finger on his lips.

"I will not abandon my family. Long Horse has been good to me. I trust he will make the right decision and choose you as my husband."

"I wish I shared your conviction," Graham confessed.

He let go of her hands and turned away. He walked a short distance to the edge of the river and leaned against a tree. It was early November. A thin layer of snow covered the grasses and shrubs. Water gurgled as it hurried around smooth, domed rocks sitting in the middle of the stream that looked like giant frosted doughnuts. He would normally pause and marvel at the beauty of this placid scene, but his mood was as dark as the sky on a moonless night. He started shivering. It wasn't from the chilly air but from the thought of losing Makawee to another man. His dream of raising a family with her was in jeopardy. Perhaps it was never meant to be. Perhaps he wasn't good enough for her.

He felt two arms encircle his waist from behind. Makawee clasped her hands around his stomach and pressed the side of her head against his back.

"Baalaásdee." ["I love you,"] she said.

He reached down and clutched her forearms.

"I love you, Makawee," he said, mechanically. He had not felt this way since the funeral for Small Heart.

"Will you fight for me?" a voice from behind asked.

Graham blinked. Her question was a punch in the gut. It stung to hear her say these words, and they snapped him back to reality. He realized it served no purpose to wallow in self-pity. He pulled her hands apart and spun around to face her.

"I came from another century to be with you," he said, grabbing her upper arms and looking into her eyes. "I'm not giving up just because I have a rival."

He said this as much to convince himself as to reassure his future bride.

She stood on her toes and tilted her head back. He leaned over and met her lips. When they separated, he pulled her close, placing the top of her head under his chin. They embraced each other, gently swaying while listening to the flowing water.

"I have a question for you," Graham said after a moment.

"What is it?"

"Do you think Little Wolf would show me how to steal a horse?"

Chapter Fifteen

Mammoth Journey

April 1874

I t was unseasonably warm for late April in southern Montana. A small crowd had gathered inside Fort Parker to witness a mass marriage ceremony. Crow families mingled with agency employees, traders, and settlers in the courtyard as they awaited Dr. James Wright.

Wright had been named to succeed Fellows Pease as the Indian agent of the Crow. One of his first acts was to rectify the practice of some white men living with Indian women without being married. The Methodist Episcopal minister had sent word and posted a letter stating any man who was cohabitating with a woman outside of marriage would be prohibited from working at the agency or buying goods from the sutler. However, the proclamation continued, Wright would officiate a group wedding ceremony on the twenty-sixth of April at Fort Parker. Anyone wishing to "get themselves right in the eyes of the Lord" could attend. Guests were cordially invited.

The Reverend Wright smiled as he stepped onto the boardwalk in front of his office building. Nearly a hundred people had assembled at the Crow Agency. Men and women chatted. Children ran among the adults playing tag. Dogs barked and chased a willow hoop as boys took turns throwing darts at the springy wheel. It was a festive atmosphere.

Graham, Makawee, Rides Alone, Little Wolf, and Black Hawk had ridden from their camp on the Stillwater River to the Crow Agency. While Black Hawk and Little Wolf tended the horses, Graham, Makawee, and Rides Alone went inside the fort to witness the marriage of their friend Mitch Bouyer.

The son of a French Canadian fur trader and a Santee Sioux, Bouyer was a guide and interpreter for the 2nd US Cavalry out of Fort Ellis working with the Northern Pacific Railroad survey team. He was also employed by the Crow Agency at Fort Parker. Mitch had lived with a Crow woman, Magpie Outside, for nearly five years. He had announced to his friends he would be "officially" married if that's what it took to continue doing business with the agency. But as far as he was concerned, he didn't need any fancy Christian ceremony to make it so.

"Ladies and gentlemen!" Wright called out, raising his hands skyward. The minister was wearing a black pulpit gown with bell-shaped sleeves over a cassock with white preaching tabs. He waited for the noise to dissipate.

"I would like to invite all those couples who wish to be joined in holy matrimony to come forward."

Bouyer took Magpie Outside by the hand. They pushed their way through the crowd. Eight other mixed couples, each a white man and a Crow woman, joined them in front.

"This is our chance," Graham whispered excitedly, as he leaned over to Makawee. "Let's get married today!"

"I will not be married like this!" Makawee said indignantly. "Those poor women are being treated like goats at auction!"

Graham was perplexed. He saw nothing inappropriate about a mass wedding ceremony.

"What's wrong with it?"

"Do you know any of these Crow women?"

He recognized one or two faces from their visits to Fort Parker, but he knew nothing about them.

"No."

"Except for Magpie Outside, they don't love their partners. The only reason these white men are marrying a Crow woman is to gain access to the land allotted to them. After they are legally married, they will own the land of their Crow wives."

Graham gulped. He hadn't been aware of such ulterior motives.

"I want to marry you. But not in a group. Not like this," she said, grabbing his biceps with two hands. "Besides, Long Horse has not given you permission. That will happen after you pay him and prove your worth. Please be patient."

Patience be damned, he thought.

As if someone was reading Graham's mind, the minister began his opening remarks.

"I will not speak long. But this is a holy ceremony. We must recognize the presence of the Lord."

He opened a leather-bound Bible to a bookmarked page in the New Testament.

"A reading from Corinthians..."

Charity suffereth long, and is kind;

charity envieth not;
charity vaunteth not itself,
is not puffed up,
doth not behave itself unseemly,
seeketh not her own,
is not easily provoked,
thinketh no evil;
rejoiceth not in iniquity,
but rejoiceth in the truth;
beareth all things,
believeth all things,
hopeth all things,
endureth all things.

The Reverend snapped the Bible shut and raised his arms.

"Let us pray..."

As Wright closed his eyes and asked God to bless the happy couples, Makawee turned to Graham and whispered, "What do those words mean?"

He could understand why she was confused. James Wright had read from the King James version of the Bible. Graham had heard these verses when he was a little boy. Thankfully, the church he attended later switched to a modern translation. But he recognized the verses from Paul's letter to the Corinthians. His mother had a framed embroidery with these displayed in her kitchen.

He turned to face Makawee.

"I will recite the same verses. But I'll use words you know. See if this reading makes more sense."

Graham closed his eyes and envisioned the small tapestry, then softly recited the words.

"Love is patient and kind."

There's that pesky patience *word again,* he thought. He wondered if the Lord was trying to send him a personal message. It was the same advice Redfield had given Graham before he left Pennsylvania.

"Go on," Makawee said in a whisper, encouraging him.

He nodded, then recited the remaining words from memory.

"Love does not envy or boast. Love is not arrogant. Love does not insist on its own way. Love is not irritable or resentful. Love does not rejoice in wrongdoing. Love bears all things, believes all things, hopes all things, endures all things."

"That is so beautiful," she said, her eyes becoming glassy.

"Gentlemen," Reverend Wright said in a booming voice, "I want you to face your bride, take her by the hand, and repeat after me."

The grooms obliged and waited for a prompt.

Wright paused. He looked down at a skinny, bearded man.

"Excuse me, sir. Please remove your hat. We are in the presence of the Lord."

"Oh. Oh yeah. Sure," the flustered man said, swiping the dusty fedora from his head and tossing it to an onlooker. He licked his fingers and used them to smooth his unkempt hair.

"Go ahead, mister preacher man."

The minister shook his head and cleared his throat. He recited the vow in segments, pausing between phrases to allow the men to repeat the words.

"I, *state your name*,"

"...take thee, *state her name*,"

"...to be my wedded wife,"

"...to have and to hold from this day forward,"

"...for better, for worse,"

"...for richer, for poorer,"

"...in sickness and in health,"

"...to love and to cherish,"

"...till death do us part,"

"...according to God's holy ordinance,"

"...and thereto I pledge thee my faith."

Reverend Wright used a hand to shield his eyes from the sun and scanned the crowd assembled in the courtyard.

"If there is an interpreter present, I would appreciate that person's help. Fellows Pease was fluent in Apsáalooke. I am not."

Makawee glanced at Graham, who nudged her with his elbow. She walked forward, pushing past the couples and stepping onto the boardwalk with the Methodist minister.

"What's your name, ma'am?"

"Makawee."

"Can you read?' he asked.

"I can."

The minister gave her the paper with the vows and addressed the couples.

"Okay, ladies. It's your turn. Makawee will read the pledge in your language."

He stretched his hand toward the crowd, inviting her to speak.

Makawee read each phrase and waited for the women to repeat the words. Graham watched with admiration as his future wife read aloud the words he hoped they would say to each other someday.

"*Ilíiaakaxpissee,*" she said, finishing the last phrase of the vows.

"*Ilíiaakaxpissee,*" a chorus of Crow women repeated.

Looking directly at Graham and speaking with conviction, she repeated the last phrase in English.

"I promise."

Graham returned her gaze. Upon hearing those two words, a chill ran up his spine. He mouthed, "I love you."

Reverend Wright took the paper from Makawee, thanked her, and raised his arms.

"By the power vested in me as a called and ordained minister of the Methodist Episcopal Church, and on behalf of the Montana Territory, I now pronounce you man and wife!"

Cheers and yells burst from the crowd. Hats were thrown. Nine couples sealed their vows with a kiss.

Makawee made her way back to her family, where they enjoyed the sights and sounds of the raucous wedding guests, many of whom began dancing when someone broke out a fiddle.

After a few moments, Rides Alone spoke above the din of music, laughing, and barking dogs.

"It is time to go," he reminded them.

As they walked out the front gates and followed the log palisade toward the area where Little Wolf and Black Hawk were waiting with the horses, Graham considered their pending journey.

Several weeks earlier, Long Horse had summoned a meeting in his lodge. Besides Graham, the chief had requested Makawee, Rides Alone, and Black Hawk to attend. Long Horse announced he was sending the quartet on a mission.

A Nez Perce messenger had sent word to Ollokot, brother of Chief Joseph, who had requested a rendezvous to discuss strengthening the alliance between his people and the Crow. Joseph had proposed to meet at a sacred site many tribes had frequented for hundreds of years. It was a place the Crow called *Shiiptacha Awaxaawe,* or Obsidian Cliff. This unique geological formation was south of Mammoth Hot Springs, inside the boundaries of two-year-old Yellowstone National Park.

Chief Long Horse saw an opportunity to test the candidates vying for Makawee's hand in marriage. He made it clear their actions and words on this diplomatic mission would help determine their respective worthiness as a warrior and a leader.

He sent Makawee along as an interpreter. His adopted daughter had a proclivity for learning languages. Shortly after she was born, both of her parents had died from smallpox. She was raised by a white man and a Crow Woman and had become fluent in English. At fourteen she was captured by the Blackfeet and learned Piegan. Four years later she was sold to a trader, who taught her French.

While living in the trading post, she learned a little of the Nimipuutímt language spoken by the Nez Perce. She also picked up Chinook Jargon, which used simplified grammar, body language, and sign language to communicate. Chinook Jargon was a *lingua franca*, a unifying language, developed by natives, trappers, and traders in the Pacific Northwest to bridge the communication barrier.

When Makawee objected to being absent from her daughter for so long, Fox Woman allayed her concerns by offering to watch the little girl while the group was away.

Long Horse assigned Rides Alone to be leader of the small group. His instructions were to listen to Ollokot and be respectful. But no one could make any promises other than to remain on friendly terms with the Nez Perce under Chief Joseph.

Graham was uncertain whether Uriah Brown would allow him to make the trip. But when he explained where they were going, the sutler's eyes lit up. He saw a trading opportunity. Brown permitted Graham to go if he would trade with the Nez Perce for rare obsidian pieces. The sutler gave him several bags of coffee and loose-leaf tobacco with which to barter.

"Kahée!" Little Wolf shouted as the trio approached. "I hear a lot of noise from the other side of the walls. Was it a good wedding?"

"Our friend Mitch Bouyer is married. Everyone seems happy," Makawee replied, glancing at Graham. She chose not to share her misgivings about the forced marriages between the other couples.

"Horses are watered. Pole carrier is ready," Black Hawk said.

Graham admired the travois attached to Makawee's horse. It was customary for Crow women to assemble and take down a tepee. She was also responsible for moving it as the clan followed the bison herds and set up the next camp. The ends of two support poles had been fastened to Makawee's horse, with the trailing ends splayed into an "A" shape. Netting had been placed between the poles to create a platform where hides, blankets, food, and other belongings were stored. They had attached the remaining sixteen poles of the small lodge to the sides of a second horse. The sledge was a simple but elegant way to bring a shelter with them.

As Rides Alone and Makawee walked around the travois and inspected the poles attached to the horse, Graham approached Little Wolf.

"Thank you again for helping me steal a Sioux horse a few weeks ago," he said in a low voice, being careful that Black Hawk did not hear him. "I couldn't have done it without you."

"I got a horse too," the fifteen-year-old said. "Counting coups is difficult. You will get better."

Graham nodded. It had been a harrowing experience to sneak into a Sioux camp at night, untie two horses, and usher them away without being seen. He recalled the fear that gripped him and the anxiety of feeling a bullet or arrow penetrate his back if they were discovered. He admitted it was exhilarating when they escaped undetected. Although Graham had gained the respect of Little Wolf after their joint exploit, he hoped he wouldn't have to be a horse thief again. He planned to purchase or trade for the two remaining horses, not steal them.

"Little Wolf, my brother," Rides Alone said as he circled back to his horse. "Watch over Fox Woman and Nahkash. After Long Horse, you are the man in our family. We will return in less than ten days."

The teenage warrior bowed to his older brother. The pride of assuming this responsibility showed in his youthful face.

Everyone mounted their horses. Rides Alone took the lead, turning his horse south.

"Shia-nuk," ["See you later"] Little Wolf replied.

Three days later, the quartet reached Mammoth Hot Springs. They dismounted and allowed the horses to drink from a small creek adjoining the massive thermal feature. The multicolored formation had been created over tens of thousands of years when hot acidic water dissolved limestone rock and bubbled to the surface before re-forming into travertine terraces and pooling as hot springs. A forty-foot conical structure known as the Liberty Cap, named by the 1871 Hayden Survey, stood at the base of the terraces. It had been formed by a hot spring that had been active for hundreds of years; minerals had slowly been deposited into a shape resembling the peaked caps worn during the French Revolution.

A strong sulfur smell hung in the air. To the north and west lay the Gallatin Range. The Washburn Range jutted up from the valley floor immediately to the southeast, and the snowcapped mountains of the Absaroka Range painted the horizon in the east.

The landscape smelled and appeared just as Graham had remembered it in the twentieth century — except for a small man-made structure sitting on one of the lower terraces.

"I'm going to check out that building," he told the others.

"We will camp there," Rides Alone said, pointing toward the Gardner River.

Graham dismounted Blade and handed the reins to Makawee. As the Crow guided their horses away from the terraces, Graham walked past the Liberty Cap toward the shanty. He was careful to watch where he stepped, as there were no boardwalks or railings. Just as he reached the six-by-eight-foot windowless shack, a man stepped out from behind the building.

"Afternoon! James McCartney," he said, extending his hand. "You can call me J.C."

"Graham Davidson."

"Pleased to meet you. I saw you folks and thought you might like to tour my humble resort."

McCartney was five-foot-six, with a medium build and a closely cropped reddish-brown beard. He wore a wool frock coat and a low-crowned derby cap. His boots were chalky white from walking among the limestone deposits of the travertine terraces.

"Is this your building?"

"It sure is. It's a bathhouse. Take a look."

The hinges squeaked as McCartney pushed the door inward. Graham stepped inside and let his eyes adjust to the dark interior. The rustic shelter straddled an oval-shaped shallow warm spring six feet long and three feet wide. Someone had conveniently placed several warped pine boards along the perimeter of the spring. The crude structure offered privacy so patrons could strip and bathe.

Graham ducked back outside.

"Nice," was all he could think to say.

"Nice? You're lookin' at one of Mother Nature's wonders!" McCartney exclaimed. "These are curative waters. People with many ailments come here. A few treatments from these springs will ease diseases of the kidney, bladder, liver, stomach, and skin. There ain't nothin' like it west of the Mississippi. These waters provide the same health benefits as Saratoga Springs and White Sulfur Springs back East."

Graham smiled inwardly at the man's enthusiasm and exaggerated claims. He sounded like a carnival barker at a county fair trying to get passersby to buy a bottle of a magic elixir that would heal anything.

"Do you have many patrons, J.C.?"

"Yes, indeed. Zack Root has a stage line that makes a weekly run from Bozeman. He brings mail, freight, and invalids lookin' for a healthy bath. I'm planning on puttin' up two more bathhouses later this year. Those will be more refined. They'll have wooden bathtubs and be fed by the warm springs. This is gonna be big business when word gets out!"

Graham nodded. He had read about some early entrepreneurs in the Mammoth area. James McCartney was among the most fervent in starting a business in the nascent park.

"Have you seen my coating operation?" McCartney asked.

"Uh, no. What's that?"

"Well, let me show you, young man."

Graham followed McCartney as he strode past the Liberty Cap and walked along the south side of the terraced springs.

"Watch your feet," McCartney said as he climbed up several levels of terraces, using boards to avoid stepping into hot water.

Graham was aghast when they reached the coating station.

The entrepreneur had constructed two scaffolds. One leaned against a terrace. It was positioned so the water overflowing from a spring cascaded onto the wooden structure.

Someone had built a trough to channel the overflow from an adjacent spring onto an A-shaped scaffold. He had suspended an assortment of articles from cross boards with wires. As the mineral-laden waters spilled over these items, it coated them with calcium carbonate.

McCartney stood on a board and removed a pine cone hanging from a scaffold. He handed the glistening white fruit structure to Graham.

"Beautiful, ain't it? You can coat most any rigid object in a day or two."

Indeed, the racks were filled with bottles of all shapes and sizes, as well as spoons, plates, picture frames, wire baskets, and even horseshoes.

"Fifty cents," McCartney said.

"What?"

"That's what I charge for my smallest coating specimens. One dollar for a large bottle. Two dollars for an encrusted horseshoe."

"No, thanks." Graham handed the coated lodgepole pine cone back to the entrepreneur.

"You keep it," he insisted. "When you get home, show it to others. Tell them where they can buy one just like it. I'll have plenty of sales when more visitors come to my little resort."

Graham stuck the cone in his coat pocket. He noted how McCartney kept referring to the springs as *his* resort. He challenged the entrepreneur on the assumption he owned what was now officially public land.

"This land and these springs are part of Yellowstone National Park. How can you...?"

McCartney held up his hand.

"It's all legal," he said, a bit defensively. "Me and Harry Horr filed a homestead claim for one hundred and sixty acres in July of '71. The park wasn't created until March of '72. I petitioned park superintendent Nathaniel Langford and got a ten-year lease from the Interior Department to operate my business."

It would take decades for the government to figure out how to run the park so it could be preserved for the public yet provide the requisite accommodations for visitors. The army would take over park administration in 1886 after little was done to prevent people from poaching animals, cutting timber, grazing cattle, defacing thermal features, or setting fires. The military was charged with maintaining order, guarding geysers and hot springs, and enforcing the laws within Yellowstone for thirty years. Congress eventually created a new agency called the National Park Service in 1916, which relieved the military of its duties that year. Most historians agree Yellowstone Park may not have survived as we know it without the army's presence in those critical early decades.

"Would you like to look at my hotel?" McCartney asked.

"Sure," Graham replied. He was curious to see the first accommodations in the park.

They retraced their steps down the terraces and skirted the base of the thermal mountain, then followed a creek upstream a short distance. Several one-story buildings were at the mouth of Clematis Gulch. McCartney stopped and described each structure.

"This is it," he said, pointing at a twenty-five-by-thirty-five-foot log building with a sod roof directly in front of them. "It's all mine, free and clear. Harry sold his shares and moved back north. Said he didn't see how a fella could make money by building a hotel in the wilderness."

"Do you see the potential for this place?" he asked Graham, leaning in so close he could smell whiskey on the man's breath.

"Yes. I certainly do."

"My cabin is next door. I also built a storehouse and a stable out back. Let me show you inside."

McCartney stepped onto the small porch and fished a skeleton key out of his pocket. He unlocked the door and opened it for his visitor.

Graham stepped inside and let his eyes adjust. The cabin had been partitioned into four rooms with wood floors, none of which had furniture. It was an exaggeration to refer to this spartan log cabin as a hotel. He turned to the proprietor and raised his eyebrows.

"I know what you're thinkin'," he said preemptively. "It ain't much. But it's the only place to stay dry within fifty miles. The rates are reasonable. Two dollars per guest each night."

"Is that for one room?"

"Heck no. That gets you a spot on the floor. You supply your own blanket. Whaddaya say?"

"About staying here? No thanks," Graham said as he stepped outside. "We brought our own lodging."

He scanned the eastern slope and noted the poles of their tepee several hundred yards away. It had not taken the Crow long to erect the pole lodge.

McCartney stood beside Graham on the porch and scratched his beard. He was clearly disappointed he would not make any money from today's visitors.

"Tell you what," he said. "I've got something I know you didn't bring along. How about I sell you some whiskey? I noticed you got a lovely squaw travelin' with you. Why not get your Injun friends drunk on a little firewater? Then you can have your way with that woman."

Graham snapped. He spun, grabbed the short man by his coat collar, and shoved him against the wall of the cabin. McCartney's hat flew from his head, and his eyes widened in fear. Graham felt a rush of adrenaline as he pinned the man against the rough-hewn logs, surprising himself with his own strength.

"I don't want your damned whiskey! You can sell your liquor to somebody else. And that woman you call a squaw is my wife!" Graham snarled, their faces only inches apart.

"Whoa, mister," McCartney said in a trembling voice, trying to free himself by pulling on Graham's strong forearms. "I didn't realize...I mean...I apologize."

Graham relaxed his grip and stepped back.

McCartney picked up his hat and straightened his rumpled coat, keeping an eye on the big angry man standing in front of him.

Graham fished the glistening coated pine cone from his pocket and threw it at McCartney, hitting him in the chest. The cone bounced and skittered off the porch.

"A word of advice," he said while pushing his cowboy hat onto his head. "Don't spend too much time or money building your bathhouses. They won't be around long."

It was an easy ride from Mammoth Hot Springs as they traveled south the next morning. After crossing the Gardner River a few hours later, they followed a small creek until the land rose on both sides and formed a shallow canyon.

At midday, they arrived at Obsidian Cliff, the remainder of a flow of lava that erupted onto the earth's surface nearly two hundred thousand years ago before pouring down the plateau. The rhyolite ridge pushed several hundred feet above the creek. An exposed seam of dark, lustrous volcanic glass near the top reflected the sun's rays like tiny mirrors. Pieces of obsidian of varying sizes lay at the base of the cliff, where they had fallen away from the face and formed a talus slope.

Rides Alone led the group to the banks of the eponymous creek flowing by Obsidian Cliff and dismounted.

"We set up camp here and wait for Ollokot."

"I will hunt," Black Hawk said as he reined his horse south.

Graham started to object to the Crow warrior hunting in a national park, but he quickly realized how ridiculous his argument would sound to a man whose ancestors hunted here for thousands of years.

Two years earlier, this area had suddenly been proclaimed off-limits for hunting because the government had made it protected land. Yet poachers would operate within the park boundaries with near impunity over the next decade, harvesting thousands of elk, bison, wolves, and bighorn sheep. Graham told himself a single elk or bison killed by a Crow Indian would be insignificant in the overall effort to protect wildlife in the park.

It was already an awkward situation riding and sleeping in the same lodge as Black Hawk, his rival who had proposed marriage to Makawee. The two men avoided conversing with each other unless absolutely necessary. Neither man wanted to incite a verbal altercation.

After they erected the tepee, Rides Alone tended to the horses. Graham and Makawee walked to the base of the cliff to examine the myriad pieces of obsidian lying there.

"How did you find the green piece for your turtle necklace? Everything here is some shade of black, brown, or gray."

Long Horse had taken Makawee to Shiiptacha Awaxaawe every year while she was growing up. She had learned the importance of this site to the many Indians who came here to collect the sharp-edged rhyolite for making arrows, spears, and scrapers. They often carved the most colorful pieces into jewelry. It was a popular place for tribes to trade with one another.

"It takes a long time and some luck to find this color," she said, gazing at the obsidian pendant on her necklace. She looked up and smiled at him. "That's why it's so special. It's a rare find."

Graham took her by the arm and pulled her toward him. He removed his hat and leaned down to kiss her. The sun reflected from the seam of the sharp-edged obsidian several hundred feet above and shone on her face. She was more beautiful than ever.

"I think you're a rare find, too. It took a long time and some luck to find you. But you are truly someone special."

Makawee smiled broadly and put her arms around his waist. She felt the handle of his Colt Cobra protruding from the middle of his back. He had tucked the pistol into his belt.

"Are you expecting trouble?"

"Do you remember the last time we were at this cliff three years ago?"

"Of course. It was not a happy day."

Graham had been with Makawee and Rides Alone at Obsidian Cliff in 1871. While they were scavenging the shards of volcanic glass at the base of the bluff, a small band of Piegan Blackfeet had captured them. They nearly killed Graham when he was mistakenly identified as a soldier who had taken part in a massacre of their people on the Marias River one year earlier. Makawee tried to convince their captors otherwise, but they were not persuaded. Fortunately, the leader of the Piegans arrived and prevented the other warriors from shooting an innocent man.

"I'm just being careful," he said. "I learned a lesson. Never leave camp unarmed."

"I understand. We can look for colored obsidian later. Right now, we should gather wood for the fire."

A few hours later, Black Hawk rode into camp with a small elk. While the Crow men field dressed the slain animal, Graham started a fire and watched Makawee prepare *timpsila*, or prairie turnips. She had brought a string of the spindle-shaped tubers and a few cooking herbs. She used a pan to brown chunks of venison, then added water, salt, and leeks. Soon an earthy aroma was filling the camp as the dried timpsila absorbed the meat juices and plumped up, inflating to twice their size. The travelers enjoyed a hearty meal under the stars before turning in, with each man taking a three-hour shift to guard the camp during the night.

The next morning, while the quartet was drinking tea made from gumwood leaves, Black Hawk suddenly stood and pointed to the south. A group of five riders was making their way downstream toward camp. They could see the visitors were Indians. But from which tribe? Were they friendly or hostile? Rides Alone picked up a rifle leaning against the tepee. Graham reached behind his back and gripped the handle of his pistol.

Makawee stepped forward, faced the horsemen, and placed her hand to her forehead and pushed it away with an open palm.

"Kla-how'-ya!" she shouted, greeting the group in Chinook Jargon.

"Kla-how'-ya!" replied the man on the lead horse.

"They're Nez Perce," she said over her shoulder to those behind her.

When the visitors reached camp, they dismounted. Their leader bowed slightly and held both arms forward, palms up, showing he was unarmed. He was tall, lean, and muscular. He had combed his thick hair into a pompadour, with two locks adorned with eagle feathers cascading down to his shoulders on either side of his face. A half dozen beaded necklaces were visible under his open white cotton shirt, which was tucked into a breechcloth worn over leggings.

"I am Ollokot, brother of Heinmot Tooyalakekt, Chief Joseph."

Makawee introduced herself and the group, starting with Rides Alone. Ollokot did the same with the tribesmen accompanying him.

Ollokot and Makawee quickly fell into phrasing, signing, and speaking Chinook Jargon, a language they both knew. Since her companions did not understand the language, she paused and interpreted frequently.

"Ollokot brings greetings from his brother. He says they have been riding nearly two weeks from their home in the Wallowa Valley and are eager to reaffirm the long friendship the Nez Perce have with the Crow people."

Rides Alone extended his arm toward the fire. He signed they were welcome. He invited everyone to drink coffee or tea while they talked.

The conversation lasted for nearly an hour. Ollokot and Rides Alone did most of the talking and signing, while Makawee interpreted. Although he understood very little of what they said, Graham could sense the Nez Perce leader was sincere.

As Makawee translated, the unfolding story of the Nez Perce shared many of the themes of other tribes. White settlers were invading their beloved homeland. They were being forced into the white man's way of life, which meant they had to become farmers to assimilate. Their people were being pushed onto a reservation and were not free to go where they had traditionally hunted for thousands of years. If they did not convert to Christianity, they were viewed as troublemakers. They had been negotiating with the government for years and hoped they could keep their lifestyle, practice the Dreamer religion, and live in peace with the white man. But their future was uncertain.

After politely and patiently listening to his guest, Rides Alone turned to Makawee.

"Ask him what he would like from the Crow people, especially from my father, Long Horse," Rides Alone said.

Ollokot sat up straight and looked into the eyes of Rides Alone when he spoke. It was a brief statement. When he finished, Makawee translated.

"On behalf of Chief Joseph, he is requesting the help of the Crow people if they cannot reach an agreement with the government."

Black Hawk immediately stood and proclaimed his allegiance to the Nez Perce, as they were indeed brothers in the fight against the tyranny of the white man. Just as the Nez Perce fought side by side with the Crow and brought death to the Sioux, they would be brothers-in-arms against the government.

Over the past year, Graham had become conversant in Apsaàlooke. He didn't need a translation of his rival's words. Black Hawk had made a bold commitment that was clearly an overreach. Chief Long Horse had given explicit instructions not to make any promises other than to remain on friendly terms with the Nez Perce.

After Black Hawk was seated, Rides Alone stood. He thanked Ollokot for coming a great distance to meet with them and promised to take the request from his father, who sat on the council of Crow chiefs. They would remain friends with the Nez Perce, but he clarified his cousin could only speak for himself, not the Crow Nation. Sits-in-the-Middle-of-the-Land would ultimately have the last word on any future alliance between their tribes. He closed by asking Ollokot and his companions to join them in sharing a meal before they returned to their homeland.

Before Makawee had finished the translation, an angry Black Hawk jumped up and dashed into the tepee. He returned a minute later with his blanket and saddle. As the men mingled around the fire and Makawee prepared a meal of elk stew, the disgruntled warrior saddled his horse. Rides Alone spoke with his cousin, but Graham couldn't hear what they said. Five minutes later, Black Hawk left camp, heading north along Obsidian Creek.

After the meal, they again pressed Makawee into service as a translator. As had been the case over thousands of years, members of both tribes took advantage of this place to barter and trade. It pleased Graham when he negotiated a dozen beautiful pieces of colored obsidian and eight mink skins for the loose-leaf tobacco and coffee from Uriah Brown's warehouse.

Graham noticed the Nez Perce had brought two extra horses. He pulled a chrome Eveready from his pack and secretly showed it to Makawee.

"Do you think they would be interested in this?" he asked.

Makawee recognized the twentieth-century invention immediately. Graham had shown her a flashlight three years earlier. Later, he had offered it to the Piegan Blackfeet leader in exchange for their freedom when they were being held prisoner in Norris Geyser Basin.

"No harm in asking," she said, shrugging her shoulders.

"Great! Tell Ollokot I would like to show him a stick that captures a piece of the sun."

The Nez Perce leader showed he understood and waited with his arms crossed over his chest for the demonstration.

Graham held the chrome Eveready flashlight in his right hand and extended his arm over his head with the lens pointing to the sky. The shiny chrome housing gleamed as he deliberately rotated it in the sun. Anyone who had never seen a flashlight would have concluded some of the sun's rays were being funneled into the small cylinder. He stepped within a few feet of Ollokot, aimed the Eveready at the palm of his left hand, and slid the red plastic switch forward. Two D-cell batteries energized the bulb, and a circle of light instantly appeared in his hand. Graham rapidly switched the flashlight on and off, making an image of the sun appear and disappear.

The Nez Perce leader was amazed. He and his traveling companions leaned toward the shiny tube to get a better look. Graham handed him the flashlight. Ollokot cautiously accepted the strange object.

"Slide the red button one way to turn on the sun's rays. Slide it the other way to put them back in the tube," Graham explained as he motioned with his thumb. He asked Makawee to translate.

Ollokot followed these instructions and marveled at the power of commanding sunlight to appear and disappear.

"It is useful at night. When the sun goes down, you can carry a piece with you." Makawee repeated in Chinook Jargon.

Ollokot rotated the flashlight in his hand, admiring the way the sun glinted off the shiny surface. He looked up and held a single finger.

"Kiu'-a-tan."

"One horse for the sun catcher," Makawee said.

"Eh," Graham replied in Apsaàlooke, nodding his head to show he accepted the offer.

Ollokot motioned for one of his tribesman to bring one of the extra horses forward. And just like that, Graham gained another horse toward the bride price for marrying Makawee.

The Crow and Nez Perce camped that evening on the banks of Obsidian Creek. They shared a pipe packed with kinnikinnick and enjoyed one another's company. The next morning, they parted ways. The group from eastern Oregon headed south, while the band from southern Montana retraced their path from Mammoth Hot Springs on their way back to Fort Parker.

As they got underway, Graham asked Rides Alone why Black Hawk had left by himself the previous day.

"Black Hawk will meet us at the camp of Long Horse. He plans to count coups and did not want us to slow him down."

This revelation took some of the luster from Graham's savvy trade. Once again, he was buying or bartering for a horse, while his rival was stealing one. It wasn't only that Black Hawk could accumulate horses more quickly than he. Black Hawk was also adding up coups, which were valuable in the eyes of Long Horse. Graham had a sinking feeling he would never measure up as a warrior. He had much to ponder on the three-day journey home.

Chapter Sixteen

Black Hills Gold

July 1874

C aptain William Ludlow reined in his horse when he reached the camera mounted on a tripod.

"Everyone will be in position in about ten minutes. Are you ready?" he asked the half-hidden photographer.

William Illingworth emerged from under the black cloth covering the camera box.

"I'm not sure how many will fit in the frame, but I'll do my best," the English-born Illingworth replied.

Ludlow turned his horse and rode back toward the massive collection of men, material, and animals. He was part of an expedition led by Lieutenant Colonel George Armstrong Custer. They had set out early in July from Fort Abraham Lincoln in the Dakota Territory. Custer had orders to explore the uncharted Black Hills. His mission also included instructions to find a suitable location for a new fort and to verify rumors of gold in the region.

Custer had departed the garrison near Bismarck ten days earlier with a thousand men from the Seventh Cavalry, two companies of infantry, dozens of Indian scouts, two miners, over one hundred canvas-covered wagons, three hundred head of cattle, three Gatling guns, one cannon, and two months of supplies. The colonel even mustered a sixteen-piece mounted brass band to inspire the troops and provide the fanfare fitting this grand military expedition. Even though the covered wagons moved across the plains in three columns and the cavalry rode on the flanks, the expeditionary force extended for over a mile when it was underway.

Now, in midafternoon on a stifling hot day, Colonel Custer had decided a portrait should be taken of the army as it crossed the plains. Ludlow ordered the men and equipment to line up in six parallel columns. The captain waited as the last of the wagons creaked to a halt and the ever-present dust settled over the dry prairie grass.

"Every unit is in position, sir," the captain said as he saluted his commanding officer.

"Very well. Signal Mr. Illingworth to take the photo so we can be on our way. If we stay out here too long without moving, this sun will cook our brains," Custer said.

"Yes, sir."

Ludlow yanked off his slouch hat and waved it over his head at the photographer several hundred feet in the distance.

Illingworth signaled he understood by waving his arm in the air. He ducked into his darkroom tent and retrieved a sensitized plate slotted into a lightproof box. Walking back to the camera, he snapped the shallow wooden box onto the back of the camera. Every part of the twenty-by-twenty-four-inch camera was covered with a dark cloth tent except for the lens. The photographer pulled a slide from the wooden holder that protected the sensitized glass plate. He removed the lens cap and peered across the rolling prairie at the massive assembly of men, horses, and wagons while counting aloud.

"One, one-thousand; two, one-thousand; three, one-thousand; four, one-thousand."

He quickly placed the cap over the camera lens.

"Dammit!" Illingworth exclaimed, as he inserted the slide over the wooden holder. He waved his arm overhead, signaling the image had been captured. Then he held both arms straight in the air and repeatedly pushed them forward.

"What's he telling us?" Custer asked.

"I don't know. Let me find out," Ludlow responded.

The captain urged his horse up the slope and trotted up to the photographer.

"Did you get the image?" he asked, not bothering to dismount.

"Yes, but I'm not sure it will be clear. Some men and horses moved while the exposure was being taken. If you can order them to hold steady for at least five seconds, I can produce a better photograph the second time."

Ludlow glowered at the young man with a horseshoe mustache and receding hairline standing by the camera.

"Mr. Illingworth, the government is paying you a handsome salary of thirty dollars per month to capture key scenes from this expedition. You were selected because of your work with the Fisk Expedition to Montana. We are not in your studio in St. Paul. We're in the middle of damned nowhere! So you'd better learn how to make the most of capturing images when conditions are not ideal. I will not go back there and ask my commanding officer to order a thousand-man army to stand still just so you can get a quality photograph. Is that clear?"

The young photographer gulped.

"Yes, sir."

"Is the image you captured acceptable?"

"Well, I won't really know until I develop it..."

"Is it *acceptable?*" Ludlow repeated with gritted teeth, leaning forward in his saddle and glaring at him.

"Uh, yes. Yes, I believe it is, sir."

"You better hope so. The colonel will want to see the image on that glass plate tonight."

Ludlow turned his horse and waved to Custer, who gave the command to proceed immediately and follow their original "order of march."

Soon, the first groups of creaking wagons were passing by the mounted camera. Clouds of dry soil floated above the prairie. Most everyone in the column was wearing a bandana across his face to keep from inhaling the choking dust.

Illingworth nervously stepped into his darkroom tent. He made the sign of a cross on his chest, then opened the holder and removed the glass plate. Holding it over a tray, he poured developer on the surface. Then he rinsed the plate with water to remove the excess chemical. Finally, he immersed it in a tray of fixing agent and washed it again.

After exiting the darkroom tent, he held the plate against a dark cloth so he could view the developed image. Illingworth breathed a sigh of relief. There were indeed some blurry figures where men or horses had moved, but the photograph looked good. It wasn't his best effort. But he had not failed.

It especially pleased the photographer the commanding officer of the 1874 Black Hills Expedition, Liuetenant Colonel George Armstrong Custer, was clearly visible on the front left side of the grand military parade. The flamboyant boy general was sitting on a dark bay Thoroughbred wearing distinctive light-colored buckskin clothing.

It was half past eight o'clock on August 2. The sun had just settled behind the sacred precipice called the Six Grandfathers by the Sioux. Decades later, relief images of four US presidents would be carved from this granite mountain into a colossal structure known as Mount Rushmore.

The expedition had entered the Black Hills from the northwest twelve days earlier after traveling nearly three hundred miles across the plains. Before Custer's expedition, the few white men who had ventured through the Black Hills, part of the Great Sioux Reservation established in the Fort Laramie Treaty of 1868, were effusive in describing its beauty. They reported a land of rugged rock formations, deep canyons, grasslands, clear streams, and blue lakes. They also claimed the region was blessed with deposits of gold and silver.

The army was camped eight miles southeast of Harney's Peak. Custer planned to stay at this site for five days and explore the surrounding area. He especially wanted to provide the miners with an opportunity to search the creeks and foothills for any precious minerals. So far, no one had spotted any signs of gold.

Colonel Custer sat behind a wooden table in his officer's tent on a camp chair, quill in hand, and stared at the blank page illuminated by a lantern. He intended to write another newspaper article about the journey, but the words escaped him. Perhaps his creativity was blunted because he was tired. He slept only a few hours the previous night after having led a small group on a successful ascent of Harney's Peak. The climbers had returned well after midnight.

It was a festive atmosphere tonight. Most men had few responsibilities other than cooking, tending to the horses, and rotating on guard duty. So when nightfall came, they were in the mood for entertainment. Quite a few unlucky soldiers were relieved of their monthly pay in card games that were ubiquitous among the enlisted men and officers. The sutler had a wagon full of wine and whiskey that he gladly sold to those with cash. A man could become wealthy by winning his colleague's pay. He could just as easily lose it all later in the evening when the effects of the booze dulled his senses and his judgment.

Custer leaned back in his chair, placed his hands behind his head, and smiled. The sixteen-piece band had played one of the men's favorite songs, adding to the convivial mood in the camp. "The Girl I Left Behind Me" was poorly accompanied by a chorus of men who couldn't carry a tune in a bucket.

I'm lonesome since I crossed the hill
And over the moor that's sedgy
Such lonely thoughts my heart do fill
Since parting with my Betsey

I seek for one as fair and gay
But find none to remind me
How sweet the hours I passed away
With the girl I left behind me

Hearing the song made him think of his wife, Elizabeth, who was waiting for him back at Fort Abraham Lincoln. Libbie was the girl *he* had left behind. She had wanted to travel with him, but Custer thought there could be trouble with the Sioux and didn't want to risk putting her in harm's way.

"Colonel, permission to enter," a man called from outside.

Custer broke from his reverie. He recognized the voice of his adjutant and brother-in-law, James Calhoun.

"Come in, Lieutenant."

"Sir," Calhoun said, saluting after entering the commanding officer's tent. "The miners just arrived in camp. They have something to show you."

Custer's eyes widened at the news.

"By all means, show them in, James."

Lieutenant Calhoun opened the tent flap and motioned for the men to enter.

William T. (Billy) McKay and Horatio Nelson Ross had been invited to join the expedition and ply their skills in locating precious metals in the Black Hills. They had experience mining near the Montana towns of Alder Gulch and Cooke City. Although neither man had struck it rich, they had made modest livings placer mining the creeks in those regions.

Billy was a middle-aged man who was almost six feet tall and rail thin. He had a gray stubble beard and large protruding ears.

"Evenin', Colonel," Billy said as he removed his hat. "Me and Horatio jes' got back from down on French Creek. Thought you might wanna see what we found. Show 'em, Horatio."

Billy's partner was older and a few inches shorter. He sported a chest-length gray beard, a bushy mustache, and short salt-and-pepper hair.

Horatio placed a glass vial filled with sand and pea-sized gravel on the table.

Custer picked up the small bottle and held it by the light of the lantern.

"I don't see anything," he said after studying the glass tube.

"Oh, use this," Billy said, handing the colonel a magnifying glass mounted on a wood handle.

Custer placed the transparent tube under the lantern and held the magnifier up to the glass. He whistled when tiny pellets of gold reflected the light and seemed to luminesce.

"Tell me where you found this," the military commander ordered, holding the vial between his thumb and forefinger.

"Horatio done most of the diggin'. He found the first pieces. I'll let him tell the story."

"Well, sir," Horatio started, stroking his bushy gray beard, "We was down at French Creek all day pokin' around. At first we just panned the surface for a while, but found nothing. Then we got to diggin' with a pick in the creek bed. We dug straight down till we hit bedrock. That's where placer gold tends to collect. Sure 'nuf, the first panful o' gravel and sand that we washed had gold. So we jes' kept at it. Diggin' and pannin' and washin'. That's 'bout an hour's work."

"How much would you say it's worth?" Lieutenant Calhoun asked.

"Oh, mebbe ten dollars, give or take," Horatio replied casually.

"You think someone could make a living mining this creek?" Custer asked.

"I could. How 'bout you, Billy?"

"Yep." His partner nodded. "Course depends on how much is there. Next place we check might come up empty. Ain't nobody knows for sure 'cept the Lord. And he ain't tellin'."

"Thank you, gentlemen. Good work. See if you can find gold at other places in the creek tomorrow. I'll keep this sample. That's all."

"Yes, sir," Billy said.

Calhoun held the tent flap open, and the prospectors exited.

"This is big news, James. I need to get word back to headquarters. The newspapers will eat this story up. Discovering a big deposit of gold in these hills could be just what it takes to get our country out of this economic depression. Plus, it gives our expedition even more credibility. Fetch our three journalists. Then find Charley Reynolds. I have a mission for him."

Ten minutes later, William E. Curtis poked his head inside the tent.

"You wanted to see me, Colonel?"

Curtis was one of three reporters invited to accompany the massive wagon train on the Black Hills campaign. He was a correspondent for the *Chicago Inter-Ocean* newspaper. Custer was politically savvy. He understood the power of having press members as part of the expedition. They could report the group's adventures firsthand. They were also more likely to be sympathetic to Custer and paint him in a favorable light since they were invited guests.

"Come in. As soon as Barrows and Knappen get here, I'll brief you on some exciting news."

"Colonel, I don't think they'll be attending tonight," Curtis said.

"Oh? Why's that?"

"They're both in a card game," he said, hesitating. "Let's just say I'm not sure either man could find your tent at the moment."

Custer shook his head. He knew some men got carried away with drinking. He turned a blind eye to this behavior with the enlisted men, so long as it didn't affect their duties. But he didn't tolerate excessive drinking among the officers. Unfortunately, he had to make an exception on this campaign. President Grant's son Frederick, who was also a colonel, was another politically motivated addition to the team. They assigned him aide-de-camp to Custer. In reality, he contributed little and was a frequent patron of the sutler's liquor supplies.

"Well, it's too bad the *New York Tribune* and the *Bismarck Tribune* aren't represented," Custer said. "I'll share this information with those gentlemen in the morning. For now, it looks like you have an exclusive."

Curtis excitedly pulled out his notebook and a pencil.

"This is the story," Custer said, handing the vial and a magnifying glass to the journalist.

The reporter laid his notebook on the table. He held the magnifier close to the glass tube and placed it in the light from the lantern.

"Oh my! So it's true! There *is* gold in the Black Hills!"

"That's right. Our miners found these gold particles in French Creek. But let me caution you. This discovery is preliminary. We need to verify gold in other places. I'd like our geologist Mr. Winchell to examine this sample. I'm sending a courier to Laramie with this news tonight. He will have a telegram sent to army headquarters. You're welcome to include what I wrote in your reporting."

He handed the correspondent his piece of paper.

Gold has been found, and it is the belief of those who are giving their attention to this subject that it will be found in paying quantities. I have upon my table forty or fifty small particles of pure gold in size averaging that of a small pinhead and most of it obtained today from one pan full of earth. —Lt. Col. Geo. A. Custer

"Lieutenant Calhoun and Mr. Reynolds, seeking permission to enter," said a voice outside.

"Come in, come in."

"Sir, Mr. Barrows and Mr. Knapper are indisposed at the moment; it seems they—" Calhoun explained.

"Yes. I know," Custer interrupted his administrative officer. "Mr. Curtis will carry the story forward."

Custer reached across the table and snatched the note from the reporter's hand. Curtis was busily writing in his book.

"Hello, Charley! I've got an important assignment for you," the commanding officer said while standing.

"Yes, sir."

Charley Reynolds had enlisted as a scout for the Seventh Cavalry Regiment. In the five years the two men had known each other, Custer had grown to trust and appreciate his skills as a marksman, guide, and hunter. The thirty-two-year-old had broad shoulders, short sandy hair, blue eyes, and a walrus mustache.

Custer handed the note to the scout, who raised his eyebrows upon reading it.

"I need to telegraph this news to General Terry in St. Paul as soon as possible. How long will it take you to ride to Fort Laramie?"

Reynolds stroked his chin.

"That must be about a hundred miles."

"More like 115," Custer replied, correcting him.

"Well, given the terrain, I should be able to make it in four days."

"Four nights. You will traverse hostile Sioux territory. Hide during the day. Ride at night."

"Yes, sir."

"You will leave in one hour. Mr. Curtis, anything you want to be telegraphed needs to be in Mr. Reynolds' hands by ten o'clock."

"Understood."

"You are both dismissed."

After the reporter and the scout left the tent, Custer sat back in his chair.

"Well, James, this is quite a newsworthy day," he said to his adjutant. "The public will soon know these hills in the Dakota Territory are black *and gold.*"

The two men grunted, sweating profusely in the scorching August sun as they struggled to pull the bear by its front legs up a rocky knoll.

Colonel Custer watched from the top of the hill, then held up his hands when they dragged the carcass to a shale ridge.

"Good enough. This is a suitable location for a photo. Captain Ludlow, can you have someone fetch Mr. Illingworth and tell him to bring his camera equipment?"

Ludlow nodded at Private Noonan, who had worked with Bloody Knife to drag the slain bear up the small hill.

Noonan saluted the captain and hurried toward the main camp a few hundred yards away.

"This is one of the biggest bears I've seen," Custer commented, walking around the bruin. "How much do you think it weighs?"

"Oh, I'd say at least six hundred pounds. Maybe more," Ludlow replied.

It was the seventh day of August. The expedition was on the journey back to Fort Abraham Lincoln and would soon depart the Black Hills.

An hour earlier, a scout had reported seeing an enormous bear in the hills to the west as the wagon train crept north. The colonel was excited about the prospect of bagging a bear. He requested Ludlow, Bloody Knife, and Private Noonan to accompany him. After twenty minutes of searching, Bloody Knife spotted the bear and summoned his boss.

The hunting party got within fifty yards of the bear before Custer dismounted, kneeled, and fired his trusty Remington .50-caliber rolling-block sporting rifle. The bear roared and lurched sideways, then lumbered away. His hunting companions pursued the wounded bear on horseback, with Captain Ludlow firing two more bullets into the animal before he fell.

"Well, he's a magnificent beast," Custer said, running his hands over the fur on the bear's massive shoulders. "My first grizzly."

Ten minutes later, Private Noonan arrived at the scene. William Illingworth followed behind with his wagon of tripods, tents, chemicals, and glass plates. The photographer jumped down and walked up the hill.

"The colonel would like a photo of the grizzly," Ludlow said to Illingworth.

"Sure. Just let me set up my darkroom tent and prepare a plate."

"Private Noonan, help Mr. Illingworth," the captain ordered.

As the photographer and Noonan walked down the hill to the wagon, Bloody Knife approached Ludlow.

"Need to speak," the Arikara scout said in a low voice.

Ludlow nodded and followed Bloody Knife. The two men walked a hundred feet along the knoll. Custer had taken a knife from a sheath on his belt and was cutting the left rear paw from the slain bear as a souvenir.

"Not a grizzly," Bloody Knife said, when he was alone with the captain.

"Looks like a grizzly to me."

"Cinnamon bear."

"Are you sure? It has the right color, and those are long claws."

"Straight face. Long ears. No shoulder hump. Not grizzly."

Ludlow grimaced. Shooting a subspecies of black bear wasn't nearly as impressive as killing a grizzly. If Bloody Knife was correct, this news would be highly disappointing to the colonel.

"Should we tell him?" Ludlow asked.

"Colonel killed large bear. Proud moment. I say nothing."

"Neither will I," Ludlow agreed.

The two men walked back to the carcass. A short time later, Illingworth scrambled up the knoll with a tripod and a sensitized plate mounted in a wooden frame. He set the camera on the tripod, mounted the plate, and ducked under the black cloth to adjust the focus.

"Okay, I'm ready," he announced.

"Come on, men. All of us had a hand in bringing down this bear," Custer said as he sat behind the animal's haunches and placed the butt of his Springfield rifle on the ground, its octagonal barrel pointing skyward. The other members of the hunting party posed behind the colonel.

"Hold still," Illingworth said as he removed the lens cap for a few seconds before replacing it. "Thanks! Colonel, I'll show you the exposed plate when we get to camp this evening."

"Wonderful!" Custer replied as he stood. "I want prints of the photo when we return to Fort Lincoln so I can distribute them to the press. Today's hunting trip will be a memorable event from our expedition into the Black Hills. Captain, have the butcher dress this animal. Let the men know bear meat will be available for dinner tonight for anyone who wants a change from beef."

Killing a grizzly may have seemed like a notable accomplishment to George Custer. But the public was much more interested in the dispatch delivered by Charley Reynolds and telegraphed from Fort Laramie. News about the discovery of gold had already reached the media on both coasts.

Prospectors would soon flood this part of the Dakota Territory seeking their fortunes. The surge of miners and settlers into the region violated the 1868 treaty with the Sioux. Although the military initially stopped white settlers from trespassing on Sioux land, over time they turned a blind eye to these illegal incursions. Within eighteen months, the government would renege on the original agreement, which designated the Black Hills "unceded Indian Territory" for the exclusive use of native peoples. When the Sioux defended their land by attacking the trespassers, the government passed a decree confining all Lakota

Sioux, Cheyennes, and Arapahos to the reservation under threat of military action. Tensions escalated.

Conflicts arose not only between the Sioux and the white settlers but also between the Sioux and neighboring tribes. As non-treaty Sioux were pushed farther west into Montana, they camped and hunted on the land of another tribe with increasing frequency. It was a tribe that had also recently been confined to a smaller reservation. It was their archenemies, the Crow.

Chapter Seventeen

Closer to the Enemy

August 1874

G raham tipped the hostler tending the horses before exiting the stable and hurrying toward the front gates of Fort Parker. He had been away from the Crow Agency for five days, visiting with Makawee and Nahkash. It would be good to get back to work and earn some money. He needed only one more month's pay to buy another horse. With the purchase of a seventh animal, he would finally satisfy the bride price set by Makawee's father.

He and Makawee had discussed a fall wedding ceremony. Perhaps they would hold it along the bank of the Stillwater River near their special cottonwood tree where they had carved their initials and sent Small Heart on his journey to the next life. The thought of marrying the beautiful woman who was the mother of his child made him smile. He started whistling the first stanza of "Bridal Chorus" by Richard Wagner. He was still whistling when he reached the gate. The sentry gave him a quizzical look as he checked Graham's employment papers. Graham didn't skip a beat. He doffed his hat and switched to humming the tune as he strode to the sutler's quarters.

The cheerful young man knocked on the door of his employer.

"Yes!" a muffled voice called from inside.

Graham entered, closed the door, and flopped into a ladder-back chair facing Uriah Brown's desk.

The sutler was hidden behind an unfolded copy of the *Bismarck Tribune*. He peeked over the top of the newspaper to see who had entered his office.

"Oh, hello, Graham."

"Hi, Mr. Brown. I got back early, so if you need something done this afternoon, I'm available."

"Just a moment," he replied. "I want to finish this article." Uriah Brown raised the paper and searched for the place he had stopped reading.

A minute later, the skinny man carefully folded the newspaper, laid it on his desk, and removed his glasses.

"Have you heard the news about the Black Hills expedition?" he asked.

"No, sir, I sure haven't. The last time I saw a newspaper was about a week ago."

"Well, look at this," he said, spinning the tabloid so Graham could see the front page.

Graham leaned over the desk and picked up the paper. The five-column weekly newspaper had devoted two columns to the latest news from Custer's Black Hills Expedition. The headlines exclaimed in bold, all-caps, "GOLD! CONFIRMED!"

Thanks to the technological marvel of the telegraph, every major newspaper had printed similar stories. As with previous reports of gold or silver in California, Nevada, Colorado, and Montana in years past, this news would propel tens of thousands of fortune seekers to the mineral-rich hills of the Dakota Territory.

GOLD! | CONFIRMED!!

EXPEDITION HEARD FROM.

Custer at the Black Hills on the 2d inst.

THE MOST BEAUTIFUL VALLEYS THE EYE OF MAN EVER RESTED UPON.

Gold and Silver in Immense Quantities.

NO FIGHTING WITH THE SIOUX.

Two Privates Lost---One by Disease ---One by Accident.

CUSTER'S BLACK HILLS EXPEDITION, AUG. 2.
Via Fort Laramie, Wyoming, August 8, 1874.
Special dispatch to the Bismarck Tribune.

Custer's Official Report!

THE BLACK HILLS COUNTRY

Gold Bearing Quartz Crops Out in Every Hill.

FIFTY PIECES OF GOLD AS LARGE AS PIN HEADS FROM ONE PAN.

FULL DETAILS RESERVED FOR FINAL REPORT.

A Band of Twenty-Seven Sioux Surrounded, but No Fight.

The Chief Surrenders, and Goes with the Expedition as a Guide.

"This is great for the country," Uriah said. "The depression that started last year with the financial collapse of the railroads has made it difficult for a lot of men to get work. The trouble is, every amateur prospector believes *he's* the lucky one who's gonna find the mother lode in those hills."

"I suppose it's good news," Graham replied placidly. "But aren't the Black Hills part of the Sioux Reservation?"

Uriah grinned. "Do you think some legal technicality about land ownership is going to keep thousands of eager men from mining those hills?"

Graham knew the answer. History would prove the sutler right. This would be one more example of a treaty broken by the government. Repeated violations by miners and settlers would anger the Sioux. Their refusal to give up their sacred land and live inside a diminished reservation would ultimately lead to a deadly confrontation in the summer of 1876 with the leader of the Black Hills Expedition, George Armstrong Custer.

"No. I suppose you're right. Greed always seems to win," Graham conceded.

Uriah Brown cleared his throat. He leaned forward in his chair and folded his hands.

"I don't know how to say this, so I'll be direct. I have to let you go."

Graham was stunned.

"What? You're firing me?"

"Not firing you. Letting you go. There's a difference. I just don't have the work. My boss Mr. Story is a businessman who is trying to stay profitable in a miserable economic downturn. He has agreed to pay you another week's wages as a way of expressing his appreciation."

Brown fished a small key from his pocket. He unlocked a desk drawer, extracted a metal box, and retrieved seven dollars in United States notes and fifty cents in postage currency paper.

"Here you go. One week's pay," the sutler said, handing the notes to the dazed young man sitting in the chair across from him.

Graham stared at the money, then looked up at the sutler.

"Are you sure you don't need an extra man for another month or two? I can work for less, if that..."

"No, I'm sorry," he said, holding up one hand. "There's nothing I can do. He has already decided."

Graham nodded. He slowly stood and stuffed the notes into the pocket of his jeans.

"Oh, Mr. Story said you can have something from our warehouse. Anything up to twenty dollars in value. You know what we carry. Something you have your eye on?"

Graham found it hard to concentrate. He was still in shock over losing his job. He placed his fingers on his temples and tried to think about what he needed most.

"I'm not allowed to stay in Long Horse's camp. I need shelter," he said. "How about a tent?"

The sutler put on his spectacles and wrote a note. He picked up a wooden-handled stamp, pressed it on an ink pad, and made his official mark on the paper.

"Go pick one out. Give this to the sentry."

Graham accepted the slip and extended his hand to his former employer.

"Thank you for giving me work two years ago. It helped get me on my feet," Graham said dejectedly, spinning the rim of his cowboy hat in his hands.

"You're a bright young fellow. Somebody will give you an opportunity. You can use me as a reference."

"Thanks," he replied glumly as he walked across the room and opened the door.

"Graham?" Uriah asked.

He stopped in the doorway and turned around.

"Do you think you'll head to the Black Hills to search for gold?"

"Nope. I will not trespass on land reserved for the Sioux."

"Where will you go?"

"Since the government moved the Crow Agency to the Stillwater River, Long Horse relocated his camp to the Bighorn River. He refuses to live in the agency's shadow, and he wants to be close to the remaining buffalo herds. That's where my family is. That's my home."

"Good luck, son."

Graham donned his hat and closed the door behind him.

He pondered his predicament as he exited the front gate with a canvas tent perched on a shoulder and turned to follow the log palisade toward the stable. He needed one more horse to match the bride price for Makawee. But he had less than ten dollars to his name. Even worse, he had fallen woefully short of Black Hawk's gifts to Long Horse. When they had returned from the trip to Obsidian Cliff to meet with Ollokot, Graham learned Black Hawk had counted coups by touching a settler while stealing his rifle and two horses.

Long Horse had questioned his nephew's decision to steal from a settler since the Crow were allied with the government. Black Hawk had simply laughed and said this white man had plenty of horses, and he would not miss the two that were stolen. He was confident they would blame the raid on Blackfeet because he yelled some words in Siksika while he corralled the horses and chased them away from the settlement. The chief nodded and congratulated Black Hawk on being clever and brave.

The deficit between Graham and Black Hawk was now three horses. It was clear his adversary's strategy was to provide *more than the asking price* for Makawee. Graham had done little to show courage in the face of the enemy. He had counted no coups. If Long Horse were to decide who would marry his adopted daughter today, it would be no contest.

Twenty minutes earlier, his heart had been filled with a joyous tune. Now he had the blues.

As Graham approached the Bighorn River, he could see why this was a desirable location for a camp. Long Horse had chosen a site several miles below the mouth of Bighorn Canyon. Several large stands of pine trees provided ample materials for lodge poles and firewood. There was plenty of forage for the horses from abundant grasses and sedges in a verdant meadow. The ever-diminishing bison herds would be easier to find in this part of eastern Montana, as most of the remaining bovids had migrated to this valley to graze.

Rides Alone greeted him as he entered camp. He told Graham that Makawee had gone with some other women to pick huckleberries and offered to show him the surrounding area. The friends rode south toward the canyon and climbed a gentle slope to a plateau. The remains of an outpost were visible among clusters of blue-green western wheatgrass and needlegrass that had overgrown the site. Chunks of charred wood were scattered within collapsed adobe walls. The tallest standing structures were four feet high. Crumbled bastions and the remnants of horse stalls were clues this had been a military post.

"What is this place?" Graham asked.

"Fort Smith. Here short time. Soldiers built to protect the Bozeman Trail. White men crossed river there," Rides Alone said, jerking his thumb over his shoulder at the waterway behind him.

"What happened?"

"Sioux Chief Red Cloud said no white man could cross land. Many raids and fights. Army gave up and left. Sioux burned fort."

Rides Alone turned his horse around to look over the valley to the north and the plains to the east. Graham reined Blade and joined him as they surveyed the expansive landscape. Several miles away, a dozen tepees of Long Horse's camp had been erected along the banks of the Bighorn River. The Powder River Basin between the Bighorn Mountains and the Black Hills surely seemed to have everything someone would need for a camp or homestead.

"We call this place *Annu'ucheepe*, 'mouth of canyon.' It is good land. It is Crow land."

Graham could hear pride in the voice of Rides Alone. As he considered the history of the abandoned fort on the plateau, a question came to mind.

"Are we in Sioux territory?"

Rides Alone slowly turned in his saddle.

"This is Crow land. Not Sioux," he said, looking at Graham with steely eyes.

"I agree," Graham said quickly. He knew from Redfield's hand-drawn map they were within the boundaries of the Crow Reservation. "But are we more likely to encounter Sioux at Annu'ucheepe?"

Rides Alone returned his gaze to the valley below before responding.

"We are closer to the enemy," the Crow warrior said laconically as he nudged his horse down the slope toward the valley.

Graham had just finished raising the canvas tent a hundred yards from Long Horse's camp when he saw Makawee walking toward him. She was carrying Nahkash on her hip. He rushed over and embraced his future bride, kissing her before scooping his daughter into his arms and giving her a hug.

"I didn't expect you to be here! Aren't you supposed to be working at Fort Parker?" she asked.

"Yeah, well, I have some bad news," he said gloomily as he put the toddler down. "I lost my job. They don't have any work for me at the agency."

"But you only require one more horse to pay Long Horse."

"Three," he corrected her. "I need three more horses to match Black Hawk. Seems like he can steal 'em faster than I can buy 'em. And now I don't even have a way to purchase any."

Makawee nodded. She could see his disappointment.

"At least you are here with your family," she responded encouragingly.

"I'm not living with you and Nahkash. I might as well pitch my tent on the Stillwater River. One hundred yards or one hundred miles. What difference does it make? Long Horse won't allow me to share a lodge with you until we are married."

Nahkash wandered into the tent through the open flap and started exploring. The strange sharp-cornered shelter must have looked very different compared to her mother's conical lodge.

"Be patient, Eagle Bear," Makawee said, wrapping her arms around his waist and looking up at him.

"Patient? It's been two years since I returned to take you as my wife. Every time we're close to getting married, something gets in the way. I'm tired of waiting!" he said in an exasperated tone. "Why don't you pack your things? Let's leave tonight!"

Makawee stepped back and turned to face the tepee village. Smoke was climbing from the apexes of the tepees as the women were preparing to make the evening meal. Three dogs were barking at several small children running between the cluster of pole lodges.

"It's not that easy. I don't want to abandon this way of life entirely. These are my people. I want to return to my village after we are married. If we leave without my father's approval, they may never welcome us back."

"Well, I don't know how I can satisfy his bride price, now that I'm unemployed," he replied irritably.

She pivoted and looked at him.

"Yes, you do. The answer is there," she said, holding her arm out and pointing to the east.

Graham furrowed his eyebrows and tilted his head slightly.

"What do you mean?"

"At this camp, we are closer to the enemy than we have ever been. Several scouts have reported a large Sioux camp one day's ride from here."

"Yes. Rides Alone told me. But how is it helpful to have Sioux close by? It seems our proximity to each other could bring trouble."

"They have many horses," she said succinctly. "And they are on our land."

To the Crow and the Sioux, it was simple. Need a horse? Steal one. Need to prove your bravery? Count coups. Need a horse *and* need to prove your bravery? Steal a horse from your enemy.

Graham had previously gone on a raid with Little Wolf. They had successfully stolen two horses. While it was exhilarating, it was also dangerous. He had vowed never to do it again. Besides, he didn't need one horse. He needed *three*. He had done very little to prove himself as a warrior in the eyes of Long Horse. Perhaps it was time to count coups like his Crow friends.

Nahkash darted from the tent and dashed to Graham, grabbing his leg. He stooped and picked up his daughter. The toddler ran her fingers through Graham's beard, fascinated with the hair on her father's face that felt like a horse's mane. He looked at her blue eyes and black hair. She was going to be as beautiful as her mother.

"I'm sure my brothers would accompany you on a horse raid," she said, grabbing his bicep with one hand while stroking the cheek of Nahkash with the other.

Graham sighed. He would do anything to be with his family, including risking his life to steal a horse. He leaned down and kissed Makawee.

"Tell Rides Alone and Little Wolf I will visit tomorrow."

The three men lay prone on a broad plateau and peered into the night at the valley below. Several hundred yards from their position, a river snaked its way north along the edge of bluffs, which rose precipitously two hundred feet on the eastern side of the river. An expansive area of rugged uplands stretched beyond the bluffs to the east. The ridge was nearly continuous along the length of the river, except for an occasional coulee or short ravine that emptied into the valley floor.

The light from cooking fires illuminated several dozen tepees pitched along the western bank of the river. A waxing gibbous moon was hidden behind a partly cloudy sky, making it difficult for the observers to discern any details of the encampment other than shadowy figures moving among the pole lodges.

"Where are we?" Graham said in a soft voice to Rides Alone, who was lying next to him in the grass.

"Greasy Grass River," came the reply in the dark.

He tried to visualize his map of Montana but couldn't remember a location with that name. The trio had risen several hours before dawn and ridden all day. They had stopped earlier to water the horses and eat, then rode for another hour until they reached this valley.

"What's the English name of the river?" he pressed Rides Alone.

"Our camp is on *Ets-pot-agie,* Mountain Sheep River. White men call it Bighorn River. This river is smaller. It is Little Mountain Sheep River."

It took a moment to digest what Rides Alone said.

Little *Mountain Sheep* River? Could it be...?

Graham looked over at his friend, who was squinting at the tepee village below. "Are we looking at the Little Bighorn River?"

"Yes. We call it Greasy Grass. Wet grass along river looks greasy."

Graham gasped and rolled onto his back. The Crow brothers did not know this site's historical significance. He took a deep breath and reminded himself the deadly battle between the Sioux and the Seventh Cavalry would not be fought here for two more summers.

Gradually, the clouds parted and revealed a half-illuminated moon. Graham grabbed his backpack, extracted a pair of field glasses, and rolled back onto his belly. He propped himself on his elbows and peered through the binoculars at the camp in the valley. He slowly scanned the area next to the river, stopping when he spotted a herd of horses at the south end of the encampment.

"Look," Graham said, handing the glasses to Rides Alone and pointing toward the picketed horses. The Crow warrior used the binoculars to survey the enemy camp, then handed them to Little Wolf.

"One guard," Rides Alone said. "We wait. When sky is dark with clouds, we take horses."

Rides Alone and Little Wolf discussed the situation. Graham was glad he had learned the Apsáalooke language so he could follow the discussion. He listened intently as they agreed on a plan. He was certainly not an expert on stealing horses.

The strategy was simple. The horse raiders would rely on stealth. They would leave their horses tied to trees at the base of the plateau and slowly advance across the open landscape. Although the clumps of grass were nearly four feet tall, the thick plants would afford minimal protection.

Little Wolf volunteered to untie the horses since he was the fastest runner. He had already stolen eight enemy horses. His voice and demeanor had a calming effect on equines. He had a gift for keeping strange horses from spooking. Little Wolf would unfasten one horse at a time and bring it back to the others waiting in the bunchgrass. If he did not alert the guard after untying the first horse, he would do the same a second time, then a third time.

After Little Wolf had separated three horses from the herd, the trio would silently lead them away from the camp. If the thieves were discovered, they would mount the stolen horses, gallop across the valley, then quickly dismount. Switching to their waiting horses, they would force the other horses up the plateau and away from the camp.

An hour later, the trio was crawling on their hands and knees through clusters of bluebunch wheatgrass. When the clouds covered the moon, they inched forward. When the moon illuminated the open landscape, they lay prone and motionless. Finally, the area where the horses were tied was less than a hundred feet away. They were picketed on ropes strung between cottonwood trees along the riverbank.

Rides Alone pointed to the sentry, a young Sioux sitting with his back against the base of a chokecherry tree on the far end of the corral. He was slumped over, asleep with his forearms on bent knees. The butt of his rifle sat on the ground between his legs, with the barrel of the weapon resting against his shoulder. Graham and Little Wolf acknowledged they saw the guard by nodding.

The Crow warrior studied the horses, watching their movements and trying to determine which would be least likely to resist being taken by a stranger. After a while, he turned to his little brother and showed which animals should be led away. Little Wolf shook his head. He pointed at two of the same horses chosen by Rides Alone but selected a different horse for his third choice. Rides Alone nodded.

Little Wolf looked at the sky. Clouds obscured the moon. He removed a knife from his belt, moved into a crouching position, and padded toward the horses. Graham felt tension in his chest as he watched the teenage warrior approach the picket line. As Little Wolf came to the first horse, he used slow, reassuring hand movements, then stroked the mare's neck. He reached under his tunic and offered the animal some dried apples before using the knife to cut the lead line. She nickered. Several horses shifted their weight, making dull thuds with their hooves in the soft earth. He slowly backed the horse away from the picket, then quickly led her to the area where Graham and Rides Alone were waiting.

Graham took the lead rope and nodded to Little Wolf, who crouched and made his way to the second horse. A few minutes later, Rides Alone was holding the lead rope of another mare, and Little Wolf headed back to the corral.

So far, so good.

Rides Alone and Graham watched from the shadows as Little Wolf approached a colt. The young horse was more excitable than the mares. He backed up and pulled against the picket line. The surrounding horses became nervous, moving their feet and snorting. Little Wolf tried to calm the yearling.

The disturbance caused the teenage guard to awaken.

Rides Alone signed to his brother the sentry had been alerted.

Little Wolf stood still and stroked the colt's muzzle.

The Sioux guard shifted his weight on his butt, crossed his arms, and gradually nodded back to sleep with his chin on his chest.

Graham realized he had been holding his breath and exhaled.

Rides Alone signed it was now safe but to hurry.

Little Wolf untied the lead line and guided the colt away from the picket line. Then it happened.

The young horse erupted into a loud snort, followed by a whinny.

The guard woke, grabbed his rifle, and jumped up from the tree. He scanned the horses, which were shifting, sensing something was wrong.

Rides Alone waved to Little Wolf.

The young Crow leaped onto the colt, turned it toward the open grassland, and dug his heels into its flanks. The horse vaulted forward.

Rides Alone and Graham mounted the stolen mares. Graham's heart was in his throat as his horse bolted toward the plateau. For an instant, it seemed like a replay of the day he and Little Wolf had snatched two horses. He could hear Little Wolf's colt galloping behind him. He felt the intoxicating mix of adrenaline in his blood and exhilaration in his brain.

Crack!

The sound of a rifle pierced the night air.

Crack!

A bullet zipped by Graham's ear.

Crack!

The bullets were coming in rapid succession from the repeating rifle.

The camp erupted with shouts and whoops as the Sioux realized there were intruders. Soon they would chase the horse thieves.

Graham was glad Rides Alone took the lead. He had lost his bearings in the dark and wasn't sure whether they were heading toward their waiting horses. When they reached the base of the plateau, the pair quickly dismounted and waited for Little Wolf.

A moment later, the young Crow warrior suddenly appeared out of the darkness. Graham could tell immediately something was wrong. Little Wolf was slumped over, holding on to the withers to keep from falling off. Graham held the horse, while Rides Alone helped his brother from the colt. He had difficulty standing. Blood soaked the side of his tunic.

"Brother, we must ride. Our enemies are coming," Rides Alone said.

"I can ride. Help me onto my horse."

"No. You will ride with me."

Rides Alone boosted his little brother onto the horse and climbed up behind him. He motioned for Graham to mount, then used his horse to herd the stolen mares and Little Wolf's horse in front of them.

They yelled and slapped their hands against their legs, causing the horses to run. Graham and Rides Alone followed closely behind the riderless mares, urging their mounts up the shallow slope to the top of the plateau. Behind them, they could hear screeches and whoops of their pursuers.

They rode hard and fast for ten minutes. Rides Alone didn't take a straight route. He rode west, then south. When they came upon a ravine with a small stream, he slowed and pushed the stolen horses into the narrow gulch. He dismounted and helped Little Wolf down, laying him under a quaking aspen.

"Gather horses together. Tie them to trees. Stay quiet."

Graham followed these instructions. Once the horses were secured under a canopy of aspen and willow trees, Rides Alone held his index finger to his mouth. He pulled a rifle from a scabbard and chambered a round. Graham extracted the pistol from his belt.

They heard the rumbling of hooves pounding the prairie above them. The sounds came closer, then faded away as the Sioux passed by the dark ravine.

Rides Alone laid down the rifle and kneeled by his brother. He used a knife to cut the young man's tunic and rolled him onto his side, revealing a bullet wound in his back just below the rib cage.

Graham gasped, then quickly retrieved a spare shirt he had tucked into his saddlebag. He kneeled by his friend and pressed the cloth against the wound.

The young Crow coughed. He looked at Rides Alone and said, "Should have taken mare."

"You were brave. Counted more coup than me. You are a warrior."

Rides Alone pulled an eagle feather from one of his braids and stuck it in his brother's hair.

Little Wolf smiled weakly. His eyelids flickered and his head tilted slowly to the side as he took his final breath.

A light breeze passed through the ravine, causing the quaking aspen leaves overhead to flutter momentarily. It was as if the spirit of Little Wolf had ascended through the trees. A moment later, the night air was calm.

Graham sat heavily in the wet grass by the stream and put his head in his hands. He tried to suppress his sobs, partly to keep from revealing their hiding place but mostly to hide his emotions. He did not want Rides Alone to perceive him as weak.

Rides Alone remained stoic as he continued kneeling. He stroked his younger brother's hair and straightened his bloody, torn tunic. Lifting his eyes toward the night sky, he raised his arms and whispered a chant.

The two men waited for several hours to be sure their enemies had given up the chase. As dawn broke on the horizon, Rides Alone and Graham wrapped Little Wolf's body in a blanket and draped it across his horse. The survivors of the raid started on their journey back to the Bighorn Valley. They had paid an enormous price for the three additional horses they were bringing to camp. They had lost a brother and a friend.

Forty miles in a saddle gave a man a lot of time to think. Graham considered the previous night's tragic outcome as the horses plodded toward the camp of Long Horse. He was grief-stricken at the loss of his friend. It was even more painful realizing he had contributed to the young man's death. If he had not asked for help to steal horses, Little Wolf might still be alive.

And why had his life been spared? One bullet from the Sioux camp had come within inches of his head.

He reached under his coat and felt the eagle-bear-claw necklace. Had this spirit protected him again? What if Little Wolf had been wearing it instead of him? He had many unanswered questions.

Graham wished Rides Alone would say something while they rode. But he was even more taciturn than usual. Graham didn't blame him. Everyone processed grief differently. Perhaps it was just as well his friend did not talk. While he wanted to console Rides Alone, he didn't know how.

It was ironic Little Wolf had lost his life in the Little Bighorn Valley. His death was a portent of an epic battle in which hundreds of Indigenous people and white men would die. Indeed, it was a valley destined to be fatal ground.

Chapter Eighteen

Stolen Bride

March 1875

I t had been a long, bleak winter in southern Montana. The temperatures had not climbed above zero for two weeks in January. Winds whipped the snow into drifts against the tepees. The horses struggled to find food and lost weight as the season wore on. Long Horse considered moving his camp farther south to locate better forage but decided against this when he concluded it would put his band even closer to the Lakota Sioux and Cheyenne. Finally, the temperatures had moderated, and the snows relented. A week in the thirties felt like a heat wave to the residents along the Bighorn River.

Graham had plenty of time to think about the past and his future on these long winter days. Although he was relegated to setting up camp a half mile from the tepee village, he could visit with Makawee and Nahkash. It was discouraging to have his family so close yet so far from him.

As he sat by a fire outside of his wall tent in early March, he recalled the aftermath of Little Wolf's death the previous autumn.

Long Horse and Fox Woman had been distraught at the loss of their youngest son. Although they never accused Graham of being responsible, he sensed they blamed him. Rides Alone had insisted the three horses captured in the raid should be Graham's. Even amid his grief, Rides Alone wanted Graham to meet the bride price. He preferred Graham to marry Makawee, not his cousin Black Hawk.

Graham recalled the events of that sorrowful day. Little Wolf had received a tree burial at the mouth of the Bighorn Canyon. The brief time Graham had spent at the burial tree was especially poignant. Although he had attended the funeral, he kept a respectful distance from the chief's family during the ceremony. After everyone had left, Graham walked to the tree where they had tied the body of his young friend. He stared at the platform that held a faded yellow blanket encased in a buffalo hide. He tried to think of the right words.

"Goodbye, my friend," he finally mumbled.

"Do not say goodbye," a familiar woman's voice said behind him.

It surprised Graham to see Makawee with Rides Alone.

Makawee hugged Graham, then stepped back while holding his hands.

"We don't say goodbye to those who have passed on to the next life," she said. "We have no word for 'goodbye' in Apsáalooke."

"Oh, I see."

Graham had become fluent in the Crow language over the previous two years. He had heard others use a phrase when they ended a conversation and parted ways. He assumed they interpreted this word as 'goodbye' in English.

"I'm confused. What does Shia-nuk mean?" he asked.

"'See you later,'" she said. "There are no goodbyes, because there is no end to life."

Graham nodded. As a Christian, he shared the Crow people's belief in life after death. The white man and the Indigenous people might interpret the afterlife differently, but they shared a common view that a person's time on earth was not the final chapter in someone's life.

"This is a good place," Rides Alone said, pointing to the tree at the mouth of the canyon where they had placed Little Wolf's body. "We are close to Annáshisee, the Medicine Wheel. The spirits will see that my little brother makes it to the next world. I want my body placed in this same tree when I die."

Rides Alone placed his hand on the trunk. "Shia-nuk," he said, before turning away.

Graham lay his hand on the tree before reverently repeating the same word.

The trio walked in silence toward camp. Graham was eager to find out if Long Horse had decided which man would marry Makawee, but he wasn't sure it was the right time. Fortunately, Makawee brought up the subject.

"Our family will be in mourning for the next few months. My father will decide who I marry in the spring." Makawee stopped and grabbed Graham's hand. She looked at him reassuringly. "We will have a decision by the time the bison are calving."

It was nice to know Makawee was still looking forward to their wedding day. But Graham was not as sanguine. He had already experienced too many setbacks to remain hopeful about their future together.

The two men sat on their horses at the edge of a bluff and gazed at the rolling prairie. It was a warm day in May. Puffy white cumulus clouds drifted lazily across the deep blue sky, casting shadows on the land below when they passed in front of the midday sun. Recent spring rains and fair weather had caused the tips of needlegrass and threadleaf sedge to transition from brown to green.

Graham had spent time over the past few months hunting and exploring the Little Bighorn Valley with Rides Alone. Ostensibly his friend visited the valley because the bison were more plentiful than along the river where they were camped.

Graham knew the truth. The Crow warrior was not only hunting bison. He was seeking Sioux. There was no doubt if they encountered the enemy, Rides Alone planned to take several scalps to avenge his brother's death. But the Sioux had set up camp farther east, and they had not crossed paths with the enemy. Although Graham could appreciate his friend's desire to extract a price for killing Little Wolf, he was secretly relieved each day the Sioux remained unseen.

The wind carried a faint, low-pitched moan across the open landscape to their vantage point. The extra horse fitted with a travois to carry their supplies and meat from their hunting trip snorted and stamped its feet, as if it recognized a tone of distress. Graham leaned over from his saddle and calmed the nervous equine by stroking its neck.

"Calf being born," Rides Alone said, pointing to a small herd of bison grazing several hundred yards away.

The sound of a bison giving birth was music to Graham's ears. Unfortunately, bison could not reproduce quickly enough to replenish their numbers. Fewer than two hundred thousand of the animals remained on the northern plains in 1875, where thirty million had once roamed. The evidence of their demise was everywhere. During hunting trips, it was common for Graham and Rides Alone to see hundreds of carcasses rotting in the sun. The beasts had been skinned, and the meat left behind to rot. After killing the bison, the hunters would peg, salt, and dry the hides before stacking them onto wagons and transporting their loads to Bismarck, where the Union Pacific Railroad had established a depot two years earlier. The rail line carried the animal hides east to be processed by tanneries on the Atlantic seaboard and in Europe.

Calving season was also a reminder Long Horse would soon announce his decision about who had been the successful suitor for Makawee's hand. The bleating sound from the pregnant bison prompted Graham to speak about the pending decision.

"Long Horse will choose a husband for Makawee soon," Graham said, glancing at his friend on the horse beside him.

Rides Alone nodded but said nothing.

"Has he decided?" Graham asked directly.

Rides Alone shook his head. "He does not speak of these things."

Graham stood in his stirrups briefly to stretch his legs before sitting down in his saddle. He didn't want to press his friend but shared his thoughts.

"No one should force Makawee to marry someone she doesn't love. I'm concerned he will choose Black Hawk."

"Both gave ten horses, three rifles."

Graham was glum. It seemed like the decision was a foregone conclusion.

"But Long Horse doesn't believe I'm a warrior."

"Are you a warrior?" Rides Alone asked.

This caught Graham off guard. He wanted sympathy, not a challenge. He felt himself becoming defensive.

"I can take care of Makawee and Nahkash. I can provide for them."

Rides Alone turned toward his baaschiile friend and asked again. "Are you a warrior?"

Why is he so damned persistent? Graham thought.

"Yes! Yes, I'm a warrior!"

"Fight for her," he said, looking into Graham's eyes.

Graham clenched his teeth and nodded. "I will."

Rides Alone held his gaze for a moment before nodding.

"Come, let us kill *bishée*," he said, guiding his horse down the steep grassy slope of the bluff toward the distant herd.

Dusk was descending on the plains when Graham and Rides Alone reached the Bighorn River. The familiar pattern of tepee poles jutting at obtuse angles into the early evening sky greeted the hunters as they arrived at the camp of Long Horse.

A young man appeared in the fading light as Rides Alone and Graham were untying the ropes holding slabs of bison meat on the travois.

"Welcome. I take care of horses. Long Horse requests you and Eagle Bear in his lodge," he said.

The friends walked together to the tepee, where Rides Alone held open the flap. Graham hesitated. It had been two years since he had been banned from the chief's lodge after Makawee had announced she was pregnant with a second child. Two years had passed while he labored to deliver an ever-increasing bride price for the right to marry the mother of his child. Two years of living in partial isolation and being frustrated. All that could change tonight, depending on the decision of the chief. Graham removed his hat and ducked inside. Rides Alone followed him.

As expected, Long Horse and Fox Woman were sitting in their customary positions at the back of the tepee. Among the Grass was on the side by Fox Woman. Makawee was seated on the side nearest to Long Horse with Nahkash in her lap. Rides Alone took a seat beside his sister. Graham strode to his family. He smiled at Makawee and gently stroked the soft cheeks of his daughter before turning to face Long Horse.

Black Hawk was standing in the center of the lodge. The chief motioned for Graham to stand beside his rival behind a small cooking fire.

"Eagle Bear, can you understand Apsáalooke?" he asked in English.

"Blaasáxchiiwaatchaache" ["It is easy to understand"], Graham replied. Living among Makawee's people had allowed him to become fluent in the Crow language. He hoped his willingness and ability to learn the chief's language would bolster his chances of being selected.

Long Horse switched to his native tongue as he addressed the young men standing before him.

"Black Hawk and Eagle Bear, both of you have asked to take Makawee as your wife. Both have met the price required," Long Horse began, shifting his gaze between the two suitors. "I need to consider other things when making this decision. The one who is most worthy must be brave. He is true to his word. He will give his life to protect his family and defend our way of life. The one who is most worthy of marrying Makawee is the warrior Black Hawk."

Graham felt a pain in his chest, like someone had punched him in the solar plexus. He struggled to breathe, and his calves quivered.

Black Hawk let out a whoop and raised both arms in the air. Among the Grass jumped up and briefly hugged her son before retreating to where she had been sitting. On the opposite side of the tepee, Makawee slowly shook her head in disbelief as she tried to process her father's decision.

Black Hawk extended his hand toward Graham, who ignored the gesture. He dropped his hat and sank to his knees. He leaned forward and placed his hands on his thighs, grappling with the weight of the chief's judgment.

"Makawee, you will give your necklace to Black Hawk as a sign you are committed to marrying him," Long Horse said. "He will return it on your wedding night, in two moons."

She lowered her head, grasped the obsidian turtle suspended from an elk-hide cord, and stared blankly at the pendant. She jumped to her feet and placed Nahkash on one hip as she hastened toward the entrance.

"Makawee!" the chief shouted.

She stopped and turned. Scared by the booming voice of her grandfather, Nahkash cried.

"If you do not marry Black Hawk, you will be banned from our tribe and this family forever. Weigh your actions carefully."

Makawee slipped outside into the early evening, wiping tears with the sleeve of her dress and comforting Nahkash as she hurried to her pole lodge.

"Makawee is upset. But she will see the wisdom of my decision. Give her time," Long Horse said to Black Hawk. "Everyone but Eagle Bear may leave."

Black Hawk nodded to the chief. He looked down at his defeated adversary on his knees, who had covered his face with his hands. *What a weak and pathetic man,* Black Hawk thought. *Long Horse chose wisely. I am the true warrior.*

Among the Grass wore a broad smile as she followed her son out of the tepee. Another loud whoop pierced the night air as Black Hawk celebrated his victory.

Rides Alone stood. He paused briefly to put a hand on Graham's shoulder, then followed his cousin out of the pole lodge.

It was eerily quiet inside the tepee. The only sound was the crackling and popping of the fire. Graham could hear his breath as he exhaled. He wiped his eyes with his hands and struggled to his feet.

"I know you are upset, perhaps even angry. This was a difficult decision but one that is best for Makawee."

Graham looked at Long Horse, then shifted his gaze to Fox Woman. Unlike her husband, she seemed to realize the pain Graham was feeling at losing his family. He could see empathy in her eyes.

Long Horse offered words of consolation intended to assuage Graham's extreme disappointment.

"You are welcome to stay outside our camp until you decide where to go. Take the ten horses you presented to me and sell them. Start a new life in the white man's world."

As the shock of the chief's devastating proclamation wore off and he regained his composure, Graham felt his anguish transition to resentment. He clenched his hands into fists at his side as he searched for the right words.

"You never liked me from the time I arrived nearly three years ago. I've done everything asked of me. Have you not seen how I care for Makawee and Nahkash? Black Hawk has no love for her. What are his qualifications to be a husband? He's good at stealing horses. Does that mean he can steal my bride? I'm the father of her child! I'm the one who will give her a loving home." His voice grew louder as he tried to control his mounting anger.

Long Horse responded by raising his voice.

"You placed Makawee's life in danger by making her pregnant with a second child when she was not ready. You were careless when raiding the enemy camp the night Little Wolf was killed. And you have not avenged his death. I lost my youngest son. I will not lose my daughter," Long Horse said defiantly.

The chief's accusations outraged Graham. These things were not true. There was no point in arguing with a man who had already decided. His only hope was Makawee. Perhaps she would finally be willing to leave the camp of Long Horse without her father's blessing.

Graham retrieved his hat on the ground. He glared at Long Horse and gritted his teeth while he spoke.

"You may be an influential leader. But you're a terrible judge of character."

He turned and walked to the entrance, then pivoted before offering a final comment.

"Give my horses to Rides Alone. Your son has earned them."

Graham walked briskly to the tepee of Makawee and Rides Alone. He poked his head inside and was relieved to see that she was the only one there. Nahkash had fallen asleep on Makawee's lap as she sat on a willow-rod backrest.

Seeing Graham at the entrance of the tepee, Makawee placed her index finger to her lips. She slowly stood, laid their sleeping daughter on a buffalo hide, and covered her with a blanket. She stepped outside the lodge and hugged him around the waist. They held each other for a minute before Graham suggested they take a walk.

A few minutes later, they were standing on the banks of the Bighorn River.

Graham turned to her, lifted her chin, and said, "You know I love you with all my heart."

"Yes."

"And you love me?"

"Of course, I do!"

"You will be the wife of Black Hawk in less than two months. Is that what you want?"

"No!" she said emphatically, turning away and lowering her gaze. "How could you even think such a thing?"

Graham grabbed her hands and pulled her toward him.

"Then you have a choice. Stay here and be married to Black Hawk, or come with me and start our life together — you, me, and Nahkash."

"Oh, Graham! Why can't I have both you and my Crow family?" she said, sobbing.

"Long Horse forced you to make this choice, not me."

He put her arms around his waist and rested her head on his chest. She cried convulsively. Soon her tears wetted his shirt. His heart pounded with anguish, and his mind was clouded with indignation. Had he come all this way to be denied the opportunity to spend his life with the woman he loved?

His thoughts turned to the advice others had given him over the years. Redfield had cautioned him to be patient. Rides Alone had counseled him to endure the wait. Even Makawee had optimistically urged him to let things play out even as Black Hawk vied for her hand in marriage. And what did this restraint gain him? A one-way ticket to nowhere.

His resentment triggered a selfish thought. *To hell with being patient! I want an answer now!*

"This is a night of decisions, Makawee," he said, grabbing her arms encircling his waist and pushing her away as he spoke. "I left my family to be with you! Come with me, or stay here."

"I...I can't decide. Not tonight. I need time to think," she said between sobs.

"Fine. I need time, too. Maybe the best time to clear my head is one hundred years in the future."

Graham released her arms, spun around, and strode toward his tent on the edge of camp. He could hear Makawee weeping as she fell to her knees. He told himself to ignore the sobbing sounds. They were coming from a woman who would not fully commit to loving him.

And right now there was no place in his embittered heart for anyone in nineteenth-century Montana.

The sun was still hovering above the western horizon as Graham stood at the summit of Medicine Mountain in the Bighorns. A light dusting of snow had coated the rock-strewn ground the previous day. Even though it was the summer solstice, a constant breeze made it feel much colder than forty degrees on the barren mountaintop. He buttoned his coat and sat down, leaning against the central cairn of Annáshisee.

The Medicine Wheel was unchanged from his last visit three years ago. Twenty-eight lines of limestone rocks radiated from a large pile of stones like spokes of a wheel. Each spoke represented one day of the lunar cycle. The ancient wheel was a disquieting reminder Makawee would be married to Black Hawk in less than a month.

As Graham waited for the sun to set and a full moon to rise, he removed his hat, placed it on the cairn, and rested his head against the rock wall behind him. He thought about the last few weeks and the journey that had brought him back to this sacred place. Until recently, he had a clear vision of his future life. He had planned to marry Makawee, settle on the frontier, and raise a family. But his dreams had been shattered with the proclamation that Black Hawk would become her husband.

Graham was enraged and exhausted from his failed attempt to secure Makawee as his wife. The crushing announcement by Long Horse prompted him to strike his camp the same evening. He had packed his belongings and moved to the site of the abandoned fort at the mouth of the canyon. The next morning, he continued to ride south. He spent the next week slowly making his way upstream along the snaking Bighorn River, stopping briefly to hunt or fish. His immediate goal was to put as much distance as possible between himself and the Crow village.

Every night he sat alone by a fire and pondered what to do. More often than not, he would change his mind multiple times before the sun rose the next morning. He was confused and conflicted.

Should he accept Long Horse's decision and return to congratulate Black Hawk and Makawee, wishing them happiness together? This would be the Christian thing to do. He could hear the voice of his minister reading a familiar passage from the Gospels.

But I tell you, do not fight with anyone who does wrong to you. But if someone hits you on one side of your face, turn the other side to him also.

Turn the other cheek? He would never accept that Makawee would soon be in the arms of another man. His heart was harder than the rocks lining Bighorn Canyon. The voice in his head switched from the religious teachings of a minister to the secular views of his mother, who always seemed to have a phrase handy for explaining hard events in the Davidson children's lives. He could hear her recite one of her favorites: *Time heals all wounds.*

But some wounds never heal. Some are so deep they become infected. They constantly fester and ooze. The resulting scar tissue torments the wounded person for the rest of his life. He thought losing Small Heart to a premature birth was painful. But losing Makawee hurt to the bone. It caused a profound ache in his heart he feared would never mend.

And so Graham found himself inexorably drawn to this sacred place where his journey to find Makawee had begun three years earlier. If time heals all wounds, then perhaps a hundred years would speed up the process. He would travel back to his time and his place in the world. He had been foolish to chase after love in a century filled with animus between so many groups of people. Graham Davidson belonged in the late twentieth century. That's where he would go.

Graham pulled the eagle-bear-claw necklace from under his coat, rubbed the smooth edges of the pendant, and touched the sharp points of the grizzly bear claws. It was his ticket home. He only needed the spirits to grant his petition to be taken back to his rightful time. He closed his eyes and drifted off to sleep, waiting for the full moon to become visible in the southeastern sky.

"Kahée!" a man's voice called out from the perimeter of the sacred stone circle.

Graham awakened with a start. He reached behind his back, pulled the Colt revolver from his belt, and aimed it in the voice's direction. The moon was high above the horizon and partially illuminated the mountaintop, but he couldn't see anyone. He rubbed his eyes and wondered how long he had been asleep.

"Who's there?" Graham asked in Apsáalooke, nervously swinging the pistol from side to side. He scrambled to his feet and peeked from behind the rock cairn while holding the revolver in a firing position.

A shadowy figure emerged from the tree line and strolled toward the circle. The man extended his arms out to his sides. His hands were open with palms forward. Graham could see he was unarmed. As the man drew closer, Graham lowered his weapon. The stranger was an elderly Indian dressed in a tunic and leggings. He had thin shoulder-length gray hair that flowed as he strode toward the center of the Medicine Wheel.

"You have learned our language," the old man said as he stopped ten feet from the cairn.

Graham stepped from behind the rock pillar and tucked the weapon into his belt. He stared at the man standing in front of him. Suddenly, he remembered he had seen this mysterious person before. He had appeared the evening Graham had petitioned the spirits and traveled back in time to 1872.

"You are Wind at Night."

"I am. And you are Eagle Bear."

Graham nodded. He was trying to comprehend how this man could exist in two different centuries. Then again, he told himself, someone could have asked him the same question.

"You are here to connect with the spirits?"

"Uh, yes. I'm...I'm seeking to go home."

"The spirits are very active at Annáshisee tonight. It is the longest day of the year."

Graham nodded. His chances of returning home seemed promising.

"Thank you for helping send me to this time three years ago," Graham said. He was trying to be courteous but wanted to start his petition while the moon was at its peak.

"The spirits are here. But they will not grant your request."

He furrowed his brow at the old man's remark.

"Why not?"

"You are not ready. And you are in the wrong state of mind."

Graham pursed his lips. He reminded himself to stay calm as he responded to these allegations.

"Why am I not ready? How do you know what I'm thinking?"

Wind at Night stepped closer. Graham could discern the wrinkles lining the old man's face and his deep-set brown eyes in the moonlight.

"Are you moving to something or running away from something?"

Graham swallowed hard. The old man had challenged him to consider the same advice his father had given before he died. *Never leave something unless you are also going to something.* He was rushing to escape a heart-wrenching experience. But would he feel less pain in the twentieth century?

"The spiritual path is not an escape. You must face the source of your pain," Wind at Night said.

Graham dejectedly sank to the ground and leaned against the cairn. He put his forearms on his knees and looked at his feet. The elderly man was right. He was running away because it was too painful to stay. He had abandoned the family he created.

A chilly breeze whistled by the cairn, then whisked through the upper branches of a lodgepole pine along the western edge of the clearing. When he looked up, the old man was gone.

A full moon was perched in the clear night sky at the apex of its trajectory. Graham held the eagle-bear-claw necklace in his fingers, debating whether to invoke the spirits. If he didn't proceed now, the moment would soon pass.

Graham rose from his seated position and knelt. He folded his hands and prayed to a God he had not spoken to in quite some time. It was a short but humble prayer in which he asked for guidance.

Who will question Long Horse's decision? Who will challenge Black Hawk's motives for marrying Makawee? Who?

In the distance, he heard a faint bird call. Graham strained to hear the sound. A winged silhouette swooped silently from the sky and perched on top of a dead tree. He recognized the great horned owl from its distinctive long tufts of feathers that resembled ears. The raptor turned its head and seemed to look directly at Graham when it emitted a deep-throated noise.

Who-who-who—you—you!
Who-who-who—you—you!

Graham shivered when he heard the owl. He grabbed his hat on the cairn and walked to the tree line on the east slope of the mountain where he had tied Blade. He removed the saddle and moved her to an area where new grass was peeking through the thin layer of snow. After picketing her to a tree, he carried his blanket and backpack to a fasting bed. It was the same one used by Little Wolf when they had first met at the Medicine Wheel. He tossed his belongings into the coffin-shaped rock structure and crawled in.

The tired young man from twentieth-century Pennsylvania lay in the primitive bed and wrestled with his decision. It took so much effort to align everything and travel to a sacred site like the Medicine Wheel. Maybe he should try to appeal to the spirits tonight. What harm would that do? He sat up when the owl raised its incessant hoot.

Who-who-who—you—you!

Who-who-who—you—you!

He lay back down and stared at the starry eastern sky. One thing was certain. He missed Makawee terribly. Perhaps he had given up too easily. In his rage, he had forced her to decide when she hadn't been ready. As her wedding day grew closer, maybe she would elope and not feel constrained by her father. He would take the advice of his friend Rides Alone and fight for Makawee. After all, if he didn't, who would?

Who-who-who—you—you!

Chapter Nineteen

Conspiracy Revealed

June 1875

Graham slid a sharpened stick through the mouth of the trout and poked it into the flesh at the rear of the rib cage. He suspended it over the fire, supporting it with several small twigs stuck into the belly to stabilize the fish while it cooked. He had consumed all the strips of dried bison days earlier. The Bighorn River had supplied him with fresh fish. These meals were a welcome change from salty red meat.

He tilted his head and peered at the waning gibbous moon. He pondered the few short weeks remaining for him to persuade Makawee to leave her Crow family and join him to start a new life together. How would she receive him when he arrived at camp? Would she be glad he had returned? Or would she resent him because he'd left in haste — without a goodbye? He wouldn't blame her if she held a grudge. He regretted his impulsive behavior.

"Thought I might find you here," came a voice from the dark.

It startled Graham. He jumped up and scanned the wooded area behind him.

"Kahée. Friend. Not enemy," Rides Alone said, as he stepped from the shadows and walked toward the fire.

Graham was relieved. He was also embarrassed because he had left the Colt revolver in his pack. He should have had it with him at all times. If someone tried to ambush him, he would be unprepared.

"I'm so glad to see you!" Graham said.

"Same here."

"What are you doing this far upriver at night?"

"Looking for you."

Why would Rides Alone be searching for me? he wondered.

"Will you share this fish with me? There's plenty for both of us," Graham said.

Rides Alone nodded and sat. Graham pulled the stick from the soft earth and repositioned it over the fire.

"You did not make spiritual journey at Annáshisee," Rides Alone said after Graham was seated.

"How did you know that's where I was headed?"

"Makawee said you go back to your time," he said. "You were angry and left in hurry."

As he looked at the Crow warrior's face in the firelight, he realized Makawee wasn't the only person to whom he owed an apology. Rides Alone was a good friend. Graham had abandoned both ten days earlier. He felt ashamed.

"I'm sorry. I was wrong to leave without saying goodbye."

Graham paused.

"I didn't want to stay after Long Horse committed Makawee to Black Hawk."

Rides Alone stared at the young man sitting by the fire. "You broke promise."

These words stung. Graham remembered the exchange between the two friends when they were hunting bison in the Little Bighorn Valley a month earlier. Rides Alone had advised him not to give up. He challenged Graham to fight for Makawee, and Graham committed to doing just that. Instead, he had turned and fled. He had broken a promise to himself and Rides Alone.

"Well... It was a mistake. I'm coming back, and I will fight for her. If she will have me."

Rides Alone picked up a stick and poked at the embers in the fire, pushing them under the fish. He seldom smiled but seemed especially somber tonight.

"I learned something two days ago. I share with you."

Graham clasped his hands around his knees and leaned forward. "I'm listening."

"I heard Among the Grass and Black Hawk talking. They are happy Sioux killed Little Wolf. Among the Grass says she can poison meat prepared for me. If I die, Long Horse has no heir. Black Hawk becomes chief."

Graham was speechless. They were glad Little Wolf was dead? And what could he say about a family member who would consider poisoning one of their own?

Rides Alone stared into the fire as he continued to speak.

"I found medicines of Among the Grass. Take them to Spotted Buffalo, medicine man in another village. She has bad medicine. She has killing roots."

Killing roots!? The midwife has poison in her collection of medicines! Graham thought.

"Have you told anyone?"

"No. There is more." He put his hand on Graham's shoulder. "Among the Grass pleased she caused baby to come early. She wounded Makawee's woman parts so she has no more babies."

Graham stood and walked around the fire, trying to comprehend what he had heard. He pieced the broken English words of Rides Alone together. Among the Grass and Black Hawk had conspired for Makawee's baby to be miscarried by poisoning her. They had lost a baby boy, his only son. And Among the Grass had punctured Makawee's uterus when she removed the afterbirth to ensure she could have no more children. That would explain her bleeding and the comments of the doctor who examined her at Fort Parker. This witch had assaulted the mother of his child and murdered his son!

He clenched his fists as he paced around the fire. His shock gave way to outrage as he screamed into the darkness.

"Aaaaahh!"

The dark walls of Bighorn Canyon echoed his outburst... *aaaahh!*

"That evil bitch! I'm gonna kill both of them!" Graham kneeled and rolled his blanket. "If we ride hard all night, we can be back in camp by late tomorrow. When we get there..."

"Eagle Bear!" Rides Alone said, holding up a hand. "Oochia!" ["Stop!"]

Graham looked across the fire at his friend, who was standing with his arms folded on his chest. He ignored Rides Alone and snatched the revolver from his pack. He opened the cylinder, confirmed the weapon was loaded, then snapped it closed. Lifting his right arm, he supported the pistol with his left hand, aimed at a tree stump on the riverbank, and fired.

Crack! The .38-special hollow-point bullet zipped past the target into the river.

Crack! A bullet disappeared into the water.

This time, he cocked the weapon to minimize the trigger pull.

Crack! A third try. Another miss.

He lowered the revolver and used his coat sleeve to wipe his eyes, then raised the Colt to fire again.

A powerful hand gripped his forearm and pushed it down.

"Oochia!" ["Stop!"]

"Get away!" Graham shouted through clenched teeth.

Rides Alone squeezed the angry young man's wrist, loosened his grip on the gun, and took it from him.

Graham sunk to his knees and shouted at the moon. "Why? Why? What kind of god are you? What do you want?"

He placed his head in his hands and sobbed, heaving his chest as he struggled to breathe. Three years ago, he had traveled to this place to start a new life. It had started with such promise. Falling in love with Makawee was the best thing that ever happened to him. And now someone had poisoned her and taken their son's life. But that wasn't enough pain and suffering. The midwife had also taken away Makawee's ability to have more children. It was too much to bear.

When Graham raised his head a few minutes later, Rides Alone was standing by his side.

"Come. Sit," his friend said, placing a hand on his shoulder. Graham obliged, joining him by the fire. Rides Alone handed him a cup of water and encouraged him to drink.

"How can you be so calm?" Graham asked, after draining the cup. "Your aunt and cousin are trying to poison you!"

Rides Alone switched to his native tongue since Graham was fluent in the Crow language.

"Like you, I was angry when I heard these things. I had drawn my knife. I was ready to take both of their lives. Something told me to stop. A voice in my head reminded me that all noble warriors have daasátchuche — patience. I left camp and went to meditate. I considered my choices and returned with a better way to deal with these wicked deeds."

Graham wasn't buying his friend's solution, whatever it was. He gritted his teeth and glared at Rides Alone with bloodshot eyes.

"There's an Old Testament reading about 'an eye for an eye.' They should pay with their lives."

Rides Alone nodded. "I can understand you would feel that way. But, let me ask you. Do you want Makawee?"

Graham was incredulous. "You know I do! Why ask?"

"If you kill Among the Grass or Black Hawk, you will lose Makawee."

"How? Your people will understand they deserve to die after they learn about the evil things they have done...and plan to do!"

"Will Long Horse accept you murdering two of his family members out of revenge? Will he believe you did the right thing? Did you forget you are the baashchiile who got his adopted daughter pregnant twice before she was married?"

"But you are his son! Won't he listen to you?"

"It would be my word against theirs. One cousin against another."

Graham rested his chin on folded hands and pondered these words. Rides Alone was right. Killing the two conspirators seemed to be the only option. Now, he could see exacting lethal revenge could harm his chances of being with Makawee. He noted the contradiction in advice given to him by Rides Alone earlier.

"Wait a minute," he said. "You told me to fight for Makawee. That's what I planned to do."

"If you kill them, you will be no better than the people you despise. Violence is not the only way."

Graham was frustrated. He slammed his fist into the ground. "But we can't let them get away with this!"

"There is another choice. One that punishes them while gaining the approval of Long Horse to marry Makawee."

These words grabbed Graham's attention. "I'm listening!"

"If my father is to take action against his sister-in-law and nephew, he needs something more than accusations. We need evidence, just like in the white man's court of law." Rides Alone pulled a small elk-hide bag from beneath his tunic and held it in his palm. "I have evidence."

Curious, Graham accepted the bag. "Where did you get this?"

"It is a medicine Among the Grass keeps in her midwife's box."

He removed a brown tuberous root with slender rhizomes. "What's this?"

"Wolfsbane. Remember the strychnine white men used to kill wolves?"

Graham recalled the gruesome deaths of the animals who had eaten meat laced with strychnine. "Yes. I sure do."

"Among the Grass told Black Hawk wolfsbane is what she would use to poison me."

The visual of Rides Alone writhing in pain as he asphyxiated from ingesting wolfsbane was unsettling. He wondered how his friend could maintain his composure when he knew a family member had plotted to take his life this way.

Graham stuffed the root back into the bag and gave it to Rides Alone, who offered a second bag. After opening this bag, he extracted a clump of coarse, dried leaves. Lavender flecks of flowers were mixed with light-green leaves. He placed the mixture on his palm and leaned toward the fire.

"And this?"

"Pennyroyal. Smell."

Graham held the herb to his nose. It had a minty aroma.

"A poison?"

"Not in small doses. But if a woman drank pennyroyal tea over many days while pregnant..."

It took a few seconds for Graham to realize what Rides Alone was telling him. When it sank in, his hands started shaking. Rides Alone reached over and took the bag of pennyroyal. Graham took several deep breaths to compose himself.

"This is what Among the Grass gave to Makawee for one week. It caused the baby to come early," Rides Alone said. "Evidence."

After a moment, Graham turned to his friend. "What's your plan?"

"I am not an expert on these roots and herbs. So I stole pieces of the plants in the midwife's box and took these to Spotted Buffalo. He is a respected shaman and a medicine man from another village. He told me what they were and how they were used. A true medicine man would not have these poisons among his herbs. They are dangerous."

Graham nodded. He could see where Rides Alone was headed.

"We invite Among the Grass and Black Hawk to meet with Long Horse and Fox Woman. You, Makawee, and I will be there. Spotted Buffalo agreed to be an expert witness. I will tell my story of hearing about their treachery. We will present the evidence. They can defend themselves and explain their actions. And Long Horse will decide their fate."

"Do you think Long Horse will find them guilty?"

"My father does not tolerate dishonesty or anything that may harm his family."

"And what would be the punishment?"

"I cannot say. But I have heard of other cases. Those guilty of crimes like these were never seen again."

Graham wasn't sure what this meant, but he would welcome a camp without Among the Grass and Black Hawk.

Rides Alone picked up the Colt revolver lying beside him and handed it to Graham. He pointed to the fish. "I'm hungry. Let's eat."

Nahkash giggled as she ran through clusters of grass, the blades of the plants tickling her arms. Her mother kept a watchful eye on her three-year-old daughter as she foraged the vast open area for timpsila. Late June was prime season for harvesting prairie turnips. Makawee rested a willow basket on her hip and carried a stout, sharpened stick as she searched for plants with light blue pea-shaped flowers. After spotting a timpsila stalk, she dug around the base of the plant, exposing the roots. She twisted off a tuberous root the size of a chicken egg, placed it in the basket, and put the soil back around the mature stalk. This allowed the perennial plant to survive long enough for its seeds to be scattered after the growing season. Her simple act of husbandry ensured there would be prairie turnips in future years.

"Nahkash! Don't wander too far. Stay close."

Makawee picked up the basket and moved downwind, knowing the most likely place for another timpsila plant was in the direction seeds were blown. A minute later, she was digging around a stalk and harvesting another tuber covered with a brown, leathery outer skin.

"I hear those taste good roasted," a man's voice said behind her.

Startled, she spun and wielded the sharpened stick as a weapon.

"Whoa!" Graham said, holding up both hands. "I didn't mean to scare you!"

Makawee's eyes grew enormous. She dropped the stick and ran to Graham, wrapping her arms around his waist and pressing the side of her face into his chest. He held her, delighting in the smell of her hair as he stroked the top of her head.

When she pulled away, she noticed Rides Alone standing a short distance away, holding the horses. He nodded but gave the couple time to talk.

She wiped tears from her cheeks before speaking. "I...I thought you had gone forever."

"That was my plan. But the spirits did not answer my petition. Rides Alone came to the Bighorn Mountains. He persuaded me to return — to fight for you. So, here I am. If you will have me."

"Yes! Yes! Of course! I'm so happy you are back!"

"Makawee, I owe you an apology. I was very upset the night your father made his announcement. I wasn't thinking straight. It was wrong of me to leave without saying farewell. No...let me correct that. It was wrong of me to leave."

"I'm sorry, too. I was conflicted. I needed time to think." She looked down at her feet and gathered her thoughts. "It's just that I didn't want our daughter to forget her roots. As a child, I was an orphan, passed along to several families. I don't want to lose this family."

Nahkash burst through a cluster of grass and grabbed her father's leg. Graham reached down and picked up the little girl, squeezing her while spinning in a circle.

"Oh, little one, Daddy's back!" he said, sitting down and putting her on his lap. Makawee sat next to them, the bliss of the moment reflected in her face.

Rides Alone approached. He punched the sharpened stick into the ground, then looped the lead ropes around it to create a picketing post for the horses. He sat across from the family before speaking.

"Makawee, we need to talk."

"What you have to say must be important. You seem very serious despite this joyous event."

Graham removed his hat and placed it on Nahkash's head. The little girl giggled when it covered her eyes.

"Listen to your brother, Makawee."

Rides Alone repeated what he had learned about the evil intentions of Among the Grass and Black Hawk. He described the midwife's poison and how she had wounded Makawee's uterus.

His sister sat motionless for a moment, then stood abruptly. She handed the reins of the horses to Rides Alone and yanked the digging stick from the ground. Without saying a word, she walked away.

Graham rose, but Rides Alone motioned for him to sit.

"She needs time alone. Stay here."

While Nahkash played with Graham's hat, the men watched as Makawee appeared to meander. She swung the digging stick back and forth, clipping the tops of the prairie grasses as she wandered toward camp. Suddenly, she raised the stick overhead like a spear. Shrieking, she sprinted toward the tepees.

Rides Alone realized her intent.

"She's going to attack them!"

He leaped onto his horse, wheeled toward camp, and raced to intercept Makawee.

"Ah, shit!" Graham jumped up. He wanted to join the chase, but couldn't leave Nahkash. He lifted his daughter onto the saddle, then mounted behind her and clenched her chest. As he urged Blade into a fast trot, he could see Rides Alone was almost in camp, but Makawee was nowhere to be seen.

"No! Don't let your anger take over! Don't be like me!" he thought.

Makawee dashed into the tepee and scanned the lodge. Among the Grass was bent in front of the cooking fire with her back to the opening. Makawee screamed as she held the pointed stick like a javelin and charged the midwife. Among the Grass turned, tripped over the stones, and fell backward. Makawee jabbed the crude spear at the woman. It missed her head by inches.

The midwife held her hands in front of her face, then rolled to one side as Makawee lunged a second time, putting all her weight behind the thrust. The muddy, sharp stick punctured the midwife's palm and passed through the back of her hand, pinning her to the ground. Among the Grass screamed in pain as she reached across her body and tried to pull her pierced hand free.

Makawee pushed the stick deeper into the ground by leaning on it. She picked up a rock from the fire circle and threw it at the wounded woman's head. It hit the midwife on her temple, causing a gash that leaked blood into her ear. Makawee continued the assault, picking up another hot stone and hurling it toward the woman's face. Among the Grass was writhing in pain, moving her head back and forth. The second stone bounced off the top of her head in a glancing blow.

As the enraged mother prepared to throw another stone, a hand grabbed her wrist. Rides Alone pulled his sister away from the screaming woman. He put his muscular arms around her waist and dragged her from the tepee. She kicked and fought his grip, but he was too strong.

"Let me go!" she screamed. Her eyes were red with rage.

A crowd had gathered outside the pole lodge. They watched as Rides Alone pinned Makawee's arms by her side and tightened his bear hug.

Graham arrived and dismounted, handing Nahkash to a village woman. He rushed to Makawee, looked into her eyes, and spoke in soothing tones while he stroked her hair. When she stopped fighting Rides Alone's grip, Graham nodded to his friend, who let go of her. She fell into his arms. Graham sat down and cradled her as she wept.

Rides Alone ducked into the tepee. Fox Woman followed him.

Among the Grass was lying on her side, gripping the digging stick, but she was too weak to remove it. Rides Alone touched the woman on her shoulder. He motioned he would pull out the spear. When she nodded, he used both hands to pull the stick from the ground.

"Ahhh!" she wailed as she clamped the wrist of her wounded hand.

The sight appalled Fox Woman. She kneeled and comforted Among the Grass while looking up at Rides Alone.

"Why did Makawee do this?"

"I will explain. She needs help. Did Spotted Buffalo arrive in camp?"

"I am here," a man said.

The shaman was standing with Long Horse at the lodge entrance.

"Can you help?"

"Where are her medicines?"

Rides Alone pointed to an area along one wall of the tent where the midwife slept.

Spotted Buffalo looked through her belongings and found a box of herbs, ointments, and cotton cloth. He kneeled by Among the Grass, who was moaning and rolling her head in pain.

"Fox Woman and I will take care of her."

Rides Alone exited the tepee with his father.

"Black Hawk will be furious when he returns from hunting and finds his mother was attacked. Come to my lodge. I want to know what happened," Long Horse said in a low voice. "If this was planned by the baaschiile Eagle Bear..."

"It was not. I will come to see you after I check on Makawee."

Long Horse spoke to the villagers. "Go back to your homes."

The spectators slowly dispersed. Rides Alone walked over to Graham, who was sitting on the ground, holding Makawee.

Graham turned her right hand over and showed it to Rides Alone. Her palm was bright red and dotted with blisters. In her rage, she had picked up hot rocks encircling the fire. She suffered from second-degree burns.

Rides Alone nodded before walking toward the lodge of Long Horse. This wasn't how he had planned to break the news of the conspiracy. He hoped it would not affect his father's judgment.

Makawee stared at the ground while tears trickled down her cheeks. "What have I done?"

Graham drew in a breath. He wanted to tell her the truth. She had exacted revenge on an evil woman who had aborted her child and left her barren. She had inflicted pain on someone who committed a heinous act. Secretly, he wanted to thank her. But he didn't.

"It will be all right," he said. "We're together now."

Inside the tepee, he could hear Among the Grass moaning. A dark thought crossed his mind.

I wonder if wolfsbane tea would help with her pain?

Chapter Twenty

Warrior Wedding

October 1875

S potted Buffalo stood at the base of the black cottonwood. A headdress of eagle and owl feathers cascaded halfway down the shaman's back. A painted otter-skin bag dangled from his neck by an elk-hide cord. His wrinkled brown skin and thinning silver hair were telltale signs of an elderly man, but his eyes sparkled as he gazed at the happy couple who were about to proclaim their love for each other.

Makawee held Nahkash's hand as Graham escorted his family to the tree. The bride was wearing a knee-length elk-hide dress adorned with elk's teeth, sky blue padre glass beads, and an obsidian turtle necklace. She wore a head wreath of braided sweetgrass decorated with sprigs of white yarrow flowers.

Graham wore a thigh-length buckskin jacket, jeans, and moccasins. His beard was closely cropped and his hair tied in a ponytail.

Long Horse and Fox Woman smiled, and Rides Alone nodded his approval at the handsome couple as they approached the shaman.

Spotted Buffalo started the ceremony with a series of lengthy spiritual incantations, most of which Graham did not understand. His mind drifted to the events of the past few months that had led to his wedding day.

Two days after Makawee had attacked Among the Grass, Long Horse summoned the medicine woman and Black Hawk to his lodge. The chief wanted to give the mother and son a chance to defend themselves against the accusations leveled by Rides Alone. He had asked Graham and Makawee to attend. Spotted Buffalo agreed to question Among the Grass and Black Hawk. He was also an expert witness on herbal medicines.

Dozens of villagers had gathered outside the tepee, awaiting the chief's decision. The allegations the mother and son had conspired to murder family members set the camp abuzz with rumors. If these charges were true, everyone knew the punishment would be severe.

Spotted Buffalo began the inquiry by showing Long Horse the wolfsbane roots and asking Among the Grass about their intended purpose. When she answered by saying she intended to plant them in the fall to provide color near the lodge, he challenged this by calling attention to their poisonous nature. He also discounted her response by reminding her Rides Alone had found the roots in her medicine chest, not with the bags of potatoes, carrots, and edible tubers.

When Spotted Buffalo asked her to explain why she had pennyroyal among her medicines, Among the Grass dismissively said she used the leaves for certain digestive disorders and headaches.

"Did you administer pennyroyal tea to Makawee while she was with child?"

"Yes."

"Why?"

"She was having belly pains."

The shaman erupted in anger. "There are safe ways to treat this affliction. This herb causes a woman to bleed more when it is her time each moon!"

"It depends on how much the patient consumes."

Spotted Buffalo asked Makawee, "How long did you drink the mint-flavored tea?"

"I drank several cups each day for at least a week."

The shaman nodded, then turned to Among the Grass. "Why would you do this?"

She was defiant. "I have been a medicine woman for twenty years. I am knowledgeable about every herb in my chest."

"Precisely," Spotted Buffalo said. "You realize pennyroyal causes a baby to come early. You know wolfsbane is a deadly root. And yet you gave pennyroyal to Makawee while she was pregnant and planned to give wolfsbane to Rides Alone. A false medicine woman like you should attempt to heal no one!"

"Don't call me a fake, old man!" Among the Grass said with clenched teeth.

"If you understand herbal medicines as you claim, there is only one explanation for your actions. You are evil."

Among the Grass narrowed her eyes. She ignored the shaman and turned her attention to Long Horse, who was listening intently to the discussion.

"You are a foolish man if you allow a white man to marry your daughter. Yes! I caused Makawee's child to be aborted! And I'm proud of it! Someone needs to watch out for the Crow people. We cannot tolerate our red blood being thinned by white men. Rides Alone may be your son, but he should never be your successor. We planned to poison him because our people deserve a leader who will fight for the Crow. My son is a brave warrior, unlike Rides Alone."

It was a stunning and brazen confession.

Chaos ensued.

Rides Alone sprang to his feet and shoved Among the Grass to the ground. The medicine woman cried out in pain as she tried to break her fall with her bandaged hand. She rolled against the wall of the tepee, causing the poles to creak as the lodge tilted to one side.

Black Hawk drew a knife from the belt of his tunic and raised it above his head. As he lunged toward Rides Alone, Graham tackled Black Hawk, hitting the warrior in the stomach and ejecting the knife from his hand. He grabbed the wrist of Black Hawk and yanked it behind his back. Placing both knees on the man's back, he pushed the tackled man's arm hard between his shoulder blades until he heard a popping sound.

"Aaah!" Black Hawk yelled.

Among the Grass lay on her side, moaning and cradling her wounded hand.

Long Horse rose and walked to the prone warrior. He motioned for Graham to release Black Hawk. Graham stood and backed away. Rides Alone gave him a nod of gratitude for saving him from being stabbed.

"Stand!" Long Horse ordered.

Black Hawk held his right arm close to his body, protecting his dislocated shoulder. He used his good arm to help his mother to her feet.

The chief shook his head as he spoke to the disgraced mother and son. "You have brought this pain onto yourselves. What you did was shameful. You are not worthy of staying with my people. I banish you from this village. I will send word to the other villages of your crimes. You are not welcome anywhere among the Crow. You have until sundown to pack your things and leave."

It was an odd feeling watching Among the Grass and Black Hawk exit the lodge. Graham felt no pity. They deserved this punishment. He was simply relieved he could soon marry Makawee.

"Eagle Bear, I was mistaken," Long Horse said after the conspirators had left. "I did not consider you worthy of Makawee. You met all obligations and paid the bride price. You have been honest and loyal to our family. We will plan a wedding suitable for a warrior."

Graham snapped back to the present, to his wedding, as the shaman continued to speak.

"... and so, we will observe a moment of silence to remember those who are not with us today. Makawee, do you wish to mention any family?"

"I would like to honor my parents, who both died of rotting face sickness when I was an infant."

"And Eagle Bear?"

"I also want to honor my mother and father."

"Are they still living?"

"They are... They will be... I mean, no. They are not."

This odd response baffled Spotted Buffalo, but he proceeded with the ceremony.

"Anyone else to be remembered?"

"Little Wolf, son of Long Horse and Fox Woman. Brother of Rides Alone," Makawee said.

Fox Woman bowed her head and wiped tears from her eyes. It was a touching tribute to her youngest son, who was killed by Sioux.

"Nahsa Eish, also known as Small Heart, son of Makawee and Eagle Bear," Graham said, looking at the tree limb above them where they had placed the aborted fetus several years earlier. Makawee smiled and squeezed his hand.

"Place a stick on the fire for each person you have mentioned."

Makawee and Graham threw branches onto the fire, watching as sparks leaped skyward from the disturbed embers.

Rides Alone handed a folded blanket to the shaman. The Hudson Bay wool striped blanket was a wedding gift from Nelson Story, owner of the trading post that operated at the Crow Agency. When Story had heard Graham was getting married, he presented the handsome blanket with red, yellow, and black stripes. The successful entrepreneur also instructed Uriah Brown to pay for the groom to be fitted by a tailor in Bozeman for a suit. Graham eschewed formal wear for a fringed buckskin jacket he saw in the display window. It was something he would use for many years beyond his wedding day.

Spotted Buffalo walked behind the couple, unfolded the blanket, and draped it over their shoulders. Graham and Makawee clutched the edges and pulled until it enveloped them.

"Each of you will become the shelter for the other. You will provide warmth for one another. You will feel no loneliness. Yesterday, you were two people. But now you share one life."

The shaman retrieved a smudging stick from his pocket and lit it from the fire. He waved the smoldering grass as he walked around the couple and blessed their union.

"May your hands be clean, so you create wondrous things. May your feet be strong, so you travel to fabulous places. May your hearts be pure, so you are guided on the right path. May your tongue be straight, so you speak in truth. May your eyes be clear, so you see what is really there."

Spotted Buffalo set down the smudging stick.

"I understand Eagle Bear and Makawee would like to seal their commitment to one another." He stepped aside and invited the couple to the base of the tree behind him.

Graham fetched a pocketknife from his jeans and whittled a shape into the thick bark. The new design featured an arrow which pierced the center of the heart he had carved when Nahsa Eish died.

"I believe a white preacher man says something at the end of a wedding ceremony. I will use it now." Spotted Buffalo's eyes twinkled. "You may kiss the bride."

Graham grinned. He turned to face Makawee, pulling the blanket with him as they became tightly wrapped in a woolen embrace. Makawee stood on her toes and tilted her head back. He kissed her lightly at first, then pressed against her soft lips. He wanted to savor every part of this defining moment in their lives.

A little over three years since Graham Davidson had returned to Makawee, they were finally married.

Rides Alone led the newlyweds to the far end of the village after the wedding ceremony. He pointed to a tilted conical lodge. Someone had set up the tepee along the Bighorn River between two clusters of tightly bunched cottonwood trees.

"Ashé," ["Home"] he said.

Graham stared at the beautiful tepee made from slender lodgepole pines. Tanned buffalo skins stitched together in semicircular shapes were draped across the poles. The light-colored skins of the lodge reflected the rays of the setting sun. The unblemished hides meant someone had erected this tepee for the first time. He could see shadows of a cooking fire burning inside, its smoke climbing lazily into the sky.

"This is ours?"

"A gift from the village. The people are happy the evil medicine woman is gone."

Makawee took Nahkash's hand, walked to the entrance, and lifted the flap covering the opening. She peeked, then turned and smiled.

"It's wonderful! There are hides, blankets, and a willow-rod backrest."

"We can't thank you enough. Please let the others know how much we appreciate it," Graham said.

"You tell them. Your family is part of our village now. And you are my brother."

He briefly hugged Rides Alone, who was bewildered by the gesture. After Graham stepped back, Rides Alone nodded and walked upstream toward his lodge.

"Come see!" Makawee said, poking her head outside.

Graham ducked inside and waited for his eyes to adjust to the low light. The tepee had ample room for six people. It was more than adequate for a family of three. One of the village women had suspended a cooking pot above the fire. A pleasing aroma from the elk stew filled the lodge. Someone had removed Graham's possessions from his tent and placed them inside. The folded canvas tent and poles were lying along a wall.

After dining on stew and bread, Graham and Makawee put Nahkash to bed. Graham fetched an armload of firewood and rekindled the fire. The newlyweds sat on a bison hide and shared the wool blanket used in their wedding a few hours earlier.

"I thought it was a beautiful ceremony," Graham said while rubbing Makawee's back.

"Me, too." She paused before asking, "Are you willing to admit I was right?"

Graham turned toward her.

"Right about what?"

"All you required was daasátchuche. It took time, but now we are together."

"Patience? Well, Mrs. Davidson, I disagree. I had to buy seven horses — and steal three. I had to work for months apart from you and Nahkash. Black Hawk almost stole you as his bride because of his ambition to be a chief. After years of fighting for you, I was close to leaving forever when I visited the Medicine Wheel. If you call that patience..."

Makawee interrupted him by placing her finger on his lips. She leaned over and kissed him.

"Was it worth the wait?" she asked, getting onto her knees and straddling his thighs.

"You're damned right it was!"

She pushed him down and unbuttoned his shirt, massaging his chest for a minute before lying on top of him. As they kissed, his hands slid under her dress. He pushed it over her hips and caressed her smooth buttocks. She stood and undressed while he took off his jeans. They lay back down and faced each other, their fingers exploring and fondling.

When he tenderly stroked her between the legs, she became wet with anticipation. She grabbed his hips and pulled him closer. He responded by getting on his knees. He gently lowered himself on top of her, feeling her soft breasts press against him.

As he slowly entered her, she flexed her hips, which added to his sensual pleasure.

"Diiawachisshik," ["I love you"] she whispered in his ear.

"Diiawachisshik."

After making love, they lay beneath the wool blanket. Makawee put her head on his chest and draped her arm across his stomach. He rubbed her back with one hand and caressed her hair with the other until she drifted off to sleep.

Graham stared at the smoke hole at the apex of the pole lodge. The opening framed a cluster of stars in the cloudless October sky. His daughter was sleeping nearby. The love of his life was by his side — and would be there "so long as they both shall live." He marveled at the tranquility inside and outside their shelter on this autumn evening.

It would not last.

A short ride to the east, where a small waterway snaked its way north past ancient buttes and deep ravines, a storm was brewing. In eight months, a clash between armies and warriors would erupt in the valley of the Little Bighorn. There was nothing Graham could do to stop it. But he could certainly avoid the bloody battlefield.

At least, that was what he hoped.

Chapter Twenty-One

Eagle Scout

April 1876

A chorus of voices echoed against the wooden walls and floor of the room at the Crow Agency. The cacophony of English and Apsáalooke made it difficult to hear unless the listener leaned toward the person speaking. Two rows of Windsor chairs and a desk faced the center at one end. Benches were lined up at the other end. The exhaust pipe of a potbelly stove extended upward from the top cook plate and exited near the ceiling. Muted sunlight from the mid-April day filtered through the smudged glass of a double-hung window.

Graham, Rides Alone, and Long Horse entered just before ten o'clock. While his father-in-law and brother-in-law greeted other Crow leaders, Graham sat on a back bench and scanned the room. He considered the invitation that had brought these groups together.

Mitch Bouyer had visited the camp of Long Horse two days earlier. Colonel Gibbon, commander of the Montana Military District, had tasked Bouyer with sending word of a council to discuss a campaign against the Sioux. Gibbon requested all chiefs and leaders to attend. It was convenient for them to come since the Crow bands had moved close to the agency in anticipation of receiving their annuities.

When his friend Mitch had relayed the news, Rides Alone was eager to take part in the council. He had been looking for a way to avenge Little Wolf's death but could not find a vulnerable Sioux camp to attack. He had confided in Graham that if the government did not act against the encroaching enemy soon, he would strike on his own.

Long Horse was also amenable to hearing what the army leader had to say. It had been a long, hard winter. The previous year's annuities had been exhausted by early February. The bison herds had continued to dwindle, and the chief had to sell ponies to buy bacon and flour. It was a humiliating experience for a man who had always provided for his family by hunting. Someone had to stop the Sioux from trespassing on Crow lands, stealing their horses, and killing the remaining bison.

The attendees had segregated into whites and Crow. Military officers and government officials were milling about on the far side of the room, while the Crow chiefs and leaders conversed in small groups on the benches. A young officer noticed Graham sitting alone in the back.

"Hello. Lieutenant James Bradley of the Seventh US Infantry," the soldier said, offering his hand.

Bradley was five-feet-ten. He had a short chevron mustache and dark-brown wavy hair neatly trimmed to cover the tops of his ears.

"Graham Davidson," he said, shaking hands with the lieutenant.

"I noticed you came with Long Horse. Do you live in his camp?"

"Yes, sir. I am married to his daughter."

"Trapper?"

"No."

"Miner?"

"No."

"Wolfer?"

Graham cringed at the word. The images of poisoned wolves flashed in his mind.

"Absolutely not."

The officer was trying to make conversation, so Graham offered a vague description of his occupation.

"I'm searching for a place to start a new life."

"And have you found what you are looking for?"

"I certainly did. I met my wife, Makawee, in Yellowstone Park."

Bradley nodded. "It's beautiful land. But dangerous, with hostile Sioux on the loose."

"I understand that's what today's council is about?"

"That is what we will discuss. Colonel Gibbon is leading a group of cavalry and infantry from Fort Shaw and Fort Ellis. We're headed to the Bighorn River Valley. We believe Sioux are in that area."

"That's quite a long march."

"Yes. It's been difficult on the men. But they're toughening up. The main reason we're here is to recruit Crow scouts. We're looking for men who know that part of the country."

"My Crow family camped on the Bighorn River. While there, we hunted bison and stole horses from the Sioux."

Graham regretted sharing this information. But it was too late. His comment intrigued the lieutenant.

Bradley placed a hand on his chin.

"That's interesting. You've lived in that area. And since you're married to a Crow woman, you probably speak their language."

"I do."

The lieutenant lowered his voice and leaned closer so Graham could hear him over the din of voices.

"If you'd like to make money, the army pays scouts thirteen dollars per month. Because you can scout and interpret, you would receive twice that amount."

Dexter Clapp interrupted their conversation. The Crow Indian agent had arranged for the officers to stay at the agency and was hosting the council. He raised his voice and asked the men to be seated. Rides Alone and Long Horse sat on the bench beside Graham. Once the room was quiet, Clapp welcomed everyone and introduced Colonel Gibbon.

The Colonel was a tall man with closely cropped hair, a short Van Dyke beard, and a bushy mustache. He delivered his opening remarks with confidence.

"I asked you to come here because I am making war on your enemy, the Sioux. They are also our enemy. They have been killing white men and your people for many years. It is time for this to stop. If you wish to join us, now is the time. If you want to drive them from your country and get revenge for killing Crows and stealing your horses, partner with us to fight."

Gibbon paused and waited for the interpreter to translate. He looked at the chiefs and leaders to gauge their reaction and was pleased when he noticed many nodding heads.

"I admire the Crow for their ability to see things a white man cannot. I need Crow warriors to look ahead and tell me what they see. We need to locate the Sioux so we can fight them. We require twenty-five brave young men. The government will pay them. They will get soldier's pay and eat soldier food. When we defeat your enemy, the Sioux, they can come back and rejoin their tribe."

Gibbon sat. The Crow murmured for a few minutes. A dozen leaders, including Long Horse, stood and said a few words. Sits-in-the-Middle-of-the-Land rose. He was among the most influential of the chiefs. He swept a corner of a robe over his shoulder to free his right arm. Everyone listened.

"The white man wants our help. Our people's land is here. The government set aside this land for the Crow. But our enemies do not respect this. They kill the buffalo on our land. They steal horses from our land. And they kill our people. It is right that the government makes war on the Sioux. You want our young men to travel with you, and I believe they should go. I cannot compel them. I can only say it is the proper thing to do. They must decide."

When the Crow chief sat, many leaders grunted in agreement.

Old Onion asked if they would force their young men to wear the white man's clothes.

Gibbon assured him they could wear whatever they wanted.

Iron Bull stood. He asked, "If our young men go with you and find a camp, they will bark like a dog. Will you fight any Sioux that are found?"

"We will. That is our intention," Gibbon said without standing.

Sits-in-the-Middle-of-the-Land stood. "You have spoken. We have asked questions. Now we must council."

"I will be here for two days. I need anyone who will join us to report to Major Brisbin before we leave," Gibbon said, pointing to a bearded officer sitting in the front row. "Most of you know the Fort Ellis post commander."

Rides Alone stood and addressed Colonel Gibbon.

"I will go. So will Eagle Bear."

"Who is Eagle Bear?" Gibbon asked.

Graham was stunned. He had not expected his friend to decide so quickly, let alone volunteer his services. Rides Alone glanced down at Graham, who stood.

"I am Graham Davidson. I'm also called Eagle Bear."

"Good. You men see Major Brisbin. Thanks for coming, everyone."

The meeting adjourned. As the Crow leaders filed from the room, Long Horse stood. He placed one hand on the shoulder of his son and the other on Graham's shoulder.

"I am proud. You can avenge the death of Little Wolf by striking our enemy and taking scalps. Come see your family before you leave."

Rides Alone nodded. The two men watched Long Horse follow the other chiefs out the door.

"Gentlemen! Come over and introduce yourselves!" Brisbin said from across the room.

The major was standing at a desk with the aid of crutches. Lieutenant Bradley and Mitch Bouyer stood beside him. Rides Alone and Graham crossed the room and shook hands.

"Mr. Bouyer and Lieutenant Bradley tell me you are well qualified to be scouts. I understand you know the country where we're headed."

Graham looked at Rides Alone, who gave a slight nod.

"That's correct. We have hunted in the Bighorn and Little Bighorn Valleys. We camped in that area last year," Graham said.

"Good. Well, Colonel Gibbon has placed Lieutenant Bradley in charge of the scouts. You will report to him. He will sign you up and make sure you get on the payroll. I'll see you in two days, when we head east."

Brisbin put on his slouch hat and hobbled across the room on his crutches. He paused when reaching the door, pivoted to face the table, and offered a last word.

"Perhaps you can convince others in your camp to join the cause."

After Brisbin left, Bradley answered the unspoken question the new recruits had about the major.

"Major Brisbin suffered an injury in the war and has severe rheumatism. He can't walk without crutches or ride a horse. An ambulance carries him to the field. But his disability doesn't slow him down. Less than a month ago, he led a two-hundred-man cavalry unit on a rescue mission to Fort Pease. I admire him greatly."

Bradley sat down at the desk and picked up a quill pen. He looked at Rides Alone before plunging it into an ink bottle.

"So, you are Rides Alone, son of Long Horse," he said, writing in the book while he spoke. "The government will pay you twenty-six dollars every sixty days. Do you need a weapon?"

"I have rifle."

Bradley opened a desk drawer and pulled out a bright red cloth armband. He handed it to Rides Alone.

"Tie this above your right elbow. If you don't wear it, the soldiers could mistake you for the enemy. Be here the day after tomorrow."

Rides Alone left the room with Mitch Bouyer. The two friends were smiling, happy to be on a mission to kill Sioux.

"Mr. Graham Davidson," Bradley said aloud as he wrote the white scout's name in the book. "We will pay you fifty-two dollars every sixty days. Do you have a postal address?"

"Uh...no. I don't."

"Any immediate family?"

"Makawee, daughter of Long Horse, is my wife."

Bradley recorded the information in his book.

"Why do you need to know?" Graham asked.

Bradley glanced up from his ledger. "If you are killed, we need to notify next of kin."

Graham gulped. This wasn't something he had considered.

"Do you need a weapon?"

Graham thought about his snub-nosed Colt. The revolver was useful only at close range.

"I could use a rifle."

"Well, I can put in a request, but we don't have any extra Springfield Trapdoors."

"An old Spencer carbine would be fine," Graham said. He had learned to fire the short-barreled rifle during the 1871 Hayden Expedition.

"I'm sure we have some of those." Bradley wrote something on a slip of paper and handed it to Graham. "Show this to the sutler. He will issue one."

"That should take care of it," Bradley said, closing the book and rising from his chair to shake Graham's hand. "See you in two days."

Graham exited the building and walked into the courtyard.

"Seems like we can't get away from each other," a familiar voice said.

A chill went up Graham's spine. He recognized the voice of Gustavus Doane. He turned to see the lieutenant leaning against a wooden support pole.

"So, you signed up to be a scout? I hope you do a better job locating Sioux than you did as a guide for Hayden in Yellowstone five years ago."

Graham grimaced at the comment, but he maintained his composure. Doane would not lure him into an argument.

"I'm trying to make a living, just like you."

"I have bigger plans than chasing Indians. Unlike career military officers who seek glory in battle, I have a talent for exploration. I'm planning an expedition down the Snake River later this year. All I need is Colonel Gibbons' approval, which I'm sure I will receive as soon as we dispatch with these hostile Sioux."

"Good luck," Graham said, donning his hat and walking toward the front gate.

"Davidson!"

Graham turned.

"When we get into a fight with the Sioux, stay out of my line of fire. I wouldn't want you to catch a stray bullet."

Six months. That's how long his marriage to Makawee had lasted before he was pulled into the war against the Sioux. Everything had happened so quickly. Rides

Alone volunteered him to be a scout. Graham couldn't refuse his friend, not in front of all the Crow leaders in the room. He would have lost the hard-earned respect of Long Horse if he had balked at enlisting in the army. Thirty minutes later he was on the government payroll, charged with scouting for the Montana Column led by Colonel Gibbon.

Graham shook his head at the irony. In his previous life, he had earned the Boy Scout organization's highest honor — he had achieved the rank of Eagle Scout. Now, the army had recruited Eagle Bear to serve as a scout. He was once again an Eagle Scout. He was no longer a teenager who excelled at earning merit badges and completing service projects. The army had hired him to find the enemy.

Graham rationalized he would not be in harm's way with Gibbon's forces. He knew they would arrive after the major battle at the Little Bighorn. He was deeply disappointed about leaving Makawee and Nahkash for three or four months. After having working so hard to establish a home life with his family, he was now swept up in a major military campaign. The upside was that he would earn money for a role that was not likely to put him at risk. And he certainly needed the cash. When he returned, he hoped to convince Makawee to move to Bozeman, where he planned to start a business. Perhaps Nelson Story, the entrepreneur, would provide seed money to help him get started.

"What are you pondering?" Makawee asked, as she lay beside Graham in the tepee.

Her question snapped him out of his thoughts.

"Oh, just how lucky I am to have you and Nahkash."

Makawee rolled toward Graham and playfully stroked the hairs on his chest.

"You're not thinking about tomorrow when you and Rides Alone leave?"

"Well, of course. I mean, I need to make sure I have everything packed. It's going to be a long ride and..."

"And you won't be lying beside me each night," she said, finishing his sentence. She rose to her knees and tugged at his underwear. After he slid them off, she pulled the elk-skin dress over her head and straddled his thighs. "You need a memory to carry with you."

Graham marveled at the beautiful woman sitting atop him. Her black hair shimmered in the firelight. He reached up and touched her smooth, firm breasts, cupping them in his hands.

She responded by moving her fingers from his chest to his stomach, then sliding them to his groin. He was aroused by the sensual movements of her soft hands as she fondled him. A moment later, she leaned forward, and he entered her. She kissed him on the neck and moved her pelvis rhythmically.

Their lovemaking was unhurried, as they both sought to extend the time they were intimate. As their passions heightened, Graham pushed the pace. Sweat beads formed on Makawee's breasts and trickled down her stomach. He thrust deeper and with more urgency. When the crescendo came, a wave of pleasure swept from his groin to his head. Breathing heavily, he pulled Makawee down onto him and caressed her back. He could feel the warm air on his shoulder when she exhaled.

They lay silently in the dark, enjoying the afterglow of their sensual experience. Graham stroked her hair. He wished he could stay inside this tepee — and inside his wife.

Makawee turned her head and whispered in his ear.

"There's a memory to pack in your saddlebag."

Chapter Twenty-Two

Where There's Smoke

May 1876

R ides Alone and Half Yellow Face eased their horses down the ravine, guiding them in a zigzag pattern to lessen the stress on the forelegs of their mounts. Rides Alone slid off his horse and reported to Lieutenant Bradley.

"Large Sioux camp. Come see."

"Sergeant Crawford!" Bradley called out.

A stocky man with a mutton chop beard came forward.

"Yes, sir."

"Take the men to the deepest part of the ravine and hide among those willows. I'm going to climb that hill and have a look. Graham, come with me."

The men urged their horses up the grassy knoll with Half Yellow Face in the lead. When they neared the summit, they dismounted.

"Hold the horses while we take a peek," Bradley ordered Graham.

He took the reins and watched as Bradley and the two scouts walked up the hill in a crouching position. As they approached the top of the ridge, the three men crawled on their knees and elbows. They disappeared into the tall grass at the summit as they lay on their bellies to peer into the valley.

It was a beautiful, warm afternoon in mid-May. Puffy white clouds scudded across an azure sky. It had been a month since the 450 men from the Montana Column under Colonel Gibbon had left the Crow Agency near the Stillwater River. Four companies of the Second Cavalry and six companies of the Seventh Infantry were presently camped along the Yellowstone, east of the Bighorn River.

Gibbon had successfully recruited twenty-five Crow scouts at the council meeting. Two days ago, scouts had reported signs the Sioux were close by, based on the number of pony tracks and recently killed buffalo. Lieutenant Bradley had asked permission to lead a detachment. He wanted to follow the tracks to see if they led to a Sioux village. Bradley had assembled a party of twenty-seven men for the three-day scouting mission — nineteen soldiers and eight Crow. The small group had taken extra precautions to remain undetected by the enemy. They used trees and ravines to stay out of sight and ran across open areas as a group. They had crossed the Rosebud and were now on the west bank of the Tongue River.

Graham watched impatiently as the three men on the ridge surveyed the land. After fifteen minutes, Half Yellow Face backed away from the summit, turned, and crouched as he scampered down the hillside.

"Lieutenant wants you to come," he said in Apsáalooke, taking the reins of the horses.

Graham nodded. He kept a low profile as he approached the top of the hill, then crawled on his elbows and knees. Bradley handed his field glasses to Graham.

"Take a look."

Graham gripped the binoculars, peered through the lenses, and adjusted the barrels to the width of his eyes. Steadying the field glasses with his elbows, he scanned the Tongue River valley. Looking to the left, he saw nothing unusual. Cottonwood and willow trees lined the banks of the river, which wound its way north and emptied into the Yellowstone River fifteen miles away. Panning straight ahead and looking east, he spotted hundreds of bison grazing on the verdant grasses flourishing on bottomland.

Bradley nudged him. "Look in that direction."

Graham lowered the field glasses. The lieutenant was pointing to the right.

He placed the binoculars back over his eyes, looked south, and used his forefinger to adjust the focus wheel. And then he saw it. Dozens of individual smoke columns drifted lazily skyward, coalescing into a thin white cloud that hung over the valley. He strained to see the familiar conical shape of a pole lodge, but the distant bluffs effectively hid the sources of the smoke trails. Graham felt his heart racing as he lowered the field glasses. They had located the enemy.

"How many lodges do you think are in the valley?" Graham asked.

"Can't tell. But I counted hundreds of columns. I propose we wait until nightfall. I think we can get much closer without being detected. A small group of three or four men could approach and count the tepees. That's the only way to know for certain how many Sioux are here."

"*Humph,*" Rides Alone grunted.

Bradley turned toward the Crow. "You don't agree with the plan?"

"Let us talk with Half Yellow Face."

"That's fair. We can't gather any more information from here. Let's retreat and..."

"Look!" Graham said, pointing to the valley floor.

The bison, which had been peacefully grazing five minutes earlier, suddenly became agitated and stampeded. Hundreds of massive bovids ran from the river toward the foothills immediately below their position. The rumbling grew louder as the herd galloped over the hill and headed straight for the ridge where the men were lying.

"Let's get out of here!" Bradley yelled, inching backward.

"Stay!" Rides Alone said, grabbing the lieutenant by his coat sleeve and pulling him down. The Crow scout got to his knees, waved his arms, and howled like a wolf. When the herd was less than two hundred feet from the men, the lead bison changed direction. The herd followed, thundering along the base of the hills until the noise gradually dissipated behind a cloud of dust.

"That was...impressive," Bradley said, wiping sweat from his brow.

"I agree," Graham said.

"Let's get back to the others. I need to discuss my plan."

They backed away from the ridge, then stood and trudged down the slope. They retrieved their horses from Half Yellow Face and led them to the tree-lined ravine where the detachment was waiting.

"Assemble the scouts," Bradley said to Half Yellow Face. "I wish to see what they think about my plan to get closer to the enemy village."

A moment later, the lieutenant explained his plan. Graham interpreted for the scouts.

"Ask their opinions. And tell them not to hold back. I need to know if it can be done."

Graham urged each Crow scout to express his opinion honestly. When all six had spoken, he looked at Rides Alone, who said nothing. He simply repeated his earlier grunt of disapproval.

"Lieutenant, it's unanimous. They say an Indian could not get close enough to count those lodges without being detected. There is no way a white man could do this. Smoke in the valley is evidence of a large village. Based on the number of streams of smoke we reported, they guess there are no less than three hundred lodges."

Bradley nodded. If this estimate was accurate, there were six hundred to eight hundred warriors in the camp along the Tongue River. As much as he would have liked to provide better intelligence, he couldn't risk being discovered. He called the men around him and announced his decision.

"Men, the good news is that we found the enemy. The bad news is they are much too numerous for us to attack. Our best course of action is to retreat as quickly as possible to our camp and inform Colonel Gibbon of this village. Feed your animals the last of the grain. We will proceed for a few hours and have supper, then travel some more before resting. But we must make haste in returning to the main camp. It will be a long night of marching."

Lieutenant James Bradley waited impatiently as the small boat made its way to the bank where he was standing. A soldier kneeled and used a long pole to propel the boat, but his progress was painstakingly slow. He was struggling to keep the wooden craft from being carried downstream in the swift current of the Yellowstone River.

"Remember, Sergeant, stay with the men until the Colonel decides what to do after he hears my report. I can't imagine he would do anything other than attack the Sioux camp. Tell the men to rest. I expect we will march all night once Colonel Gibbon learns of the large Sioux village."

"Yes, sir. I sure hope so. I'm tired of marchin' and campin'. That's all we've done since we left Fort Shaw two months ago. I'm itchin' for a good fight."

As soon as the dinghy bumped into the muddy north bank, Bradley stepped aboard and sat on the bottom. The soldier deftly pushed off toward the middle of the river. His passenger held on to the narrow gunwales and tucked his knees to his chest. The diminutive craft was just large enough for two men.

Fifteen tedious minutes later, the boat nudged against the opposite bank. Bradley leaped onto dry ground and hurried to the commanding officer's tent.

"Lieutenant James Bradley to speak with the colonel," he said to the sergeant guarding Gibbon's wall tent.

"Bradley! You're back! Enter!" a bass voice called from inside.

James Bradley removed his hat, pushed the flap aside, and stepped inside.

"Sir, reporting from the scouting mission."

"At ease, lieutenant," Gibbon said, as he pulled off his reading glasses and looked up from a map spread on a small table. "No need to be formal. Just get to it. Did you see or learn anything?"

Bradley summarized their venture. He emphasized their observations from the ridge overlooking the Tongue River Valley. Gibbon raised his eyebrows when Bradley reported at least three hundred lodges in the village.

"Sergeant!"

"Yes, sir!" he replied, ducking into the tent.

"Have all officers report here in ten minutes."

The sergeant saluted and exited.

"After your fellow officers hear your report, I will decide on a course of action. While we are waiting for them, I have a question. What do your Crow scouts want to do?"

Bradley replied without hesitation.

"Fight."

On the opposite bank of the Yellowstone, Rides Alone, Half Yellow Face, and Graham sat in the shade of a cottonwood tree and stared at the camp.

"Why take so long?" Rides Alone asked. "The enemy could move farther away."

"It's called chain of command. There's a lot to consider. Two other columns of soldiers are marching toward this area. My guess is the generals are trying to coordinate the movements among those armies."

"The white man thinks too much. Find the enemy. Strike the enemy," Half Yellow Face said.

Rides Alone nodded.

Almost an hour later, the trio stood when they spotted a boat making its way slowly across the river. The pole-pushing pilot had a passenger. A cavalryman was sitting in the craft. He gripped the reins of a horse, which was swimming behind the boat.

As challenging as it was for the soldier to direct the boat toward the opposite shore, the horse struggled even more. The animal tired in the swift current and started drifting away from the boat. Her owner desperately clung to the reins, but the drag of the horse nearly upset the boat. When they were a hundred feet from shore, the large mare pulled the soldier overboard. The desperate man surfaced and gasped for air. He grabbed her mane, and the horse pulled him through the water. Fortunately, they reached the opposite bank safely a few minutes later. Man and animal were exhausted.

"Whew!" he said, as Graham and Rides Alone helped him straggle ashore. "I sure hope we don't have to do that again!"

The boat pilot informed the sergeant what they had already surmised — the colonel had given the order to attack. Except for one company assigned to guard the camp, the army would cross the river. The cavalry would go first, followed by the infantry. This operation would take most of the day since only two small boats were available. Once everyone had traversed to the south side, they would march to the Tongue River.

Rides Alone interpreted the news for Half Yellow Face, who smiled broadly and ran toward the area where the Crow scouts were resting. Shouts and shrieks of joy erupted from the Crow contingent. They broke into a war song and danced, holding their weapons high above their heads.

"Sounds like our friends are happy about the news," Graham said.

"Yes. We are," Rides Alone said.

The soldiers in Bradley's detachment were also jubilant. They slapped one another's backs and joked about who would be the first one to kill a Sioux. The consensus seemed to be the quicker they fought and defeated these heathen Indians, the sooner they could return home.

The exuberance on both sides of the Yellowstone River dissipated over the next three hours.

Only ten horses and riders crossed safely in the first hour. Several times, the horseman and pilot nearly drowned when the boat capsized or the animal was carried downstream before being lassoed and dragged to shore. The results were no better during the next sixty minutes. Of the eight horses that attempted the crossing, one drowned. When three horses drowned and two soldiers had to be rescued in the third hour, it was clear the plan for the Montana Column to cross the river was not working. More horses and possibly some men could be lost. And it would take days, not hours, for the army to reach the other side.

Word finally came from an exhausted boat pilot that Colonel Gibbon had abandoned the river crossing. He gave orders for everyone on the opposite bank to recross the river. There would be no attack on the Sioux camp — at least not today.

As Graham stepped onto a boat to be ferried across the river, he noted the faces of the Crow scouts. They were crestfallen at not being able to attack their hated enemy. They were also angry and disgruntled. How could the simple act of crossing a stream prevent a large army from advancing toward the enemy? As if to prove a point, the Crow did not wait. One-by-one, they entered the river, grabbed their horse by its withers, and swam with their mounts across the stream. They made it look effortless.

It was dark when all the men and horses had recrossed the river. Since it was a clear sky and the soldiers had taken down and packed the tents, the army bivouacked for the night. They would continue the slow march down the Yellowstone in the morning.

Graham walked down to the river to brush his teeth with a chew stick after dinner. Lieutenant Bradley was standing on the bank and peering across the swollen Yellowstone.

"Look."

The lieutenant pointed to the large open area on the opposite bank where the scouting detachment had waited only hours before.

Four dozen Sioux warriors were in plain view. They had built fires and were cooking meat from a freshly killed bison. It seemed they were thumbing their noses at a white man's army that didn't have the skills or courage to cross a river and fight.

"Their camp is safe for now. But they can't hide. We will find them again. And when we do, it will be a helluva fight."

The lieutenant was right. There would be a battle.

But the young officer couldn't have imagined the outcome.

General Alfred Terry stroked his long, bushy goatee and scanned the grassland along the riverbank while standing in the pilothouse of the *Far West*. When the shallow draft steamboat had arrived a few miles east of the mouth of the Rosebud on June 21, Terry had ordered the captain to moor on the south bank of the Yellowstone River. A courier reported the Seventh Cavalry had just arrived. Terry was eager to get the war planning meeting underway with his senior officers. Colonel John Gibbon and Major James Brisbin were relaxing in the main cabin. Everyone was waiting for Lieutenant Colonel George Custer.

Just before two o'clock, Custer walked up the gangway. The self-confident officer took the steps to the cabin deck two at a time. He paused at the top of the stairs to salute his commanding officer. Terry returned his salute and led Custer to the central hallway between two rows of cabins. Gibbon and Brisbin were leaning over a long table covered with maps and charts. The officers exchanged cursory greetings before Terry got down to business.

"Gentlemen, have a seat. We have a lot to discuss."

The three officers each pulled up a chair. The general remained standing as he explained his plan, using a map to show key waterways and troop movements as he spoke.

"Based on Captain Reno's scouting mission and reports from our Crow scouts, we can say with certainty the hostiles are on the headwaters of the Rosebud, the Bighorn, or the Little Bighorn."

He pointed to each of the rivers on the map.

"Since we do not know their exact location, I propose the following. The Seventh Cavalry will seek the Indians by riding up the Rosebud. If no hostiles are found, the Seventh will continue to the Little Bighorn. Meanwhile, Colonel Gibbon's Montana Column will march up the Yellowstone to the mouth of the Bighorn, where the *Far West* will ferry his troops to the south side of the river. They will travel up the Bighorn to the Little Bighorn and prevent any Indians from escaping. One of your armies will surely encounter the enemy. Although we have not heard from General Crook's Wyoming Column, I expect he is marching from the south as we speak. He will prevent any escape in that direction. With a bit of luck, he may even join in the fight."

General Terry sat in a chair at the head of the table. He placed his arms on the table and interlocked his fingers.

"What do you think?"

"I think it's a splendid plan," Custer said immediately.

"Of course you would say that," Gibbon said. "The Seventh can travel a lot faster. Major Brisbin's cavalry can cover ground quickly. But I also have six companies of infantry. It's obvious who is likely to engage with the enemy first."

"Yes, that's true. That's part of the strategy. Custer's cavalry has a large mobile force that can strike the enemy. Colonel Gibbon — your column serves as the smaller blocking force. They are equally important."

Brisbin shifted in his chair to relieve the pain in his arthritic joints. "With all due respect, sir," he said to Colonel Gibbon. "If Custer is most likely to engage the Sioux first, perhaps my four cavalry companies should join forces with the Seventh."

"Thanks for the offer, Major. But the Seventh can handle any Indians we encounter," Custer said confidently.

"Some reports estimate the Sioux village has over four hundred lodges. If this is true, then..."

"No help needed, Major," Custer said tersely.

Brisbin shook his head, folded his arms across his chest, and leaned away from the table. There was no sense arguing with the cocksure officer.

"Major Brisbin raises a good point. You may not need more men. But you might benefit from the Gatling gun battery," Terry said.

"There's no way I'm taking those mechanical disasters. I had a Gatling with me during the Black Hills Expedition, and it was nothing but trouble. They jam easily. The guns are mounted on enormous wheels that are hard to maneuver. And they have to be pulled by four horses. They will slow me down."

"You wouldn't need to take all three. Even one might prove valuable if the enemy is larger than expected."

Custer sighed. "General, if you want me to catch these Indians, I have to live and travel like them. That means fast and light. No Gatling."

Terry's face reddened, and his jaw tightened. He would not let his junior officer's insolence go without a reprimand.

"I don't want *you* to catch the Indians. I want *all of us* to catch and punish them. This is not your personal battle. Is that clear?"

"Yes, sir. It's clear."

Brisbin and Gibbon exchanged a glance. Everything they had heard about the vainglorious officer was true. He may be a damned good soldier on the battlefield, but to his fellow officers, George Armstrong Custer was often a pain in the ass. If they were going to defeat the Sioux, the forces of the Dakota Column and the Montana Column would have to cooperate. This was not a time to seek individual glory.

"Colonel Gibbon, the Seventh Cavalry is traveling into country unfamiliar to our Arikara scouts. Since you will travel known waterways to the mouth of the Little Bighorn, you will transfer six of your best Crow scouts to Custer's command. And make sure you select one or two who can interpret," Terry said.

"But, General, Lieutenant Bradley is in charge of our Indian wolves. He doesn't speak their language. How will we communicate with our remaining Crow wolves?"

Terry chafed at the slang Gibbon used when referring to the Crow.

"You will refer to these men as scouts, not Indian wolves, Colonel Gibbon. They have an important job, and we should give them the respect they deserve."

"Yes, sir."

"To your question about communicating with your Crow scouts, use sign language. I'm sure you'll figure it out," Terry said, waving his hand dismissively. "It's critical Custer has good intelligence from those who know the Rosebud and Little Bighorn Valleys."

"Yes, sir. Right away." Unlike his blond-haired, insubordinate colleague, Gibbon would not publicly question his commanding officer's orders.

"I'll send Mitch Bouyer and Bloody Knife to meet with Lieutenant Bradley. We recruited Bouyer as a Crow interpreter and guide. And Bloody Knife is our most reliable of the Arikara. I trust their judgment in selecting the Crow scouts," Custer said.

"All right, gentlemen. We have a plan," the general said. "Have your quartermasters get your supplies from the *Far West* this afternoon. We ride and march in the morning. Any comments or questions?"

Chairs screeched on the wooden plank floor as the officers stood and saluted General Terry. Custer opened the door of the cabin.

"Lieutenant Colonel!" Gibbon called out.

Custer stopped and turned around.

"If you arrive at the village first, wait a short while. Give my men from the Montana Column a chance to fight. They deserve it."

George Armstrong Custer smirked. He donned a slouch hat and disappeared from the doorway. The three officers heard Custer laughing as he scampered down the stairs to the main deck and hurried off the gangway.

The *Far West* nudged against the north bank of the Yellowstone River, its twin tall stacks billowing wood smoke into the early evening air. Major Brisbin hobbled down the wooden planks on crutches. Colonel Gibbon, Mitch Bouyer, and Bloody Knife followed. Lieutenant James Bradley saluted the senior officers as they stepped ashore. Gibbon continued walking toward his tent, leaving the other men on the riverbank.

"We saw your signal from the opposite shore. I understand you wanted to speak with me," Bradley said.

"That's right," Major Brisbin said. "This is Mitch Bouyer and Bloody Knife. They are two of Lieutenant Colonel Custer's scouts."

The three shook hands.

"We will transfer six Crow scouts from your group to Custer's command, effective immediately. You will work with these men on the selection. The *Far West* will ferry the six scouts and their horses across the river. Captain Marsh is expecting them aboard the ship within two hours."

"I'm sure we can identify six from our twenty-four."

"Lieutenant, my orders are to provide the six best Crow scouts."

"Yes, sir. As long as I have someone among the remaining group who can interpret."

"Your six *best* men, Lieutenant. If they have language skills, even better," Brisbin said, with a hint of sarcasm.

Bradley nodded. He could see from Brisbin's demeanor he was not pleased with these orders and wondered what was said at the meeting with General Terry aboard the *Far West*.

"I'll leave you men to sort this out. Report to me when the scouts and their horses are aboard."

"Yes, sir."

Brisbin limped toward camp, using crutches to provide additional support for his arthritic legs.

"Let's go to my tent. I have a list of the Crow scouts among my papers. We can discuss over a cup of coffee," Bradley said.

They stopped by the cook fire for a coffee and a chunk of bacon, then proceeded to Bradley's tent. The two scouts sat cross-legged, while the lieutenant read each name from the enlistment papers. Mitch Bouyer knew many of the recruits from his time with the Second Cavalry and interacting with the Crow at Fort Ellis. As Bradley read the list aloud, he placed a mark beside a name when Bouyer recognized the man as someone with a noteworthy reputation.

"All right, I have marked five names," Bradley said, after reading the last name on the list. "Half Yellow Face, Hairy Moccasin, White Swan, Curly, and Rides Alone."

Bradley looked up from his paper. Bouyer was talking with Bloody Knife in the Arikara scout's native language, explaining each man's qualifications and why he was an excellent choice.

Bouyer gulped some coffee, then asked a question.

"Who's your best scout among those remaining?"

Bradley knew the answer, but he equivocated.

"Well, it would be White Man Runs Him or Eagle Bear."

Bouyer nodded. "Summon the five men we selected. We'll ask them."

Ten minutes later, the recruits were standing in front of Bouyer, Bloody Knife, and Bradley. Mitch explained why they were here. He could see the excitement in their eyes. They would finally have a chance to strike the enemy under Custer instead of holding back for the perfect moment to attack under Gibbon.

"We need one more scout and are considering two men. White Man Runs Him or Eagle Bear. Who should go with you?"

"Déaxkaashe-Daxpitchée!" Rides Alone said immediately.

The other Crow nodded approvingly.

"His name in English?" Bradley asked.

"Eagle Bear."

James Bradley closed his eyes. *There goes my last interpreter,* he thought.

"I do not know this man," Mitch Bouyer said.

"He is my brother-in-law. We have hunted bison and stolen Sioux horses in the Little Bighorn Valley. He also speaks English."

"Can you ask him to join us?" Bouyer said to Bradley.

The lieutenant nodded and asked Rides Alone to fetch the white man scout.

When Graham arrived at the meeting site, he was puzzled. His friend had not told Graham the reason Bradley wanted to see him. He recognized Bloody Knife from their brief encounter four years earlier. And the Arikara scout seemed to recall him as well.

Mitch Bouyer held out his hand. "Graham! Graham Davidson! I haven't seen you since the mass wedding at Fort Parker!"

Graham shook the hand of the affable French-Sioux half-breed. "It's good to see you, Mitch."

Lieutenant Bradley explained Brisbin's order to transfer a half dozen Crow scouts to Custer's Seventh Calvary.

"We need a sixth scout. Rides Alone nominated you."

Graham was aghast at this turn of events. He was unlikely to see any fighting with Gibbon's Montana Column. But hundreds of Custer's men would not survive their battle with the Sioux.

"I said you are good scout. You know country. You speak Crow language," Rides Alone said with pride.

Graham cringed. His friend meant well by nominating him. How could he know the danger ahead?

"Is this true? You know the Little Bighorn and you can interpret?" asked Bouyer.

"Yes."

"Then you're our man!"

"Well, what do you say, Graham?" asked Bradley. "I'm giving you a choice. You can stay with the Montana Column and interpret for me. If you decide to stay, I will assign White Man Runs Him as the sixth Crow scout for the Seventh Cavalry."

The lieutenant seemed to signal from his words and body language he hoped Graham would decline. But Graham couldn't abandon his friend. He had to keep Rides Alone alive. He was partially responsible for Little Wolf's death at the hands of the Sioux. There was no way Long Horse was going to lose his only surviving son to the enemy. Not if Graham could help it.

"I will scout for the Seventh," Graham heard himself say.

Bradley sighed and pulled a watch from his trouser pocket.

"Very well. Rides Alone, please tell these men they have one hour to report with their horses and belongings to the river, where a boat will transport them to the opposite bank. Gentlemen, good luck. Hopefully, we will see you after a victory on the battlefield."

Rides Alone and Graham arrived at the river with fifteen minutes to spare. After loading their horses and gear onto the shallow steamer, they leaned against the railing at the stern. As the setting sun illuminated Rides Alone's face, the normally sedate Crow warrior smiled. It pleased him to be headed to war with the enemy. He would finally avenge his little brother's death.

The paddlewheel churned and slapped against the water as the captain steered the steamer away from the bank and headed across the river. Sailors had neatly stacked short lengths of dry cottonwood on the main deck — fuel for the insatiable appetite of the wood-fired boilers. A week from now, wounded men would crowd the deck. The *Far West* would be transformed into a hospital ship.

Graham removed his hat and let the cool evening breeze tousle his hair as the steamer chugged toward the southern bank of the Yellowstone. He marveled at the size of the armed encampment. Soldiers had set up tents, which stretched along the riverbank for a half mile. Smoke and tiny embers fluttered skyward from hundreds of campfires. As he listened to the muffled voices of men laughing and talking, he wondered how many would return home, how many would be injured and placed on this ship, and who would be buried where they fell.

Now that he was a scout for the Seventh Cavalry, Graham had a singular goal. Return home safely with Rides Alone.

Chapter Twenty-Three

Bloody Greasy Grass

June 1876

T he color sergeant plunged the staff of Custer's regimental flag into the soft earth, then used both hands to push it deeper into the ground. He stepped back to make sure it was parallel to the pole holding up the commanding officer's tent. A light evening breeze lifted the swallow-tailed flag, revealing a design of equal horizontal stripes of red over blue with two crossed white sabers in the center. Satisfied he had secured the guidon, the regimental standard-bearer headed to his bivouac, eager to grab a meal of hardtack and bacon. He was looking forward to getting some sleep after a hard day's march up Rosebud Creek.

George Armstrong Custer stepped out of his tent. He was wearing a fringed buckskin jacket over a dark blue blouse with wide collars. His buckskin pant legs covered the tops of his dusty boots. He smoothed his reddish-blond hair with his hand before donning a gray broad-brimmed hat. Custer was still getting accustomed to short hair. At the colonel's request, a barber had cut off his curly locks at Fort Lincoln. He didn't know how long he would be chasing Indians. Short hair would be more comfortable as summer approached.

"Lieutenant Cooke!"

Custer's adjutant was writing notes under a nearby willow bush. He dropped his pencil and hurried to the tent. William Cooke had been Custer's administrative aide for five years. The tall man was distinguishable by his Dundreary side whiskers. The long bushy whiskers worn without a beard formed an inverted *V* which reached down to his chest.

"Yes, sir."

"Have the men eaten?"

"I believe so, sir."

"Good. I need to call an officers' meeting."

Cooke turned to summon the trumpeter, but he stopped when Custer spoke again.

"No trumpet calls. We don't know how close we are to the hostile camp. Find Reno and Benteen. Tell them to pass the word. I want every officer present — right down to the second lieutenants."

Fifteen minutes later, a cadre of thirty-one officers sat in front of the commanding officer's tent. It was unusual for all of them to be assembled in the field. They were curious to hear what Custer had to say.

"Men, I want to set expectations and discuss what lies ahead of us," he said, pacing with his hands clasped behind his back. "First, we all know the pack train has been holding us back. I'm going to assign a junior officer to make sure they keep up. We can't let seventy-five mules dictate the pace of the cavalry. But we need those supplies, and especially the ammunition they carry. So, expect some changes to our rear. Until further notice, no trumpets. Pass all orders in person. We don't want to give away our position."

Custer placed his hand on his chin and stroked his Van Dyke beard before continuing.

"Now, about the size of the Sioux camp. I'm sure you've heard rumors. I'll be straight with you. It's unclear how many fighting men we will face. My best guess is about a thousand warriors. Perhaps fifteen-hundred, but no more. You also may have heard the Montana regiment offered us a Gatling gun. Well, if you think a pack mule slows a cavalry, try pulling one of those heavy big-wheeled monstrosities."

A few nervous chuckles erupted from the officers.

"And one more thing. Major Brisbin suggested adding his four cavalry companies to the Seventh. I declined his offer."

A low murmur rippled through the audience. Custer's words were incongruous. They could face up to fifteen hundred Indians. But Custer had turned down a Gatling gun and additional cavalry!

"Here's why we don't need help. The Seventh Cavalry is the best fighting force in the army. Our men will defeat these hostiles. It doesn't matter how many lodges we find!"

Major Marcus Reno and Captain Frederick Benteen were sitting next to each other. Custer's two senior officers would have critical roles in the coming battle. Both men despised their commanding officer. They chafed at serving under the flamboyant cavalry commander. They had separately challenged Custer in the past for different reasons but ultimately followed orders. Reno leaned over and whispered to Benteen.

"If there's a man with a bigger ego west of the Mississippi, I have yet to meet him."

The forty-two-year-old Reno was of average height. He had short dark hair, brown eyes, and was clean-shaven except for a chevron mustache. He had become morose and pessimistic when his wife died after giving birth. It was no secret the major drank heavily.

"I will do whatever it takes to bring these hostiles to justice," Custer said, raising his right hand in the air for emphasis. "Have your farriers and blacksmiths double check the horses' shoes. We have some hard riding ahead. I intend to follow this trail until we encounter Indians. We will ride as far as horseflesh will take us."

Captain Benteen leaned toward Reno and responded with his own cynical comment.

"Easy for him to say. He has two horses. The rest of us have one."

Frederick Benteen was the same age as Marcus Reno. But he looked much older, with prematurely graying hair and a salt-and-pepper horseshoe mustache. His fellow officers referred to him as the "Old Man." He had commanded H Troop of the Seventh Cavalry for nine years and shared Reno's dislike of Custer, considering him a braggart.

"One more thing," Custer said. "The enemy will challenge us soon. It is important that we fight as one unit. You may not agree with all my decisions. Some have questioned my judgment in the past. But I expect every officer to follow my orders without complaint."

"Sir," Benteen said loudly, leaning forward from his seated position. "Are you accusing someone here of disobeying orders?"

The cluster of officers turned toward the senior captain, then back to the field commander. Almost everyone knew the two officers were not on good terms. They could feel the tension rise in the air.

Custer clasped his hands behind his back and looked at Benteen with exasperation.

"My remarks were not directed at anyone in particular. I am imploring everybody to follow orders. We should not waste time questioning authority."

Benteen leaned back and crossed his arms on his chest. He did not reply.

"All right, gentlemen. Let's synchronize our watches. It is 8:35 Chicago time. Make sure your men get a good night's sleep. We will be saddled by 5:00 a.m."

As the officers checked their pocket watches, a wind rustled the branches of the willows along the bank of the Rosebud. The sides of Custer's canvas tent billowed. The regimental guidon fluttered and flapped before being pulled to the ground, with the finial on the staff pointing away from the Little Bighorn Valley.

Lieutenant Cooke jumped up and retrieved the battle flag, brushing mud from the crossed white sabers. For the superstitious, the fallen guidon was a bad omen for the Seventh Cavalry and its commander.

The men were in a pensive mood as they dispersed to their bivouacs for the night. The giddiness and optimism of whipping an inferior enemy had dissipated. Reality had set in.

This was going to be a big fight.

Six men peered west into a valley in the first gray light of dawn. They were sitting on a divide between the Little Bighorn and the Rosebud. Rides Alone pointed to an area about twelve miles distant. Lieutenant Charles Varnum leaned forward and squinted, trying to visualize what his Crow scout had seen.

Custer had named Varnum chief of scouts. The Arikara had given the twenty-seven-year-old the nickname Peaked Face because of his receding hairline and large, pointed nose above a bushy mustache. The six Crow scouts from Gibbon's command reported to him, along with thirty-seven Arikara and two civilian guides who had been with the Dakota column since they departed Fort Lincoln.

Lieutenant Varnum left the main camp six hours earlier with Mitch Bouyer, Rides Alone, Graham, Curly, Bobtailed Bull, and Red Star. He had orders to confirm a sighting of the Sioux village by several Crow earlier. Now he was straining to discern what the Crow and Arikara claimed was there. He removed his kepi and retrieved a small telescope from his haversack. Extending the spyglass, he held it to one eye and pointed it toward the distant river valley.

He rubbed his eyes, blinked several times, and refocused on the horizon. Then he saw it. A group of tiny insects was moving along the river. Across the stream, faint wisps of smoke drifted lazily skyward.

"Are those things that look like ants actually horses?" he asked no one in particular.

"Yes. A large herd of ponies," Bouyer said.

"And the camp is on the other side of the river," Graham said. The white smoke was difficult to see because it blended in with the early morning clouds. But he had excellent eyesight and was confident what they were seeing was not an illusion.

Varnum nodded. He led the scouting contingent off the ridge and into a swale below the summit where Red Star was holding the horses. The lieutenant scratched a brief note and folded the paper. He instructed Red Star and Bobtailed Bull to deliver it to Custer. The memo stated a Sioux village had been spotted and that he would wait on the hill for Custer. The main column had ridden all night and was camped only a half hour away.

While Varnum wrote in his diary, the others climbed back to the crest of the hill and looked to the west.

"Little Wolf and I stole Sioux horses from this valley," Curly said in his native tongue. "I'm a better shot, but he was faster than me."

The young Crow's comment was unsettling to Graham. Curly had been best friends with Little Wolf. Graham recalled the day at Fort Parker when the two were vying for honors by throwing spears through willow hoops and shooting arrows into the air. Curly's recollection also brought back the painful memory of the night Little Wolf was killed by the Sioux when attempting to steal horses.

He wasn't fast enough that night, Graham thought. He glanced at Rides Alone and wondered if he was thinking about how his little brother's life had ended — at the hands of the Crows' hated enemy.

The dim light cast a shadow on the Crow warrior's face. It highlighted gray streaks in his black hair, premature for a man in his early thirties. His prominent cheekbones protruded like small, flat rocks as he stared at the camp and clenched his teeth. His dark eyes narrowed and glistened as he spoke.

"The enemy is on our land. I will avenge my brother's death."

Graham reached over and placed his hand on his friend's shoulder. Rides Alone planned to take Sioux scalps. He would be brave and perhaps reckless in his mission to exact revenge. Yet Graham was desperate to ensure his friend survived the coming battle.

Looming even larger was the pending death of hundreds of the Seventh Cavalry, as well as many Sioux and Cheyenne. What if he could alert the Sioux camp? Wasn't that the right thing to do to save lives? Or would it only delay the inevitable deadly clash of cultures? Even if he could secretly leave Custer's column and ride ahead to warn the Sioux, he would almost certainly be captured or killed before he said a word. Besides, warning the enemy would be treason. And he would betray the Crow people, who were now part of his family. He closed his eyes and wished for a solution to this Gordian knot.

A birdlike call snapped Graham from his thoughts. Curly had cupped his hands in front of his mouth and made a *caw-caw* sound several hundred feet from the crest of the ridge. He signaled for the others to look down the western slope.

A mile away, seven Sioux were riding toward them. Bouyer, Rides Alone, and Graham lay flat on the hill and anxiously watched them approach.

Mitch Bouyer scampered down the opposite side of the hill and fetched Lieutenant Varnum, who grabbed his carbine and followed the half-breed guide to the crest. Varnum laid the rifle on the grass in front of him. He motioned to the others to spread out along the ridge and form a firing line. The lieutenant held up his hand. He wanted everyone to hold fire until he gave the signal.

Everyone in the scouting party was thinking the same thing. The warriors below could not be allowed to discover the regiment. But if they started shooting, the gunfire from the skirmish might alert the Sioux camp.

A few tense minutes later, the mounted Sioux veered to the north. It appeared the cavalry had remained undetected.

Suddenly, the lead horse halted. Its rider pointed at the hill, waved his arm, and let out a high-pitched yell. The group turned and galloped west, receding into a ravine before reappearing on the opposite side. They soon disappeared from view. Something had spooked them.

Lieutenant Varnum looked behind him and motioned for the others to do the same. A massive dust cloud from Custer's regiment hung over the trail like an approaching storm. It was a telltale sign of an army on the move, and the Sioux had seen it.

Graham realized this close encounter made moot all options for an alternative outcome. Custer was hell-bent on pursuing the Sioux. They knew he was coming. Bloodshed was inevitable on this fatal ground.

Six hundred men took turns watering their horses in the clear, cold water of a stream that flowed west toward the Little Bighorn River. Custer had ordered a halt of the Seventh Cavalry's advance around noon on June 25. The junior officers and enlisted men awaited word from their commanding officer on his strategy for attacking the Indian village less than ten miles downstream.

Custer gathered his senior officers under a large willow along the stream bank to escape the midday heat. Custer's adjutant, William Cooke, took notes while Major Marcus Reno, Captain Frederick Benteen, Captain Myles Keogh, and

Captain George Yates listened. Lieutenant Charles Varnum had also been asked to attend because he was in charge of the scouts.

"I've given this considerable thought since we entered the valley earlier this morning. We've almost certainly lost the element of surprise. But the enemy has a weakness we need to exploit. We will use the same strategy that worked well at Washita in '68 when I defeated Black Kettle. The key is to capture a significant number of women and children from the village and hold them as hostages. If we do this and run off most of their ponies, they will surrender."

He looked at the officers and was pleased to see some nodding heads.

"In order for my plan to work, I'm dividing our regiment into three battalions."

Reno and Benteen exchanged a glance but remained silent.

"Major Reno, you will command companies A, G, and M. Captain Benteen, you will also have three companies — D, H, and K. My battalion will comprise companies C, E, F, I, and L. Captains Keogh and Yates will each command a wing of my battalion. And of course, Lieutenant Varnum will command the scouts. We will allocate the Crow and Arikara to those groups who advance to the enemy first."

He used a long stick to draw a map in the soft mud.

"Major Reno will lead the left wing. I will lead the right wing. Both battalions will proceed downstream until we encounter the edge of the village. One battalion will strike the enemy head-on, while the other circles around and attacks it from one side. The scouts' principal job is to scatter the pony herds. Our aim is to capture as many noncombatants as quickly as possible and force their surrender."

"And my battalion?" Benteen asked.

"Yes, of course. My primary concern isn't how many Indians are in the village. It's how many will scatter and escape before we can surround them. If they get away, we'll be chasing Indians all summer. Captain Benteen, your battalion will scout those bluffs." He pointed to the southwest. "We need to force any Sioux camped along adjacent streams into the main camp. If you find any hostiles, engage them and send word to me. If not, rejoin and reinforce the other battalions in the fight."

It peeved Benteen to be given this mission. It was clear Custer had orchestrated the assignments so he could grab the accolades of a victory. But he wasn't surprised. This was predictable behavior for the glory hound.

"Yes, sir," the captain said through clenched teeth.

"Questions?"

No one spoke.

"All right. Pass the word to your junior officers. We mount in fifteen minutes."

The battalion commanders saluted and walked back to their units.

"Sir, I would like you to speak with the senior scouts. It would be helpful for them to hear firsthand what you expect," Lieutenant Varnum said.

"Sure. Fetch them. Be quick about it. The Sioux may be packing up their village right now."

Varnum saluted and jogged upstream. He returned a moment later with Half Yellow Face, Mitch Bouyer, Bloody Knife, and Graham in tow.

Custer briefed the scouts on his plan, then emphasized their roles. Graham translated for Half Yellow Face since he did not speak English.

The Crow shook his head. "It is not wise to split your men. There are too many Sioux. We need to fight together."

Mitch Bouyer nodded in agreement. "I have never seen an Indian village this large, and I've been scouting for almost thirty years. I agree with Half Yellow Face."

Bloody Knife was silent. He was one of Custer's most trusted scouts. But Graham sensed the confident Arikara was uncomfortable by the way he shifted his weight from one foot to the other while looking at the ground.

The colonel shed his buckskin jacket and tossed it to Cooke, who folded it over his arm. Custer's neck flushed red in anger. He struggled to keep his composure as he contemplated the advice from the scouts.

"Let me be clear," he said. The colonel's voice grew louder as he spoke. "You will scout and herd the enemy horses. No one is asking you to fight. Leave that to me and my men. Since I will do the fighting, I will decide how, when, and where we will fight."

Graham translated.

"General," Bouyer said. "I'm not afraid of anyone. There's no way I'm staying back while the blue coats fight. I'm going with you."

"Very well. But can you take that off?" Custer asked, pointing to the half-breed guide's black-and-white piebald vest he wore over a soldier's blouse. "The Sioux can spot you from a mile away. You are a mounted target. Sitting Bull already has a bounty on your head."

"No. It stays. If I'm going to die, I want to wear my finest. Besides, you're easily seen with that bright red kerchief around your neck."

"When we get into heavy fighting, I need my men to find me so I can rally them."

Graham noted the cavalry commander had said *when*, not if, they got into heavy fighting. He wondered if Custer had a premonition of what would unfold.

"Then we'll both look good when we meet in Hell."

Custer laughed. Bouyer's comment broke the tension.

"One more thing. Remind the scouts they can keep any ponies they capture. That's all, men. Good luck."

"We need to move out ahead of the regiment. Bring the scouts forward," Varnum said to Half Yellow Face and Bloody Knife.

Graham was shocked when they assembled near the tepee a few minutes later. Half Yellow Face and Rides Alone had applied war paint. Rides Alone had three bright red strokes that started on one cheek, crossed the bridge of his nose, and ended on the other cheek. He had blackened his forehead and stripped off his shirt. He was in a warrior mindset.

Rides Alone handed Graham the strip of red cloth and held out his arm. Graham tied it above his friend's right elbow. He was glad Rides Alone did not eschew wearing the red armband. It was a critical identifier the wearer was a friend. In a few hours, Crow and Arikara would be among Lakota Sioux and Northern Cheyenne. In the heat of battle, it would be easy for a soldier to shoot an ally by mistake.

Two hours later, Varnum and a lead group of scouts came upon an abandoned campsite. Bobtailed Bull held his hand over the ashes of a cooking fire. He signed to the others that it was still warm. The group rode another half mile to the end of the site, where two tepees were standing. While the men dismounted, several Arikara scouts rode up to the lodges and ripped them open with knives.

The Sioux had constructed a burial scaffold in one tepee. They had wrapped a warrior in a buffalo robe and placed the body on a crude wood platform. A repeating rifle, bow, arrows, pipe, and elk-hide medicine bag were lying next to the deceased.

As they inspected the scaffold, Graham recalled the day they had placed Little Wolf's body in the cottonwood tree along the Bighorn River. Rides Alone snatched the Winchester and ammunition from the platform of the dead warrior. He scrutinized the weapon, compared it to his army-issued 1873 Trapdoor Springfield, and handed the single-shot weapon to a young Arikara scout who was armed only with a bow and arrows.

"Lieutenant!" Bouyer shouted from a small bluff.

Varnum mounted and rode to the ridge. The guide pointed west. A mile away, fifty or sixty warriors had kicked up a cloud of dust as they sped from the campsite toward the Little Bighorn. The Sioux were scattering.

The two men turned and galloped back to the tepee, arriving just as Custer approached. Varnum reported what they had seen from the bluff.

"No time to waste. I will not let them escape."

Custer barked orders in rapid succession.

"Lieutenant Varnum, make certain your scouts keep after those Indians. Don't lose sight of them. Lieutenant Cooke, burn that tepee. And where's Reno?"

"I'm sure he's behind us and will be here soon."

"Well, I have to get my battalion on the move. When he arrives, relay this order. The Indians are a few miles ahead and are running away. Tell him to overtake them and attack. He will have my support."

"Any word from Benteen?" he asked Cooke.

"No, sir."

Custer shook his head, turned, and headed across the stream with Mitch Bouyer.

Lieutenant Varnum motioned for Half Yellow Face and Curly to go with Custer, while Bloody Knife, Rides Alone, and Graham should stay with Reno.

Shortly after Cooke set alight the tepee and burial scaffold, Reno rode into the abandoned camp.

"I have orders," the adjutant said to the major. He repeated Custer's directive.

Reno nodded. He paused for a moment to watch the tepee in flames, then wheeled his horse and rode toward his command. He passed Custer's battalion on the way back going the opposite direction. The colonel's troops did not ford the stream. Rather, they stayed on the north side of the waterway and moved toward the bluffs. How was Custer going to support Reno's attack from the other side of the river? Perhaps Custer planned to cross farther downstream. Reno remembered Custer's admonishment about following orders without complaint. He urged his mare into a trot.

One fact was obvious. They had found the Indian village. And Reno had the honor of attacking first.

Reno's battalion forded the Little Bighorn at a well-used crossing that was three feet deep. As the last of the horses reached the west side, Graham, Rides Alone, and Bloody Knife galloped toward Lieutenant Varnum. Graham reported their latest observation. Varnum turned and rode to Reno with the news.

"Major, my scouts report the Indians we've been following are no longer retreating. They reached the main village and have recruited others. They are coming our way. Look!" Varnum said.

A cloud of dust was rising above the prairie, about two miles away. It could only mean one thing. Lots of men on horses.

"I need to report this to Custer," Cooke said. The adjutant had ridden with Reno since they left the lone tepee. He turned his horse, made his way through the other men, and recrossed the river. The lieutenant's Dundreary whiskers bounced against his chest as he galloped toward the bluffs and Custer's battalion.

Marcus Reno extracted a flask tucked inside his canvas cartridge belt. He loosened the cap, took a pull, wiped his mouth, and screwed it on the slender metal container. After returning it to his belt, he turned his horse to face the soldiers.

"Tighten girths!" he yelled.

"Tighten girths!" three company captains repeated.

One-hundred-and-forty troopers dismounted. After making sure their saddles were secure, the soldiers swung back onto their mounts.

"Advance!"

Moving in battle formation at a fast trot, the battalion crossed the open area west of the river. Varnum ordered his scouts to ride in the rear with the third company.

The size of the enemy became more clear as they drew closer to the camp. This was not a village of one hundred lodges. There were at least five hundred. It stretched north along the river as far as a man could see through the dust.

Two miles into the charge, the battalion came to a large bend in the river. A dense pocket of cottonwood trees and willow bushes filled an area where the Little Bighorn almost flowed back into itself as it meandered to the northwest. Major Reno saw the number of warriors on horseback ahead, assessed the strength of his troopers, and looked among the bluffs to his right for a sign of Custer's promised support. No mounted cavalrymen were coming to his aid.

"Battalion, halt! Dismount and prepare to fight!" he ordered.

The soldiers dismounted, and every fourth man led the horses into the cottonwoods along the river bend. The remaining troopers spread into a single line, each man spaced about three or four yards apart. Bloody Knife and Rides Alone handed the reins of their horses to Graham. The Arikara and the Crow joined the skirmish line. One hundred men began walking toward the village, firing as fast as they could reload their Springfield Trapdoor carbines.

No! Graham thought. *Rides Alone can't be fighting with these men! It's too dangerous!*

Graham accompanied the other horse handlers to the woods, frequently turning around and squinting through the smoke to see if the two scouts were still standing. As he reached the edge of the woods, he saw Lieutenant Varnum ride up behind Bloody Knife and Rides Alone. The officer tapped them on their shoulders and motioned for them to fall out of line. The scouts grudgingly obeyed. The skirmish line closed the gap of the missing men, who followed Varnum back to the timbered area where Graham held their horses.

"I need you as another set of eyes. Stay here and wait for orders," Varnum said.

The scouts were not pleased. They would not have applied war paint unless they intended to fight.

The soldiers advanced and fired at the village several hundred yards away. When a band of Sioux counterattacked, Reno ordered a halt in an area pocked with prairie dog burrows. Some men knelt and continued shooting. Others lay prone and used the mounds as breastworks. The Indians retreated when the soldiers wounded or killed four warriors.

Fifteen minutes later, the tide of the battle turned. Hundreds of Indians gathered their ponies and weapons. They rallied and joined the fight, becoming more aggressive when they realized the soldiers were fighting on foot. Some rode around the left end of the skirmish line. Soon they had encircled the aggressors.

When Reno became aware Indians were firing from the rear, he ordered a retreat to the trees. Some soldiers turned and ran, but the officers yelled for a disciplined withdrawal from the prairie to the timber. The troopers regained their composure and maintained a firing line as they made their way to the wooded area, their backs to the river.

When Indians started attacking from across the river, the situation deteriorated. All the battalion's horses were being held in a meadow near the water. Now bullets and arrows were raining on the troopers from all sides. Men alternated coming back from the firing line to retrieve ammunition from their saddlebags, as most had exhausted the fifty rounds they carried. Gun smoke and a choking dust filled the hot afternoon air. The sound of wounded and dying horses mixed with soldiers shouting and warriors yelling. It was impossible to communicate in the chaotic battleground.

Graham pulled his Spencer from its scabbard and led the three horses into thick underbrush. He tied the reins to a bush and joined the troopers who were protecting the rear of the battalion. Sioux warriors were riding along the river eighty yards away, firing or launching arrows into the trees. Graham cocked the carbine. He cycled the trigger guard down and back into place, aimed, and squeezed the trigger. He missed his target. Three more attempts. Three misses. He quickly discovered it was difficult to hit a man riding a horse. He looked down and saw his hands were shaking. There was no way he would hit anything unless he calmed himself.

As Graham took several deep breaths, a familiar voice shouted to him.

"Iichíile!" ["Horse!"]

Graham saw Rides Alone running toward him forty yards away carrying the Winchester. The Crow warrior's chest glistened with sweat. Graham rushed to the bush, untied the horse, and held out the reins. Rides Alone sprinted to the waiting horse but stunned Graham when he ignored the outstretched reins. Instead, he shoved his friend to the ground. The Crow knelt, lowered the rifle, and fired two quick shots. A man screamed and fell from his horse a few feet from Graham.

Rides Alone pulled a knife from his waistbelt, straddled the injured man, and plunged it into the side of his neck. Blood splattered onto Rides Alone's chest and arms. He let out a terrifying shriek while holding the knife high in the air. Grabbing the man's hair, he yanked the dead man's head up and harvested the enemy scalp. He held it above his head, then tucked it into his waistbelt.

Rides Alone dashed to his horse, mounted, and glanced at Graham, who lay dazed on the ground. Without another word, the Crow Indian let out a high-pitched yell and urged his horse toward the river and more incoming Sioux, firing his Winchester as he galloped away.

Graham was appalled at the savagery displayed by his friend. It was a side of him he had never seen. He would not soon forget the look in Rides Alone's eyes as he celebrated the death of his enemy. He would witness more brutality before the day was over.

A bullet zinged by Graham's head and snapped a branch behind him. He retreated to the edge of the woods where the two horses were tied. The chaos continued as men from the prairie side of the firing line poured into the timbered area, calling out the name of the fourth man who had been tending to their horse. Amid the shouting and panic, he heard someone say there was an order to mount.

A moment later, Bloody Knife came running and confirmed the rumor.

"Mount," the Arikara said calmly.

"Where are we headed?"

Bloody Knife swung into his saddle and pointed to the bluffs overlooking the river upstream. He turned his horse and rode toward the other end of the meadow at the edge of the timber. Graham mounted Blade and followed the Arikara scout.

Major Reno was on his horse but seemed undecided about what to do to save his men. He signed to Bloody Knife, trying to get the scout's opinion on what the enemy would do if they vacated the woods. Meanwhile, the Indians had taken advantage of the sudden lull in firing to draw closer to the soldiers.

As Bloody Knife was signing to Reno, a bullet struck him in the back of the head. Bits of bone and brain matter splattered on Reno's face as the Arikara scout slumped, then fell out of his saddle. His horse panicked and ran into the woods.

"Dismount!" Reno yelled.

Those who heard the command got off their horses. Those who were not within earshot asked one another what order had been given.

Graham dismounted and pushed Blade away so he could fire on the ever-encroaching Sioux. When his firing attempt ended with a click, he realized he had emptied the seven-round magazine. He dashed to his horse to retrieve the Blakeslee ammunition box.

"Mount!"

As Graham reached for his saddlebag, he heard Reno's voice above the din of shouting, shrieking, and gunfire. He swung onto Blade. A crowd of soldiers gathered behind the major at the edge of the timber.

"Any men who want to escape, follow me!" Reno bellowed.

Major Reno charged out of the woods and onto the prairie, retracing the path the battalion had taken when they forded the Little Bighorn less than an hour earlier. The men galloped across the open field toward the Sioux, who parted and fell back at the bold move of the approaching bluecoats. After Reno's men broke the enemy lines, the Indians regrouped and gave chase, attacking the fleeing soldiers from the flanks.

Reno desperately searched for a place to cross. He veered to the left and led the column to the river a mile and a half downstream from the original crossing. After hesitating, Reno urged his horse to jump into the water, which was four feet deep at this point. The queue to access the river grew as frantic soldiers sought to find a way across and away from the Sioux. It was every man for himself.

While the riverbank was only three feet high and gently sloped on the entry side, it was ten feet high, with a steep slope on the opposite side. A narrow ravine wide enough for one horse was the only way to exit the river and access the bluffs. While soldiers continued to jump their horses into the water, they discovered the constricted area on the east side prevented a rapid escape.

Most of the men forded the river and climbed out the other side. But not everyone made it. Some drowned when the swift current pushed them out of their saddles. Others were killed by the Sioux, who lined the riverbank and shot the soldiers as they awaited a chance to climb out. Still others were swept away when their horses were shot from under them. This was the fate that befell Graham.

Graham was halfway across the river when his horse screamed and toppled over, spilling him into the water headfirst. Graham surfaced but couldn't stand in the chest-deep water. The strong current pushed man and horse downstream, away from the pandemonium at the crossing. He grabbed the saddle horn and held on. Rocks battered his legs as he bounced along the river. He reached across the horse's neck and felt a large hole where the bullet had exited near the throat. Blood gushed from an artery. Blade was dead.

The noise of battle receded as he washed downstream. Graham scanned the bank for a place to climb out, but a long escarpment overhung the east side of the river. He wanted to save his carbine and saddlebags. Ahead, he noticed a willow tree had fallen into the stream. He kicked and pulled on the saddle, trying to steer himself and the carcass toward the half-submerged tree near a bend in the river. Graham strained as he tugged on the horn and spun the horse so its head faced upstream. With one last shove, he launched the carcass toward the willow and watched as its legs caught in the branches. The tree held, and the water flowed around the dead animal.

Graham struggled to keep his balance as he slogged to the willow-tree-and-horse dam below an earthen overhang. He stood on the upstream side of his dead horse and leaned on its flank, exhausted from the effort of positioning the carcass along the far bank. After taking a minute to catch his breath, he attempted to recover his carbine but discovered it was missing. The short-barreled rifle had fallen out of its scabbard. His saddlebag with the Blakeslee ammunition box was accessible. The ammo was worthless without the Spencer. The other saddlebag was under the horse. But he couldn't flip the heavy carcass over.

"Helllpp!"

A garbled voice called out from the middle of the river.

Graham looked upstream and spotted a soldier bobbing and tumbling as the swift current carried him down the river. He pushed his way through the roiling waters and stood where the end of the willow jutted into the river. He braced himself. A moment later, the trooper crashed into Graham, who clutched a stout limb while snatching the man's shirt.

"Grab a branch!" Graham yelled.

The desperate man flailed for a few seconds until he latched onto a sturdy limb. Graham dragged him toward the carcass. The soldier tried to stand but was weakened from his chaotic journey down the Little Bighorn. After much effort, the two men were holding on to the saddle, gasping for air.

"I thanks ya' for savin' me hide," the soldier said, after catching his breath.

"Glad I could help. I'm Graham. Graham Davidson. A scout."

"I be Sergeant Patrick Carey of Company M," the man said, holding his shoulder and wincing. "You can call me Patsy. That's what I was called as a lad in Éire."

"Are you injured?"

"Aye. But I be alive."

They could hear gunfire and shouting upstream. Smoke drifted downwind, creating a haze over the river. The pungent aroma of gunpowder permeated the late afternoon air. The noise seemed to have moved to the base of the bluffs.

"Whaddaya think we should do?" Graham asked.

The two men looked upstream at the cloud of gun smoke. They turned and peered through branches toward the Indian village downstream. The eroded escarpment overhanging the river concealed them from anyone riding along the east side. The willow tree and carcass kept them hidden from any Sioux on the west bank.

"Shite!" Patsy said, scratching the stubble on his chin. "What choice have we but to stay here?"

"I agree. If we try to leave the river, we'd almost certainly be killed."

"You have a gun?"

"Only my pistol." Graham wondered if the Colt Cobra would fire after being drenched. Luckily, it was lodged in his belt and had not fallen out during his raucous ride down the river.

"Ain't gonna kill many feckers with that," Patsy said. "Done lost my rifle too. I'm supposin' that's what we do, then. We wait and leg it up those hills after dark. I hope the boys in my company stay in those trees and do the same."

"How many did the major leave behind when he led the retreat?"

"Don't know for sure. Ten. Maybe twelve. What a buck eejit, the major! I was a goin' to get help from yer man when my horse got killed and I ended up in the drink."

"Yep. Same here."

Patsy held up his hand, signaling Graham to be silent.

A series of whoops and the shrill tone of an eagle-bone whistle grew louder as a group of horses rumbled upstream from the village on the eastern side of the river. Graham and Sergeant Carey got on their knees on the riverbed. The cold water rushed over their shoulders and around their necks as they pressed their backs against the wet clay of the embankment. A moment later, hoofbeats thundered overhead as the warriors headed toward the bluffs. When the sound faded, they stood and gripped the saddle.

"Night will come in no length, please God," Patsy said.

They stood in the river and listened to the gunfire and shrieks. There were two battles raging. One was upstream along the bluffs where Reno had led his men. The other was downstream, across from the Indian village. Graham knew what was happening at the second site. Custer and his battalion were fighting for their lives. It was a fight they would lose.

"I'm knackered. Watch my back while I take a quick kip," Patsy said. He draped his arms across the horse, laid his head on the saddle, and drifted off to sleep.

The sergeant's ability to nap standing up in cold water while a battle raged nearby amazed Graham. But he was not about to pass judgment. These men had slept fewer than three hours the past two days. Everyone was exhausted.

Graham was drained, and his nerves were frazzled. He focused on keeping Patsy from slipping off the saddle and waited for sunset.

As he stood chest-deep in cold water beside the slumbering sergeant, he noticed the water swirling around them had a reddish hue. His gaze shifted a hundred yards upstream. Three soldiers and four horses killed during the crossing had washed downstream. A carcass was stuck on a large rock in the middle of the river. Subsequent victims had stacked up behind the first carcass, creating a macabre jumble of bodies and horseflesh. Blood oozed from the mortal wounds, circulating around the rock and forming a crimson streak that meandered downstream. Greasy Grass was awash in blood, and the battle was far from over.

The gunfire from the bluffs became more sporadic as the sun slipped below the horizon. Hopefully, they could find their way to the regiment under cover of darkness.He draped his arms across the horse

Graham shivered. His body's reaction was caused by the chilly water and by the realization of how close he had come to dying. He thought about his mother and his commitment not to be with Custer on June 25, 1876. He had kept his promise. Fortunately, he had not been assigned to the colonel's battalion. But there was no guarantee he would survive another day with Reno's troops, who were surrounded and badly outnumbered.

He wondered what Makawee and Nahkash were doing while he was hiding in a river from thousands of Sioux warriors. And he hoped Rides Alone was still alive.

Chapter Twenty-Four

Shadow of Death

June 25, 1876

After digging in the hard clay for almost an hour on his knees, Graham looked at his hands. Pus-filled blisters had formed on his palms. His shoulders and lower back ached. He gazed at the lid of the hardtack box and shook his head. How could a battalion have only two spades, forcing the men to use box lids, tin cups, and knives to dig rifle pits and build temporary breastworks?

He was grateful to be alive. But he had moved from a valley with plenty of trees for cover to an open ridge. A few hours earlier, he'd had access to millions of gallons of fresh water. Now there was nary a drop. As Graham finished his breastwork by heaving two sacks of oats on top of the dirt pile, he considered the circumstances that had placed him on top of a bluff with no water and scant natural defenses.

Two hours after sunset, Graham and Sergeant Carey had agreed to make their way to the ridge. While there was no gunfire on the bluffs, they could hear intermittent shooting from the village. The Indians had built enormous bonfires and were celebrating their victories by singing.

They abandoned the fetid, bloating carcass and slogged their way along the muddy bank. Sergeant Carey led the way, scanning the east side of the river for a place to scale the steep embankment. After ten minutes of searching the slopes, they arrived at a tiny stream trickling into the Little Bighorn. A millennium of erosion had created a narrow path from the river to the top of the escarpment. The sergeant clambered to the top of the crevasse and cautiously poked his head into the flatland. Swiveling his head like a prairie dog, he looked in all directions, trying to discern if any Sioux were in the area. Satisfied, he scrambled down the narrow ravine.

"I took a quick gander. Ain't no one around. Let's crack on. Got your pistol?"

Graham nodded and pulled the Colt Cobra from his belt. He was thankful the Irishman couldn't see the revolver clearly in the dark. He didn't want to explain the snub-nosed weapon.

"Since you're armed, are you willin' to take the lead?"

"Sure."

"Grand. I'll be right behind you. If we see any red devils, we'll hafta leg it up the hill and hope we don't get shot."

That's a helluva strategy, Graham thought. But he couldn't offer a better way to rejoin the battalion on the bluff.

Graham climbed up the crevasse, with the sergeant following close behind. He paused at the top to get his bearings. They would have to run across a grassy plain for 150 yards to the base of the bluffs. A sparse assortment of trees and bushes grew on the slopes. This vegetation would provide minimal cover as they made their way to the summit. He glanced at his revolver. The .38 Special seemed like a woefully inadequate weapon.

"What's the story?" Patsy asked from below.

"Just making sure I know which way to run."

"Sure, look. It'll be grand. Give it a lash."

Graham took a deep breath, exhaled, and pushed out of the tiny ravine onto the grass, wet with evening dew. He sprinted toward a cottonwood while scanning the base of the bluffs for the enemy. When he got to the tree, Graham looked behind him. Patsy was running awkwardly, holding his injured shoulder close to his side. Thirty seconds later, the sergeant joined him at the base of the tree.

"Stall it. I need to catch me breath."

They paused for a minute. As Graham started his ascent, Sergeant Carey grabbed him by the arm.

"Shout somethin' when we get close. Wouldn't wanna get shot by one of our fellas."

Graham nodded.

Five arduous minutes later, they were lying behind a bush five hundred feet from the ridge. The outlines of boxes and bags stood against the night sky. They could hear men talking, the soft snorts of horses, and the low moans of wounded soldiers.

"Don't shoot!" Graham yelled.

A rifle appeared on top of the breastwork.

"Who goes there?" a sentry demanded.

"We're Reno boys!" Patsy called out.

"Come ahead!"

The exhausted men in sodden clothes quickly covered the open ground and scrambled over boxes, sacks, and dead horses to the battalion's crudely fortified position.

"Jesus, Mary, and Joseph!" Patsy exclaimed. "We be jammy to get outta that fierce mess."

The newcomers stripped off their wet shirts and jackets and wrapped themselves in blankets. After Sergeant Carey told their story of hiding in the river, others wanted to know if they had brought any water. Truth was, neither man thought about needing water on top of the hill.

They learned Captain Benteen had arrived late in the day with the pack train. The combined battalion had fended off a series of attacks but had lost at least thirty men before the Sioux stopped firing at dark. Indeed, Graham and Patsy had stepped over three stripped and mutilated bodies on their ascent.

The Sioux had forced the regiment onto a bluff with a shallow depression at the summit. The enemy had a higher vantage point on an adjacent bluff several hundred yards away, well within firing distance. Besides rifle pits excavated from crude digging tools, temporary breastworks were being constructed on all sides using whatever materials were available. The men had erected two canvas tents for Dr. Henry Porter, the surgeon riding with Reno's battalion, to use as a field hospital. They corralled the mules and horses around the medical tents to afford some protection for the wounded.

"Davidson!"

The voice of Lieutenant Varnum summoned Graham's attention.

"Yes, sir."

"Glad you made it. I wondered what happened to some of my scouts in all the chaos down below."

"My horse got shot from under me in the river. I stayed hidden in the river with Sergeant Carey until dark."

"Yeah, a dozen other boys hid in the timber. They showed up a short while ago. Are you injured?"

"No, sir."

"Do you still have your carbine?"

"No, sir. Lost it in the river."

"Your pistol won't do much good unless we are fightin' in close quarters. Go over to the hospital tents where we stacked the supplies. We've got extra Springfields from the dead and wounded. Pick one out. And try to get a few hours' rest. They'll be coming at us again tomorrow."

"Yes, sir."

"Well, I'll let you get back to it," Varnum said, pointing to Graham's crude dirt parapet.

"Lieutenant, have you heard from the other scouts?"

Varnum rubbed his temples and looked at the ground as he spoke.

"Mitch Bouyer and Curley went with Custer. I've accounted for most Crow scouts. Bloody Knife is dead. The Arikara scouts are on their way back to the Powder River, where we agreed to meet them after the battle." He paused. "Sure wish they would have stayed and helped fight, now that we know how many Indians are in that village."

"So you haven't heard from Rides Alone?" Graham asked, hoping the chief of scouts would have news of his friend.

"No. Perhaps he rode forward and joined Custer's battalion. It's also possible he was captured or..."

"Lieutenant!" a soldier said, lying on his belly and peeking over breastwork. "There's a man waving his arm."

Varnum and Graham looked where the soldier was pointing. It was difficult to see the man's face in the moonless night. But one thing was obvious. He was wearing a red cloth above his right elbow. He was a scout!

"Don't shoot!" Varnum yelled to the soldiers along the line. He removed his hat and waved his arms, motioning for the man to walk forward.

Rides Alone emerged from behind a bush leading a saddleless pony and carrying a Winchester.

Graham recognized his friend's familiar gait and couldn't contain his joy. He threw off his blanket, ran to Rides Alone, and embraced his friend. The Crow warrior managed a thin smile. Graham pulled away and walked with him to the protective circle at the apex of the hill.

"Welcome back," Lieutenant Varnum said. "Private, picket this man's horse."

After the soldier took the lead rope, the Crow scout sank to the ground on his knees. He placed his hands on his thighs and stared ahead with glassy eyes. Dried blood was spattered across his face and bare chest. Clumps of mud stuck to his hair. He reeked of perspiration and horse sweat. He had tucked four Indian scalps into his belt. Blood from one of his victims had dripped onto his leggings.

Varnum glanced at Graham, who grimaced at the gruesome appearance of his friend.

The lieutenant got down on a knee beside the scout and leaned against his rifle. "Any sighting of Custer or his men?" he asked.

"Too many Sioux for Son of Morning Star and his men," Rides Alone said, shaking his head.

"Is Custer okay?"

"They were fighting. Curly and I chased away enemy ponies."

"Where is Curly?"

"Got separated. Do not know."

"Is Custer okay?" Varnum impatiently repeated his earlier question.

Rides Alone lifted his head and glared at the officer. "Enemy has powerful medicine."

Varnum wanted to press the Crow scout further, but Graham grabbed the lieutenant's forearm and shook his head. Rides Alone needed rest. He was physically and mentally exhausted.

"Okay," Lieutenant Varnum said. "I'm assigning both of you to Captain French's M Company. No need for scouts. We know where the enemy is — all around us. Right now, we need every able-bodied man on a Springfield. You will take orders from Captain French until further notice."

The weary lieutenant stood and headed toward the hospital tents, where Reno was resting. He needed to report this news to Reno. Rumors within the camp were that the major was drunk. He had coped with the horrific events of the day by filling his flask from the lone barrel of whiskey from the pack train.

Graham fetched a spare blanket and some hardtack for Rides Alone, then led him to the dirt parapet he had built from the box lid. The two friends sat wrapped in blankets and listened to the songs of the enemy echoing in the valley below.

"Someone told me they are singing war songs of the victorious," Graham said.

Rides Alone tilted his ear toward the river and listened.

"Not all war songs. Some songs of mourning. We lost men. Sioux also died." Rides Alone turned toward Graham. "I avenged Little Wolf. I am at peace."

Graham stared at the four scalps on his friend's belt. He felt queasy as he recalled the grisly scene of Rides Alone scalping the warrior near the timber. He had performed the gruesome deed three more times.

"The enemy will come again at dawn," Rides Alone said, as he wrapped in the blanket and rolled onto his side. A few minutes later, he was asleep.

Graham tried to tune out the wails and shrieks from the valley. The agonizing sounds of the wounded lying in the hospital tent permeated his brain, keeping him awake. Most men fell asleep behind their makeshift breastworks, dreaming of a cool drink of water.

The Sioux had rebuffed several attempts to reach the river earlier, killing two men and chasing three others back up the hill with empty kettles. Graham wished he would have thought to retrieve his canteen and fill it with water before they scaled the bluff. The battalion had plenty of food. But they would gladly give up most of it for a few gallons of water.

As he lay in the darkness, a man's voice rose above the moans and wails. Initially, Graham couldn't hear what the man was saying. Then he realized a soldier was reading from the Bible. Graham propped himself on his elbows and listened to the words. He recognized Psalm 23.

The Lord is my shepherd;
I shall not want.
He maketh me to lie down in green pastures;
He leadeth me beside the still waters.
He restoreth my soul;
He leadeth me in the paths of righteousness for his name's sake.
Yea, though I walk through the valley of the shadow of death,
I will fear no evil, for thou art with me;
Thy rod and thy staff, they comfort me.
Thou preparest a table before me in the presence of mine enemies
Thou anointest my head with oil;
My cup runneth over.
Surely goodness and mercy shall follow me all the days of my life;
And I will dwell in the house of the Lord forever.

When the unknown soldier finished reading, the distressing moans of the wounded and the sorrowful lamentations of the Sioux once again dominated the night air. On a hot Sunday in June, the shadow of death had enveloped the Little Bighorn Valley.

Graham closed his eyes and said a quick prayer. After asking God to care for Makawee and Nahkash in his absence, he ended his petition by repeating one phrase in the psalm.

"Yea, though I walk through the valley of the shadow of death, I will fear no evil, for thou art with me."

Graham opened his eyes, looked to the heavens, and added, "Lord, be with me and Rides Alone tomorrow. Amen."

Graham slept fitfully for a few hours, then rose before dawn. Since a few sentries on the bluff were the only men awake, he stumbled along the perimeter until he discovered a spade lying beside a sleeping soldier. He used the digging tool to help

Rides Alone construct an earthen breastwork five yards from the one he had built earlier. They completed the second rifle pit and dirt barrier after thirty minutes, taking turns shoveling the hard clay. When they were finished, Graham inspected his palms. The blisters on his left palm had broken. Clear fluid oozed from the skin and mixed with dirt. It hurt when he made a fist. It was going to be painful to cradle a rifle. He pulled a bandana from his pocket and tied it around his stinging hand.

Just as the first rays of sun edged over the horizon, several rifle shots echoed through the valley. Within minutes, the beleaguered men on the hill were exchanging fire with Sioux and Cheyenne warriors on all sides of their defense perimeter.

As the morning wore on and the day heated, the fighting became more intense. The warriors came closer to the ridge top with each hour. While Major Reno cowered near the pack train supplies and hospital, Captain Benteen became the de facto commander of the battalion. Benteen walked along the perimeter, encouraging the soldiers while they tried to hold off the attacking enemy.

"Look, boys! We have scouts to help us out! They have good eyesight, and I hear they are marksmen!" Benteen said loudly, as he walked behind Graham and Rides Alone.

Benteen walked casually as he spoke to the troops. Bullets zipped past him. Some poked holes in the folds of his trousers and blouse. But he remained calm, even as the situation became more desperate and the odds of escaping the hilltop alive seemed overwhelming. Graham was impressed with the captain's courage. Was it bravery? Or was he simply testing fate? Regardless, it was inspiring to see an officer who was cool under fire.

Fifteen minutes later, a large whoop erupted from the north perimeter. Graham looked over to see all the men jumping over their breastworks and running down the slope, yelling at the top of their lungs. The tactic obviously surprised the enemy, and they quickly retreated. Benteen had taken the offensive and was leading a charge. A moment later, the soldiers scrambled up the hill to their defensive positions.

"We should do same," Rides Alone said, turning to look at Graham from his prone position behind the parapet.

"What? You mean charge the enemy?" Graham asked incredulously.

"I am a warrior. Not a coward who hides."

"We report to Captain French. If he wants us to charge, he will give that order."

"I do not need permission to strike the enemy," Rides Alone said, getting to his knees. He chambered a round into his Winchester, pulled a knife from his tunic belt, and placed the back side of the blade between his teeth.

Graham's heart raced. He envisioned his friend dashing down the slope, only to be cut down by a torrent of bullets. What could he say to dissuade him from this foolish action?

"We're going to bolster Benteen's line!" Captain French suddenly yelled from a distance. "If I tap your shoulder, follow me!"

French ran along the perimeter and tapped every third man. When he came to the area defended by Rides Alone and Graham, he skipped them and recruited the soldiers on either side.

"Hold our position, men! I'll be back!" French shouted as he escorted a third of his company to the south side, where the firefight had intensified.

Rides Alone removed the knife from his teeth and slumped forward, leaning on his rifle. He could not leave a large section of the perimeter unguarded. Bullets whizzed by the Crow warrior, but he was indifferent to the danger.

Graham scooted to his friend and pulled him down behind the breastwork.

"You are the bravest man I know," Graham said, putting his arms across the warrior's shoulders. "You have proven yourself and avenged Little Wolf's death. Now is the time to defend, not attack."

He could see Rides Alone was considering his words.

"I promised Makawee I would return. And Long Horse needs a son," Graham pleaded.

A soldier immediately to their right suddenly cried out in pain. Blood spurted from his neck. He briefly clutched at the gushing wound before rolling onto his back. His body went limp.

"I've got to get back," Graham said, trying to disguise the fear in his voice.

Rides Alone nodded. He placed his rifle on the parapet and sighted down the barrel, seeking a target.

Graham scooted on his hands and knees to his breastwork. It took a half dozen shots before he found the range of the Springfield. Just as he lined up a shot on a Cheyenne warrior, he felt a sharp sting in his left upper arm. He let out an anguished howl and instinctively grabbed his triceps with his opposite hand. When he lifted his hand away, blood oozed from a bullet wound.

"Dammit!" he yelled, slapping his hand against his arm to stop the bleeding.

Rides Alone hurried to his friend. He pulled Graham's hand away and inspected the wound.

"Bullet went through. Come with me to doctor."

Graham winced in pain as he lay on his back. "No. We can't leave our posts. Can you bandage it?"

Rides Alone nodded. He untied the red cloth from above his elbow, wrapped it tightly around Graham's arm, then tied a knot to secure it.

"I'll be fine. You better return to your position."

The soldiers held their own for the next four hours against the overwhelming number of warriors, who gathered in bunches and periodically charged up the hill, only to be rebuffed when the defenders responded with a hail of bullets. The besieged battalion gained some relief from the relentless heat when a group of men successfully made their way down the slope and returned with kettles and canteens of water from the river. Captain Benteen ordered the wounded should receive the fresh water first, with the rest distributed among the parched troopers guarding the perimeter.

Late in the afternoon, the firing from the attackers ceased. There was an uneasy feeling among the Seventh Cavalry members entrenched on the hill. Were the Sioux and Cheyenne planning a last surge? All the soldiers could do was wait.

An hour later, the warriors set fire to the grass, creating a gigantic cloud of smoke that hung above the valley floor. Captain French summoned Benteen to a small knoll on the western perimeter. He handed field glasses to the acting battalion commander.

"Looks like they're packing up and leaving."

Benteen peered into the binoculars. He saw an enormous procession of Indians and horses through the smoky haze. The camp was heading south toward the Bighorn Mountains. While the women had dismantled most tepees, they had stripped the buffalo hides from the lodges and left most of the pole frames standing. Benteen slowly swung his field glasses to the north. He estimated the cavalcade stretched for almost three miles. A group of warriors sat on horseback by the river, protecting the group's flank as they paraded by.

"Now there's something you'll never see again," Benteen commented. "Pass the word. Leave a sentry at all corners of the perimeter. Tell the men to gather on this side and look into the valley. I want them to see how many Indians we held off. They should remember this sight so they can tell their grandchildren about it."

Some thought the departure was a deception and were wary about one last attack. But as nightfall approached, it was clear the Indians had departed the valley. Major Reno ordered the battalion to move their encampment from the high ground to the base of the bluffs. This accomplished two things. It provided access to water for men, mules, and horses. And the venue was a welcome change of scenery from the stench of dead horses and the bodies of their comrades who had yet to be buried.

The mood in camp that evening was a mixture of sadness and relief. The troopers grieved over those who had died. They also rejoiced inwardly at their good fortune to have survived a ferocious attack from a determined enemy.

As Graham lay under the stars near Rides Alone, he counted himself lucky to be among the survivors. But was it luck? He pulled the eagle-bear-claw necklace from under his sweat-stained shirt and rubbed the bear claws. Other than a bullet that passed harmlessly through his arm, he was unscathed. If the bullet had landed six inches to his right, it would have pierced his heart. His body would be among those awaiting a hasty burial in the morning. But the necklace had protected him again. Or at least, that's what he believed.

He knew tomorrow would bring grim news for the survivors of the Seventh Cavalry. Most men clung to the belief that Custer had rested his battalion after a long fight. Surely, they reasoned, the colonel would rejoin forces with Benteen and Reno in the morning.

Selfishly, Graham didn't want to think about the men on both sides of this fight who had lost their lives during the past two days. He was simply glad the shadow of death had not touched him and Rides Alone.

His arm ached from the bullet wound, and his blistered palms stung. Graham pushed these pains to the back of his mind by focusing on the future. Hopefully, he would be home within a week. With that happy thought, he fell asleep dreaming of Makawee in his arms.

"I don't believe it," Captain Benteen said. "There's no way they could have killed Custer's entire battalion!"

General Alfred Terry nervously tugged on his bushy goatee while he spoke. "It's true. We just came from the battle site. Most of the bodies are horribly mutilated, but there's no doubt. Custer and all his men are dead."

Terry and Colonel Gibbon's column had arrived midmorning to the cheers of the survivors of Reno's and Benteen's battalions. But the mood quickly changed when the news of Custer's demise reached the rank and file.

"How far downriver?" Major Reno asked.

"About four miles."

Reno cleared his throat. "Well, sir, we had our hands full right here, that's for sure. I tried to provide support to Custer, but the hostiles surrounded us up there," he said, pointing to the bluff across the river. "If only..."

"Major! There will be plenty of time to assess what happened later."

Benteen glanced at Reno and shook his head. But he chose not to question his fellow officer. This was not the time or place.

"How can we help?" the captain asked.

"I need men from both battalions to help Colonel Gibbon locate and bury the dead. Our surgeons will assist Dr. Porter with the wounded. We need to figure out how to get those men to the *Far West* as quickly as possible. Our first order of business is to bury the dead and care for the wounded."

"Yes, sir," they replied simultaneously while saluting.

"Oh, one more thing," General Terry said. "Search the coulees and ravines for body parts. Based on what I saw, they dismembered some men."

Lieutenant Varnum assigned Graham and Rides Alone to a group charged with searching the timber, the site of Reno's initial retreat before ordering his men to cross the river. A half dozen soldiers walked through the wooded area, poking into bushes and looking under trees for victims. The Indians had scalped and stripped the clothing from every victim, oddly leaving only socks on the feet of any man whose legs had not been amputated. The burial detail marked each fallen victim using tepee poles from the Indian village. They completed their gruesome task by locating any missing arms, legs, or head and stacking these on top of the body. More than once, a soldier ran to the river to wash out his mouth after he gagged upon seeing the mutilation.

Graham walked to the edge of the woods after observing one of the macabre scenes. The smell of death invaded his nostrils, and he needed to breathe fresh air. He bent forward and placed his hands on his knees, trying to calm himself. Rides Alone followed and placed his hand on Graham's shoulder.

"The Sioux are my enemies," he said in Apsáalooke. "But I do not blame them for what they have done here."

Graham was incredulous. He turned to stare at his friend.

"What?"

"If someone attacked my family, I would do the same," Rides Alone said. To make his point, he lifted the hair from the four scalps tucked in his tunic belt.

I would defend my family to the death, but I can't imagine committing such heinous acts, Graham thought.

"Well, all I can say is..."

A faint, high-pitched squeal interrupted Graham.

"Do you hear that?"

Rides Alone tilted his head. At first, they only heard spades sinking into the earth, where soldiers were digging shallow graves for their comrades. A moment later, they heard something like a cat's meow.

"It sounds like a baby," Graham said. "I'm gonna check it out."

"It might be a trick. Wait here."

"But..." Graham said.

"Eagle Bear must have daasátchuche," Rides Alone said, holding up his hand. "I will let you know if it is safe."

Graham sighed and crossed his arms. "Go ahead. I'll wait."

The Crow warrior chambered a round and held the butt of the Winchester against his shoulder. He cautiously moved across the partially burned grassland toward the abandoned village. The sound grew louder and more incessant as he approached a small ravine, where a young woman was lying facedown in the tall grass under a bush. The dead woman had an infant in a cradleboard strapped to her back. Despite continuous soft wails, the baby was so dehydrated he did not produce any tears.

Rides Alone slipped the strap of an otter-skin water bag over his head and carefully poured a tiny amount of water into the baby's mouth. The child instinctively moved his lips and eagerly sucked, coughing when a small amount entered his windpipe. Rides Alone loosened the swaddling blanket and peeked between the infant's legs. It was a boy. After securing the baby, he rolled the woman's body to one side, then the other, to remove the leather straps from the woman's shoulders.

Holding the cradleboard and child aloft, he shouted to Graham at the edge of the woods.

"Huúlaa!" ["Come over!"]

Crack!

A gunshot echoed through the valley. Rides Alone sank to his knees and fell backward. The child started crying anew when the cradleboard thudded beside him.

Graham sprinted across the prairie to his friend. When he arrived, he slid on his knees in the charred grass. The Crow warrior was holding his side. Blood soaked the right side of his tunic.

"You've...been shot! I'll get a doctor. Hold on!"

Graham didn't know who had fired. He could be the next victim! He pivoted on his knees and desperately tried to locate the shooter.

"It was me!" a voice called out from several hundred feet away. A man on horseback trotted toward Graham.

Graham immediately recognized the man when he drew near. It was Lieutenant Doane.

"You son of a bitch! You shot a scout!" Graham stood and shouted as the cavalry officer halted ten feet from the scene.

Doane looked down from his horse at the bleeding Crow.

"It was an honest mistake. I thought he was Sioux. It looked like he aimed a weapon at you. I shot him to protect you."

Graham struggled to contain his rage. But the most important thing was to get medical attention for Rides Alone.

"Fetch a doctor!"

Doane nodded, reined his horse, and galloped back toward the camp.

"Eagle Bear," Rides Alone said. His voice was weak.

Graham kneeled and leaned over his friend, who spoke in his native tongue.

"Take the child. Makawee will care for him."

"Come home with me. We will raise him together," Graham said, his words catching in his throat.

"I am going to the next life."

Rides Alone coughed and wheezed, wincing as the blood continued to ooze from his side. Graham pressed his blistered hand wrapped with the bandana against the wound, trying to stop the bleeding. The thin cloth was quickly soaked with blood.

"I want to..." The wounded warrior stopped to draw a breath and finish his thought. "... be with my little brother."

Tears rolled down Graham's cheeks as his friend lay dying. He pressed harder on the wound. *Where is Doane with the fucking doctor?* he thought.

"You won't die," he whispered. "You can't die! Not after all we've been through!"

He closed his eyes and laid his head on the Crow warrior's chest. There was no rise and fall. There was no heartbeat. His friend had started his journey to the next life.

Graham sobbed. The painful loss numbed his senses. He didn't hear the horses as they came to a stop. He didn't notice the doctor dismounting and pulling him away.

"Davidson!" Dr. Porter said, raising his voice to get Graham's attention.

"Huh?"

The doctor told Graham what he already knew. "I'm sorry. The Crow is dead. I'm very busy caring for the wounded. Do you want me to take that baby back to camp?"

The Sioux child was crying vociferously, adding to Graham's sorrowful mood.

"No. No, I'm gonna take care of him."

"Are you sure?"

"Yes."

"All right," the doctor said, shaking his head. "Come see me later if you want some advice on caring for an infant. I've got to get back to my patients."

Graham nodded. He sat with his hands clasped around his knees and stared at the body of his friend.

"Just one more casualty of this battle, I guess," Doane said from his saddle.

The lieutenant's voice momentarily snapped Graham from his despair. A pulse of rage surged through him as he stood to face Rides Alone's killer. He reached behind his back and grabbed the handle of the Colt Cobra tucked into his belt.

Doane reacted to the threat by pointing a Spencer carbine at Graham's chest.

"I wouldn't do that, Davidson. Not unless you want to join your friend in the afterlife."

Graham let go of the revolver handle and slowly brought his hand to the front. He pointed his forefinger at Doane.

"You are a murderer! And I'm gonna see you pay the price. I'm reporting this to General Terry."

"Go ahead," Doane said. "I did nothing wrong. It was his fault for being shot."

"How?"

"Where's the colored cloth above his right elbow that identifies this man as one of us? I could only assume he was the enemy. He wasn't wearing a red band." Doane pointed at Graham's bandaged arm. "But you are."

The arrogant lieutenant's comment stunned Graham. He gazed at the band wrapped around his upper arm. Rides Alone had taken it from his arm and used it to bind Graham's wound when they were on the bluffs. He had contributed to his friend's mistaken identity.

"I'll tell the men in the timber there's another body to bury out here," Doane said from his saddle.

"No! I will take the body. I will bury him according to Crow customs."

"Suit yourself," Doane said, shrugging. "I'm going to report what happened here to my commanding officer. I'm confident he will absolve me of any wrongdoing."

The lieutenant reined his horse toward the camp at a trot.

Graham reached behind his back and pulled the Colt from his belt. He pointed the revolver at the middle of Doane's back, placed his left hand under his right, and pulled back the hammer with his thumb. For a second, he envisioned the .38 caliber bullet severing the spine of Rides Alone's killer, sending him tumbling from his horse.

But his hand started shaking. He lowered the weapon and sat down heavily beside the body of his friend. As he de-cocked the revolver, a myriad of emotions assailed his brain. His enmity for Lieutenant Doane had nearly caused him to do something that would have been disastrous. Not only for himself but for his family.

Graham told himself to focus on the here and now. He needed to figure out how to transport Rides Alone home.

As he considered these things, the child strapped to the cradleboard reminded him of another obligation by crying even louder. He had committed to delivering the baby boy to Makawee. He picked up the otter-skin water bag and dragged the cradleboard under a bush to shelter the baby from the blistering sun. After leaning the board against a low branch, he tilted the bag and let tiny amounts of water trickle onto the infant's parched lips and down his throat. In that instant, he realized his world had expanded. Life wasn't just about satisfying his needs and desires. He had additional family obligations. And a commitment to make sure his friend would receive a burial worthy of a warrior.

Before leaving the valley, death had claimed one last victim.

Chapter Twenty-Five

Shia-nuk

June 30,1876

G raham waited patiently to board the *Far West,* moored at the mouth of the Little Bighorn River. He traveled with those who transported the wounded from the battlefield. Because they had to carry the men over difficult terrain on improvised litters fashioned from tepee lodgepoles, it had taken two days to travel twenty miles. The captain cleared space on the venerable boat to accommodate over four dozen soldiers needing medical attention.

As the space on the decks filled with wounded, Graham worried if there would be room for him, his horse, and a mule. He had outfitted the horse Rides Alone had stolen with a bridle and saddle. There were many to choose from since the army burned the extra saddles and bridles. They had no way to carry the tack because dozens of horses had been killed or wounded. Half Yellow Face helped Graham wrap Rides Alone's body in a blanket and tie the corpse on a pack mule.

Three days earlier, fifteen mules had carried extra rounds of ammunition to the Little Bighorn. The regiment needed only two mules to transport the unfired cartridges. It was a stark reminder of how close the survivors of the fight had come to running out of ammo.

"I dunno, son. I've got a lot of cargo and people," Captain Marsh said, observing the loading process from the base of the gangplank.

Grant Marsh was the riverboat pilot and captain of the *Far West.* General Terry praised the captain's nautical skills when he spoke to the wounded as they were being prepared for the overland journey to meet the steamboat. He assured them Marsh was a man who could get them quickly and safely to Fort Lincoln.

"I understand your priority is to get the wounded to Bismarck," Graham said. "But all I need is to cross the Bighorn."

Marsh glanced at the infant sleeping on the cradleboard Graham had strapped to his back.

"Lieutenant Varnum tells me you're one of his scouts. Damned if I can figure why you wanna take a dead Indian and a baby across that river."

294

"I'm just trying to get home."

"Aren't we all?" Marsh asked. He gazed wistfully at his ship. The crew had transformed it from a supply vessel to a floating hospital under his direction.

The captain ambled up the gangplank and watched as troopers carried the wounded on litters and assisted others to hobble onto the boat. He would occasionally bark orders and direct soldiers to a specific area of the deck.

"Davidson!"

Graham turned to see Lieutenant Bradley striding toward the steamer. It surprised Graham when the young officer embraced him.

"I'm so glad you survived!"

"It's good to see you, lieutenant."

"I heard the Crow scouts performed their duties admirably. Most are on their way back home, but it saddened me to hear about Mitch Bouyer and Bloody Knife. What happened to Rides Alone?"

Graham walked a half dozen steps to his picketed mule and placed his hand on the rolled blanket.

"He's right here."

"Oh…oh, I'm sorry," Bradley said. "He was a good man. I know the two of you were close."

"I'm taking him home. His father, Long Horse, has camped at the mouth of the canyon on the Bighorn. At least, that's where he was in early May."

Bradley nodded. "Well, I was certainly glad to have you as one of my scouts. I will recommend you to my commanding officer if you're interested in…"

"No, thanks," Graham said, holding up a hand. "I've got other plans."

"All right. Just thought I'd mention it. I hope we see each other again."

Bradley stuck out his hand. Graham accepted it, and they shook. The lieutenant hurried off toward the officers' tents, where discussions were taking place about whether to assemble a battalion to pursue the Sioux into the Bighorn Mountains.

The Sioux child started fussing, so Graham slipped off the cradleboard, leaned it against a large rock, and pulled an otter-skin bag out of his saddlebag. Dr. Porter had been tremendously helpful when asked how to care for the child. The doctor estimated the baby boy to be about six months old and thought he was slightly underweight. He advised Graham to find foods he could cook and soften so the baby could digest them. Graham spent an evening cooking dried apples, potatoes, and beans. He soaked chunks of hardtack in water and added them to the mixture. After mashing the softened foods with a fork, he added water until it was the consistency of oatmeal. Then he filled the bag.

Graham squeezed the vegetable-fruit blend into the neck of the bag. *Well, it's not Gerber, but I guess it's edible,* he thought. He was careful to offer water to the baby every few bites, as he was worried the boy might become dehydrated in the heat. He kept a small chunk of salt pork handy for the child to suck on between meals.

"Is that everyone?" Captain Marsh asked Major Reno, who had escorted a wounded soldier onto the steamer.

"That's the last man," Reno said. "Take good care of these fellows. General Terry and Colonel Gibbon will meet you where the Bighorn meets the Yellowstone."

Marsh walked up the gangplank and surveyed the decks. Graham saw the captain direct a few men to be moved, then turned toward shore.

"Come aboard!" he said, motioning with his hand.

Graham shouldered the cradleboard, untied the mule, and led it up the gangplank. After handing the reins to a ship's mate, he hurried to fetch his horse. He led the horse aboard and found a space along the wall of the cabin.

It was a morose atmosphere on the ship. They had laid the most severely wounded shoulder to shoulder, with barely enough room for the doctors to step between them as they tended to the patients. Those who suffered from less debilitating injuries sat on the stairs or leaned against stacks of cottonwood. Fortunately, ample supplies of laudanum and whiskey were available. The surgeons administered liberal doses of the opium tincture and alcohol. Both dulled the patients' senses and reduced the incessant moaning of the traumatized, which was a relief to their fellow passengers.

A crew member untied the mooring ropes, tossed them onto the deck, and jumped aboard. The captain engaged the paddle wheel and shifted the rudder to point the vessel toward the middle of the river.

As the steamer headed across the waterway, a soldier with a bandage around his leg slumped against a wall near Graham. The man glared at the mule's cargo.

"Who's rolled in the blanket?"

"A Crow scout."

He leaned over and spat tobacco juice on the plank floor. "You shoulda buried him."

"Why's that?"

"Cuz he smells like cow dung. Many of these boys be lookin' to die. They don't need somethin' else ta make 'em swimmy-headed."

Graham gritted his teeth. "I'm just going to the other side."

The soldier didn't respond. He closed his eyes and tilted his head back against the wooden wall.

Fifteen minutes later, the *Far West* had crossed the river. The captain turned the boat 180 degrees and eased the flat-bottomed hull against the muddy bank.

A sailor lowered the gangplank, and Graham disembarked with his mini equine entourage. He watched as Marsh pointed the boat downstream. He saluted the captain standing in the wheelhouse. The captain reciprocated, then turned his attention to navigating the steamer through the myriad of sandbars, small islands, and sharp bends of the Bighorn River.

Graham fetched a piece of salt pork from his saddlebag and handed it over his shoulder to the baby. The child grasped the fatty chunk of meat and made a slurping noise. Graham grabbed the lead rope of the mule and mounted his horse, being careful to keep the cradleboard upright as he swung into the saddle.

"Okay," he said aloud to the Sioux child on his back and the deceased Crow warrior. "Let's go home."

The following afternoon, Graham sat on his horse while he surveyed the Crow village two miles away. He had thirty miles to think about how he would break the heart-wrenching news to Long Horse and Fox Woman. Their oldest son was dead. Nothing he said would ease their anguish. All he could do was assist with the burial and mourn with the family. He took a deep breath and urged his mare toward the camp.

A young man rode out to meet him with a rifle aimed at his chest. When Graham gave a Crow greeting and explained who he was, the man lowered his weapon.

"Who is that?" he asked, nodding to the blanket tied onto the mule.

"Rides Alone, son of Long Horse."

He let out a shriek. Reining his horse, he galloped toward the camp, announcing at the top of his lungs Rides Alone was dead.

Graham grimaced. He had hoped to tell Long Horse privately before others found out.

Within minutes, he could hear wailing in the village. People greeted him as he came to the edge of the camp. Women screamed when they touched the blanket that encased the body of Rides Alone. Men cried and shouted at the sky. Dogs jumped and barked. And children stared in bewilderment at the adults' behavior.

Graham rode to the tepee of Long Horse, who was standing with arms crossed in front of his lodge. Two men untied the rolled blanket from the mule. Long Horse and Fox Woman joined the procession as they carried the body of the fallen warrior above their heads, weaving in and out of the pole lodges.

Graham dismounted, removed the cradleboard from his back, and set it on the ground. Incredibly, the baby had slept through all the noise. No one seemed to notice the infant. All eyes were on the body being carried through the village.

He handed the reins of his horse and mule to a young boy. Picking up the cradleboard, he leaned it against a nearby tepee.

As the mourners snaked their way to the other end of the village and their lamentations faded, Graham heard a voice behind him.

"Are you here to stay?"

He turned to see Makawee holding the hand of Nahkash.

"Oh, Makawee!" He rushed to meet her. He lifted her off her feet and kissed her.

"Daddy!" Nahkash said, looking up. Graham had almost forgotten his daughter spoke both Crow and English.

He picked Nahkash up, kissed her on the cheek, then hugged her and swung her in a circle.

"I'm so happy to see you, little girl!"

Graham set her down and held her hand as he gazed into Makawee's eyes.

"This is such a bittersweet homecoming," he said. "I can't tell you how many nights I dreamed of this moment when we would be together again. And yet..."

"Yes. I know."

"I'm so sorry I couldn't keep Rides Alone safe!"

"I'm sure you did everything possible," she said, standing directly in front of him and squeezing his upper arms.

"Ow!"

Graham's reaction startled Makawee. She let go.

"What's the matter?"

"I have a wound. It's a little tender," he said, touching the bandaged area under his shirt. "Can I hug you with one arm?"

Graham embraced her with his uninjured arm. He wondered if what Makawee had said earlier was true. Had he done everything possible? He thought about his role in Rides Alone's demise. If only he had made sure his friend had put a red band back on his arm that identified him as an ally, he might still be alive. A man like Lieutenant Doane would look for any reason to kill an Indian. And Graham had provided that reason. Tears welled in his eyes, but he wiped them away with his fingers. He regained his composure and stepped back.

"Makawee, I want to show you something."

He led his wife and daughter over to the cradleboard sitting against the wall of a tepee and kneeled. She leaned over and gazed at the baby.

"He's beautiful!" she exclaimed. "It is a boy, yes?"

"Yes."

"Why do you have a baby? Who does he belong to?"

Graham looked at Makawee and smiled.

"He belongs to — us. If you will have him."

Makawee raised a hand to her mouth. She stroked the child's round cheeks and smoothed his black hair with her fingertips.

"Why is he ours?" she asked in a skeptical tone.

"He's an orphan. Rides Alone thought perhaps we could...we might...provide for him."

"His mother was killed?"

"Yes."

"She was Sioux?"

"Yes." Graham paused. He tried to discern his wife's thoughts by reading her facial expression. "Does that matter?"

Makawee looked at her husband. "Not to me. If he needs a home, we should give him one."

Nahkash unexpectedly leaned over and kissed the sleeping child. "Mommy, can we keep him?" the four-year-old asked.

Makawee and Graham laughed.

"Well, I guess it's settled. We have a new family member!" Graham said. "Yes, Nahkash. We can keep the baby. He is your little brother."

Makawee stood on her toes and kissed Graham on the cheek.

"We have a baby boy," she said. "I will care for him as if he came from my womb."

Graham was relieved. He had hoped his wife would accept the little boy but was uncertain because of the child's provenance. A rare joyous outcome from the terrible battle at Greasy Grass was this wonderful gift to their family of an innocent child.

The noises from the mourners grew gradually louder as the procession made its way back to the center of the village.

"Tell no one we have adopted the baby. I must find the proper time to inform Long Horse and Fox Woman," Makawee said. "Right now we are only caring for the child until we can find a home for him. We need to focus on grieving the death and honoring the soul of Rides Alone."

"Agreed."

When the mourners returned, they stopped in front of a tepee, lowered the body from their shoulders, and carried it inside.

Today, Graham and Makawee welcomed a new life into their family.

Tonight, after being apart for months, they would become intimately reacquainted.

Tomorrow, Rides Alone would receive a tree burial.

The residents of Long Horse's camp gathered in a cottonwood grove along the Bighorn River on a humid afternoon. Fox Woman and several women of the village had painted the face, neck, and hands of Rides Alone with vermillion. They dressed the corpse in a new tunic and leggings before wrapping it in a blanket and encasing it in a tanned buffalo hide, flesh side out. Ironically, the same rifle Rides Alone had taken from the dead Sioux warrior on the scaffold in the Little Bighorn Valley was now strapped to the hide. Long Horse had tied the four scalps taken by his son to the barrel of the stolen Winchester.

Graham and Makawee walked with the other villagers to the cottonwood grove by the river in midafternoon. A few old women remained in camp to watch the youngest children. Earlier in the day, men had constructed a platform out of lodgepoles and wedged it between two sturdy branches eight feet from the ground. They used ropes to hoist the corpse onto the horizontal tree scaffold.

When the crowd had gathered, the chief motioned for a young man to come forward. He was leading the mare Rides Alone rode in the Little Bighorn Valley. It was the same horse that had brought Graham home to the Crow camp. The horse was wearing a neck rope but no saddle. He led the mare under the tree and handed the grieving father a Colt 45 single-action revolver. Long Horse stroked the neck of the Appaloosa. He cocked the hammer, placed the muzzle in the middle of the forehead just below the ears, and pulled the trigger.

Crack!

The horse screamed briefly before crumpling to the ground.

Graham flinched. *What the hell was that for?* he thought.

As if reading his mind, Makawee whispered to her husband: "Rides Alone died in a battle with his enemies. He is afforded the gift of a horse to take with him into the next life."

Graham shuddered as he looked at the dead horse at the base of the tree. He had witnessed many men and animals being killed in battle. Why add to that tally at a funeral?

The villagers started chanting and singing songs of mourning. Fox Woman and Makawee walked under the burial tree. Using scissors, they took turns cutting off each other's hair at the neckline.

Graham was silent when his wife rejoined him. It had shocked him when Makawee had cut her hair after losing Small Heart to express her grief. It didn't surprise him she had done the same thing when her brother died. He didn't like it. But he understood.

"Please tell me you will not cut yourself," Graham said over the singing and wailing.

"It depends on how I feel later."

He envisioned Makawee with scores of cuts on her arms and legs. He desperately wanted to avoid a horrible repeat of her self-mutilation when she had lost their baby.

"Rides Alone was my closest friend. I have grieved his death for many days. My sorrow is no less than yours. But I don't need to inflict pain on myself as a reminder of how much I hurt inside."

Makawee looked up at him. "I must do something, or the others will think I do not care."

"What about your family? I need you. Nahkash needs you. And your baby boy needs a healthy mother."

His last comment hit home. He could see by the look on her face Makawee was considering his words.

"A few cuts?"

Graham couldn't believe he was discussing how many incisions his wife could make on her skin.

"Two shallow cuts on each arm. No more."

"I agree. Thank you," she said.

Makawee left his side and joined a group of women slowly circling the tree and chanting.

As Graham listened to the doleful sounds of the women, he reflected on the tragic deaths of Little Wolf and Rides Alone. Just as it was for scores of Sioux and Cheyenne and hundreds of soldiers, the Little Bighorn Valley was fatal ground for the two sons of Chief Long Horse. There was one significant difference. Little Wolf had been killed by the enemy. Rides Alone died from so-called friendly fire.

Graham harbored a deep-seated hatred for Lieutenant Doane, who had shown no contrition for shooting Rides Alone. Graham debated whether to share this information with Long Horse or Makawee. He concluded there was no benefit in disclosing how Rides Alone had died.

He donned his hat and looked up at the platform in the tree. He recalled the way the Crow say farewell. It was the same phrase he had used at the burial of Little Wolf.

"Never say goodbye," Makawee had admonished him. *"That is too final. Say, 'see you later.'"*

"Shia-nuk."

Makawee sat under the trees by the river and observed the baby as he crawled off the buffalo hide. She laughed when the boy touched the prickly blades of a green needlegrass plant, backed away from the bunchgrass, and looked at his hands.

"Hey, baby!" she said. "Here come your father and sister."

Graham and Nahkash had returned from a walk along the river. They joined Makawee sitting on the buffalo hide.

It was a beautiful day in mid-September. Although the days were still warm, evenings had turned noticeably cooler. The cottonwoods and willows would shortly turn shades of yellow. Fall was just around the corner.

"Your little brother will walk soon," Makawee said to her daughter as she picked up the baby and sat him on her lap. "Then we will have to watch him closely."

"You always call him 'baby' or 'little brother.' Will he ever have a name?" Nahkash asked.

Graham looked at Makawee. "Your daughter wants to know. So do I. Have you decided?"

"You will accept whatever name I choose?"

"We talked about this. It's your decision."

Makawee lifted the baby under his arms and bounced him on her lap until he giggled. She hugged him and kissed the back of his neck.

"We know nothing about his first family," she said to Graham. "But I wanted to give him a name that reflects who he is. I lost my mother and father when I was an infant, and I felt lost for many years. Our son will know something about himself from his name when he is older."

Graham removed his hat and tossed it beside him.

"So, what will we call him?"

"*Dakkoótee.* It is the Crow word for 'Sioux.'"

"It's a beautiful name!" Graham said.

Inwardly, he cringed at her choice. What would the others in camp think of a boy who shared the name of their blood enemy? How would Long Horse and Fox Woman react? Makawee had explained she was only caring for him until they traveled to the Crow Agency in late September. She said she intended to ask the Indian agent, Dexter Clapp, to find a home for the child with a white family.

"Dakkoótee!" Nahkash said, repeating the name and following the baby as he crawled on the buffalo hide. "I like it!"

"It's been over two months since Rides Alone passed away. Your family will soon travel to the Stillwater Valley Agency to receive annuities. It's time to let your parents know we are adopting him," Graham said.

"Yes. We will tell them tonight. I'm sure they will be pleased."

Graham wondered if Makawee was trying to convince herself it was true. He wasn't as sanguine about the prospects of his in-laws accepting Dakkoótee into their family.

Nahkash grasped a long wooden spoon and reached into a pot suspended over the cooking fire. Fox Woman placed her hand over her granddaughter's, and together they stirred the elk stew.

Makawee was gratified her adoptive mother was teaching Nahkash how to cook at an early age. The older woman had taken a renewed interest in Nahkash since the death of Rides Alone. Having lost two sons, she took great pleasure in spending time with her granddaughter. She had never spoken to or picked up the baby boy since Graham had shown up with him two months earlier. Makawee hoped this would change when she announced the child was now part of their family.

After a hearty meal, Long Horse packed a pipe with kinnikinnick and passed it to Graham. The men exchanged it several times before Makawee spoke.

"I have exciting news! Graham and I are adopting the boy." She looked down at the sleeping child on her lap. "We have named him Dakkoótee."

Long Horse removed the pipe from his mouth and laid it in front of him. His eyes narrowed as he leaned forward.

"I was generous in allowing you to care for the boy because he is an orphan. You said he would be given to someone else. If you adopt him, he will not be welcome in my lodge."

This was not what Makawee had expected. She appealed to his sense of fairness.

"Eagle Bear and I decided he will be part of our family. Surely you would not punish an innocent child."

Long Horse leaned back and crossed his arms on his chest.

"Our enemy killed Little Wolf and Rides Alone. And you want to raise a child with Sioux blood? A child who bears the enemy's name? Every time I look at him, I remember how his people took my sons' lives. Do you realize the pain you have caused with your decision?"

Makawee put her hand over her mouth. She glanced at Fox Woman, who was fighting back tears. Her adoptive mother clasped her hands around her knees and stared at the ground.

Graham's prediction about how Long Horse would react to their announcement had been accurate. He pondered whether to set the record straight on Rides Alone's death. He had not been killed by Sioux. A white man had murdered him. But he dismissed the thought. This revelation would only add to the chief's anger. Graham tried to think of something that might sway his opinion.

"Chief Long Horse, I have great respect for you," he said in Apsáalooke. "May I remind you I was a stranger in your lodge years ago? You did not like me because I am a baashchiile. But you eventually welcomed me into your family. Please give Dakkoótee the same chance."

The chief turned to the side and spat on the ground. He placed his hands on his thighs.

"I will never forgive my enemy. And I will not have Dakkoótee in my lodge," he said, pointing a finger at the Sioux baby. "Give the child up, or leave my camp."

This ultimatum incensed Makawee. She wiped tears from her cheeks using the sleeve of her dress. She stood, balanced Dakkoótee on her hip, and took Nahkash by the hand.

"Do you have nothing to say, Fox Woman?"

The wife of Long Horse looked at her husband with pleading eyes and placed a hand on his arm. The chief stared straight ahead and ignored her touch. Realizing her remaining family was dissolving, Fox Woman covered her face with her hands and wept.

"Goodbye," Makawee said, with quivering lips. She turned and exited the tepee with her children.

Graham's heart ached to see this family torn apart. Perhaps her father would view things differently in a few days. He gathered his hat and stood to face Long Horse. Makawee had said her farewell in anger. He wanted to leave the door of reconciliation open with his parting word.

"Shia-nuk."

Graham tossed branches onto the fire. He peeked inside the tent at Nahkash to make sure she was asleep, then sat cross-legged beside his wife. Makawee was rocking back and forth, singing a lullaby. Dakkoótee had fallen asleep in her arms, his mouth open in a small oval.

Graham sighed as he thought about the distressing conversation that had culminated in his family leaving the camp of Long Horse a week earlier. Makawee was adamant they depart the next morning. Graham had received permission to take four horses. They spent a half day readying for the journey. Nahkash rode the mule, which also carried some belongings. He attached a travois behind Makawee's horse and lashed a platform between the poles to hold additional items. They took turns wearing the cradleboard, with Dakkoótee strapped in place.

As they headed west, Graham assumed their destination was Bozeman. He had talked with Makawee for over a year about locating a plot of land to settle and finding work in the growing town. But she surprised him during the evening meal the first night with a stunning proposal. She wanted to move away from Crow territory and pleaded with him to take their family to the Wallowa Valley to live with the Nez Perce. He had argued against this idea, as they had no guarantee the Nimiipuu people would welcome them.

But Makawee was persuasive. She reminded Graham of their meeting with Ollokot, brother of Chief Joseph, at Obsidian Cliff. The Nez Perce and Crow remained staunch allies. They had been friendly for many generations. Makawee was confident their family would find a home with those who shared the Sioux as an enemy. After all, Makawee argued, she was the daughter of an influential Crow chief. Ollokot would see the advantage of accommodating a Crow family to further strengthen the diplomatic bond between their people.

After Graham agreed to her plea, he realized they needed to prepare for a much longer journey. They stopped at the Stillwater Crow Agency and received their share of annuities. These included flour, salt pork, coffee, sugar, dried apples, and beef. Graham traded two horses for a Spencer carbine, ammunition, and a large wall tent.

Tonight, they camped near Mammoth Hot Springs. Tomorrow, they would enter Yellowstone Park. They would travel south through Norris Geyser Basin, then west along the Madison River into Idaho Territory. Makawee had experience as a guide. She had traveled throughout this region as a young woman with Rides Alone. Graham had confidence they could make their way to the Nez Perce camps. But it was the last week of September, and they would ride over high elevations. He worried about traveling through deep snow.

"He's a beautiful little boy, isn't he?" Makawee said, interrupting Graham's thoughts.

"Huh? Oh, yes. And he's lucky to have you as his mother."

Makawee beamed. Graham marveled at how her somber mood waned as they rode west.

"I need to ask one more time if you're sure about leaving Crow Territory."

She turned her attention from Dakkoótee and scooted close to Graham, who put his arm around her.

"I'm tired of watching men kill one another. All this killing poisoned the mind of Long Horse. He is not the man who took me into his lodge."

Graham nodded. He was not the same man either. Not after witnessing the brutality at the Little Bighorn. Many nights he would wake in a cold sweat. Horrific images of death and dying on the battlefield plagued his dreams.

"And you're sure about our destination?"

"Yes," she said, without hesitation. "I wish to live in a place that is far from where my brothers lost their lives. When we spoke with Ollokot two years ago, he was confident the white man would leave the Nez Perce in peace. That's where I choose to raise our family."

Some Nez Perce had signed a treaty, given up their ancestral lands, and moved to a reservation. But Chief Joseph's band resisted the coerced relocation of his people. The government would soon consider his followers hostile. Rather than dissuade Makawee from her dream of moving to the Wallowa Valley, Graham hoped they could settle with a different Nez Perce band. But that was a discussion for another day. Right now, he needed to get his family to northeastern Oregon before winter.

"Once we exit the park and enter Idaho Territory, there's no turning back," he reminded Makawee, pulling a blanket over their shoulders to shield against the chilly night air.

"I know." She looked down at the baby boy sleeping in her arms, then up at Graham. "Someday Dakkoótee will return to his people. Until then, I will give him a loving home. I believe that home is with the Nez Perce."

Graham leaned down and kissed the boy on his forehead, then kissed Makawee. While their exile from Long Horse's camp was painful, the journey to the Wallowa Valley provided an opportunity for a new life together. It was an uncertain future. But one he would face with the love of his life.

And that was all he could ask for.

About the Series & the Author

The Story Behind the *Frontier Traveler Series*

Burning Ground is the award-winning novel that was published in July 2021. It is a saga about a young man who travels back in time to 1871 and joins the expedition that explored the Yellowstone region before it was a national park. It is part autobiography, part historical, and part fiction.

Two seminal events in my life inspired the book. I met Redfield, a Crow Indian, as a teenager. He lived a simple life but had a profound effect on the way I saw the world. As a young man, I spent a summer in Yellowstone National Park giving guided tours on Yellowstone Lake. The cultural and geological history of the park fascinated me. When I was not working, I spent my days exploring all corners of that magnificent land, often in the backcountry.

I envisioned my historical fiction debut as a stand-alone novel. Unexpectedly, it garnered several book awards. Equally surprising, readers asked when the sequel would be released.

Sequel? I had not planned to write a series, but...

Graham Davidson will have more adventures!
The following stories are part of the Frontier Traveler series.

- *Burning Ground* is <u>Book 1.</u> It is the beginning of Graham's travels across the American West, starting with the Hayden Expedition through Yellowstone.

- *Fatal Ground* is <u>Book 2.</u>
  (If you enjoyed this story, please consider leaving a review on Amazon or Goodreads. Thank you!)

- *Bitter Ground* will be <u>Book 3</u>. Follow Graham and Makawee as they travel through Yellowstone Park in 1876 and seek a new home with the Nez Perce tribe.

The Author

David Allan Galloway grew up in rural Pennsylvania near Gettysburg. After a long career in manufacturing and writing a bestselling nonfiction book, *Safety WALK Safety TALK*, he launched a second career as a novelist. He enjoys reading about adventurers and explorers, traveling internationally, riding a recumbent tandem bike, and spending time with his four grandchildren. David lives in Springboro, Ohio, with his wife, Leesa.

If you would like to read about news or history related to Yellowstone or our national parks, or be notified when the next novel in the Frontier Traveler series will be released, subscribe to David's newsletter on his website: dagalloway.com/contact

Acknowledgments

F or those readers who are historians, researchers, archivists, military experts, or enthusiasts of The Battle of the Little Bighorn, a disclaimer is in order. One literary source claims over three thousand books have been written on this topic. Few military engagements have been analyzed and critiqued as much as this one. I aspired to write the concluding chapters of my story based on our understanding of what happened not only during those two days of June in 1876, but also in the years preceding this seminal event.

To be clear, *Fatal Ground* is not a definitive description of the events leading up to and culminating in the famous battle. It is a work of fiction inspired by southern Montana and Yellowstone history between 1872 and 1876. I encourage those who want to read a thorough account of the battle to consider the many nonfiction books and references about this historical event, including the ones listed below.

In *Fatal Ground*, the protagonist interacts with key historical figures throughout the story. Period photographs augment the reader's experience. You can find more information about these people and images on the "Notes" pages.

Among the many sources I used for writing this novel, the following are noteworthy.

- The reference I most relied upon when researching the people and the conflict was James Donovan's *A Terrible Glory*. He wrote an excellent book that brings the reader into the minds of the participants and onto the battlefield.

- Because one of the principal characters in *Fatal Ground* is a Crow scout, it was vital to include perspectives of the battle other than those recorded by white historians. Orin Libby interviewed nine surviving Arikara scouts in 1912. Libby's interviews are documented in *Custer's Scouts at the Little Bighorn: The Arikara Narrative*.

- The park rangers and guides at the Little Bighorn Battlefield National Monument in Crow Agency, Montana were extremely helpful in providing additional insights. I encourage readers to visit the battlefield. Tour the visitor's center, which has a plethora of information about this historical event.

- Custer's Expedition into the Black Hills is well documented in Donald Jackson's short book published in the 1970's, *Custer's Gold: The United States Cavalry Expedition of 1874*. Jackson relies on a compilation of government documents from the National Archives, as well as reports from newspaper reporters and journals.

- *The Montana Column: March to the Little Bighorn* provided valuable insight into the regiment that was approaching the Bighorn Valley from the west. The book, based on James Bradley's papers donated by his widow to the Montana Historical Society, allowed me to imagine the difficulties of that long march and the growing anxiety as Bradley's Crow scouts first spotted the Sioux camp.

- Turmoil wasn't confined to the Bighorn Valley in the mid-1870s. Along with other tribes, the government forced the Crow onto a dramatically smaller reservation during this time. The Crow Agency was moved from Fort Parker near Livingston to present-day Absarokee before being relocated a third time to its current location. The information from the *Extreme History Project* about Fort Parker was a tremendous help in writing that part of my story.

- Montana State University has digitally archived a collection of articles and letters written by residents of the Crow Agency or historians from its first days in 1869 through the 1930's. These accounts were valuable in determining what daily life was like in southern Montana. It also shares stories of settlers, government officials, and the Crow people.

I am grateful to those who read some or all of the manuscript and provided feedback or advice. Thanks to Heidi Archer, Laurie Baker, Brenda Barrett, Lee Bendtsen, Dean Benjamin, Wes Bolyard, Monica Bond, Dave Bonistall, Lisa Briem, Daniel Clark, Kathy Collins, Cherie Davis, Cindy DiMaggio, Vicki Dismuke, Christina Duddy, Janelle Erwin, Lori Fahrbach, Deb Fisher, David Fitz-Gerald, Jill Frego, Gail Gardner, Nancy Hart, Becky Havey, Tamsen Hert,

Kathleen Howard, William Igoe, Christiana Kettelkamp, Kay Kinney, Katie LaSalle-Lowry, Carol LeCrone, Rich Leever, Dan MacDuff, Greg Marchand, Bill Markley, William Martin, Marilyn Mcleod, Sherrill Medley, Bob Newton, William Platt, Joleen Ramirez, Robyn Rofkar, Mickey Rup, Connie Sauerbrei, Hans Schmellencamp, Jamie Seagroves, Yvonne Siemer, Adam Simpson, David Sinkhorn, Dan Small, Bill Smith, Diane Sperber, Jim Steele, Betsy Steele, Mark Swenson, Kent Taylor, Wanda Titman, Deborah Turman, James Tyrone, Joette Van Ness, Linda Waits, Melanie Wallace, Frank Wallis, and Richard Warner.

A special thanks to Brian R. Smith, a firearms historian who generously advised me on weapons and other story elements. His attention to detail and feedback strengthened the historical accuracy of the novel.

A professional editor is essential for an author's work to shine. Ellen Tarlin did a superb job finding and fixing all those things that make a book more readable. Cindy Marsch was also an enormous help. She completed a manuscript assessment and offered suggestions to improve and tighten the story.

An enormous thank-you to my bride of forty-three years, Leesa. She made invaluable edits and suggestions for each chapter. Her love and encouragement kept me going.

Notes

Chapter One (Ashes to Ashes)

"Rock of Ages" lyrics by Augustus Toplady. Psalms & Hymns for Public and Private Worship. July, 1776.

Chapter Three (Go West, Young Man)

Image: *Map of the Yellowstone and Missouri Rivers and their tributaries* explored by Capt. W. F. Raynolds, Topl. Engrs., and 1st Lieut. H. E. Maynadier, 10th Infy. Assistant, 1859-60. Revised 1876. [Washington, D.C.] : Office of the Chief of Engineers, 1876 [i.e.1877]. Annotated by D.A. Galloway.

Chapter Five (Portals to the Past)

Photo: *Dragon's Mouth* by Diane Renkin, National Park Service.

Photo: *Devils Tower* by Todd Trapani. Edited by D.A. Galloway.

Photo: *Medicine Wheel,* a Native American sacred site and National Historic Landmark in Wyoming. The Forest Service of the United States Department of Agriculture. Source http://www.fs.fed.us/r2/bighorn/

Chapter Six (Humbled by a Hatchet)

Photo: *Bloody Knife*, Custer's scout, on Yellowstone Expedition, 1873 - NARA - 524373.tif U.S. National Archives and Records Administration.

Bloody Knife (NeesiRAhpát) was an Arikara who served as a scout and guide for the U.S. 7th Cavalry Regiment and a favorite scout of Lt. Colonel George Armstrong Custer. In 1874, he took part in the Black Hills Expedition. During the Little Bighorn campaign, Bloody Knife repeatedly tried to warn Custer there were too many Indians to fight. Despite the overwhelming odds, he refused to stay out of the battle. He was killed while assigned to Major Marcus Reno's battalion.

The terms "Lakota" and "Sioux" are often used interchangeably to refer to the tribe of native peoples of the Dakotas. The word *nadouessioux* was created by French traders and later adopted by the English as just *sioux*. It is said to come from the Ojibwe word *natowessiwak* meaning "little snakes", as the Lakota were traditionally enemies of the Ojibwe. The words *Lakota* and *Dakota*, however, are translated to mean "friend" or "ally" and is what they called themselves. Many Lakota people today prefer to be called *Lakota* instead of *Sioux*, as *Sioux* was a disrespectful name given to them by their enemies. https://blackhillsvisitor.com/learn/lakota-or-sioux/

In the context of this story, they were viewed as an enemy by the government and the Crow tribe. For this reason, I refer to these people as *Sioux*. This is not meant to be disrespectful.

Chapter Nine (Fireworks)

Photo: First structure at *Fort Parker*, Montana. William Henry Jackson Photograph, ca. 1872. Public domain. The first Crow Agency (1869-1874) was constructed about eight miles east of present-day Livingston, Montana on Mission Creek.

Fellows David Pease was born in Tioga County Pennsylvania in 1835. In 1861 he entered the Yellowstone country and organized a fur trading company. In 1869, he became Indian agent under General Sully in Blackfeet country, Montana. He was chosen to succeed E.M. Camp at the First Crow Agency in 1870 and served through 1873. Pease was fluent in English, Santee Sioux, and Crow.

Nelson Story was a pioneer Montana entrepreneur, cattle rancher, and miner. He was best known for his 1866 cattle drive. His team brought approximately 1000 head of cattle to Montana along the Bozeman Trail. It was the first major cattle drive from Texas into Montana. His business ventures in Bozeman were so successful that he became the town's first millionaire. He played a prominent role in the establishment of the Agricultural College of the State of Montana (Montana State University) in 1893 by donating land and facilities.

On the night of October 30, 1872 the agency buildings in Fort Parker caught fire. The *Bozeman Avant-Courier* reported that a former employee threw warm ashes on sawdust in the north bastion, which caught fire early in the evening. Although the flames were extinguished, the fire re-ignited about 2:00 am, and the bastion was soon engulfed in flames. Heavy winds spread the fire rapidly, resulting in a total loss.

During the summer of 1871, *Lt. Gustavus Cheyney Doane* took part in the military escort supporting the Hayden Geological Survey of 1871 of Yellowstone under the leadership of Ferdinand Vandeveer Hayden. This was Doane's second major foray into the Yellowstone region. Although Doane's pathfinding skills were praised by Hayden, the Hayden explorations (not the Washburn-Doane explorations of Yellowstone in 1870) got most of the credit for the creation of the park. This caused a long lasting resentment by Doane. The man was entitled and egotistical. He had a checkered past that made him unlikeable. His most egregious offense was the active participation in the massacre of innocent Piegans on the Marias River in 1870.

Chapter Twelve (Shrinking Land)

Photo: *Crow Chiefs at Fort Parker* [Left-to-right: Poor Elk, Sits in the Middle of the Land (Blackfoot), Long Ears, He Shows His Face, and Old Onion]. William Henry Jackson. 1871. Albumen silver print. The Daniel Wolf Landscape Photography Collection. Denver Art Museum.

Awé Kúalawaachish/Sits In The Middle Of The Land, was also known as Blackfoot. He was the principal Crow leader in the mid-1800's and was credited with using the metaphor of the four base tipi poles to describe the borders of Crow Country. He became the head chief of the entire Crow Nation, uniting the River Crow and Mountain Crow for the first time. His name was too much for some people in government, who shortened it to "Chief Blackfoot." When the white man began the westward expansion into the Crow Nation's ancestral lands, Blackfoot negotiated with the United States and gained many advantages for his people. He led an Indian delegation of lesser Crow chiefs, such as White Swan, Shot in the Jaw, Poor Elk, and Wolf Bow, to the important Fort Laramie treaty council of 1868.

Felix Brunot was appointed as President of the Board of Indian Commissioners in 1868. Brunot spent four summers, over the six years that the Bureau was active, visiting Native Americans and Indian agencies throughout the western territories to provide the federal government with recommendations on the treatment of the Native American peoples. In 1873, he was dispatched from Washington with Eliphalet Whittlesey, another board member. Dr. James Wright, a Methodist minister, was also asked to assist with the negotiations to cede a portion of the Crow reservation to the United States.

Chapter Thirteen (An Only Child)

Ashishishe (known as *Curly* and *Bull Half White*), was a Crow scout in the United States Army during the Sioux Wars. He was best known for having been one of the Indian survivors at the Battle of Little Bighorn. Curly was assigned to scout for Lt. Colonel Custer, but did not fight in the battle. He watched from a distance, and was the first to report the defeat of the 7th Cavalry Regiment.

Chapter Fourteen (Second Suitor)

Photo: Burton Historical Collection, Detroit Public Library. *Bison skulls* await industrial processing at Michigan Carbon Works in Rogueville (a suburb of Detroit). Bones were used processed to be used for glue, fertilizer, dye/tint/ink, or were burned to create "bone char" which was an important component in sugar refining. Unknown photographer.

Columbus Delano served as President Ulysses S. Grant's Secretary of the Interior during a time of rapid Westward expansionism, and contended with conflicts between Native tribes and White American settlers. Delano argued the best Indian policy was to force Native tribes onto small reservations in the Indian Territory, and cede their land to white people. In his view, the reservation system humanely protected Native tribes from the encroachment of western settlers, aiding in Indian assimilation into white culture, language, attire, culture, and religion. To compel the Native tribes of the west to move to reservations, Delano supported the slaughter to the near extinction of the vast buffalo herds outside of Yellowstone, which were essential to the maintenance of the Plains Indians' way of life. His legacy includes the harsh treatment of Indians and the endorsement of slaughtering buffalo.

Photo: Julius Ulke and Henry Ulke, *Apsáalooke Delegation*, 1873. Back row (standing) from left to right: Long Horse; Thin Belly; Bernard Prero (interpreter); unknown name, wife of *Awé Kúalawaachish* (Sits In The Middle Of The Land); Major F.D. Pease (agent); unknown name, wife of *Uuwatchiilapish* (Iron Bull); Frank Shane (interpreter); and Bear In The Water. Front row (seated in chairs) from left to right: Bear Wolf; White Calf; *Awé Kúalawaachish* (Sits In The Middle Of The Land); *Uuwatchiilapish* (Iron Bull); One Who Leads The Old Dog; and *Peelatchixaaliash* (Old Crow [Raven]). Front row (seated on the floor) from left to right: Stays With The Horses, wife of Bear Wolf; and Pretty Medicine Pipe, wife of *Peelatchixaaliash* (Old Crow [Raven]). Albumen silver print from glass negative, 8 x 10 in. National Anthropological Archives, Smithsonian Institution.

Chapter Fifteen (Mammoth Journey)

Photo: *Liberty Cap and bathhouses of J.C. McCartney*. From Aubrey Haines. The Yellowstone Story. 1:197. (photograph by W.H. Jackson, 1871).

James McCartney came to the Montana Territory in 1866. He first passed through Yellowstone in 1869 and joined the Cooke City gold rush. In 1871, he partnered with *Harry Horr* to stake a claim of 160 acres at the mouth of Clematis Gulch at Mammoth on July 5. They built two cabins that became known as McCartney's Hotel, which was the first lodging in the park.

Photo: *Coating specimens. Mammoth Hot Springs*. Yellowstone National Park. Hayden Survey, William H. Jackson, photographs, compiled 1869 - 1878. https://catalog.archives.gov/id/516606

Chapter Sixteen (Black Hills Gold)

Photo: *Column of cavalry, artillery, and wagons*, commanded by Gen. George A. Custer, crossing the plains of Dakota Territory. By W. H. Illingworth, 1874 Black Hills expedition. National Archives.

William H. Illingworth was an English-born photographer from St. Paul, Minnesota, who accompanied both Captain James L. Fisk's 1866 expedition to the Montana Territory and Lt. Colonel George Custer's 1874 U.S. military expedition into the Black Hills of the Dakota Territory. Illingworth was selected as photographer to Custer's 1874 military expedition by *Captain William Ludlow*, who was the Chief Engineer of the Department of Dakota, and was to map the expedition's route. He provided the photographer with necessary equipment, rations and supplies, and added him to the civilian payroll with a salary of $30 per month.

William Eleroy Curtis spent most of his life as a journalist for two Chicago newspapers, the *Inter-Ocean* from 1873 to 1886 and the *Record Herald* from 1887 to his death in 1911. Primarily a traveling correspondent, the articles he wrote concerning such places as China, Germany, Italy, Russia, Spain, and Latin America. While working for the *Inter-Ocean*, Curtis interviewed the notorious James and Younger brothers. During this time in his life, he accompanied George Custer on a campaign into the Black Hills.

Photo: *Our First Grizzly, killed by Gen. Custer and Col. Ludlow.* By W. H. Illingworth, 1874, during Black Hills expedition. National Archives.

Chapter Seventeen (Closer to the Enemy)

Image: *Bismarck Tribune.* August 12, 1874. Volume 2. Number 5.

Chapter Eighteen (Stolen Bride)

Photo: *Rath & Wright's buffalo hide yard in 1878, showing 40,000 buffalo hides, Dodge City, Kansas. Department of the Interior.* National Park Service. National Archives.

Chapter Twenty-One (Eagle Scout)

Mitch Bouyer was an interpreter and guide. His father was a French Canadian and his mother was a Santee Sioux. He was recruited as a guide for the 2nd U.S. Cavalry and worked with the Northern Pacific Railroad survey team. From 1872 on, he was employed by the Crow Agency and the US Army. In 1876, Lt. Col. George Armstrong Custer requested that Bouyer be transferred to the 7th U.S. Cavalry as an interpreter for the Crow scouts when *Gen. Alfred Terry* ordered the 7th to search for hostile Indians. Custer's regular scouts were Ree (Arikara), including *Bloody Knife*. However, for this mission, Terry assigned six of *Lt. James Bradley's* Crow scouts to the 7th (including Curley).

Lieutenant James H. Bradley was the chief of scouts of the 7th Infantry under *Colonel John Gibbon*. Bradley was one of the first persons to find the remains of Custer and his men following their defeat at the Battle of the Little Bighorn. In the Summer of 1877, Colonel Gibbon & several companies of the 7th Infantry were ordered to intercept Chief Joseph & the Nez Perce, who had fled from Oregon. Bradley was killed at the beginning of the Battle of Big Hole.

Major James Sanks Brisbin was an American educator, lawyer, historian, author and soldier. He served as a Union Army officer during the American Civil War. He remained in the military for the rest of his life, and authored several works on a variety of subjects. Brisbin was in command of the 2nd Cavalry of General John Gibbon's Montana Column at the time of the Little Big Horn campaign. Brisbin offered four companies of his 2nd Cavalry to General George Armstrong Custer at the final command meeting of Generals Terry, Gibbon, and Custer just prior to the final march into the Big Horn valley, but Custer declined it, stating that the 7th Cavalry alone could defeat the hostiles.

Dexter E. Clapp was Crow Indian Agent from 1874 to 1876, succeeding *Dr. James Wright*, a Methodist Episcopal minister.

Colonel John Gibbon was a career United States Army officer who fought in the American Civil War and the Indian Wars. Gibbon was in command of the 7th Infantry of the Montana Column comprising the F, G, H, L of the 2nd Cavalry under James S. Brisbane from Fort Ellis and of his own regiment of 7th Infantry stationed at Shaw, Baker and Ellis in the Montana Territory, during the campaign against the Sioux in 1876.

Gustavus Doane returned to Fort Ellis in the fall of 1876. He planned an exploration of the Snake River regions south of Yellowstone. Doane believed this exploration would garner accolades similar to those given Hayden for Yellowstone and John Wesley Powell for his exploration of the Grand Canyon. Although he had permission to make the exploration from *Colonel John Gibbon*, Doane went over the head of his immediate commander, *Major James Brisbin*, the post commander at Fort Ellis.

Chapter Twenty-Two (Where There's Smoke)

Photo: Steamship *Far West* docked somewhere along Missouri River. Denver Library Digital Collections. Public Domain.

General Alfred Howe Terry was the military commander of the Dakota Territory from 1866 to 1869, and again from 1872 to 1886. Terry was the commander of the U.S. Army column marching westward into the Montana Territory during the Centennial Campaign of 1876. A column of troops under his command arrived shortly after the Battle of Little Bighorn and discovered the bodies of Custer's men. In October 1877, he went to Canada to negotiate with Sitting Bull. He was still in command in Montana during the Nez Perce War and sent reinforcements to intercept Chief Joseph.

Chapter Twenty-Three (Bloody Greasy Grass)

William Winer Cooke was the adjutant for George Armstrong Custer and was killed during the Battle of the Little Bighorn. He was an excellent shot and one of the fastest runners of the regiment. He was known for his long side whiskers.

Major Marcus Albert Reno served under George Armstrong Custer in the Great Sioux War. He is most noted for his prominent role in the Battle of the Little Bighorn, where he failed to support Custer's position on the battlefield, remaining instead in a defensive formation with his troops about 4 miles away.

Captain Frederick William Benteen was appointed to commanding ranks during the Indian Campaigns and Great Sioux War. Benteen is best known for being in command of a battalion (Companies D, H,& K) of the 7th U. S. Cavalry.

Lieutenant Charles Albert Varnum was most noted as the commander of the scouts, who were civilians, army personnel, Crow Indians, and Arikara Indians. His duty was to delegate scouting missions and coordinate the resulting reports. The Crow and Arikara scouts in his unit discovered the location of a huge Indian village with hundreds of lodges. Varnum accompanied the troops of Marcus Reno and Frederick Benteen and survived the battle.

Chapter Twenty-Four (Shadow of Death)

Captain Grant Prince Marsh was a riverboat pilot and captain noted for his many piloting exploits on the upper Missouri River and the Yellowstone River in Montana from 1862 until 1882. He was pilot of the *Far West*, a shallow draft steamboat operating on the Yellowstone River and its tributaries, which was accompanying a U.S. Army column that included Lt. Colonel George Armstrong Custer and the 7th Cavalry. After the Battle of the Little Bighorn, Marsh piloted the *Far West* down the Yellowstone and the Missouri Rivers to Bismarck, carrying fifty-one wounded cavalry troopers. Marsh set a downriver steamboat record, traversing 710 river miles in 54 hours.

Made in United States
Troutdale, OR
02/02/2024

17390714R00186